ACROSS 110th

New York almost explodes with racial tension when a powerful white Mafioso decides to teach Harlem's black crime king a lesson. Caught in the middle of the Mafia in-fighting are a bitter police captain, an integrated pair of detectives—and a city about to come apart with fear. . . .

"Here is a slam-bang cops-and-crime yarn full of tense action, violence and bloodshed. . . . the plotting and action are ingenious and the pace is furious; the racial tensions are handled boldly and the underworld scenes sound convincing. Ferris has written a story that crackles."

—*Associated Press*

ACROSS 110th

by
Wally Ferris

WARNER

PAPERBACK LIBRARY
NEW YORK

WARNER PAPERBACK LIBRARY EDITION

First Printing: June, 1971
Second Printing: June, 1972
Third Printing: November, 1972

This Warner Paperback Library Edition is published by arrange-
ment with Harper & Row, Publishers.

Warner Paperback Library is a division of Warner Books, Inc.,
315 Park Avenue South, New York, N.Y. 10010.

Chapter 1

Twilight sun touched the glassed-in penthouses with orange, was reflected in the windows of the fashionable stores and shone across the horse-drawn Victorian cabs lined along one side of the fountain in front of the Plaza Hotel.

The whistle was shrill and demanding and stirred the fat man, sitting next to the driver, out of his drowsiness. The fading daylight had speckled the buttons and braid of a uniformed doorman, transforming him into an obsequious toy general bowing and bouncing to a silken woman and her evening-dressed escort as they entered the cab he had commandeered. The doorman palmed the tip, not looking at it until the cab drove off, then his face soured. The stout man turned away.

"It's really hot for this time of year, ah, Mr. Rizzo?"

The driver's sweaty face gave proof to his words as he waited for the light. With a commuter's boredom he glanced at his passenger. The fat man's blunt face contrasted with his expensive suit and white-on-white shirt, the silk tie and highly polished wing-tip shoes. The company always alternated the drivers and the passengers. There was the conservatively dressed Lombardi, who spoke affectionately of his home life, his wife, his children; the smiling Savarese, who liked the ponies and women and liked to exchange ribald jokes. Lombardi and Savarese didn't care what avenues or streets were used just as long as they got up there and back in the shortest possible time. But lately during his stint as chauffeur, he had been catching Rizzo and the route was always the same, through the park, and then silence. Now the fat man barely grunted an answer.

The dying sun shredded through the trees onto the elderly who sat as though in despair and watched the young walk past in shorts and sweat shirts, carrying tennis rackets like swagger sticks, while children climbed

5

through the maze of monkey bars and soared skyward on swings. The park road twisted and turned and occasionally they could see Fifth Avenue, could see the spiraling Guggenheim Museum and later Mt. Sinai Hospital over the trees. The rows of apartment houses had been changing; the doormen had disappeared and the canopies covering the entrances had become faded and torn, until now only skeletal pipe frames remained.

When they left the park at 110th Street it was dusk and the street lamps had come on. They turned right onto Seventh Avenue and the tempo of traffic and the city picked up as the beat of a heart and accompanied the inconspicuous car carrying the two white men as they crossed the perimeter and began to move along the ghettoed canyons of Harlem. At 121st Street the traffic crawled through a surge of foaming water that spilled in a rush across the grimy avenue where shouting kids, their lithe onyx bodies glistening, ran through the spray of an opened hydrant. But their gleeful voices were muffled by high-pitched laughter, radios spewing ball games, raucous music and the idle, endless talk of the people, sitting on the stoops of decayed tenements that hovered over them like sentinels of depression. Big-busted Negresses stared broodingly down from the windows of the crippled buildings, like benign goddesses in cunning towers watching the crowded, agitated street below them. And above it all the incessantly clanging bell of a white ice cream truck pealing its cry of coolness.

At 125th Street the two white men looked disinterestedly at a crowd listening in anger to a black militant on a stepladder who was rousing them to assenting murmurs and nods with his cries of united black power, as he added his own heat to the evening with his "hate the whites" harangue; then the light clicked green and they turned left into Harlem's main street.

In the sluggish traffic they passed the flaring neons of liquor stores, movie houses and restaurants. Music blared from bars and record shops, a mélange of staccato beats that were picked up by the hipsters lounging along the curb eyeing the high-assed girls going seductively by. The occults and fortunetellers worked their trade from second-story perches and the married couples window-shopped

6

below in the five-dollars-down, five-dollars-when-you-catch-me jewelry and clothing stores. The Loew's was again double-featuring *Pinky* and *I Passed for Black* and the window of the Savoy Bar was missing. As they passed the outdoor clock in front of Blumstein's Furniture Store it registered nine as though tolling Harlem's fermenting life into a nocturnal bloom. Inching right at Eighth Avenue, they passed blacks and browns and high yellows who crossed on the green in front of them, and drove, about another mile, deeper into this ebony belt of impoverishment.

Then the inconspicuous car turned into a side block and came silently to a stop. A few teen-agers were gathered under a street lamp, harmonizing an imitation of the latest rock-and-roll hit. A couple of houses away a mother called, "Estelle, Estelle" impatiently from an upper-floor window. "You come up here now, you hear what I say?" And a man staggered by in the clothes of a laborer, moving as if he had bellied to a bar far too long after work and now was on his way home to a tongue-lashing wife. This was a block less congested than most, three-story brownstones sitting back from the street, their stoops leading to second-floor vestibules that still showed semblances of once-proud turn-of-the-century elegance.

The big driver got out of the car. His dark eyes and leathery face had now lost some of the boredom. He scanned the street briefly, barely conscious of the curious, hostile stares from the people sitting on the darkened stoops; they meant nothing, he scarcely saw them, for they were the normal still lifes. His cursory glance was looking past them for an irregularity but it found only a Harlem slum street. The fat man had leaned over the back seat and come out of the car carrying a large valise. He followed the driver up the front stairs to the second-floor vestibule of the house in front of which they had parked. They didn't pause to look for a name or ring a bell but pushed through the lockless inner door. Dim gray light from the rear halls washed across them through the spokes of the banister as they climbed the stairs to the top floor. They moved along the dark hall, almost groping, to the front of the house. The driver knocked on the door and both men waited, listening to the muted footsteps coming

7

toward them. The door opened slowly to the extent of a chain. A black face, crushed and coarse, hung above the taut lock, its eyes surveying them warily, then the chain was released and the door swung open.

The room they entered was heavy with heat and sweat. Its shades were drawn and an old-fashioned cloth-shaded lamp hung low from the ceiling, throwing its yellowish glow onto a table, which was completely cleared except for a very large amount of money piled loosely into bundles. Two well-dressed Negroes standing beside the table nodded a greeting. The one who had let them in relocked the door and casually leaned against it. The stout white man laid the suitcase on the end of the table, opened it and took a small notebook from his inside pocket. His driver stepped back and blended into the background.

No time was wasted on formalities. The white man, sweat now running freely down his face, stopped occasionally to wipe his brow and began to write down certain figures. The three men, cigarette butts hanging loosely from the corners of their lips, became completely engrossed in the tabulations, the ancient lamp above their heads distorting their faces with its harsh light. A squat old-fashioned clock above the artificial fireplace tolled the half hour with the boldness of Big Ben, for the room had become completely silent except for the sorting of the green paper.

The sound was heard first by one of the men at the table. His brow furrowed, his eyes flicked up, he darted a glance at the door and then relaxed. Just an innocuous footstep in the hall. Other people live in the building; nothing to worry about. The transfers were never done in a completely clandestine manner. Except for the fact that the collection room was always well guarded, the pickup of the weekly take was carried on against an active background. The organization emulated the banking corporations that, when transferring large sums, used the busy time of day, the crowded streets and a limited number of guards. The era was past of torpedoes riding up in touring cars and emptying hoods onto a street to scare a neighborhood with intimidating scowls and bulging guns under form-fitting coats.

The knock came like an explosion. Each man tensed,

his insides knotting. Each looked quickly, nervously at the others and stood for what seemed an incredibly long minute. Then the knock came again; just as insistent. The Negro guard at the door peered anxiously from the shadows at the two white men. The driver of the car, who had been lounging lazily, now straightened up with a gun in his hand and moved next to the heavy, perspiring collector.

"See who it is."

The fat accountant's voice cut through the tension of the room with a hardness that belied his appearance. The guard pulled a gun from under his coat and aimed it at the door, while his other hand opened it cautiously. He looked through the small opening and his body froze. Then slowly he turned back to the table. His face, shadowed, was controlled, but his tenseness was evident from his hushed, perplexed voice: "It's two cops!"

The words bounced off the walls like an electrical charge.

"Take it easy," the white man said in a low tone to one in particular. He motioned the men to put their guns away, then nodded slowly toward the door. "Okay, let them in," he said, realizing it was too late to hide the money. He knew the cops would make the scene at a glance and he wanted them to. He wanted them to have no doubt about what was going on in the room. He had calculated quickly and decided that a C note apiece would be a generous buyoff.

The chain was released and in they came. One big, one average, both black. They wore their hats down low, just above their eyes. Perspiration had stained their dark-blue shirts under the armpits and their pants were wrinkled as if they'd been sitting too long in a radio car. They stopped vigilantly just inside the door, their eyes covering the room. The big one had his hand pressed to his side, his fingers hidden behind his back. He looked like a cop unsure of himself, ready to go for his gun.

"What's the matter, officers?" The white collector forced a smile to his lips. He had ruled them off as blunderers, confused by the display of so much money in a mixed room of whites and blacks, men who realized this was too big to touch and now didn't know how to exit grace-

9

fully. Dumbheads, the fat man thought, and his face held the smile but his voice couldn't hide the annoyance and sarcasm that crept into it. "What's the trouble? Am I parked by a hydrant or something?"

The cops' foreboding silence continued as they separated and took a careful step farther into the room. The guard at the door retreated before them, as if mesmerized by the big uniformed policemen. The Negroes at the table shifted self-consciously while the fat man slowly, assuredly took some bills off a pile and gratuitously folded them in a show of contempt. The guard continued to stare at the big cop and suddenly he realized what was happening. In that stifling, inflammable room he could feel his flesh ripple and a sickening chill go up his back.

"They're not cops!"

His words burst forth more in astonishment than in warning. But it was too late. The hand that was partially hidden behind the uniformed man's back swung quickly around, leveling and snapping a Sten gun into its full length in a single motion, its metal click filling the room. The intimidation was complete. His partner's hand now held a .38 Police Special.

"Get them up."

The words came from the man with the submachine gun. In the stunned shock of silence no one moved. Then the voice of the white man, part in disbelief, part in anger, rolled up from deep in his throat.

"Why, you lousy black bastards!" The words tumbled from his mouth as his arms slowly went above his head.

The bogus cop handled the weapon like a pro, using it to motion them away from the table and money. But when he spoke, the tremor in his voice betrayed him.

"Over to the window, all of you. Spread out and face me."

The collector realized further talk was useless. The gunman was wound with tension, nervous as a big cat, and in his tightness was capable of squeezing the trigger at the slightest provocation.

"Now, nice and slow you throw the guns onto the floor." His voice trembled, but the ugly weapon emphasized the words and their guns fell.

The accomplice quickly returned the .38 to his holster

10

and worked his hands behind his back as he stepped to the table and pulled from under his uniform shirt a large folded cloth bag. He started to scoop up the money, throwing it hurriedly, aimlessly, into the open mouth of the bag. The five men facing the automatic weapon stood immobile. Gray cigarette smoke curled listlessly about their heads in the hot, humid room. The eyes of the man with the Sten gun shifted nervously, as he held the men in their positions by his grit and the gun. His confederate, the bag almost filled, swiftly reached over for the remaining money in the suitcase. In his emotional, pent-up haste his hand caught the top of the valise, knocking it to the floor with a jarring crash that startled the gunner, whose raw, jagged nerves reacted. He turned from his captives and glanced over his shoulder.

It was the mistake the Negro who had let them in was waiting for. He bent quickly, silently. His fingers had already curled around the grip when the bogus cop turned back. The white accountant had made his own move, his heavy frame surprisingly agile. But his move was not toward the gunner, for his attention was riveted upon the snub-nosed gun rising in the guard's hand. The fat man's voice was high-pitched, as if only he had the imagination to guess what was going to happen.

"No, no, don't!"

The bellowed screech of warning was lost in the explosion of sound from the submachine gun. The bullets tore into them, spinning them and driving them back against the wall and front windows. A body hung, momentarily welded to the partition, its eyes wide open in disbelief; then slowly, grotesquely it slid to the floor. The sound of glass from the shattered windows tinkled on the cement of the street below.

The assassin stood motionless, his ears still pounding from the now-quiet gun while a thin trail of vapor waved up past his face from the gun's heated nozzle. In front of him a leg twitched, a hand moved and from the wall a beseeching cry of repentance: "Jesus, oh, Jesus, Mary and . . ." Then a terrible silence. He stood transfixed, looking across the slaughter. His body seemed elongated as though he stared from some great height, detached from what had transpired. Then the room tilted and

11

spun around him and he could feel the nausea rising from the depths of his stomach, through his chest and into his throat. He turned from the carnage and the sight that greeted him restored his mind to sharp awareness. His accomplice was doubled over, one hand holding the table for support, belching vomit onto the overturned valise. The gunner moved stiffly across the room, grabbed the arm of his partner and shook it. "Goddammit, man, you don't crap out on me now. Not now." His voice guttered with distortion as he fought back his own terror, his own sickness.

"I'm okay," said the bag man, like a drunk with his head over a toilet. He wiped his mouth with the palm of his hand and pulled his hand across his shirt. "I'm okay." He bent down to scoop up the scattered money on the floor, trying to prove he was all right. But his retrieving was too slow for the gunner, who held the bloated duffel bag open for the remaining bills.

"Okay, that's enough. Let's get out of here." He yanked the draw-cords closed on the bag, jammed it up under his arm and turned to the door. But his partner held back for a fleeting second, his eyes returning to the butchered bodies in the front of the room. "Goddammit, let's go, man," the gunner yelled. He pulled the bag man past him, pushing him toward the door. "Come on, move, move."

Out the door they went, the big one almost running up the heels of his partner, who stumbled in the semidarkness ahead of him. They turned at the end of the hall and pounded down the flight of steps. They were halfway down when the outer door was pushed open and two uniformed policemen filled the vestibule entrance. Their drawn guns reflected the dim light from the low-watt bulb in the rear of the hall. In the dimness their strained bodies seemed to slack gratefully, as they recognized the uniforms. Their guns came down and pointed to the floor. The shallow grayness of the outside street lamp came through the door, partially silhouetting their bodies and blending them into barriers to escape.

"What's up?" There was a catch of caution in the cop's voice as he squinted quizzically up at the two men on the stairs. The submachine gun cleared the banister.

Again the deafening staccato burst, and the two policemen fell as though a child had moved a heavy hand, downing tin soldiers. The bullets had chopped across their faces, leaving them in their twisted dead positions with incredulous blood-soaked stares.

In the vestibule the gunner slipped going over one cop, who had been blown back through the door. His knee went across the chest, forcing a gasp of air from the dying man's lungs.

The gunmen hit the sidewalk in a rush of panic. A car, its headlights out, came up fast, cutting in toward the curb and just missing the empty prowl car, and it slowed barely enough to receive the men as they frantically tore open the doors and piled in. The gears shifted and the car took the corner on skidding, screeching tires, leaving the brownstone, the street and the surrounding area in a stunned quiet.

Chapter 2

Piercing sirens wailed along Convent and St. Nicholas Avenues, flaring up over Edgecombe and the sliver of Colonial Park. The angry shrieks rose, wave upon wave, meeting responding shrieks from Eighth and Seventh and Lenox Avenues, until all of Harlem seemed saturated with the sounds.

The wall of people parted as the siren growled just enough to clear a path to the wooden barricades holding the curious back. The cop by the blockade pulled part of it aside and waved the detectives through. They eased the car into the block, which now vibrated with a perverse excitement. They could feel it as they stepped into the street and threaded their way between the haphazardly parked patrol cars and unmarked detectives' cars with police radio frequencies rolling out static monotones. The detectives walked past the cars of broadcasters and newspapermen. The rolling police lab was next to the curb and clusters of cops and detectives stood in small talkative circles.

The tenement telegraph had sent its message and the teeming multitudes had responded. They pressed against the roped-off areas in front of the brownstone and every window on the block was darkened by bodies that leaned precariously from the ledges. People stood on the roofs and hoods of automobiles, caught in the long splashes of scarlet mixed with amber from the flashing lights atop the prowl cars, and hundreds more had gathered at the intersections. The street possessed a morbid carnival air that forced the two detectives to quicken their pace up the glass-littered stoop. The window panels were blown out of the doors and the vestibule was pockmarked with bullets. The cop assigned to the death watch glanced dolefully at them. A blood-soaked shoe lay in the corner and the bodies had been pulled from the entrance and placed along the inner hall. A twisted blue trouser leg stuck out from one of the canvas covers. The detectives continued up the stairs. At the landing they had to squeeze past civilian-clad inspectors and other detectives, who stood outside the room nodding and talking in the hushed tones one would use at a wake.

Inside, the harsh floods the photographers used reflected off the gold-braided hats and shiny buttons of grim-faced police chiefs. Lab men were dusting the table and the walls, and taking the identification prints of the dead, who lay within chalked outlines. Shadows of profiles and full figures jumped along the walls, as the artificial brightness transformed the room into an abstract black-on-white world.

"Christ, this is going to be some night," a young detective said, easing past the two men who had just come in.

"Any leads yet?" one of them asked.

The young detective stopped, seemed about to say something, then shrugged and stepped past them, his voice coming back softly over his shoulder. "You find out," he said, and disappeared into the hall.

The taller of the two detectives was a Negro, his lean, athletic frame enhancing his conservative dark tropical suit. His high cheekbones and aquiline nose gave

14

him almost the look of an American aborigine, but the soft brown eyes and the heavy lips underlined the African heritage proclaimed by his amber-brown skin.

His partner, white and ruddy-faced, nudged him. "Come on," he said in a whisper.

The two of them walked over to the precinct captain, who stood in civilian dress in the center of the room, conversing with a dignified-looking elderly man. They stopped just short of overhearing, but in a position to be seen, and waited.

To an avid reader of inexpensive paperbacks, the white detective might have taken on mythic dimensions: square jaw, pugnacious nose and the deep narrow eyes in an Irish face that supposedly spelled "cop." He was taller than average, but his stocky, muscular frame shortened his appearance. Under the hat his hair was sandy and his clothes had a slightly rumpled, uncared-for look.

The old man talking to the captain shook his head to signal the end of the official conversation and, picking up the unmistakable black leather bag of a medical examiner, walked past the detectives. They held their distance a moment longer, as Captain Paul Matthews looked around broodingly at the crowded, active room. He seemed relatively young, but as they walked up to him the lines around his eyes, magnified through the horn-rimmed glasses, exposed his age, along with the deep contours around his mouth and neck.

"I thought you'd still be on sick leave, Frank. Everything all right now?" Matthews asked the white detective in a tired tone that somehow still carried genuine concern.

Frank Sullivan stared at him before answering, trying to read another meaning into the question, but he found none in the deep gray eyes. "I got a clean bill of health from the surgeon's office this morning." He paused, then added reassuringly, "Everything's all right, Captain. I'm fine."

They held the stare for a couple of seconds. "Good," Matthews said finally. "I'm going to need every man on the squad." His gaze drifted toward the front of the room and settled on the covered bodies lying in front of the bullet-pitted wall and broken windows. "We got

15

a hell of a mess on our hands, Frank. Four got it up here and you saw what was in the hall."

"How about witnesses, Captain?" the young Negro detective asked. "Are there any people we can start to work from?" His articulation was sharp.

Matthews turned to him. His face hardened and the gray eyes came through the horn-rimmed glasses with all their twenty-five years of cop behind them. "Sure," he said. "All that shooting and the front windows laying out in the street, I would say maybe fifty people got some kind of a look at who did this. Enough witnesses to where we could have a good composite, but we can't get one of them to come forward. We've already checked the street and talked to the people in the adjoining buildings, but nobody's seen a thing." He didn't try to conceal the contempt he felt for the neighborhood. "Because these people don't want to know from nothing. They're cop haters and if a couple of cops got killed tonight, fine, that's fine. It's two less they have to hate."

Bill Pope knew the moment he asked the question that it was a mistake, that he should have cooled it and waited, letting his senior partner carry the inquiries. But the words weren't as stinging as indictment against race as they sounded, for in the short time he had worked under this hard-nosed man he had found him to be an honest, fair superior who seemed to treat the black cops under his command the same as he treated the whites. Paul Matthews undoubtedly was afflicted with the human failing of prejudice as much as or maybe more than most men because of his job, but professionally he surmounted it and was capable of separating the man from his color when it came to doing his work as a policeman. And that was really all you could ask, because Pope, since being assigned to Harlem, had learned how exceedingly difficult it was just to separate himself emotionally from the environment.

The three of them had fallen silent, watching the death detail move in. The ambulance attendants, with their stretchers and canvas bags, pulled off the hasty coverings the police had thrown over the bodies and started to bundle the dead to the waiting ambulances for the ride downtown to the cold slabs of Bellevue's morgue. They

16

turned a twisted body onto its back, the black face now ashen in a strangely peaceful repose as if death brought beautiful sleep. Sullivan took a quick glance at Matthews, then back to another face—another Negro—but this face held the horror of the killing. The open eyes stared blindly, the lips were parted wide, and Sullivan could almost hear the scream that had rolled out of the purple mouth.

When the last weaving stretcher had passed him, Sullivan said, "They're Doc Johnson's boys." His voice was flat and controlled, but the surprise came through as he realized how big this shooting was, the ramifications it could have, and now he knew why Paul Matthews seemed tired and old and so deeply concerned. "I had no idea, Matt," he said. "I thought this was strictly amateur night in a shooting gallery."

"Professionals," Matthews answered him, letting the words sink in. His eyes went across both detectives and settled on Sullivan. "This thing had to be cased too well to have amateurs behind it. But they must have been shitting in their pants pulling it off." He motioned toward the caked and drying vomit lying across the overturned suitcase. "It looks like Johnson was turning over the weekly take." The voice droned on in the city accent that seemed so colloquially appropriate to New York cops. "The white guys figure as the collecting arm for the downtown crowd. That's what I meant about it being well cased. They're always careful about the pickup, but I guess they thought they'd never be hit up here, so their guard must have been down. They didn't seem to put up a fight; we don't know if they were in any sick plan to go or if the machine-gunner panicked."

Pope looked at the shades hanging shredded and torn at the windows, the pools of blood on the floor coagulating to brown smears, and he remembered the bodies being packed onto stretchers. He thought of the savage violence that must have been behind the gun. Panic or not, he knew it took a cold calculation to premeditate a crime such as this, a coldness that sent a chill across his imagination. "They didn't take any chances on missing," he said.

"How could they with the arsenal they were carrying?" Pope heard the captain answer, and he turned back to face him. "And that partially explains why the patrol-

17

men downstairs didn't get any shots off." The captain spoke slowly, reexamining his first impressions more analytically now, as if he were using them as a sounding board. "It's one of those unfortunate situations of being in the right place at the wrong time." He paused, the lights in the room reflecting off his glasses; behind them his eyes seemed to be searching for answers. "I guess that's the part that bothers me the most." His voice lost the tough tone of authority. "I just didn't think I had anyone in my command who when they seen that gun wouldn't have dropped them where they stood or at least got some shots off." His words trailed off and he shrugged into silence, but his words hung in the seething heat of the room, chafing in the stilled cigarette smoke above their heads like a neon light one could see flickering through night fog. Matthews had voiced the silent query of every police official there. He knew it would be the first question asked in downtown headquarters at Centre Street tomorrow morning. An isolated cop killed in the line of duty: part of the job. Two cops killed together in a violent death: there'll be an investigation. A quiet one? He could try to cover it in a screen of lies: Precinct Captain Paul Matthews at the scene of the crime expressed the opinion that robbery of a high-stakes card game between white and Negro professional gamblers was done in hasty awkwardness by amateurs and culminated in the slaughter of . . .

There were inspectors, deputy inspectors and lieutenants from Manhattan Detectives North. The commissioner and his chief inspector made their customary appearance, mouthed the clichés and disappeared. But the press were aware Matthews was the precinct captain, so they went for him. They stuck their radio mikes and television cameras into his face; the brass stood on the side as though not wanting to get involved but stayed close enough to hear what he was going to say to reporters, who recorded and quoted with quick scribbled notes. Then most of them disappeared with his fabrications to make late-news shows and morning pictorials. Harlem was the new news beat now. Los Angeles had its Watts and Chicago its South Side and Detroit its gutted slum, but New York had the biggest and best black ghetto of them all. And it sold papers and filled commercial air time. News people told of the rallies of black nationalists and militants, their marches and picketings, and echoed the black power cries of the activists. But Matthews detested the superficial coverage. Why no lurid headlines about the four murders last week and three the week before, which helped add up to twelve homicides in a typical month in the community called Harlem? But he knew New York was fun city, so why jar the great white multitudes in their middle-class world: aren't there enough of them moving to the suburbs? So don't mention it; don't give the town a black eye, and remember the politicians and the tourists board and the merchants' associations; black kills black—the hell with it because New York's a summer festival.

A uniformed cop walked into the room and quickly spotted Matthews. The throng had thinned out, the police photographers had doused their floods and were packing their gear. Several of the gold badges and braid still lingered, talking among themselves, their presence lending authority. But it was Matthews' precinct, his command, and he would handle the details. Only the laboratory men were still working, in the painstakingly deliberate movements of their trade.

"Captain." The young patrolman's voice was edged with an urgency that pulled Matthews around.

"Yeah?" The demeanor of command returned. "Yeah, what is it?"

"A call came over the intercom for you, sir. They picked up the man who rents this apartment and he's being questioned at the precinct."

"Good," Matthews said. "Tell them I'll be right over." He turned back to the detectives, tiredness still hanging over his face, but he had pushed the perplexities to the back of his mind because the tedious task of tracking down leads had begun. "I want you two to go over to the emergency ward of Harlem Hospital; one of Johnson's men is still alive. How the Christ he ever survived this, I don't know. But as long as he's still breathing I want a statement. I want you to try to get as much information out of him as you possibly can. I got every man on the squad working tonight and I told them what

19

I'm telling you two." He lowered his voice, not wishing to be overheard. "By tomorrow morning I want to have a report that can be put together against a lot of questions from downtown. So I want everything—quotes, details, everything and anything that's pertinent to this case." They both stood motionless; the order seemed too general, so they waited a moment longer for specifics and then realized they were being given initiative to move as they saw fit. They nodded confirmation, turned and were at the door when his voice stopped them. "Sullivan." There was no command in the tone. The white detective walked slowly back; his Negro partner waited at the door.

"Frank." Matthews hesitated as if he had something difficult to say. His eyes held with Sullivan's for a few seconds, then broke away uncomfortably. "I'm throwing the papers in, Frank."

"What?" Sullivan's ruddy, blue-eyed face showed its sudden concern. "I figured you all the way for a full thirty, Matt."

"No," Matthews said flatly. "I can't stand this shit anymore. I guess my type of cop has had his day, so I'm going to get out and try a couple of things I always wanted to do while I still can."

"Matt, if they don't want your type anymore, then the department's in a lot of trouble."

The captain's lips moved in an imperceptible smile that seemed to say thank you. Theirs was a mutual respect that leaned toward admiration. Frank Sullivan had worked under him for two years, ever since Matthews had taken command of the precinct after the shakeup. They had found that both were cut from the same rough cloth of middle-class Irish beginnings. Matthews had had to work it using the books and rode arduously up through the competitive tests of civil service. He found his ambition equaled in Sullivan's rise to first-grade detective. But this was a different, more fatalistic drive, which Matthews at times found barely understandable, for Frank Sullivan was trouble, something every precinct commander tried to avoid. Still the captain had protected him, held on to him. Not because he knew some people had labeled Sullivan as a brutal nigger-hating cop with an unenviable record of three killings, all done in the line of duty. There was a possibility of truth on the surface. But he also knew the man underneath, his innate honesty and the pride that he carried in the swaggering walk. Sullivan was an anachronism, a throwback to the detectives of another era who had moved through the streets and clubs and dives and earned reputations for toughness that put respect and awe into the meaning of the word "cop." Matthews held on to him for another, more selfish reason. He was a nostalgic mirror, though blurred by time, reflecting the view he had held of himself fifteen years before.

"So if I seem a little edgy, now you know why," Matthews said softly. "It took me quite a while to decide to pack it in." There was a wistfulness in him that made Sullivan want to grasp his hand and wish him luck and tell him that he had made the right decision. But in that busy room with its stink of death it would have been fraternization of the worst kind. There will be a testimonial and he will be there to sing the cheers with the others across the table full of Scotch and pitchers of beer, and that will be the right and proper way to do it.

"If this is going to be your windup," Sullivan said quietly, "then we're going to miss you, Matt."

"This is the last one, Frank, I guarantee you that. That's why I want everything done just right. I"—again he groped for the right words—"I guess I want to leave as a cop. They say the last one you work on is the one you remember." His eyes went about the room as he assured himself he was not being overheard. His voice became hoarse, almost a whisper. "So I'm going to handle this as it should be done. I'm going to bug a lot of bastards who need to be bothered, because this is going to be played the old way for a change. That's why I'm taking the leash off you and every man in the precinct."

A smile started to cross Frank Sullivan's face, as he caught the permeating excitement of the words. He knew the repercussions it could create, and if it was to be a strong exit he was grateful to be a spear carrier in such a final act. "What's your theories, Matt?" Sullivan was surprised to hear the emotional charge of his own voice.

"I think this was a local affair." The natural gruffness came back into the captain's tone; his moment of disclosure was past. "This was no hit or miss; it had to be plotted. You know as well as I whites would be pretty conspicuous casing something like this." The gray eyes widened behind the glasses as if in some kind of begrudging tribute. "It took a lot of balls to pull this off, but more than that, it took some inside knowledge. Maybe Doc Johnson's got some insurgents on his hands." He shrugged and shook his head. "I don't know, but it's still something to think about."

A paunchy, aging police official standing with an assistant inspector was clearly impatient to give some kind of parting instructions to Matthews. He signaled that he wanted to speak to him. "If you don't get anything at the hospital I want you and your partner to stay in the streets and play it by ear." Matthews took a step toward his superior and stopped. "And, Frank, any methods you use, I'll back you." Their eyes held for a moment and then Sullivan nodded, acknowledging the authority he was being given.

He turned to his partner and the two of them moved down the stairs past the two now-empty chalked outlines on the floor and out into the simmering street.

Chapter 3

The stone fence ran the length of the spacious lawn, rising up out of the shadows like a foreboding barrier, insisting on privacy for the rambling, imposing houses behind it. The man had parked discreetly on the quiet tree-lined street and now he walked up the graveled driveway. His footsteps seemed a paradox in the evening heat, for they echoed like strides across freshly fallen snow. He had gotten the call and driven quickly up Manhattan's West Side Highway, across the George Washington Bridge to this palatial house atop the Palisades of New Jersey. He had wondered about the call and thought maybe the old man was dying and The Family being summoned to pay its last respects. But no extra cars were parked in the driveway or street and there were only a couple of lights on in the house. Let 'em surprise me, he thought, pressing the button, and the chimes played their subdued chord behind the heavy oaken door. There was a wait and then the knob turned once, twice and the door flung open and he stared down at a curious, wide-eyed child. The dark curly hair of the boy needed trimming and it jounced on his head as he quickly, furtively turned back toward the approaching stout woman in the white uniform of a domestic.

"Antony." Her voice was barely composed and she would have yelled at him if the man weren't there. "You no supposed to open the door. You grandfather tell you, I tell you."

But the boy ignored her. His large dark eyes had already begun their search of the stranger in the doorway. Her starched uniform crinkled as she grabbed the boy's hand from the knob and pulled him protectively behind her, looking hard at the trim olive-skinned man. A perceptible aura of disquiet about him that seemed to manifest itself in his deep-set almond eyes forced a wary respect in her tone of inquiry.

"Yessir, mister, what'd you want?"

"I have an appointment with Mr. Giaccano." His voice was a murmurous rasp, the thin tight mouth barely moving. "Tell him Nick Difalco is here."

She stared at him, trying to decide what business this ominous-looking man had with her employer. Then her eyes dropped as she remembered the many stories of rumored enterprises based on illegitimate business. But she didn't want to believe any of it; her employer seemed to her truly kind and gentle. . . . The boy broke away from her grip and started down the wide chandeliered hallway.

"Grandpa, Grandpa," he called, then opened a door and disappeared.

The servant sighed in exasperation and motioned the stranger reluctantly into the coolness of the air-conditioned house, closing the door behind him. Nick Difalco's eyes took in the crystal chandelier, the ornate white staircase leading to the upper floor and the paintings hanging along the wall. He removed his hat and waited. His black hair, receding slightly, was combed straight back, blending into the high-cheekboned face. The tight body in the dark Continental suit was trim and cared for.

The woman had followed the path of the boy down the long carpeted foyer and gone into a room near the foot of the stairs. She emerged a moment later. "Okay, Mr. Giaccano he wanna see you."

Difalco was about to pass her. "Mister, you no stay too long, huh?" She said it quietly with a touch of pleading in her voice. "Mr. Giaccano he no feel too good and . . ." Difalco's impassive stare cut her words short. She lowered her head and backed off, embarrassed.

As Difalco opened the door, he could hear the squeal of the child and the laughter of the man; her concern didn't seem to be shared by Giaccano.

"Come in, come right in, Nick." The old man's hoarse voice filled the study, but his appearance came as a shock. The boy, sitting on the arm of the chair cuddled next to his grandfather, became silent again. Some pictures hung on the wall with little lights over them, as in a museum. A sculptured Madonna and Child stood in one corner and a dark cherry-wood stereo was against another wall, the shelves above it filled with records and books. The child was annoyed at the stranger; he wanted to continue the impromptu romp. But the old man ended it. "Okay, Tony." He slapped him gently on the rump. "You go with Angela and get your bath now." The child went reluctantly. He looked back at the old man, who smiled paternally, as Angela took the boy's hand firmly and quietly shut the door. "Some kid, huh?" Giaccano mumbled, and continued to gaze at the closed door.

Then he looked up at the humorless face of Difalco. "Sit down, Nick," he said, pointing to a seat opposite him.

"How do you feel, Mr. Giaccano?" Difalco's tone was metallic and unsympathetic but the words were respectfully correct.

"Hah!" Giaccano waved his arm in a disdainful gesture of dismissal and Difalco knew he shouldn't continue the synthetic commiseration.

He hadn't seen the patriarch in over six months. The word had filtered down that the old man was very sick; Difalco had discounted it as wishful talk of the ambitious. But he believed it now as he watched Giccano pour wine into crystal glasses from the serving table. The gray hair was whiter than he remembered, the body had shriveled, and there were indelible lines of age across the sunken face. But it was mainly the eyes which told the story, red-rimmed, tired and now too big in his head. The thin hand, lost in the sleeve of the expensive satin robe, pushed a drink toward him. The old man looked up and caught disillusionment in Difalco's gaze, which he misread as sadness.

"Everybody get sick, Nicky; it's just my turn."

"How bad is it?"

Giaccano picked up his drink, lights catching in the vermilion liquid as he twisted the glass slowly in his hand. "They cut me open, take something out and sew me up and now I wait to see what happens. It's a funny thing: most of the time I feel okay."

Difalco wanted to tell him, You'll be all right. But he could see death in the old man, he could see it stamped across his face. He picked up the drink and held it toward him, "With God's help," he said, and took a sip.

The don showed no acknowledgment of the salute. "How old are you now, Nicky? Thirty-five, thirty-six?"

"Forty-two, Mr. Giaccano."

The old man shook his head thoughtfully. "Time, you wonder where it goes. I remember when you were just a kid; I was moving up and you were just coming in." A wisp of melancholic smile touched the tired face. "You were just a button then, a lousy punk kid. But you did all right; you built a good reputation for yourself, Nicky, with the family. I get good reports about you all the time."

Difalco felt a certain gratification at the words being put to him by this ranking patrician, but he didn't know which direction the old man was taking the talk, so he averted his eyes and remained silent. Giaccano's smile disappeared and he stared at the younger man as if ascertaining his future value.

"I guess you'd like to move up a little higher, huh, Nicky?"

Difalco looked up quickly, found the old man's eyes boring into him. "I never said that, Mr. Giaccano," he answered slowly, full of caution.

"You don't have to; ambition she's written all over you. You're wearing two-hundred-dollar suits and forty-dollar shoes and I bet your shirts are made to order. You got style, Nicky. You're a couple of cuts above the average guy that I got working for me and somehow you got lost in the shuffle, huh?"

Difalco watched the old don rise with a noticeable effort. The emaciated body labored as he walked to the picture window facing the Hudson. In the distance the lights flickered like tiny jewels in Manhattan's skyline. A tug's whistle rolled up mournfully from the river and there was the dull, aggressive drone of a jet reaching for altitude. But Nick Difalco never heard a sound, for his mind was too full of this enigmatic, almost threatening old man. Giaccano wanted it that way. He wanted Difalco's sleek hardness to squirm, he wanted to remind him that he could have him dead within a couple of hours after he left the house if he gave the order. That he controlled the destinies of shylocks, bookmakers, pimps and whores, pushers, labor unionists, extortionists and executioners. That he held the most prestigious of the Cosa Nostra dominions in the country. For the New York—New Jersey area was divided into five uneven sections and his was the most lucrative, with gang money to pour into the takeover of legitimate banking, investment and real estate firms, trucking and garbage collecting companies. He supervised control over recordings, jukeboxes, vending machines and Big Board securities; and he was going to die. He was on the national commission, maybe the biggest one of them all, and some sheeny bastard of a surgeon cut him open, sewed him up, then sent him home, telling him he had maybe six months to live. He could feel the bitter rage swelling up in his emaciated body. He, who had put the key working fix on union and business executives, elected officials and the indispensable cops, was going to die. He had to smash out against the tomb that was closing about him, to prove

26

to himself that he could still make his world crawl at his feet. He turned and looked at Difalco.

"I think tonight I give you a big opportunity." The gray head nodded slowly. "Yeah, maybe after tonight I move you up from behind the hatchet to some kind of a piece of the action. You like that, Nicky? Hey, I don't have to ask, huh? I can see it in your face. The trouble with you, you're too good in doing your job. In our thing a guy can stand still for a long time because we"—he left no doubt the "we" meant himself—"think maybe there's nobody around that can fill a good man's place if he goes up. I farm you out for contracts all over the country; the other families they want to use your talents all the time. But I become blind, I keep you nothing more than a special soldier. Now maybe I move you up to a capo. There's an opening now and I think it's about time some new blood starts pumping up. But I'm gonna tell you something, Nicky." The wrinkled face showed disgust. "I got a lot of stupidos working for me, guys moving up through the organization that the worst they ever do is make book or work a shit muscle. In the old days I don't let them shine my shoes." He shook his head sadly. "But these are the times so you live with what you got. But you, Nicky, you got the credentials. I think maybe you make a good capo in our regime."

Difalco sat perfectly still. Giaccano was well known for offering inducements, but if a prize was to be gotten he knew that in the end it had to be paid for, as the old man always got his pound of flesh in return. Still, he couldn't deny the excitement the offer generated as he watched the don walk toward him. He could see the change in the old man, the anger behind the eyes, which suddenly didn't seem as tired, the flaccid mouth and neck, which somehow had firmed into a semblance of the man he remembered. Even the leaden gray face took on the color of health.

"You know what happened tonight, Nicky." It wasn't a question the way Giaccano said it, but a statement. "We got hit good. The full Harlem take. I lose five guys in the heist and the sloppy bums that did it also kill a couple of cops."

It was the first Difalco had heard of it. He had received a phone call and was told to get over to the old man's house right away and nothing more. Now, as he sat staring up at Giaccano's wrath, his mind clicked like a computer, calculating the significance. "The full take," he said aloud, and almost whistled thinking of the amount of money it must have been. But he knew it was suicidal. Whenever the Syndicate was hit in the past, and this had been rare, they all had the same endings written off in red ink, but their code, their very foundation, dictated that the ink would be supplied by the blood of whoever had done it. Now Nick Difalco knew why he was here. Still, why the don was toying with him, offering a possible jump up in The Family, didn't jell. It didn't need a specialist on a kill like this. Rumors based on facts would filter through the organization, for everybody would be seeking out the smell of hot money. He had no doubt that the perpetrators would be found; a day, a week, a month, it didn't matter. Then whoever had done it would be dead; as simple as that. It didn't warrant a bonus. Any button in The Family anywhere in the country could handle the execution.

Giaccano spread his arms, his hands palm up, as if his problems were too large and he was asking help from some personal deity. "So what do I do, huh? Do I call that *scimmia* who's running things for us up there, give him a slap on the wrist and tell him you no lose any more money and let him go on like before and wait for it to happen again?"

Difalco knew he didn't want any answers; they had been thought out beforehand and if they hadn't he was not going to suggest any, because if they went wrong he knew he might have to pay for them.

"Oh, I knock off who's responsible. Maybe it take some time, but we get them eventually, hey, Nicky? But what do I do now, right tonight, huh?" The old man shut off his rage like a faucet, containing it in his eyes, which compounded with the inner fury of his strategy. He sat down on the sofa again and leaned forward, his voice lowering. "I tell you what I do: I teach him something they don't forget." His thin fingers moved out of the silk robe and pointed like a gun aimed at Difalco's chest. "I'm giving you the contract, Nicky. I want whoever pulled

28

this caper off to lay dead like nobody ever died before."

Difalco lowered his eyes to the marble-top serving table and his hand toyed absently with the wineglass. Giaccano shrewdly read the meaning.

"I know what you think, Nicky. You feel anybody could do that kind of a job, that I'd be wasting your talents." The old man leaned back and shook his head slowly. "But you're wrong. What I got in mind is going to take a specialist with lots of moxie. That's why I sent for you. This is going to be handled like nothing you ever done before because I'm sending you up there with only two guys, and you pick them long on guts because I think they're going to need it."

Difalco didn't look up, not wanting the old don to see the problems he foresaw in this.

"The way I'm going to set this up is have that spade Johnson do the leg work. Then he is going to stand by while you do his job. That way we let all his black crowd know that we don't consider him big enough to do his own enforcing on something like this. And remember, you're acting in my name, Nick. You let them know who's boss, you understand?"

Difalco nodded his head affirmatively, but how could he permit himself to be sent to Harlem on such a nebulous mission? He realized that his appearance would show the dissatisfaction at the top, that he could blast Johnson verbally for letting it happen. But that was as far as he could go until they found out who did it, and it didn't figure that Doc Johnson would be able to finger anyone this quickly. He would have to explain this to the old man, tell him not to expect wonders, that it would take time. He looked up at the intense, haggard face, again drained of color.

"What happens, Mr. Giaccano, if he can't turn up anybody?" Difalco's soft, raspy voice began subtly to manipulate the old man back to the standard procedures of reality. "I'm not coppin' no plea for him, Mr. G., but it's kinda doubtful that he can roust out whoever did it on such short notice. It's a lotta town to go through, especially when somebody don't wanna be found."

Giaccano leaned forward impatiently, the fingers of

his hand bunching together. "Nicky, this was a nigger hit."
The younger man's brow furrowed, the eyes narrowing
still further in his high-cheekboned face. "Hey, they
didn't tell you on the phone?" Giaccano's voice carried
surprise. "I thought you knew."

"I didn't know. I just took it for granted it was a
white man's heist."

"Yeah, I find it hard to believe, too," the old man
snarled, "but I got a call from Johnson. One of the cops
he got on the payroll up there told him it was blacks that
done it, that's why he's got to produce fast or he's going
to be in a lot more trouble than he is right now. I won't
have any bullsh—"

The cough came suddenly and made Giaccano bend
over with pain. His hand groped inside the robe pocket
for a handkerchief and he pressed it across his mouth.
Difalco started to rise to help him but the old man
waved him down. It took him fully a minute to gain control of his spasmed body. His eyes watered and he
wiped spittle from his lips. He was embarrassed by the
attack and stood up, wanting to get away from Difalco's
stare of sympathy, detesting the pity he thought he saw
in the dark eyes of his underling. He paced the floor
slowly, pushing back sickness by the remembrance of
who he was and what he represented. And then he was
the don again, the Mafioso head of an invincible Family,
who had built his rank and reputation on a violent temper and quick retaliation. He stopped in the middle on
the floor, whirling around to Difalco. "I been hearing
about this nigger wanting a bigger piece of the take, but
every time I see him he's an Uncle Tom slobbering all
over me. I got a problem, though: no matter who I put
up there it's going to be the same thing, because when you
get an outsider to run a store for you you take a chance.
They start to see all that money and begin to get big-
shot ideas, and the only way to keep them in their place
is fear. You know what I mean?"

Difalco's dark heavy brows arched questioningly. "You
think he engineered the hit?"

"I thought about that, too," the old don answered
slowly, "but I don't think so. He's got to have more brains
than that to try to pull something as loud as this. But
30

that don't get him off no hook. I'm still going to give him and that whole goddamn black area up there a lesson they don't forget soon. I want whoever pulled this shit to lay on display in the middle of Harlem so nobody else will have the guts to try something like this ever again."

The old don's eyes burned into his enforcer's with all the malignant passion of one fully savoring the power of reprisal, and by force of habit he leaned forward, his voice shading down to conspiratorial growls, as if he were plotting across a checkered tablecloth and it was twenty years ago in a Little Italy restaurant on Mulberry Street, on the Lower East Side. "But to do that, Nicky, I'm going to have you operate out in the open. No back alley stuff on this one, because I want you to flash the muscle so everybody can see it. Let them know we run things and nobody"—the thin-veined fingers again curled into a gnarled fist and he raised it in front of Difalco's face—"but nobody goes against us and lives. And I want that lesson given to them tonight while this thing is still the hot uptown talk. I know"—he nodded his head at Difalco's muteness to show that he respected and recognized the validity of his enforcer's earlier question—"I know he may not turn up somebody this quick, but he's got to have some idea who pulled this off. Maybe he ends up guessing on a couple of punks, and it don't matter if they did it or not because we're gonna use them anyway, we're gonna pin the rap on them for a quick showcase. And if you can't find some of the names he gives you, Nicky, I want you to go after somebody in their families— a wife, a mother, father, I don't care who, just so long as you cut them open and lay them dead in the middle of the street."

Difalco stared at the old man. Only minutes before he had doubted the old man's competence and now he marveled at the quick retribution he had planned. It was Chicago and prohibition and all the things the Syndicate in its sophistication now tried to avoid. It was a brutal reprisal and he realized that it was so right for this thing it was almost classic. He was going to bring back the stone age of trigger men in cruising sedans surreptitiously shooting up a street some mark was on, then

31

hightailing it away; he was going to work with only two others and they would stay and hopefully, methodically, pile the dead one on top of the other for all to see. It didn't bother Difalco that he might have to kill the innocent; they had been killed before and that was almost classic, too. Now he knew why he was there, but he wondered if Giaccano knew how difficult a contract he was giving him. He had always prided himself on the seclusion of his hits, well-thought-out acts of privacy with exits; but now the cops would be moving up there. Since they lost two they would be shaking the streets with their own code of retaliation.

He listened to the old don filling him in on the take from Harlem's narcotics and policy rackets, the gambling and loan-sharking, the strings of clubs, bars and whorehouses, and on the kickbacks to politicians and cops that kept them in business, and finally on Doc Johnson's commission and how much it cost to maintain his black help to run their uptown vices. He watched the gray head punctuate the words with gestures and nods, half hearing the sick, hoarse voice and thinking that he was being given a smell of the brimming, rich, corrupt pot, but the lid would close before he had an opportunity to dip down into it if he didn't execute Giaccano's orders. Well, he'd deliver, but good. He resented others he considered his inferiors moving up in The Family because of strong blood lines, the right Sicilian marriages and better connections. Yeah, he'd go up to Harlem and do the risky, dirty job because he was Nick Difalco. Giaccano was dying, but as long as he lived he was still the boss and the organization would listen when he told them "Difalco moves up."

The knock at the door brought the don to silence. The domestic, without waiting for an answer, came into the room holding the hand of the scrubbed, bright-eyed child, now dressed in short summer pajamas. "Antony wanted to say good night before he went to bed," she said, acting as though the stranger weren't there. And the old man did, too. The wizened face broke into a grin, he opened his arms and the boy came running to him, then he closed them about the small body, and the dark, haggard eyes

32

flashed with unexpected vitality. But there was a sadness, too. And it was possible to see tears as the don stared above the small tousled head buried in his chest.

"Some kid," he said. "Some kid."

Chapter 4

They pushed through the emergency entrance of Harlem Hospital, the small reception area surprisingly empty except for a nurse sitting behind a desk. Bill Pope flashed the badge and was about to speak when she pointed languidly. "Turn left; he's in Receiving Room Two," she said, and went back to her two-finger struggle with the typewriter, taking advantage of the momentary quiet to fill out reports before the next screaming crisis rushed at her through the swinging doors.

As they turned down the corridor they saw the uniformed patrolman stationed at the end of the hall, and the hospital smell reached out fetidly for Frank Sullivan. Walls once white reflected the dull overhead lights screwed into the ceiling as they walked past wheelchairs and rolling stretchers down the passageway. Sullivan could sense the hopelessness that inhabited the aging building, nesting above him in the rooms of the insured and wards of the impoverished, and with it came memories he had tried to bury. . . . The truck had been around the bend and seemed to materialize out of nowhere. He hit the brakes but the car had been going too fast—too fast. The brakes had locked and the passenger side turned into the impact. The windows had blown in a sickening crash of metal that bent the frame like a toy. He'd been thrown clear. . . . The clicks of their heels on the polished linoleum floor echoed loudly down the silent hall. To Sullivan the sounds were dreadfully similar to the steps he had taken beside the highway patrolman in that upstate hospital. He remembered mumbling a rosary into an incoherency, his eyes jumping frantically between the stretchers on which his wife and child were lying silent

33

and bleeding, with the blankets pulled up almost over their faces. He was told to wait outside the room and he watched them, as the hospital personnel rushed past into the emergency room, their faces grim in silent prognostication, their strained eyes as they came out telling the story of what was happening behind the doors. The priest trotted down the hall, again the echoing steps, and he went into the room. Then the old nurse yelling to the elevator operator: "Hold it, hold it, we're taking her up." And her dress lay in shreds beneath her where they had cut it off the crushed body. A tube ran into her arm from the bottle of plasma hooked to a hinge above her head. "And what about the boy, the *boy?*" he screamed. And they told him he was dead. He buried his face in his hands, covered with their blood, and turned to the wall, and nobody came near him, nobody knew what to say. An hour later she died on the operating table.

"Hey, Howie, how's it going?" Pope called affably to the cop standing outside the door.

Sullivan returned the cop's smile with a curt nod and followed his Negro partner into the brightly lighted white-tiled emergency room. A bottle of blood tubed down into the naked dark form that lay on a cushioned slab below the hot overhead lights. A colored nurse looked up absently, then went back to assisting the intern. The youthful doctor, his bland features beaded with sweat, seemed unaware of their presence, for his attention was riveted on the probe he moved through the rent flesh that was peeled back by clamps tying off the veins and arteries to hold back the flow of blood. The body lay still, silent as the dead and unmindful of the ravishing probe plunging into it, spreading and tearing the puckered flesh into red, raw meat.

The detectives, standing one on each side of the table, had grown morbidly fascinated by the pincer as it penetrated into the oozing flesh and extracted flattened lead. The clang of the lead as it was released into a tin basin seemed exceedingly loud in the quiet room. The head moved and a gurgling torment tore unexpectedly up at them; they looked at the intern, for the pained cry rolling deep from the throat of the wounded man touched their experience, the sound not unlike the rattle of death.

"Is he going to make it, doc?" Sullivan's voice carried no concern, his tone doubting he would.

The intern's glasses reflected the light, his face twisting in concentration as he found another bullet, this one embedded near the groin. They watched him ease it gently out of the pliant flesh; the basin clanged again.

"I don't know if he's going to live," the intern answered tiredly, not looking up.

"Can we talk to him?" Pope asked, and his eyes drifted back to the ashen black face staring up, unseeing, its eyes dilated and half open.

The doctor mumbled something to the nurse and leaned across the wounded man, the thin probe again digging into the racked body. "I just gave him another sedative to deaden the pain." His voice was edged with irritation. "He'll be going upstairs in a moment."

"How long before we can question him?" the white detective asked, his voice falling into the flat monotone of his profession.

He waited for an answer, but none came. The detective scowled with open annoyance. The intern was holding them back with his hunched-over medical possession of the body, concerned only with his probing and extracting and patching together of what was left of the victim. And in a few minutes they would lose him altogether to the injected sedation and then to the more experienced surgeon waiting somewhere in the hospital.

Frank Sullivan leaned toward the doctor, his face hanging above the body. His voice was low, but the tone cut with a jagged emphasis. "That's a prisoner you're working on. He's the only witness to a multiple murder that included two patrolmen. Now I want to know how long before we can talk to him."

Crude bastard, the intern thought, and for the first time he looked up. He was surprised how close the detective had pushed his face to his. He looked into the acrid blue eyes staring out from the pugnacious, ruddy face. "No sooner than forty-eight hours, if then," he said, not trying to hide his own tartness. His youthful face showed its fatigue, the eyes behind the glasses were strained, and he appeared older than he was.

"You mean he's going to make it?" Pope said from his side of the table.

The intern looked indignantly at him. "I didn't say that. He has a chance if you two will let me continue without these interruptions."

"That's no answer, doc." Sullivan said it with a baiting, calculated roughness. "What we want to know is if this guy's going to be alive two days from now."

The doctor looked at him curiously, then at Pope, and realized he was caught. He knew they were taking liberties with him they wouldn't take with an older, more worldly man. He could yell at them to go out, but he doubted that they would, and maybe they were right. Maybe a more seasoned, practical man would let them do their repulsive job while he labored over his. He shrugged off his medical stance and stared down at the black, bullet-punctured body. "I doubt he'll make it," he said quietly. "I think I'm fighting a losing battle. He's just shot up too much."

"Well, then, we really don't have a choice, do we, doctor?" Sullivan's voice eased and commiserated with the intern's frustration. "It's either question him now or maybe never."

"I don't know if you'll get through," the intern replied, taking a fresh syringe from the nurse. "This man was in a semiconscious state when he was brought in. He's under drugs now, but in his condition of pain"—he shook his head—"I don't know if he went under completely. You still might be able to get through to him." Then a caustic smiled played about the corners of the the intern's mouth. "Now I hope you don't mind if I continue; I'll try not to bother you."

They ignored his touch of sarcasm, their interest absorbed by the nearly dead man stretched out before them. His eyes were closed and dried blood and fresh spittle clung to his lips, the mouth twisted apart as if anticipating the next charge of pain.

"Hey, man, you hear me?" Sullivan said, leaning down toward the anguished face. "Who got you, man?" Only labored breathing came from the Negro hood, and Sullivan thought, This son of a bitch is going fast. He had an impulse to touch him, shake him, and then thought how

36

ridiculous it was fighting the intern for a shot-up body that couldn't respond. But he leaned closer and tried again. "Who shot you, boy? You hear me, man? How many were in on the holdup?" A guttural moan rose from the man and his head tensed in a new spasm of suffering. Sullivan's brow creased as he glanced at Pope, encouraged that life still ticked beneath him. He motioned to his partner to take over the questioning.

The Negro detective knew what he wanted. He bent down close to the prisoner's ear. "How many cats made the scene tonight, man?" Pope's voice lost the education and went to the streets, wrapping itself heavily in the black man's intonations. If it was still possible to get through the layers of pain and morphine, this was the kind of talk that might be understood and responded to. "How dey make it into dat room without you cats jumpin' 'em, huh, man?" Again the moan, and the sweating head wove on the vinyl-covered pillow against the piercing probe working in to a final laceration.

The doctor mumbled something to the nurse and she went hurriedly across the room to a glass cabinet that housed surgical instruments, large jars of cotton and gauze. Bill Pope let his eyes drift down to the clamp digging into the body. He looked at the other open punctures across belly and groin, which seemed to be spilling out the man's stomach and intestines and bowels in a seepage of blood and raw flesh. Pope was no stranger to death; he had seen it before lying in the filth of Harlem streets. Then there had been an impersonal detachment that insulated him from it. Now he heard the guttural cry again and knew this black man lingered miraculously past his time.

"Hey, man," he heard himself saying, "man, you're not gonna make it, you hear me, because you're gonna die."

A startling crash came from behind them. A large glass jar the nurse had picked up slipped from her hands and smashed loudly onto the tile floor. The wounded man, who had seemed to lie dead only a second before, sat bolt upright on the table. His scream was not unlike a woman's, its shrillness stunning them into spectators as they watched the grotesque form sit up with a crimson, oozing belly, bellowing with fear while the clamps still clung to the tied-off arteries. His feet swung to the floor as the intern grabbed for his shoulders. The tube from the transfusion bottle ripped from his arm, the blood hitting the floor in a scarlet splash. The cop outside came running in as the Negro gangster shrieked a piercing lament of sorrow. He started to stand and it was then that the detectives moved to restrain him. His heavy, sweating body shuddered in their grasp and pitched forward at Frank Sullivan, the face buried against his shoulder. Then silence. They lifted him gently back upon the emergency table. The nurse grasped his arm and reinserted a tube into the vein.

The doctor turned on the detectives, his face drained of color and his eyes mingling rage and fright. "What the hell do you think we're running here?" His voice quivered. "My God, this is a hospital, not a police station. I don't care what you wanted to question him about. I don't care because he didn't deserve this and neither do I. I don't think you two comprehend or even care what I've done here. For your edification, I've been trying to save a man's life and that *has* to be more important than any kind of information he could give you. And now what you've done is . . . is . . ."

He stood facing them, wanting to add more, but his emotion knotted the words up inside him. Abruptly he looked away, his face showing his disgust, and picked up the stethoscope, then leaned over the now profusely bleeding form. The cop who had come running into the room turned and slowly went back outside to his post. The detectives watched, in sphinx-like silence, the fatigued face of the intern as he searched for a pulse. His eyes closed against the beads of sweat that saturated his brows and ran down the bridge of his nose. He stood motionless in that hunched position over the body for what seemed an endless moment, then slowly he straightened up, continuing to stare down at the ravaged remains.

When he spoke his voice was subdued, the words barely audible. "I'm truly surprised he even lasted this long; he must have had a tremendous will to live." Tiredly he turned from the table and removed the stethoscope from around his neck, stripped the rubber gloves off, fumbled in his pocket for a crumpled pack of cigarettes and took a long-needed drag before he looked at them. "I'm new up here, but tell me: is this a normal situation with the police when they want to question an emergency victim?"

The detectives stared at him, his quiet moral reproof making them feel far guiltier than if he had shouted obscenities. "No, it isn't, doctor," Frank Sullivan said, regret in his tone, "and we owe you an apology."

The intern stuck out his hand and said his name was Levy. "I'll be doing my internship up here for the next couple of years, so I guess I should know you fellows. I expect I'll be seeing you again, but under better conditions, I hope." They shook hands and introduced themselves and moved out of the nurse's way as she gathered the surgical instruments in a basin and covered the body. The intern looked at the sheeted form. "In medical school they told me there would be days like this."

"You're in a combat zone, doc," Sullivan said dryly. "This is the hundred-year war you heard about."

The intern looked at him and saw that he wasn't smiling. "Well, I guess I'll get plenty of experience up here then, if this is any indication."

"Oh, you'll be kept busy, doc," Pope said. "By the time you've finished your schooling up here you will have it all and maybe a few other things they don't write about in the medical books."

Levy could sense the ironic humor behind the immobile face. "But no more with questioning detectives. I've already learned my lesson on how to handle that in the future," he said smilingly, and crushed out the cigarette. "And now, if you'll excuse me, I'm beat and I'm still on duty and have to make out a death report and then, if I'm lucky, I'll get some sleep." He walked away from them through a back door that led into the interior of the hospital.

"Well, now we start from scratch," Pope said quietly as they stood for a moment watching wet red patches spread slowly on the white cloth shrouding the body.

"I think we start by turning over some rocks," Sullivan said, and turned away from the dead man.

"A hell of a rock pile, Frank. I can think of a dozen to begin with."

"What we're going to look for is one that is damp and soggy," Sullivan answered, "and I think I know the creep that would crawl out from under it. You remember me pointing out the Nightman to you?"

Pope nodded that he did, but he wasn't sure; there was so much the white detective had told and shown him in such a short time, he couldn't quite put the face and name together.

"He's a small-time hustler," Sullivan continued. "That's the best kind to have working for you. They move around a lot and aren't noticed." They started to walk slowly toward the door. "When I grabbed him initially he was dealing drugs for Johnson. I guess I scared him pretty good, because he's been steering clear from anything that could bust him for more than ninety days. He hadn't been working long for Johnson but enough to know the score and that kinda makes him the best bet to check out."

"How reliable is he?" Pope asked.

"I used him a couple of times in the past and the information he gave me was okay." Frank shrugged almost apologetically. "But you never know with bastards like this. You can't count on them too much, but still . . ." In the hall Sullivan looked at the uniformed cop. "You won't be needed here anymore; the prisoner died. When you check into the precinct let them know at the desk."

Chapter 5

The ancient, high-ceilinged room lit by pale lights and with a scuffed marble staircase in the rear was reminiscent of an era of fat, red-faced men speaking in brogues, of domed hats and single-breasted tunics and horse-drawn trolleys. But now this musty, turn-of-the-century building served a different age. Tonight it was presided over by a desk sergeant called Bilinski, whose shrewd pale-gray

40

eyes stared down from behind the high desk and tarnished old railing that separated him from the busted and the enraged. It had been an active night for the blotter; the cells in the basement were being filled up by arrests that would normally go unheeded. Detectives worked upstairs in the cramped squad room, questioning the undesirables and informants they had rounded up for leads that would lend substance to the mumbling words of a dying man's cry: "Blacks, blacks."

To Bilinski, the patrolmen and detectives seemed to pass in a soft blur, some acknowledging him, others inordinately quiet, all sensing in the charged atmosphere that the Centre Street brass had arrived. He placed the phone back in the cradle; the calls had been coming in with a monotonous rapidity—addicts breaking and entering; a white store owner worried about a colored kid loitering outside just waiting, he was sure, to come in and rob him; rape, assaults, automobile collisions. It was as though the robbery and the killing in the brownstone had set off a chain reaction of violence across Harlem in a rising wave that was breeding the fear that Bilinski heard in the panicked voices over the telephone pleading for a policemen. The desk sergeant from his high perch glanced at the closed door at the rear of the room and then turned back to the prisoner being booked. The pimp standing before him had had his kink straightened into a slick pompadour and his mustache was evenly trimmed over his upper lip. His chartreuse sports jacket was blood-splattered. He seemed bewildered. He hadn't been touched for over a year. The sergeant knew the arrest was a mistake.

"Were there any weapons on him?" he asked in a voice that seemed to carry indifference.

The young plainclothesman placed a large folded stiletto on the desk. "Just this knife," he said, keeping his expressive Italian-American face impassive.

The sergeant barely looked up from his writing. "Was there any resistance when the arrest was made?"

Despite himself the detective allowed a smile of self-satisfaction to crease his face. "A little," he said.

"Where was he apprehended?" Bilinski's pen seemed to start across the blotter before the answer was given.

41

"The place is called the Tick Tock. It's over on the East Side near Madison," the detective said tonelessly. "I didn't figure it for a change-your-luck joint; all I was doing was giving it the quick once-over. My partner stayed with the car and I went in alone to avoid suspicion. There were a few white guys mixed in with the crowd and I didn't see nothing out of order"—he motioned with his thumb to the ruffled Negro beside him—"until this punk comes up to me at the bar and starts to pimp for a couple of high yellows down at the other end of the room, and at twenty bucks a throw."

The sergeant had stopped writing. "I guess, officer, you don't look too prosperous; the price is generally higher."

The young detective, his expression assuming a quizzical scowl, again pointed with his thumb at the now smirking prisoner. "You know this creep?"

"Wipe that smile off your rotten face or it'll be knocked off for you." The sergeant's voice didn't rise but it turned mean. The prisoner complied quickly. The sergeant made a final notation in the ledger and then motioned toward the back of the house. "Okay, Feminella, you can take your prisoner downstairs and put him in a cell." He was going to add, "Nice arrest," but felt he shouldn't be facetious to this bright-eyed rookie detective who had been transferred to the precinct only a week before and couldn't know that after his prisoner's telephone call to the inevitable lawyer he would be back operating out of the slime of the same cesspool in a matter of hours. As he watched them disappear down the steps the sergeant wondered about the identity of the issuer of immunity to this night crawler, who greased his way to operate in the open by giving kickbacks—to a politician, a ward heeler, a cop?

"Sergeant." The voice was loud; it startled him. He turned quickly to the grimly serious face of the patrolman standing in front of the desk.

"What is it, Russell?"

"The prisoner I was assigned to cover at the Harlem Hospital is dead." Bilinski realized that the patrolman was well aware of what was happening and knew that the death of the only witness could only add unwanted

42

agitation to an already precarious case. The desk sergeant steeled himself for a long, unpleasant night ahead. He looked away from the dark, somber face staring intently up at him and started to fake some writing across the blotter. "Captain Matthews is in interrogation," he said, not looking up. Then, as if in casual afterthought, "You'd better tell him."

Patrolmen, freshly shaven, their uniforms pressed, stood in small groups and talked in hollow, hushed tones, waiting like soldiers to form lines and move out onto the streets in the midnight-to-eight trick. Detectives, whose eyes showed the strain of double shifts, traversed the time-worn stairs seemingly in step with the unceasing ring of telephones that echoed throughout the archaic building. And over it all hung the heavy intimidation of authority, which now was among them.

The interrogation room was small, without windows; a ventilating duct was cut crudely into the ceiling. A single 500-watt lamp with a reflecting shield at the top poured a circle of intense white light onto the black man who sat directly beneath it in a straight-back wooden chair. The heat was repugnant to the patrolman, who stepped quietly into the room. The smell that assailed him seemed not to come from sweating bodies in close confinement but from the open fear of the man in the chair; it poured from him, beading his face and wetting his hair as if he had been doused with a bucket of water. In the shadows the patrolman could barely distinguish the motionless forms rimming the circle of light.

"You say you lived in the place for over a year." He recognized the captain's voice coming through the obscuring haze of cigarette smoke.

"Yessir." The answer came slowly, respectfully from the downcast head.

"And you still tell us you don't know who used your apartment tonight or any of the people who were there." Paul Matthews' tone rankled with disbelief.

"No, sir, I don't know them," the man said with a Southern Negro drawl, then hesitated. "I—I don't know who they are or why they were there."

Matthews stepped abruptly into the light. "Williams, you're a goddamn liar." His voice climbed with his im-

43

patience as he towered angrily over the cringing, bowed head. "Look at me, Williams." The prisoner, his open-collared white shirt saturated with sweat, continued to stare at the floor. "I said look at me!" Matthews shouted. Slowly the Negro lifted his gaze, his shining face moving up into the harsh light. Sweat on his forehead formed into rivulets and rolled down the sides to his cheeks. His eyes squinted and his face tightened as though he was going to cry. The captain's body slackened. Once more the interrogating room let in the sounds of a ringing phone, and a muffled voice could be heard calling out a duty roster.

"We checked your alibi out," Matthews said softly. "We know you weren't there when the robbery took place. And from what we know of your history we doubt you would have planned something like this. I'm willing to concede your innocence on all counts, except one. It was your apartment where the killings took place and you knew at least one of the Negroes and maybe all three, because I'm sure this wasn't the first time your place was used as a pickup. Doc Johnson uses a half a dozen spots that he thinks are safe. He moves them around to keep people guessing, and your apartment is one of them. So it makes no sense for you to be busted on a big charge, because you're protecting something we already know about." Matthews paused and waited and took a step back to ease the prisoner's apprehension. But only cowering timidity came from the thin Negro, who continued to hold his face up into the light. Then he closed his eyes as though hoping that when he opened them again the hot, shut-in room with its bright light and questioning white man would somehow have disappeared. Outside, the noises that had filtered through stopped and silence held the prisoner and the captain and the shadowy sentinels, till someone shifted his weight and the floorboards creaked under the movement.

Matthews turned and stepped over to a shadowy figure leaning against the wall. Their words were mumbled whispers; then he came back to the cowering man, who again had let his head drop down toward the floor. Slowly Matthews lit a cigarette and held it out to the
44

Negro, who took it in a noticeably nervous hand, quickly filled his lungs with its momentary comfort.

"Williams, I'm prepared to offer you a deal, and under the circumstances it's more than you could hope for. You give us what we want and we'll give you a clean bill of health. No arrest, no charge; you can walk out of here right now." The prisoner raised his head, his eyes seeking Matthews, who stood just outside the perimeter of light. "All we want from you," the precinct captain said, "is a signed statement telling us how you were contacted, how much they paid you and how many times Doc Johnson used your apartment as a drop for Syndicate money."

The expression on Williams' face still held the stress, but his eyes narrowed against the trail of cigarette smoke as he pondered the new proposal, which would free him from the stink and dread of this black box of a room.

"I can understand why you let them use your place. The few dollars they gave you must have been like found money. You weren't hurting anyone. They come and go and you don't see them until next time. If this didn't happen tonight, Williams, we wouldn't have even known you existed. You just happened to be unfortunate; your place was marked for the knockover, and that misfortune has put you into this up to your ears." He paused again, letting the words sink in. "But you can pull yourself out of it, you can get out clean, just by giving us a simple statement of facts." Williams took another long, worried drag on the cigarette, his kinky head glistening under the light. His expression conveyed little. "All we want is a signed statement; I guarantee you will walk out of here a free man tonight."

The prisoner, his head seemingly too heavy for the thin body, lowered it so that his chin was almost resting on his chest and he gaped at the floor as if he were deaf and incapable of comprehension.

"Don't you dummy up on me!" Matthews' voice shredded the previous agreeable tone. "I just gave you an out. If you're not smart enough to realize it, it doesn't stop us from getting what we want. Only then you're going to rot your ass off doing time, because an accomplice rap is going on you so tight you'll end up doing five to seven."

45

The patrolman standing in the shadows cleared his throat before speaking and Matthews turned toward the door. "Excuse me, Captain," the cop said. He had been waiting for the proper moment to breach the interrogation and had become so immersed in watching the pressuring of of the uncommunicative prisoner that he wondered now whether he'd waited too long.

"Yes, what is it?" Matthews asked impatiently.

"The prisoner, sir, the one who was taken out of the brownstone tonight—he died before they could get him to surgery."

"Did he give a statement before he died?"

"No, sir, he didn't."

Matthews stared at the shadowy patrolman as he eased out of the room. He had hoped for a quick resolution from a dying man's declaration that would give them people they could corner immediately. Now that hope was gone. He would even have settled for descriptions, and taken the tedious route of deductions and suppositions that would have methodically put names on them. But that possibility, too, had expired with the dead man.

He turned back to the prisoner. Williams was just a grab-bag surprise, a bonus he had intended to use against the seemingly untouchable Johnson. For years Johnson had flaunted Syndicate connections and power payoff in the face of numerous precinct commanders in Harlem, for he was legally immune with a business front and wise in the ways of spreading fear among those who would dare inform against him. Sweat the time out, fuck 'em, why bother now?

But now he had him. Had him through an insignificant prisoner sitting terrified before him. Johnson was the great big achievement, the one that people would remember him for. And all that would be needed to start it was a signed statement and Williams on the stand. The district attorney would go after a grand jury indictment that could expose all the vices and corruptions that sucked the ghetto like a many-headed leech. It was the kind of story the papers would love and exploit, and from the investigative explosion, cankerous fallout would rain down on the respectables hiding on the periphery behind their full bag of take money. The chain reaction

46

could knock over politicions and crackle right on into headquarters, forcing the premature retirement of some brass. Yes, they'd remember him all right, and it would all be started by the testimony of a cringing black man. Matthews could smell the indictment; could almost hear the cell door clanging on the convictions that would follow.

The obscure forms standing back in the darkness sensed the change in Matthews, in the way he stepped under the light and pushed his face down to the prisoner's. "Okay, Williams, we're through playing games. I told you I'm prepared to let you out of this. You won't do a day. Your only involvement would be a simple statement on how you were being used." Matthews waited for an answer, but the bowed black head remained staring at the floor. "You're going to give us a signed statement or you're going to wish you were never born." The captain's voice had a magnetic chill that pulled the plainclothesmen toward the circle of light, their indistinct pallid faces hanging in the grayness like crudely painted masks.

"I—I swear to you, I don't know who they were." He sensed what was going to happen and tried to forestall it in a piping, squeaky voice. "I don't know any of them men who were in the house tonight and I don't know nothing about anybody named Johnson. Not a thing. You just gotta believe me because—because . . ." He stopped as suddenly as he had started, and became silent.

The back of Matthews' hand struck Williams across the side of his face. In the boxlike room it should have made a louder sound, for its force drove him halfway off the chair. But he made no response. One of the detectives stepped into the light and pushed him back roughly into the seat. Once more the captain's hand blurred out of the darkness, across the other side of his face. The sound seemed louder. It was like a flat stick striking a wall. The hand had caught the sweaty black face across the mouth, forcing the teeth to cut into the lips. They started to bleed.

"You're going to sign that paper." Matthews growled his aggravation, but the perspiring, matted head, riveted by its eyes to some crushed speck of dirt lying at the captain's feet, refused an answer. Matthews struck again,

47

spinning Williams' face and sending a spray of blood out across the brightness, which splotched both of them in a wretched unity. He hit once more, driving Williams to the floor and waiting until he made it back to his knees. Hands came out of the gray shadows and started to lift him. But Matthews was already bending, pulling him up. He pushed him back into the chair, cupped his hand under the black chin and forced the face up into the light. Williams blinked against the sweat running into his eyes. Blood leaked from his smashed mouth and rolled down across Matthews' fingers. "You're going to sign," he heard the white voice say. His eyes widened, searching the silhouetted head towering above him, then found and returned the rigid stare.

"You can hit me all you want, but I'm not signing nothing because I ain't going against that big cat Johnson. He'd have me killed real quick, man, and I'd rather do time than be dead."

Paul Matthews continued to hold the prisoner's jaw, but was suddenly unsure of his depth, afraid of this swift, unexpected current of truth. He could still see trepidation etched across the battered face, but the eyes were laced with candor. There were not many prisoners who had been victorious in this cakelike room, where suspects agreed to deeds beyond their imagination. But this frail, bleeding, insignificant man had succeeded. He rode it out on a fear of what a man named Johnson could do to him that far surpassed the intimidations of a local precinct captain.

Matthews took out a handkerchief and wiped the drops of blood from his hands. He cleaned his fingers slowly, methodically, still staring down at Williams, then handed the handkerchief to him; Williams took it gratefully and pressed it to his rapidly swelling lips.

"Book this punk as an accessory." The irritation came rolling out from Matthews in a tone of bitter frustration.

The door opened, letting noise and a burst of light into the room. The occupants seemed frozen in their positions.

The two detectives who had assisted Matthews lost their frightening anonymity, becoming middle-aged, graying men in rumpled jackets; and beyond them the apparition that the prisoner could barely perceive materialized as a youngish man leaning against the wall with his arms folded casually as someone waiting for a bus.

Sergeant Bilinski took a step farther into the room. "Captain, you said you wanted to talk to the night tour. They're ready to go out now."

They stood four lines deep in regimental form. They had gone through roll call and now were at semiattention, their dark-blue, freshly pressed uniforms already clammy against the night. Not many were over thirty. The arduous task of a lonely chase down a dark alley dictated continuous turnover in a precinct that favored the spartan and the young. Their gun belts hung around lithe bodies and the caps were squared above their eyes. Some turned their heads slightly, others their eyes, as they followed Matthews. They watched him mount the couple of steps and move behind the railing and elevated desk and stand like some informal magistrate with his jacket and collar open and tie pulled down. They didn't notice the civilian-clothed deputy inspector who had come out of the interrogation room and now stood authoritatively against a back wall. The captain, his gray eyes showing strain behind the glasses, scanned the faces of the ruddy, the swarthy, the pale and the black, all glistening with sweat. Some averted their eyes, while a few stared back insolently. But most returned his look with a passive indifference that reached up across the desk and slammed gallingly against Matthews' indignation. He could feel the acrimonious sting rising in his chest. It was his duty to speak about the loss of two patrolmen, to touch briefly on the atrocious robbery, then to let them go, for they weren't the investigators who would have to shift through the shit of the Harlem underworld. Their purpose was to prevent crime by the show of a uniform on the street and if someone busted a law, bag and book him and let the so-called brains put the case together. That hopefully would bring a conviction. He knew that many of the uniformed men before him turned their back on infractions, their attitude being why get involved and then lose a day off in court to see a shyster free their collar. And sometimes he wondered if they weren't right. But now this rising anger against their apparent unconcern about

49

a matter so foul pushed this tolerance into the back of his mind. He knew that this tour, especially this one, had to go out in a mood of aggression and fuck the civil-rights caution. He started slowly, trying to hide the timbre of irritation in this tone.

"Tonight two policemen were murdered in the line of duty. I'm not going into the fact that they were fellow officers and friends. I'll leave that up to the chaplain; that's his job, to speak for the dead. My job, as precinct commander, is to speak to the living by seeing that you answer this vicious crime. Answer it the only way a cop on the beat or in a patrol car should answer it, with all the traditional force and authority that is loaded at the end of night stick."

He leaned forward, his palms going flat on the desk, the lamp shade throwing a greenish pallor across his taut features. "The backbone of law is the man in the uniform. But his commanding image has slowly deteriorated and has been stripped and chipped away with threats of civilian review boards, liberalization of the laws, and political shackling, to the point where he is asked to turn the other cheek. Well, that's a grand theory for a man of the cloth. But to a policeman it can be fatal. For by sheer necessity of the job it's required that he gain respect by exercising his authority. And that's what I want you to do tonight."

An alien hush filled the building as his voice firmed and rose to the upper floors and detectives came out of the squad room and stood in shirt sleeves on the marble steps. "I want you men going out on this late tour to send a message to everyone in Harlem. I want it sent to the whores and their pimps, the pushers and the junkies, through after-hours joints and bottle clubs and to anyone on any corner who dares to give a word of backtalk." The flexible ranks now seemed to stiffen. There were no scowls or lethargic glances now, for their eyes cleaved to his as they grasped the controlled anger of this man made strange by the power of his concern. He straightened up and as he did he lowered his voice, and the lines of men almost turned their heads seeking his words.

"The vast majority of people in the community, like
50

anywhere else, are honest, law-abiding citizens who want and need protection. And now these people are going to be watching the behavior of the police to that minute proportion of undesirables who have given Harlem a bad name. And that small gang of punks are also going to be gauging our reaction to them. So to leave this viciousness unanswered is to invite it to happen again and again. By tomorrow morning I want every man, woman and child to receive the message of a fundamental truth: Nobody kills a cop and gets away with it. Tonight"—his voice thickened and reached down to them—"all wraps are off."

For long seconds no one moved in the oppressive silence, not realizing he had finished. Then Bilinski, conscious that his commands were too loud in that quiet hall, turned and moved them out onto the street. Matthews watched the police ranks disappear through the doors. At the rear of the room he caught a glimpse of the deputy inspector stepping into an office whose door was marked "CAPTAIN P. MATTHEWS," in chipped lettering. Let him wait, he thought, and forced his eyes down to the open ledger on the desk as if to study the pages, but his eyes were closed against the scribbled words. He could almost smell the sudden imagery of a patch of woods that overlooked a stream and he heard the laughing voice of his boy beside him as they sat in the lazy sun ignoring the poles and the fish, enjoying the contented talk and not caring about the tomorrows.

John Croton, lean, almost slender, sat with his back to the door. He now turned partially around. "Nice speech, Matt." The only light came from the fluorescent desk lamp and it put his face in a semisilhouette.

Matthews came to the other side of the desk and looked down into a face that seemed too young to be that of a deputy inspector. Croton smiled wryly but his cold eyes showed what he really thought of the captain's pyrotechnics. "Yes, some speech. I haven't heard a talk like that since I was in the service. You almost had me getting a night stick and wanting to go out with them." The monotone was so flat that the sarcasm couldn't be disguised. John Croton had the mythical look of the aspirant. It showed in the pinched features: high bones

51

and hollow cheeks, pale eyes that stared icily at him without blinking, and a thin, tight mouth.

"You seem surprised," Matthews said, faking docility and sitting down opposite him. "Don't you think what happened here tonight called for me to say something as strong as that?"

The deputy inspector seemed to find lint on the arm of his gray suit. "Ten years ago," he said, not looking up, "they would have put it in the manual under proper procedure." He rolled the lint around in his fingers. "Now we're in the process of reediting the book. It's being updated with more realistic viewpoints that are essential to an efficiently run department." He looked at Matthews from under a furrowed brow. "We have to understand the times we live in. Things are continuously changing. What was practical and right yesterday can be terrible and wrong today. It's a necessity that our people, no matter what their personal feelings, go along with what is happening. . . ."

Paul Matthews stopped listening. He had read the memorandums that came down to the local precincts from the burgeoning elite who suddenly seemed to have filled headquarters in Centre Street. By now the bottle should have been out on the desk with two shot glasses already emptied, along with the easy talk of contemporaries and no thought of rank. But there was no fraternizing with Croton, a man Matthews' junior by more than a dozen years. He was a Fordham graduate in the liberal arts and held a master's degree in the social sciences, and he wore these qualifications the way other men wore a uniform, using the Police Department and its civil service examinations as stepping-stones to success, grabbing notice by his quick rise, his membership in the right clubs and the appropriate political connections. And then, to move up further after there were no more examinations to take, he ingratiated himself with the proper people in the city administration, who were looking for images to point to in stressing the new breed, the intellectual cops. The schooling and drives of men like Croton carried them to membership in confidential squads, as public relations advisers of a new order. And, in John Croton's case, as a hatchet man.

"Why should it be any different now?" The captain's voice had a needling bite.

"What?" Croton asked, his smoothness stopped.

Matthews leaned across the desk, his heavy hands folded in front of him. "I said why should there be any difference now in our reaction when two cops get killed in the line of duty than it was ten years ago, or twenty, or even thirty? Aren't we supposed to react anymore, or do we have a new code to go by that I don't know about?"

Croton's eyes narrowed perceptibly as he gazed at Matthews' rigid, lined face. Croton's presence and rank usually forced precinct commanders to anxious nods of agreement about most things he said, especially when they had trouble. He seemed intrigued by Matthews' candid resentment. He was a jump in rank above this gray man in the department and still ascending. There were not many who took liberties with rank, and especially with him. He rippled the mental index of the security file he kept in Centre Street of what he considered key personnel jobs. Matthews, Paul J.; age, 51; schooling, fundamental; married, three children, two in subsidized colleges; captain five years; mode of living, comparable to the wage; moved into Harlem after precinct gambling shakeup two years ago; good authoritarian; no scandal. The surface growl not in dossier but now will be added with a question mark after it until a more microscopic examination analyzes this open indifference. The deputy inspector smiled, trying to cover the pause.

"Well, let's say circumstances are, or should be, examined a little more carefully now. Besides"—Croton's smile broadened as if he were dismissing the question with a forced sense of good fellowship—"that's the way the department wants it so who are we to argue, eh, Captain?"

The smugness of the inspector's patronizing answer goaded Matthews into a deeper exchange. "Well, then, don't you think it's about time we started to ask some questions? If things are changing that much, Inspector, we're going to have the Indians running the reservation and then we're all going to be in a lot of trouble."

"Get with it, Matthews. You talk like you don't read the newspapers, or the memorandums and reports coming out of headquarters." Croton didn't raise his voice but there was an unmistakable inflection that carried the warning: Don't go too far.

The hum of the air-conditioner in the window, a gift from a Harlem appliance shop to the previous commander, seemed to get louder. Matthews' eyes dropped from Croton's; his resentment of the deputy inspector and all he stood for was carrying him too far. Twenty-five years of a semimilitary life were too deeply ingrained; the rank deserved respect. He held the silence for a long moment, showing his distaste for the man behind the façade of professionalism. When he looked up he felt it safe to go on in the same vein, but now without endangering himself by insubordination. Still, indignation seeped through his tone like smoke under a closed door.

"Inspector, I'm sorry if I seem out of bounds. But if I ran this precinct completely by that new book you're talking about, this black community would eat us alive. We might as well tear the building down for a parking lot, because the only semblance to law and order would be the governor sending in the troops to protect the white store owners' interests and us from the snipers. And again I'm not talking about the straight people up here, I'm talking about the underworld element we have to cope with every day. They're the animals who are not going to give us even grudging respect, because when we try to herd them our hands are tied. This new liberal approach to police work they talk about may look fine on paper but let them come up here and pull eight hours a day. I think their eyes would be opened to see what we're up against."

Croton's eyes had wandered to Matthews' family picture on the desk, up to an iron-mesh window and down again to the filing cabinets pressed against the walls, and to pictures of wanted men, profiles and full shots, tacked to a small bulletin board. He tried to avoid showing his irritation, but felt it must be conspicuous. He disliked Matthews for copping out behind an apology and then using it as a guise to continue to talk against fresh insights and policies. He had to deal with the old guard, those great protectors of the middle class, at every biting level of resentment in the department and their provincialism in the face of change more than annoyed him. In Paul Matthews he found the archetype of them all; antiquities who grew up reading the overpublicized exploits of the Johnny Brodericks and the Barney Radutskys and still held to the police boff-and-bang style of the thirties. Croton hated their phoniness, their hiding behind their badges like dogmatic tin gods; they contributed nothing and seemed to give vent to their dissatisfactions only when their twenty-five or thirty years on the job were clocked, posing as pillars of wisdom, espousing their narrow perspectives, and maybe better than half of them with cans full of graft buried behind their drab, one-family, look-alike houses in the acrid back yards in Brooklyn and Queens, John Croton could feel his aggravation being pursued by his anger. He had been sent up here to oversee regulations, to give instructions on what to tell the press and to blend unobtrusively into the general background while ensuring protection for the Department. But Matthews' indifference to his position had turned him around and made him part of what he felt was an illegal interrogation. For the right to have a lawyer present during questioning was so quickly mentioned and so hazily declined, along with the prisoner's other legal rights, then even if Matthews had got what he wanted Croton doubted the testimony would have stood up in court. It was the vehement, uncalled-for speech, however, made without clearance as if his, a deputy inspector's, presence in the precinct had sanctioned it, and now this, the prodding of policy with such smoldering sarcasm, that split their official relationship into an open antagonism that had to be rebutted. He would get him, later, methodically cut him up in a formal report. But that would be later when his temper had a chance to cool. What was called for now was an immediate answer and John Croton proceeded to break one of his cardinal rules: he let anger dictate his thoughts; he decided to go after him now.

"We fully realize, Matthews, that there are extenuating circumstances in a number of commands, and as you know, we let each precinct captain have a certain amount of authorized freedom in judging his own problem area." He paused as though condoning the captain's discontent, then he leaned forward, the winter in his eyes searing away the composure while he held on to a semblance of his style. "But when you send patrolmen out on the street with a win-one-for-the-gipper speech, I've got to consider you a joke, but a very dangerous one. Because I don't think you comprehend the trouble you could be inviting for the whole Department. The men you send out"—he shook his head in repudiation as if admonishing an errant child—"they don't need a talk like that. We've been trying to indoctrinate them into a broader understanding of the times and the temper of the country, and to bring that knowledge into the neighborhoods and beats they patrol. Just their appearance on the street tonight would have been sufficient intimidation for tightening up the area. But you fired them up and gave them your blessings to go out and bust heads in an indiscriminate display of force that's going to catch a lot of innocent people who are going to resent being pushed around. And then, maybe, we get a few other militant black organizations parading outside crying police brutality, just asking for a fight. You displayed a lack of responsibility, Captain, to the men under your command, to your job and to the community you're supposed to protect." His hands grasped the sides of the chair as if about to rise. "And you can be certain, Captain, that everything I just told you is going into my official report."

Paul Matthews knew Croton had been goaded past the point of no return and strangely he didn't really give a damn. In fact he found it exhilarating to clear some of the liberal air that had slowly been suffocating him over the last few years. He was dead with Croton, dead before he had even walked into the room, and now he was glad that he had pushed him and found out how the deputy inspector was planning to bury him. But Matthews would add footnotes to the report that even this representative of the new order could not ignore, nor a few old-line cops he had come up with who thought like him and still held important desk jobs in the Department.

"Well, then, Inspector, you'd better note down the reasons behind my actions or your papers won't be complete." There was no growl or bitterness in Matthews' voice, just a cold realization that his justification for his behavior would be read in headquarters along with Croton's prejudicial accusations. "In the past, when the

Department lost a man, a suspect was generally apprehended at the scene or a short while after because they were senseless, spur-of-the-moment killings. What took a place up here tonight is unique." The captain leaned on his folded arms, his eyes holding on to Croton's silence. "It's different because of the situation surrounding the case. A Harlem gang leader loses a lot of money and some of his boys are knocked off along with a couple of white syndicate men. It's the biggest crime to hit Harlem in years. But what compounds it is we lose two patrolmen. The word is spread and now Harlem is waiting for the backlash, fully expecting us to storm out through the streets in a fit of reprisal. And I'm not going to disappoint them, because this I believe to be basic police psychology in *any* ghetto."

His hand tapped the desk emphasizing the words, and his close-cropped gray head pushed toward Croton, and was reflected in the desk's glass top like a face in a pool pool of smooth water. "If we don't react with a quick show of strength, especially now in the next few hours, they will begin to wonder that maybe our fights with civilian review boards, our distaste for the administration led by our great silver-spooned proletarian mayor, who has put a clamp on the Department in his chasing of black votes, have softened us up. What I'm simply saying is if we don't respond we lose some of our edge because we lose respect: Because I'm worried about the two-bit black bastards with the get-rich-quick ideas. They're the ones with the guns stashed away who didn't have the guts to use them before. And now they maybe start to look around for nice clean stickups and fuck the law."

He couldn't resist it. He raised his hand and pointed his finger authoritatively. "My first responsibility, Inspector, is to do my job as well as I can and that includes letting the punks, the oddballs and the junkies know right away that that goddamn hidden arsenal up here stays right where it is. Hidden. But more important to me is to let the public know the pride a cop can still take in his job. Maybe that sentiment is too old-fashioned today for that new book of regulations, but it's one I was brought up on and I'm not about to change now." He stopped as if he had finished, then added softly, "And if you can't remember everything I just said, Inspector, I'll be glad to repeat it in person to whoever you hand your report to."

The deputy inspector had dropped his eyes to his subordinate's pointing finger. When the hand pulled back Crotton again looked up, exasperation written on his face, and he seemed to sigh. He stood up, "Captain, I fear you're almost a blind man, for you can't see past the boundaries of your own precinct. In truth, you can't even see what is happening right under your nose. A couple of years ago, half the officials in the Department would have been up here hogging the microphones of the television reporters and making sure that their rank and name were recorded properly for the papers. Now they send someone like me up here to try to make sure it's played down as much as possible."

His sallow face receded from the light as he moved around and stood behind the chair. "And do you know why, Captain? Because they're afraid. They're frightened that something they would say might be misconstrued and be the spark that could again ignite this tinderbox community into a holocaust." He flattened his tie against his shirt and buttoned his jacket. "Yes, we have a mayor who walks the ghettos, with proper publicity recording it, and in a couple of weeks will announce what a peaceful summer we had. You and I know it hasn't been too peaceful, but he's delighted because nobody threw a Molotov cocktail and caused a Newark or Detroit here, and he's absolutely right. But it's more than that, Captain. It's Washington pouring federal money into this area to keep the potential kid rioters cooled down with meaningless activities, like cleaning lots and painting and fixing buildings that should have been torn down years ago. They don't have many answers either, so they try to buy out of trouble before it can start. You may not like this system, but surprisingly it has worked in New York for the last couple of years. So don't you go and try to turn it all around in one night, Captain, and that's an official order. From here on in we play this thing down until it's a dead issue with the people up here, and with the men working under your command, and especially with the press for the most valid reason of all. Because what happened tonight could be easily misinterpreted, particularly after our statement that it was a local heist of an inconsequential sum. If it got out that it was a big syndicate robbery, it might seem exactly as it sounds to some eager reporter looking for a story. And our two dead patrolmen will come out like they were riding shotgun for a large illicit take."

Croton stood looking at Matthews, letting him consider what the repercussions of a charge like that would bring, then he walked to the door. His hand was on the knob when he stopped and looked back at the captain, sitting in the spray of light, surrounded by the dingy room. "Matthews, it's pretty obvious you're packing the job in," he said firmly, "or you wouldn't have had the courage to talk to me the way you did. Well, your papers are going to be held up, because I'm going to personally go over your record and have you thoroughly investigated, and if you took a dime or a graft and I can prove it I'm going to bring you up on a departmental trial and I'll try to bust you to where you won't be able to collect a penny of retirement pay. You're going to be my example for every man in the Department." Croton opened the door and closed it softly behind him.

Through the rippled glass Paul Matthews could see the outlined figure recede, then disappear. He continued to stare at the door, at his name engraved on the glass with its chipped and peeling letters.

Chapter 6

Sullivan turned into Lenox Avenue, rode with the traffic for a few blocks, then inched slowly along a double row of parked cars. The Harlem Club, its lights snaking around the electric sign on the building, announced its expensiveness glaringly from the middle of the block. It was one of the few remaining nightclubs that still drew downtown whites. But their number had fallen off since the militants and the riots and it was mostly well-heeled blacks who got out of cabs and expensive cars tonight in front of the canopied entrance. The doorman, his white admiral's uniform laced with elaborate decorations, salaamed humorlessly to the modish women and shuffle-danced the men toward the entrance, then bowed them in to overprices. If they left an automobile at the curb entrance, then he snapped his fingers to a waiting attendant and majestically motioned him to take it away to a lot around the corner. But that was generally too crowded, and the boys double-parked the cars along the avenue. The admiral was a show, taking comic threatening steps toward passing girls while he traded lines with studs along the curb who leaned on their shiny cars as if they were paid for.

His eyes caught the unmarked squad car, watched it roll slowly past the entrance, then ignored it. They were The Men, screw them; who needs trouble? But when they stopped he yelled, "Hey!" as if he didn't know who they were, "Hey, man, you can't park there," and trotted out between automobiles as if to chase them away. He leaned down with pretended annoyance and looked into the car. He was older up close, and his brown face broke into a wrinkled smile. "I knew it was you behind the wheel, a block away, Frank. Only the police drive beat-up cars in Harlem." And he looked at the Negro detective sitting beside Sullivan and winked as if it were some kind of inside joke.

"Still comin' at them, hey, Lincoln?" Sullivan said, returning the smile.

"I'm just an old hoofer doing my routine and staying in shape," he answered. "You never know, I might get busted again for somethin' and my kinda dancin' still goes over big at the Prison reviews."

Bill Pope liked the doorman's humor. He threw a glance at Sullivan, whose face had become serious as if the banter with the doorman had gone far enough.

"Is The Nightman inside?" Sullivan asked indifferently. But the realization that they weren't just killing time took the laughter out of Lincoln.

"What he do now, huh? He all messed up again with the law?"

"Is he inside?" Sullivan asked.

Lincoln shook his head solemnly and sighed. "That

60

cat he ain't been around here in over a month and I don't think he gonna show up around here either. The boss he holdin' a tab on 'im and he lookin' for 'im, too. You know what I mean?"

"Where's he hanging out now?"

"I don't know, man. He like the night. He could be anywhere. You know him."

"Where's he hanging out now?" Sullivan asked as if he hadn't heard him, and his voice thickened.

"He mean nothin' to mc, man." There was a touch of annoyance in the doorman's tone. "If I knew where that cat were I'd tell ya." There was a lull, and the doorman thought maybe he had been to firm in disassociating himself from The Nightman. He didn't like the way Sullivan stared at him from the shadows of the car. He knew that the detective's reputation for toughness was legitimate. He had seen it at work. He also knew he was unpredictable. "Now don't you be gettin' your mad up, Frank. I don't know nothin' about him. The only thing I can tell ya, he was sharin' a pad with his cousin. You know, the one that plays piano."

"Okay, Lincoln," Sullivan said, letting him know everything was all right. "Yeah, I know Zack. Is he still playing at Toxie's?"

"Uh huh, he's still playin' there."

The piano was playing. A candle was stuck in the saucer on top of it and other candles flickered on a few tables along the wall, making faces barely distinguishable in its reddish glow. Toxie, a short, balding black, had let them in through the irongrated door in the basement, which he always kept closed, admitting only people who were in good standing with him. And if somebody got sloppy with drink or was nasty or too loud, he personally threw him out, for Toxie ran his restaurant and bar without a license. It was an after-hours joint that had no hours. The customers paid for the booze but he gave them an unwatered honest measurement. And his down-home food was known all over Harlem. A swinging door opened at the end of the hall and a white-shirted waiter came out of the kitchen. He squeezed in between the conversing Sullivan and Toxie, the platter of ham

61

hocks, turnip greens and black-eyed peas smoking deliciously as he passed Pope and went into the candled room. Another waiter, on the other side of what was once the main room of a parlor floor and basement, used a pocket flashlight to make change. In its fringe of light Pope was surprised to see how many people were in the room. All the tables were filled and all the eyes seemed to be staring at him.

The candle on the piano didn't cast enough light to read music by, but it didn't matter. Zack couldn't read it anyway. He was blind. With tinted glasses on, hunched over the piano, he played the melody caressingly, repeating a particular chord he liked and never replaying it exactly the same way. The song was somebody else's, but the music was his and he rearranged it to suit his talents and taste. To some he seemed to be distorting it in the fits of improvisation, but to the purists who knew what jazz was all about, Zack had it all.

Sullivan stood beside the piano with Pope and watched the blind man's easy rhythm as he flourished the end of the number. "When are you going to leave this dive, Zack, and give Garner a run for his money?"

"Hey, who's that?" He grinned and cocked his head toward the voice.

"It's me, Zack. Frank Sullivan."

"Hey, man, how ya doin'?" And the smile broadened. "Long time no hear."

"And what I hear is still good," Sullivan said. "You're playing better than ever."

"Yeah, thanks. But it's like me and you and maybe some cat sittin' off in the corner are the only ones that know about it today, man. Maybe I should plug a couple a batteries into the piano and wail a little rhythm and blues." His hands hit a couple of heavy chords imitating a rock-and-roll beat, and he laughed.

"Hey, Zack, I want to introduce you to my partner, Bill Pope." The blind man hung his right hand above the keys. Pope leaned over and shook it. "Nice meeting you, Zack. And Frank's right, you do play great."

"They're still teamin' you up with a black man, hey, Frank?"

"The Department's determined to integrate me yet." Sullivan smiled.

"Hey, haven't you heard?" Zack said. "The black man he don't want integration. All he want now is the money to buy gas for the Cadillac and he got black power."

The three of them laughed as the piano player toyed with the melody just loud enough to cover their conversation. "What are you two ballin' tonight, Frank?"

"No, we're working, that's why we're here. We're trying to find The Nightman."

Zack made a sour face. "You mean Sportin' Life. That cat he cut out on me owin' two months' rent. I had to go around feelin' for the furniture to see if he sold it out from under me."

"What's he doing now?" Sullivan asked.

"He ain't broke. I hear he doin' all right."

The plate was tapped on top of the piano. The waiter said, "Request from a customer, Zack. 'Fly Me to the Moon.'" He laid the accompanying dollar beside the candle. The blind man reached up and folded the bill into his pocket and began to play loudly enough to please the customer but quietly enough that they could still talk.

"Yeah, I hear he doin' the hustle for Big Alice and a few of her smelly cunt. But he better not get wind of you lookin' for him or he's gonna take off, makin' money or no, 'cause he always said you were always bad news to him." Zack's head came up and he smiled. "That is unless he thought he would gain some points."

They had come down Amsterdam Avenue past Lewisohn Stadium and stopped in the shadows of Columbia University's blocks of sprawling buildings. The coffee-shops, pizza parlors, clothing and book stores were closed, but surrounding streets and buildings were alive with noise and people. Big Alice had used the peephole, recognized them and opened the door. She was a tall, jet-black woman of Jamaican birth and in her forties she was turning to fat, but when business backed up, she still turned the trick.

"Now I don't want no police trouble. I pay my ice the first and the fifteenth," she said, leading them down a

63

short hall and into the curtained front room, "and I'm all square and I got my paid-up connections, so don't you two be disruptin' my business."

Two young whites, looking as though they should have taken the downtown subway home when their classes ended, sat apprehensively on the edge of the sofa. They dropped their eyes, embarrassed under Sullivan's baleful stare, and both stood up unsurely and started to edge toward the curtained door.

"Now where you boys goin'? You sit right down, you hear. It won't be long. I'll have a couple a my gals ready for you in just a minute. It'll be worth your wait, I promise." Big Alice's voice stopped them. They looked at her, then at the detectives, then banged into each other in their haste to get to the street. Irritated, she turned back to the detectives, the loose robe bouncing in an overflow of cleavage that gave evidence it wasn't for her height that she was called Big Alice. "Now see what you do. You see. You scare a couple of live ones away."

"You're better off, Alice. They look like a couple of wild ones," Frank Sullivan said with a straight face. "You know them college boys fool around a lot and you don't want your girls takin' a chance on gettin' a dose now, do you?"

"Huh," she snorted, and waved disdainfully at his humor. "That kind of joke don't cover what they were goin' ta pay. What you two want here anyway?"

"The Nightman," he said. "We want to talk to him."

Her eyes squinted suspiciously and she started to shake her head in denial.

"Oh, he's clean," Sullivan said, "as clean as that punk's ever going to be. And if it makes it any easier for you, we're not here to bust him."

She stared firmly back at him and shook her head. "I don't know where he about."

They heard footsteps go down the hall and the front door open and close. The curtain that hid the rear bedrooms was pushed back and out came a girl wearing a cheap rayon robe tied tightly about her. She had just run a comb through her dark hair. Her features were plain, her skin more white than brown. She was about seventeen. Her bored eyes were a lot older as she looked

64

over the detectives, apparently thinking they were a couple of new johns. But she became skeptical, then alarmed by their sternness, and mumbled something to Big Alice in Spanish.

"You just go back in there and cool off, honey," Alice answered. "It's okay. Everything's all right. This ain't business for you."

The three of them watched her go languidly back through the curtain. Sullivan looked at Alice. His mood had changed, manifesting itself in a grim scowl. "Now what are we going to do, act dumb?" he snapped. "I told you I want to talk to The Nightman and I don't want to see you shake your head at me again because I don't care who you're paying off. I'll close you down right now, and you better believe it."

"Take it easy." She raised her hand in a placating gesture. "Take it easy. I was gonna tell ya. I don't know where he at this minute. He were here a little while ago but he went back out on the street like he were gonna bring some trade. But for all the business he bring around I like to starve." She shook her head, annoyed. "You know that boy's big vice, he think he some kind of a pool champ. He more than likely out tryin' to take somebody's drinkin' money away from them when he supposed to be out hustlin' up some customers for me and my girls."

Chapter 7

The black sedan with bogus plates nosed up the midtown ramp to the elevated West Side Highway and headed north. It passed the billowing luxury liners, their tonnage berthed with a ponderous dignity, wearing strings of night lights like nouveau riche women wearing garlands of jewels. The car made the quick sudden turns along the cobbled and worn road, passing the tired, once proud heavy old apartment buildings that now pensively share Riverside Drive perches with new high-rise middle-income buildings. On the left, farther uptown in the distance, cars crossed to New Jersey on the George Washington Bridge, flickering commuting fireflies in formation rushing to the wombs of suburban garages.

Nick Difalco looked across the darkened river, looked at the Palisades lights and geographically tried to approximate the don's home along the blackened Jersey cliffs. He had made his call from a public booth as soon as he left Giaccano. "Get me Morello and Parini. Have them meet me in an hour at the Mancian Hotel."

They didn't flinch when he briefed them on what they had to do. He didn't elaborate, but gave them just fundamentals. No questions were asked; they knew better than to pry too deeply. He told them they were both working on bonus money and this helped in covering the open hits. From their disciplined silence and eyes, Difalco sensed that they were proud that he had singled out their muscle from the dozens of button men he could have tapped, that he had recognized their grim talents of violence. And they also knew a job as big as this would not go unnoticed in The Family.

The highway lamps flashing past threw streaks of pale light inside the car, silhouetting the beefy shoulders and wide neck of Tony Morello, his dark hair glistening behind the wheel. Through the rear-view mirror Difalco caught a reflection of the coarse face of Mario Parini, sitting beside the driver. He was smaller than Morello but had the granite, flat features of a fighter. His swarthy skin, shades darker beneath the hat, and his eyes were lost in the sunken shadows of his face.

In a straight rub-out, Nick Difalco would have preferred a couple of the older, more experienced soldiers, but he knew these out-in-the-open contracts called for more balls, more brutal ambition than an older man might possess, and he had to be sure of his backups working on such strange turf. So he went with the young and he felt satisfied with his choices.

The car plunged down a darkened ramp, emerging into a cobblestoned, shadowy street. They moved slowly now along the wide, mean avenue, emptied of its daylight clamor of trucks and shouts and smells of men. They rolled around a junk cart piled with the price of a bottle and pushed by a derelict. The tugs moored to rat-infested docks seemed to pull at their lines, trying to escape from the rotting wharfs and condemned warehouses. The garage's red bricks were blackened by years of soot and they almost missed the sign hanging tilted and loose: "LIMOUSINES, 24 HOUR SERVICE."

The wino stumbling past in a nightmare of alcohol stopped, discerning a touch, but as he stood there weaving, watching the three men come out of the car, he hesitated and said nothing, for their truculent eyes frightened him. Their sardonic silence broke in impatient raps on the door of the garage and the wino lurched down the desolate street and away from their menacing presence.

A burly Negro guard opened the door. Single file, past gleaming Cadillacs sitting incongruously in the low-ceilinged squat dusty garage, they followed him to a panel door in the rear.

Four flashily dressed blacks standing around a desk turned at their entrance, frowning. Difalco's dark, vitriolic eyes in the forceful, high-cheekboned face moved them with servile steps back into the corners of the room, away from the desk.

"Nick Difalco!" The bass voice rumbled out of a large, fiftyish, graying Negro. Seated in a high-back leather chair as though on a throne, he dominated the room with all the elegance of a potentate surrounded by his retinue. Pushing back theatrically from behind the large onyx desk, he strode heavily across the rubber-tiled floor. On a knotty-pine wall above a mahogany bar, his portrait looked down benignly, like an ash-black African king. He was a fleshy man in an expensive, well-cut suit, who moved with a surprising agility that belied his bulk. Like a former athlete gone to age and fat. But Difalco knew the surface softness was a sham; it covered a ruthless drive that had pushed Doc Johnson to the top of the steaming black underworld. In a ghetto that respected few, Doc Johnson was a revered living legend. To many downtrodden Negroes he was truly an American success story, which had started twenty-five years before when he arrived in New York with just the clothes on his back, one jump removed from a Georgia chain gang. But he didn't walk into an arid black belt like so many other new arrivals from Alabama and the Carolinas and Mississippi, hoping for industrial work. He was an industry unto himself. He had a vast talent for turning the quick, dirty buck that led him into cutting dice games, the hustle of numbers, and dope, which was just making it big on the scene. So he dealt it. He started cornering a corner, then a block, then a neighborhood, and building a reputation, always knowing what and who was ahead of him. Some said he handled the gun himself when the former black Mafioso front man's life was blown out of him on a Harlem street. It left a void and he was the logical successor so they nominated him and he filled it, bringing in more money than old man Giaccano thought could ever be squeezed out of uptown.

"Nick, how are you?" he said, with the smile of a thousand amiable darkies flashing across his mouth. Halfway across the room, he extended his hand, but the brown eyes were hostile.

Difalco ignored the hand; the taut skeletal face stared as if viewing some foul object. He held this look for a long moment, then brushed past the large man, purposely, filling the room with tension. The silent arrogance excoriated Johnson and his black hoods, who held to the walls of the room as if pressed there by the white man's searing contempt. Difalco turned and sat at the edge of the desk and folded his arms across his chest. Johnson had now moved, his assumed smile gone, and Nick Difalco could almost see the anger crawling under the black skin.

Doc Johnson knew Difalco's reputation better than he knew the man, and he was surprised to see him. It wasn't their style to send up somebody this soon and certainly not one of the syndicate's top enforcers—not in Harlem on this night when every cop would be out busting his ass to smell out any kind of lead. He had thought old man Giaccano would cool it for a couple of days, waiting to see what floated up to the surface before he'd ask for an explanation of how the money was lost, along with their two grays and his own blacks. He knew the best approach was a straight story. It was going to be hairy for a while but he could face their immediate anger—unless they thought he rigged the job and pocketed their money. Slowly, ever so slowly, Johnson forced the bogus smile across his broad black face again. A distasteful putdown was hard to swallow in front of his own.

"They didn't waste much time in sending you up here, Nick." His tone was friendly. Accepting Difalco's affront seemed to ease the tautness of the room slightly.

"What happened tonight, Doc?" Difalco's raspy voice came like a controlled bark from the thin mouth that barely moved.

Johnson's hands parted patronizingly in a gesture that seemed to say to his black underlings: This is the way to play it. "That's what I'd like to know. Right now you know as much about it as I do. Nothing's changed since I called the old man, except now we've got a lot of helpers. The bulls are on the street shaking everybody down for some kind of information. It's like them and us are all on the same side tonight," he added with a faint smile.

"How much was taken tonight?" Difalco snapped, ignoring Johnson's attempt to mollify him.

"Like I told Giaccano, the full weekly take. It was all up there and they took every penny, every last goddamn dime, and a few people, too."

He felt conspicuous with Nick's men standing behind him like white robots. He walked away from the door with shoulder-rolling arrogance, past a serving bar, without offering a drink; that would seem too much like an act of submission. Casually he went around the desk and spread his bulk assuredly in the chair.

"You told Giaccano this was a colored hit. How do you know?" Difalco asked, half sitting, half leaning on the edge of the desk, hanging rapaciously above him.

Slowly Johnson pushed back in the chair and hiked his feet, in their sixty-dollar shoes, to the top of the desk. He snorted humorous contempt, his eyes going across the room to his Negro muscle as if Difalco had said something funny. He looked up at him. "Yeah, that's right, no big bad Charlie planned this; this was strictly a black man's gig. I got that straight from the scene, but didn't need to be told, 'cause no white man outside the

69

organization would know how I operate up here. And even you people downtown don't know all about the guys and the collectin' styles I use. No, it couldn't be cased by no Charlies, 'cause even if they had the guts to nose around, they would have stood out like a white hooker at a black revival."

"How do you know fuzz didn't engineer this?" Defalco lashed at him. "They got a book on you that might have interested some ambitious cop. I think you'd be an easy mark for a greedy man trying for a big score."

"Oh, I'm ahead of you," Johnson answered. "Yeah, they're takers all right, and maybe they could have pulled it off, but the cats that did this were reachin' all the way, they were willing to bet their lives against the money, and I ain't seen a cop willing to go that far yet. And there's another reason why I threw the idea out. He'd still have to work up here, holding onto the front and being worried about the guys he was in with and all the while knowin' how easy it is to get anyone, including a cop, in Harlem." Johnson shook his head, a derisive grin ticking the corners of his mouth. "No, sir, man, no cop pulled this off."

Difalco sensed a subtle Negro put down, which was echoed by the sly grin on the face of one of Johnson's lackeys lounging in a leather chair near the desk. He remembered his instructions: *"You go up there, Nicky. You make that son-of-a-bitch jig work for you. You let him know we just consider him nothing but hired help who's responsible for us to lose a big pay date. You tell him, Nicky."*

"Your guy who was covering the entrance of the house —how come he didn't do something?"

"Because he was in the tally room upstairs," Johnson answered defensively.

"We send a guy up to protect the money when it's bein' counted." Difalco's grating voice still probed for an opening. "Your guy's supposed to cover the front door and you tell me you had him up in the room." His face twisted and he shook his head disdainfully. "I came up here expecting to hear a better story than that. That's gotta sound like you don't give a shit or maybe you're losing your touch."

70

"Who the hell expected this!" Johnson shouted, for Difalco was now belittling his abilities to manage the district, and pride wouldn't let him hold still for this kind of assault. "I been turning the collection over to downtown for ten years and not once"—his finger moved up in front of Difalco's face, emphasizing his pride and rising animosity—"not once have I been hit. There's a first time for everything, so you go easy, Nick. I'm no punk running numbers in the back room of some gin mill. I worked too mother-fuckin' hard in building Harlem into one of the best money areas the organization has, and it always got an honest count, so nobody tears me down for one losing night—you, Giaccano, nobody."

Johnson's blacks bluffed casualness along the sides of the room and Difalco's two whites peered inconspicuously from the door. But for all their silent, professional calm, they were rooting spectators intensely watching their rated fighters verbally maneuver, and lead and counter, and they were a little awed by the way Johnson had suddenly turned things around and was taking control.

"When he sees you, Nicky, he'll know I'm not fuckin' around. He'll know I'm putting him on trial, and if he don't come through, well, then, maybe I look around for a replacement and you still get a contract, Nicky—him."

Difalco's mouth tightened into a chilling semblance of a smile. "Oh, you're no punk," he said softly. "That's why I'm up here. You're getting personal service." The smile jumped off his face. "But when you give me stinkin' answers like what a good job you've been doin', you're pilin' up the past to cover a bad present. *Now* is what matters, Johnson, not the last ten years. You screwed up, and I want to know what you're doin' about tryin' to remedy it." His hand swept scornfully toward Doc's Negro help. "And how about them, or are they just dummies you keep around for laughs to tell you what a big man you are?"

Johnson stared scowlingly at him. He knew Difalco was talking for the Giaccano family and that sobering thought was reason enough to check his temper, but to ensure his keeping calm he slid his feet off the desk, his hand went to a humidor and he unwrapped a cigar, using the time to cool himself down. Still, why the hell was Difalco push-

71

ing him so hard, as though he was trying to force him into an outburst he wouldn't be able to back off from? No, they could have no idea what he was thinking; it was just a coincidence. . . .

"Don't you worry about it," he said evenly, making a show of lighting the cigar. "I got most of my guys out bird-doggin' the area. If they'd come across anything out of the ordinary, I'd have known about it, and I was just about to send out a couple more just before you gentlemen arrived," he added mockingly, rolling the cigar along his protruding pink lips. He looked at a burly, well-dressed black who sat in a cushoned chair. "JJ, you take Swinger and you move along Lenox from a Hundred and Tenth, right on up. Check the bars and clubs and restaurants and the whorehouses for the action that's not normal, man. Talk to the bartenders and managers and if anybody asks you why, you tell them Doc's interested. You'll get cooperation." One Negro hood got up slowly, another pushed away from the wall. "And, JJ." Doc's voice halted their steps. "You spread the word I'm laying a thousand out on each head I can chop off."

JJ nodded and was about to leave when Difalco's strident voice stopped him. "Hey, you, boy." His caustic tone turned them around, their eyes showing hate for his white-boss arrogance. "If you get lucky," Difalco said, "don't touch them. You call back here. You understand?" He turned and looked down at Johnson, "And you can tell the rest of your boys that, too." Surprise and irritation made Doc stare up at Difalco. "Yeah, you heard me right, Johnson, nobody touches them; this is our kill."

"Hey, I don't need you up here to do my enforcing," Doc snapped, but the unexpected order had shaded the tone. "If you want to stick around and see how I operate, okay. But I don't want no white man doing my hatchet jobs, not in this black man's ghetto."

Nick Difalco slowly shook his head. "Not this trip, pal. This is the corporation's contract. All we want is your boys to find them." A scornful smile caught the side of his mouth. "And you don't even have to get off your black ass to help."

Johnson was out of the chair, snarling above him, his

battle for control lost in a burst of temper no longer able to be contained against this ridicule. "Now, goddammit, you just hold a minute, white man. I been sitting here taking your bullshit since you arrived, just out of respect for the Syndicate. But I want to tell ya, I don't dig it. If Giaccano got a bitch the way I'm running things up here, let him tell me to my face without sending his guinea muscle to do a contract I'm well capable of handling. I been given this district to milk long before I heard of Nick Difalco and I don't need you now to show me how to run the business—"

Difalco smashed his fist down onto the desk, jarring everyone in the room into immobility. "Your business is running our business," he shouted in a voice that ripped up at Johnson. "You may be somethin' up here, but below a Hundred and Tenth Street you're just another fat nigger." His face constricted, the eyes vanishing behind vitriolic slits. "Giaccano pulled you out of the stink of a back alley and put you up front to represent the Organization; he calls the shots and if he tells you to shit, you better start squattin', fat man. And that's just what he's tellin' you now. He put you in and he can put you out, and you better believe it. Because anybody that loses money is a bad risk and tonight you lost a bundle."

A whispered story told over a drink, or gossip let slip at a gathering by some boozed-up Sicilian vicariously enjoying a compatriot's exploits, words, hearsay, pieces of information that come together and build reputations that are only half believed—all this might form the background to such a man as Difalco, but now as Doc Johnson stared at him he knew there was nothing false about the man. He was psychotic, the Syndicate prize with a prowess in executions that had earned him frightening respect. But the swarthy hood, for all his reputation, had not frightened Johnson, not even intimidated him. Now, however, Johnson would go no further in fighting for the respect he felt he had long ago earned from the Giaccano family. He worked for them but his relation with the hierarchy was a little different from that of many whites who ran other sections of the city for the old don. For he knew they needed a strong buck who could

73

control the turf and move the vices for them in a ghetto that would be too threatening, from its police and its black population, for their white skin to operate out in the open, and he was paid, accordingly, a fraction of the take. It was a true gauge of respect and it had always walled him from the crudities of the Nick Difalcos. But now this breach of the white specialist into the black district to do Johnson's assassinations had ominous undertones of a beginning of an end. However, he had other plans and he wasn't about to demolish them with an insane shooting match with Difalco. Nor would he let the man carry back any more than he already had. He would allow him the story that Johnson backed off, that when the chips are down he's a yellow nigger and you don't have to worry about him being out of line anymore. He hadn't taken his eyes off Difalco. Okay, he said to himself, you want the contract, take it, you wop bastard, it's all yours. And he eased back into the chair.

"The heist on top of that bad killing you pulled off a couple of months ago." Difalco ignored Doc's flag of silent truce and continued to hammer at him. "They're really startin' to worry about you. Maybe you're losin' your juice, lettin' things run this loose."

Johnson stuck the cigar back in his broad face, rolling it into the corner of his sullen mouth. "I explained that hit to the old man. It was a must job. Because it was a white cat didn't change a thing; it had to be done."

"But you can't explain this." Difalco jumped him verbally. "One guy in his proper spot could have cut down anyone leavin' the building. In fact, they wouldn't even have got up the stairs in the first place. But where was your guy with the hardware? Up there to be taken like some slob."

Doc squinted against the smoke curling up past his eyes. "I'm not the first guy in the organization that ever lost a take in a stickup. How about that Los Angeles job last winter when almost as much was taken as they got tonight?"

"They were caught and the money returned," Difalco said quickly, "and it didn't make the papers. And they

74

didn't kill anybody, especially cops, because it was pulled by no hophead shines."

Johnson ignored the derogation as if it had never been said. He released a wafer of smoke from between his heavy lips, his brown eyes watching the cigar cloud rise toward the ceiling and rip apart in an air-conditioner draft. "This wasn't pulled by no hophead." Johnson's intonation was as soft as the rising smoke.

"You got something?" Difalco forgot the castigations, his tone falling back to a milder rasp of anticipation.

"JJ, what the hell you standin' there for, man?" Doc's voice boomed out to the burly Negroes standing at the door. "Didn't I tell you two to go and check along Lenox?" To the three white men, the tone was anger, a quick-rising, domineering annoyance against the slowness of an underling. But to the two Negroes at the door, his voice and his eyes carried much more. Johnson was telling them he didn't need their assistance, he had control, nothing foolish would happen, and he really wasn't taking Difalco's shit, no matter how it seemed. And like mutes participating in a subtle sign language, JJ and Swinger turned and walked out of the room. "Them boys, they sure slow when you want somethin' done. I think I'm gonna make some changes around here," Johnson said, looking toward the two remaining Negroes, sitting on each side of the room. The telepathic joke, such as pass between blacks when whites are present, was received; they didn't smile.

"Okay, Doc, let's cut out the horseshit," Nick's voice cut in sarcastically. "What have you got?"

Johnson looked up quickly into Difalco's lidded eyes and wondered if he was really that hip. "Just deductions," he answered flatly. "I had good boys up there tonight, some of my best. They weren't letting any amateurs take them, and this bunch ain't no amateurs. They carried a chopper and took out five guys with one blast. I got a real feelin' about this; I think they were playin' it that way. They didn't want no witnesses. This thing took mother-grabbin' knowledge of how I operate, and guts."

Nick Difalco, no longer playing a part, was as mesme-

75

rized by Doc Johnson's analysis as were the others in the silent room.

"I figure it has to be inside, so I check my group first and they come up clean. Then I start to think about the cats that used to work for me; I had to go through a lot of them because the cat I was lookin' for wouldn't be too close to me, but at the same time he had to know the story. You know what I mean? He needed a lot of things goin' for him and there's one guy shapes up as fillin' that bill. He was one a them that worked in numbers, did some strong-armin' and once in a while escorted the money on collection day. He didn't work for me long, but he knew the whole setup. About a year ago I lose him. He got messed up for carryin' a gun; bein' an ex-con they had him on a Sullivan rap and he took a one-to-three-year fall." Doc shrugged his shoulders and his eyes moved toward the others, then went back to Difalco. "Now I could be wrong about this cat; for all I know he might still be doin' time. But until I find out otherwise, I gotta figure this grabber to be our man."

Chapter 8

"Jim Harris, you goin' to be a rich man." The laughter was wild, uncontrollable, like that of a gleeful, exuberant child. But in the squalid tenement kitchen it wasn't a time or place for laughter. The mirth sounded strange as it echoed off peeling yellow walls and worn oilcloth. It bounced off a stove, which still held food in a pot, and over a sink piled with unwashed dishes and down to the filled paper bag of garbage by the bolted door. The two men at the table stared morosely at him. A yellow shade was drawn over the window and a bottle of booze and an over-stuffed bag of money lay open on the table.

"Yessir, man, I give you credit. You had this mother figured cold. And you, too, Joey boy, I'm not forgetting you."

The little man with the scraggly, pencil-thin mustache

and dull flat eyes protuberant in his coal-black face jerked his head toward the shot glass he held. The glass was filled to the rim and some slopped to the floor as he downed the drink with one quick movement. His exuberance had not abated since their return to the apartment. Henry Jackson had never possessed more than a couple of hundred at any one time in his life, and now the sight, the touching, the counting of the fortune before him was too rapturous a joy; if they had let him, no doubt he would have thrown the money over his head to let it rain down upon him while he danced out all the glad dreams of his life. The fact that his exultation gained momentum from the belts he took from the bottle seemed to force the two men at the table into deeper shells of silence and his toast to them had brought no response. They had been successful beyond their hopes, but in their victory came no elation, just a cold, frightening memory of their fear. The severity of the crime was still too appallingly vivid to let them unbend.

"I was sure enough worried when you two went up them stairs," Henry Jackson said, becoming serious and walking toward the table. "And when that gun went off blowin' out them front windows"—he stopped and shook his head, letting his eyes roll mournfully—"I'll tell ya, man, and I'll be honest with ya, I came this close"—his fingers barely parted—"this mother-fuckin' close to hot-assin' it out of there." The two men at the table looked at each other as Jackson leaned over and greedily fingered the money. "But I tell ya, I ain't worried no more, yeah, no more," and again the childlike laughter burst from him.

The burly man looked up at Jackson. "Henry, I wouldn't advise any more liquor." His voice was subdued in its admonishment, but it checked Jackson's hand as it moved from the money to the bottle.

"What's the matter with you, Jim?" The humor was now suddenly blown out of Henry Jackson, punctured by the warning and the aura of disquiet in the hazel eyes set in Harris's muscular face. Henry stood staring at him, not understanding the melancholy, then he leaned down and touched his shoulder. "Hey, man, I don't dig this sadness. You and Joe sit here like a couple of losers. Jimbo, it's not every day a man makes his fortune; we got a lot to celebrate about. Come on, it's past. It's time to relax and just think about how you don't ever have to bust your hump again."

They looked at him, each seemingly immersed in his own thoughts. Then Joe Logart broke the silence. "Oh, let him have a blast, there's no harm now." Logart's voice was weary, almost despairing, in ironic contrast to the features in his reddish-black face. The scar on one cheek ended at the lip and twisted the corner of his mouth into a perpetual smirk, as if he were constantly amused by some inner joke whose punchline he alone knew. "We could all use one, I guess," he added, and poured out three drinks. And Jim Harris shrugged as if rescinding his caution.

Harris rose and stood half a head above Jackson. "It's too hot for booze," he said, and walked to an almost dead refrigerator pushed up next to the sink. His hair was cropped close over a cocoa-color broad face and wide nostrils. He was a thick-set man and his T-shirt stuck to his sweating body like another layer of skin. They watched him snap open a can of beer and lift it to his mouth and they watched the muscles of his throat work as he drank. Henry Jackson sat down at the table and lifted his shot glass in another ambiguous gesture that forced Joe Logart to down a drink with him. Somewhere across the court a radio was playing blues and its fading sounds came through the open window, around the pulled-down shade and dimly into the room. The faintly heard lyrics wrapped barriers of detachment about them and they listened to its conclusion, each isolated in thought. Only minutes before they had turned their own radio off. They had heard a news broadcast that dispassionately told of their success. There were no leads, everything seemed safe. They had pulled it off, they were home free, and it was time for congratulations.

"I was scared up there tonight, man," Joe Logart said softly. "Like never in my life was I that scared." Henry Jackson's hand moved to the remaining drink and pulled it to him and Logart turned and looked at Harris, leaning against the sink. "I never want to be afraid again, man. You know what I mean, Jim?"

"Yeah, I know what you mean." Harris shook his head, his eyes mirroring the answer.

"I'm—I'm sorry I slowed you down, Jimbo. I kinda went to pieces on ya up there, didn't I? Thanks for pullin' me outa it. I—"

"You didn't slow me down, man." He wanted to tell him he did fine, he wanted to lie to him that they were both great, but they had both been there and that would be ludicrous. "We got what we went after," he said softly, "and we're still alive, Joe. We're here having a drink and talkin' about it and that's got to mean something."

Sweat rolled down Logart's face, caught the crevice of his scar and crept over the twisted flesh at the corner of his lip. "I didn't think it was goin' to be that rough; I expected it to be tough, but not like it was, not like that."

"Why don't you forget it, man." Harris's tone was pliant with understanding, but he wanted to yell at him to stop the morbid playback. "It's over and done with; let it lay," he heard himself saying.

But Joe Logart couldn't. It hung graphically in front of him, visions with afflicted screams in the air, bodies strung against the wall and slowly sliding downward, eyes disbelieving, and moans, and the low lamentable cry to Christ.

"Everything leading up to it was solid like you could feel and touch it, you know," Logart whispered. "I musta told myself over a hundred times this was it, we're goin' for the big one; the biggest thing I ever gonna do in my life. But it don't hit me until I start to climb them stairs and I feel high, like after a long pull on pot when everything starts to be unreal. But only more so, man, oh, more so. Even the shots goin' off, they sounded like they come from a mile away. And my legs, my legs, Jimbo, they felt like I'm standin' on stilts and the floor like startin' to move." He stared at Jim Harris, immobile at the sink, listening with his head down. "They died bad, Jimbo, they shouldn't have cried that way, it should've been quick, no sounds . . . no sounds." His voice trailed off and the tenement kitchen was a stilled chamber of memory that pulled Harris back to the broken men dying

79

at his feet and the choking, sickening smoke twisting up past his face from the gun barrel in a—

"Hey, hey, come on, you two!" Henry Jackson's shiny face creased into a grin. His hand hit the table but he didn't spill the drink; he had already downed it. "This ain't the right kind of feelin' for a party. You gotta shake the blues loose by thinkin' about all the good action that foldin' money here is gonna bring." He turned his head toward Harris. "You, too, man. Come on over and sit down with us and have a drink." He began to laugh again. "Yeah, baby, it's no more scratchin' for a lousy buck from now on. It's goin' to be high street on velvet, silk shirts and suits and—"

"Get off your cloud, Henry. We ain't home yet." Harris's authoritative growl bit into Jackson, freezing the flat features into irritation.

"Hey, baby, you been callin' the signals from the very beginning," Jackson protested. "Now that it's over, man, and we're winners, how about lettin' up, huh, and lettin' us live our lives and start enjoyin' some of our feelings?"

Harris walked back to the table, his big body filling Jackson's view. "I'm still callin' the shots, Henry, and don't you forget it. If you think we're over the hump you better guess again. From here on in we gotta cool any thoughts about swingin' with the money for a long time, and you just better believe it."

Jackson worked his mouth into a pacifying grin without mirth. "Oh, I'm not quittin' you, Jimbo. I just figure some joy talk gonna make you and Joe feel better. That's all, just tryin' to cheer things up. And I'm goin' along like you planned, you know, like all the way."

Satisfied, Harris softened his tone and spoke to Logart. "How about you, Joe? Now that we scored, any doubts in your mind about me callin' it to the end, or do you want to jump out now?"

Logart returned the questioning stare. "You sold me a wild scheme," he answered slowly. "I had my doubts from the start, but I bought in because I was movin' to nowhere and I knew it was the only chance anybody ever goin' to offer me to get out of the shit." He nodded toward the money and his hand gently touched one of the stacks of counted bills. "If I died goin' for this tonight, at least it would have been goin' down for something big." He shook his head. "No, I ain't about to knock success. You proved your point, man. I stay with the scene right down the line."

"Well, I'm glad you still feel that way. Yeah, I'm glad you both feel that way"—Harris's eyes stayed with Logart's, waiting for a reaction—"because things have changed. I'm not goin' to hole up as long as I said. I'm breakin' up the rest of the plan. I'm goin' to sit on the money for a lot less time than I said. The day after tomorrow, thirty-six hours from now, we take our shares and run. If I thought I could move on them now, I'd give you both your shares and I'd cut out."

Joe Logart didn't disappoint him. Harris saw the scar along his cheek pulse as he pulled his lips into a twisted, inadvertent smile of suspicion. Logart looked over to Henry Jackson for support. "You been preachin' from the very beginnin'," he said, choosing his words cautiously, "that we gotta stay with the plan. Once we start, you said, we don't jump around; no matter what happen we live with the scheme." Logart came forward, almost leaning on top of the money. "A week was needed to cool down the hunt and you said that would be tight. But there goin' to be some safety after that to move around and it made good sense and, man, we agreed to sit and sweat it out because it was the backbone of the whole hit. Our safety valve, you called it." Now he was thoroughly back in the present, his mind attuned to his share of the money in a bag that overflowed voluptuously like a big-titted woman. "I don't like changin' dice in the middle of a hot roll, man. You been right so far; now you don't sound so right no more. Like you're not so sure anymore, man."

Harris listened impassively. He felt Logart had the right to question him. Jackson didn't count. He was on a gravy train. Twenty thousand dollars just for wheeling them away in a hot car. But it was different with Logart. They had been friends for years and he had called him in Detroit and brought him in and hooked him on a proposition that he knew was the longest of shots. And he had laid down strong, inflexible rules and Logart had listened, respecting his toughness and relying on his inside knowledge. Now this sudden change made Logart suspect a cop-out. Maybe he had seen the crack in the hard-guy surface. It was there to be seen. For Jim Harris now doubted that he could have stayed cooped up with so much gold, knowing the final phase of the plan and what was on the street looking for them. He knew now that the temptation to run was too big to have held him still for a week. Yes, Joe Logart had the right to question him.

Harris's hand parted as if grasping for the right words. "I wanted to stay with it, Joe; I mean I meant to play it like I called it, man. Right down to the final blueprint. And I would have——" He caught himself and was embarrassed by the thinly disguised apology, embarrassed by their eyes staring silently up at him. His voice hardened and his big frame came out of its slouch. "Baby, this mother fucker changed when them two cops came in that hall. I didn't figure the law in on this. It was goin' to be tough enough just goin' up against Doc Johnson. He moves real big up here, but he don't have that many guys. And when he gets a no-show he gonna have to wait to see where the money starts flowin' because it's the only thing he can do, man, and a week of hidin' would of cooled the trail. Cooled it enough where we'd be able to travel a lot easier."

The extraneous sounds coming through the windows had ceased for Joe Logart and Henry Jackson as they sat intently, watching Harris's big frame hover above them. "The cops they won't sit back like Johnson; they don't work that way. They're gonna keep on comin'." All they could hear now was his rigid justifications. "They'll blanket this whole black area, man. They'll talk to everybody and they look everywhere. They'll turn Harlem inside out and they're never gonna stop. Because they got the troops to keep goin' at it. And the longer I sit chained up here with all this money, the more chance we're givin' them to find me." Logart dropped his eyes from Harris's and his fingers began to worry the empty shot glass. "And there are other things now to consider, Joe. Things I put down before but now look kinda strong, like maybe people livin' in this building start thinking I'm an oddball cat, all the time stayin' in the room, never

82

showin' my face. They get curious, start talkin'; maybe they even think that now. Course, ever since I rent this place I been tryin' to duck them. Or maybe what's worse, some strungout junkie tries to bust in, figurin' nobody's home, it's so quiet, and he got an easy touch. I'd have to burn him and I don't want to be sittin' here with no dead body." His voice trailed off tonelessly. The pallid light jammed into the ceiling made the three of them appear to be black waxwork figures that through some mechanical miracle were able to perspire, giving their mute, still forms a more lifelike appearance.

"He's right, man." Henry Jackson shook his head seriously. "Jimbo's right," he reiterated in a tone he felt emulated Harris's quiet authority. "When you waste a couple of fuzz, you got big trouble. They got a tough code. If Big Jim here want to change the plan, it sound all right to me." He looked over at Logart. "Because, man, if word ever got around he sittin' up here with this kinda money, he wouldn't have enough bullets to shoot all the people that would be tryin' to come in here and take it from him." Being an optimist, he thought Harris had covered the dangers, but he went along with it because it would put him closer to twenty thousand dollars, five days closer to changing his dreams and avaricious hopes into realities.

Logart, his finger tracing a line through some of the spilled liquor, acted as though he hadn't heard Jackson at all. He said to Harris, "I guess you know what you're doin', man. It's just that—"

"If you think I'm pullin' somethin' cute, Joe"—Harris cut into his halfhearted submission. His voice was detached; no anger, not even annoyance. Nigger, nigger, he cried to himself, and he could feel his nerves being pulled tighter, I lead you by the hand into a promised land of a hundred thousand dollars, lay it at your goddamn feet, and—"then stay here with me," he said softly. "I got room, you can pad right up here. And if you really got your doubts, man, you can sleep right on top of the money."

Joe Logart dropped his eyes from Harris's blunt stare and slowly, self-consciously, shook his head. "I'm sorry, Jim, if it sounded like that. Don't mind me, huh? I'm not

83

thinkin' too clear yet. You know what I mean, man? It's just we came so far from what you laid down in the beginning, I just don't want anything lousin' up now, that's all."

"I don't know what you goin' on about." Jackson bounced his hand off the table, letting his true character flow back and almost spilling the drink he had just poured. "The sooner we get our cuts, the better. That there money weren't meant to be sittin' around nohow. It's meant to spend. That's right, ain't it, Jimbo? Like enjoy, huh, man?" He raised the shot glass to his lips and downed it.

Harris pulled a chair around and sat down at the end of the table between them; his concern now was Jackson's eagerness and he tried to modify it, at least subdue it for a time with what he felt to be the truth. "Henry, after you get your cut I can't tell you how spend it. You and Joe well earned your shares; you can do anything you want with them. But I want to warn you, if you're lookin' for a long life you'd better take it slow, nothin' flashy."

"Now, Jim," Jackson answered, rolling his protruding eyes in his black, shiny face and playing for laughs, a character that seemed suited to him. "I don't intend to spend big, baby, because my share is just a little ol' portion of that there money. Oh, I ain't complainin', you two cats did all the chance-takin', especially you, an' you put it all together and made it work. But I got enough out of it, that satisfyin'. It's goin' to let me treat myself well. Yeah, it sure will!" and he rolled his eyes again and laughed. His arms spread out as if he held them in a cooling breeze and he grabbed at some of the bills lying on the table and let them fall through his fingers. His likable ease and the communication of his laughter reached toward Logart.

"What you gonna do with your money, Henry?" Logart asked. "You goin' to get one of them downtown gray bitches and do some swingin'?"

Jackson lit a cigarette, taking a long, pompous pull as he relished his thoughts. He blew the smoke toward the peeling yellow ceiling and then leaned importantly over the table and looked at Logart. "I'm goin' into business.

I'm bustin' outa this deadbeat, dead-assed town and I'm goin' to Chicago and look for a nice bar to buy over on the swingin' black South Side."

"That's a fine hip business, Henry. You can always make a good buck on that. There's always a demand. But what kind of owner you goin' to be, you goin' to spring for every fourth round?" Logart let himself relax still further into Henry Jackson's easy optimism, for Henry was again bubbling, exuberant, giving himself freely to happy visions.

But then Henry looked at Jim Harris and his good cheer faltered. Harris's solemn gaze directed back at him made the smile stick to his face. He felt as if Harris were pitying him, as if he were staring at some dumb creature caged behind bars in a zoo. Quickly Henry turned around.

"Hey, Joe," he said, trying to sustain the conviviality, "why don't you come with me, man? We can go in partners and instead of a gin mill we can maybe buy a fancy cocktail lounge. You know, like one of them white cheatin' joints where they got them low lights that makes all them gray bitches look good, while they foolin' around with all them married guys. Why, man, a couple o' sharp cats like us, we'd do okay in that town."

"No, thanks, Henry," Logart said softly. "I got plans, too, but in the opposite direction. Like France and Italy and maybe a touch of Spain. My old stompin' grounds during the service bit. I always wanted to go back someday"—his hand motioned to the money—"but never thought in this kinda style. Henry, my share's gonna look like three, four times the amount over there." His eyes gleamed in kinetic remembrances of being stationed in Frankfurt and farther south at a base in Bavaria, of the accumulated leave he had used and the three-day passes to Paris and Rome and Barcelona, of the good wine he had drunk and the whores he had jugged, and the sights he had seen. "You gotta see the towns, Henry, they're old with lots o' history, with pictures hanging' on museum walls that are worth a million dollars. And the people, you ask them for directions and they all take their time and tell ya, sometimes even drawin' you a map. And they all seem young with smiles on their faces, even the old ones. I tell ya, man, it's all beautiful."

The idea of picking up and putting down in a foreign country seemed too strange an abstraction for Henry Jackson to imagine. He had been born and bred in the black ghettos and felt comfortable only with the familiar. America was his country and he wanted to live and die there and the hell with the foreigners; so he stopped trying to fathom Logart's talk and put him down as a lame.

Fresh blues were audible once again, flowing at them from somewhere. And Harris and Logart went back into their silence. But Jackson had an avuncular feeling for the two younger men and he assumed it was his duty to pull them from their gloom. He looked at Harris. "How about you, Jim, where you goin' to light to?" he asked. "You goin' to go down South to one of them cracker towns and buy one of them big houses on the hill that's goin' to look down on all that white trash?"

Harris stared somberly at him for a long moment, then answered slowly. "I just want to get out of Harlem alive, Henry."

Jackson raised his hands in mock fear. "Don't say that, man." He shook his head sadly. "Now don't say it, you hear. You are the most frettin'est cat I know. Here you engineered the biggest bang-bang heist that happened around here for twenty years, and you may not know it, Jimbo, but it's gonna be talked about for the next twenty years. And you're frettin'."

Harris ignored him. He got up and walked to the corner of the room where they had piled the blue police uniforms, and extracted two .38 automatics from the heap. He came back and laid the guns on the table. Then he reached into the pile of money, methodically counting out five hundred dollars twice, and pushed it to them. "Here, it's off the top. You can call it expense money, I don't care what, just so long as you use it to set up your transportation and have enough left over to pay any tabs, like hotels, or anybody holding chits on you. No sense in tryin' to skip out, still owin' somebody, where they're goin' to remember and talk about you. Pay your bills tomorrow so when you get your cuts you can get directly out of town." He spoke in a flat, almost indifferent tone and now centered his gaze on Henry Jackson. "And if you got to take care of somebody with more than just a few dollars, you can always send it through the mail later and like with no return address for a thank you, if you know what I mean." Leaning over the table, he shoved the hand guns at them. "I want you both to hold on to these awhile. I don't expect any trouble, but you never can tell, right, Henry? No chance-takin' now, baby."

"I don't need no gun, daddy." Henry's voice suddenly took on a strange, inimical growl, his face twisting as his hand disappeared below the table and then quickly flared up. The knife snapped open, the large gleaming blade flashing in his hand in a decisive ugly motion. His lips parted still further into a grotesque grin. His eyes showed the contempt he felt for Harris's solicitude. "Any mother fucker come near me, I'll cut their goddamn belly out. You hear me, I don't need no gun to protect myself, Jimbo."

Joe Logart stared across the table in surprise at the abrupt change. But Harris knew what was eating at Henry. He realized he offended him as if the repeated warnings were meant as a simple putdown to someone he didn't have confidence in. He picked up the gun and held it in front of Jackson. "You take the piece, baby," he said consolingly. He didn't want to lose him and looked for words to soothe the ruffled feelings. "I want you both packed for better action than that there sticker can give, Henry. You're too good a man to go down for the want of a weapon." With his other hand he gently touched his shoulder. "And besides, man, it's gonna make me feel a lot better sittin' up here knowin' you two are packed for some kind of protection. I'm gonna sleep a lot easier knowin' that, Henry."

Slowly Henry Jackson took the gun. He kept his gaze on Harris for a couple of seconds as if silently apologizing, and then slipped the gun into his waistband. Jim Harris straightened up from the table. There didn't seem to be anything more to add. Logart caught the finality of his movement and stood up, too, stuffing the other gun into his pocket.

87

Henry went for the bottle and poured a drink into the shot glass. Then he stood up and raised the drink. "One for the road," he said, and his head went back as he downed it.

"Henry, if you want you can stay here tonight," Harris said. "We can keep each other company. I got plenty of room; you could—"

"Why, man?" Henry smiled. "Because I had a few lousy drinks? Hey, you know me better than that, Jimbo. You know I can carry my booze." His lightheartedness didn't ease the look on Harris's face. "Would you stop worryin', man? I'm all right. Johnson's cats don't know us. You're the only one that has to hole up and, besides, I got no time to stay with ya. You forgettin' you changed our timetable. I'm gonna be busy clearin' up a few things before I'm able to move out feelin' free and I'm gonna need tonight as well as tomorrow to take care of it."

Harris looked at him for a long moment as if deciding what to do. "Okay," he said, "but you just make sure you play it cool." He turned to Logart. "I'll see you both back here; make it twelve noon the day after tomorrow."

"You know it," Logart answered, his eyes wandering to the money lying at the end of the table. "Guard it good, Jimbo. I'm only going to be a rich man once."

"Don't worry, baby, it's like it's in a vault. They'd have to crawl over me to get at it," Harris said unsmilingly, then he turned, walked to the door and unbolted it.

Jackson stopped on his way out and shook hands. "I'll see ya in a couple of days, and don't worry about me, man, okay? You just relax and get some sleep." And he stepped out into the hall and started down the steps.

Harris grabbed Logart's arm as he passed him. "I don't want nothin' kickin' wrong now, so you keep an eye on him. You know what I mean?"

Logart nodded, then stepped out into the blackness and followed Jackson down the stairs. Jim Harris listened to their receding footsteps, then closed and rebolted the door.

Chapter 9

The cue stick wove above the ivory ball on table one like a magic wand in the hand of the big dusky in the pink shirt. With a disdainful motion of his head he signaled the corner pocket, where he intended to drop the sixth consecutive ball in his run. The hand cupped on the green felt and the cue moved liquidly, professionally through the curled fingers. The eyes narrowed below a forehead rippled in concentration. The stick paused in its backstroke, then flicked forward just as the shooter caught sight of them coming through the door. The ball hit with the lazy sound of a missed shot. The player's small, consumptive-looking opponent, staring down at the table, flashed yellow teeth and suppressed a sarcastic laugh. Pop Gibson, the proprietor of the academy, sat hunched over a glass case by the window reading the morning line of horses and he squinted in the bad light as he followed them back past the second table, where the shark of the house practiced in solitude, unmindful of the three teen-agers stiffening in the high chairs along the wall, silently watching them move back past the darkened third and fourth tables. The two men in a game of straights at the back of the room were too absorbed to look up. The short man, his expensive silk suit reflecting the green shaded light hanging from the ceiling, leaned across the table professionally. His cue slowly rode back, lining up the shot, then a hand picked up the ball. The shooter whirled his mouth, ready to explode words in a rush of anger, but the pockmarked face froze. "Hello, Nightman," the voice said as he squinted up into the pale-blue eyes of Frank Sullivan. The other player stood trancelike, the cue at his side like a bed-player stood trancelike, the cue at his side like a be-draggled soldier, waiting as though the intrusion were a
"Take a walk," the detective said sharply. But his voice failed to stir the shabbily dressed player across the

padded felt table. "Get the hell out of here." Sullivan's tone tightened into a physical threat but the immobile face remained impassive. The purple lips parted and started to form sounds, then stopped.

Bill Pope walked toward the man, his hand ready to grab the collar to turn him around and boot him in the ass in the direction of the door, but the dreamy-looking Negro stopped him when he spoke.

"I beat him." He raised his hand and pointed at The Nightman. "I whipped him clean and he owe me a fin." The voice seemed to wallow in addiction.

Sullivan studied the face, then turned to The Nightman. "Pay him."

They watched as The Nightman pompously laid the cue stick across the table, his hand going in a big movement to his wallet, and he opened it as if it were a Bible, rippling the bills, and pulled out a fiver. His dreamy opponent took it, his expression never changing; he turned, stuck his cue stick in a rack along the wall, and seemed to shuffle out on a cloud. Frank Sullivan's lips pressed across his teeth, but he wasn't smiling. Instinctively The Nightman turned his head, his body tensing. He felt he was going to be hit.

"Are you pushing the shit again?" The detective's voice was barely audible.

"Now you know I'm not messin' around with the junk no more, man." The answer came quickly. "You got a tap on the community; you know I been clean. I'm an independent now; I move for myself, and pushin' the drugs ain't one of my things. A man can get busted too easy for that." The blow hadn't fallen and The Nightman seemed to find courage. "If that cat's on it he didn't get no duji from me and you know it, man. Go ahead, search me."

The other people in the urine-odored hall stood silently waiting for the hipster to disappear between the tables, to be dropped there by the stocky white detective. Bill Pope scowled at them and they turned slowly, uncomfortably back to their games. The three teen-agers had left already. The Nightman could feel a knot tightening in his stomach, his fingers twitched. He knew Frank Sullivan, he knew how this cop operated. You Irish prick, he thought to himself as he tried to force a bored expression on his face. "What you guys want?" He kept the voice respectful and raised it slightly to carry the hall, playing to the small audience up front.

Sullivan was aware of the little hustler's bit of show and purposely held his own voice down. "I'll give you three guesses what we want."

The detective's restraint seemed to lend courage to The Nightman and his hand, a diamond glittering on the pinky, flung out in a wave of rejection. "Man, I don't want one of your guesses. I don't like playin' games. If you lookin' for somebody for the question-and-answer bit, you ain't gonna find him in me."

Pope took a step to him. "Hey, punk, you watch your mouth or it'll end up droppin' blood." Like his partner, he had not raised his voice.

"Okay." Sullivan nodded, not taking his eyes off him; he sensed The Nightman was looking for a cover against the inquisitive glances coming from the silent players at the front of the room. "I'll draw you a picture," the detective said quietly. "We want a lead on who robbed Johnson tonight and with it killed two cops that got in their way."

"Now how the fuck should I know about that?" The Nightman's ridicule spilled out in a stream of scorn that he was unable to stop, for the idea that he was even remotely connected with such a big-league hit came at him with surprise. But he desperately wanted to recall the disrespect, to bring it back to a silence or a grunt or a shrug, for he knew he had overplayed his act.

Bill Pope's large, whitish-brown palm rode up from somewhere below the table and caught him along the cheek. It jolted and turned his head, its sound slapping off the walls and bouncing to the front of the hall. The Nightman's hand went to the side of his face, the eyes wide in fright above the wide-bridge nose as he looked at the young Negro detective.

"What you do that for, man?" His veneer was gone and his voice was a whisper. "I'm only asking a legit question. What I say for you to hit me?"

"The next time, joker, I close the hand." Pope said it as if he wanted to hit him again.

91

The Nightman turned quickly to Sullivan, who stood hefting the ivory cue ball in his hand and staring at him ominously. The pool hall was now theirs. The other players had deserted it; their sticks lay across empty tables; the players were already on the street. Pop Gibson's white-topped Uncle Tom head could be seen through the front window, as the owner stood outside as if trying to catch a nonexistent breeze. The Nightman's eyes moved to the ball in Frank Sullivan's hand and his body constricted in sickening anticipation.

"You got a lot of mouth lately, Nightman, and a short memory," Frank Sullivan said, his voice as soft as before. "I don't know who you got going for you"—he shook his head sadly—"but whoever you're greasing, it won't be enough."

"Hey, wait a minute, huh. You're goin' too fast. I got a right to know what I bein' rousted for, man." His voice squeaked and his hands parted and he blinked up at Sullivan. "I been a good bag for you, but it's always been private talk, you know what I mean. And now you come in and lay it on me that you want information about cop killers. Hey, you scare me, man, right down to my feet. For all I know you lookin' for a fall guy to take the rap. Like maybe I don't got no witnesses to cover my time for a couple of hours and then I'm dead, huh? Man, a cat got to fight for his rights nowadays."

"You're dead anyway, Nightman." The detective's voice didn't rise, but the sardonic tone dug deep into the Negro's fear. "I think it's about time I stopped using you as a source and closed you out real good. I can run you in any time I want. With your sheet any one of a half dozen charges would do, but if you're looking for a frame, I'll give it to you, you son of a bitch. I'll plant a dope rap on you into a seven-to-ten-year fall and I'll color it with enough background that'll ensure you pull the whole stretch."

The Nightman had lowered his eyes before Sullivan's stare, the threats overwhelming him. He tried for coolness and scanned the racked sticks and empty stool-like chairs along the wall, the barren green tables with their score indicators stretched on taut wires above them, and he looked past the detectives to the open door, to the street and escape. He could feel the sweat break from his pores, running from under his armpits down the sides of his body, as memory flooded his mind. . . .

There had been an outbreak of cabby holdups, a couple of drivers killed, and the papers jumped in with a hard sell. Hopheads, they screamed in three-inch headlines, which brought the inevitable police crackdown. Nothing moved on the streets. The organized pushers went underground to wait out the heat and the addicts started to climb the walls. The Nightman, on the fringe, fighting for a piece of the narcotic action, pushed his meager diluted supply down from the rooftops of tenements to the backs of their halls, then ignorantly out onto the streets, where he would wait under the gray lamps hustling his now overpriced wares to the dark-skinned recipients. The lights flicked on from the battered car that pulled away from the curb and moved through the cold January street and it eased toward The Nightman, a heavy-set middle-aged Negro at the wheel. He ignored it—for he was too busy dealing drugs to an addict— until it stopped and from the other side of the car there appeared a white face topped by a snap-brim hat. It was Sullivan's eyes he remembered most of all. They seemed not to have any pupils, just ovals of cold gray slush that came at him, frightening him by their deadliness, herding him into the back of the car. Three years, he thought, they're going to take me off the street for three years, while the car drove slowly toward the station house. Three years: that would begin with his booking, his trial, his—

But the car stopped. Piers loomed in the darkness of the deserted warehouse street. The door opened, the hand of the white devil pulled his collar, dragging the cowering Nightman a decent distance away from the cigarette-lighting Negro at the wheel.

"Open your coat, nigger"—the voice was barely heard through the whipping roar of the wind—"and get your palms against that wall." A shakedown; the white bastard is shaking me down. But in this thought there was an elation: he wasn't going to jail. Sullivan's hand went through his pockets; pulling out a wallet, he read the name and his fingers indexed the few hundred stuffed inside it.

The other hand had come up with a slim packet of brown paper. He opened it; his finger touched the powder and he brought it to his lips. His face soured. He let the powder blow away, its whiteness disappearing in a gust of wind. "Nigger, turn around." Sullivan's fist smashed into his face, driving him back, and he sagged against the wall. The detective's right fist drove deep into The Nightman's stomach. He measured the pain and hit him again, and again, and once more, the other hand keeping him pinned against the wall. Then he watched the sick black face follow the crumbling body to the pavement. His hat rolled into the gutter and he lay at the detective's feet and Frank Sullivan had to hunch over him so his words wouldn't be lost by winter blowing in from the bleak piers. "I'm going to give you a break; I'm not going to bust ya. But from now on you're my pigeon. When I want to know something, you tell me. If you don't, you find out. You hear me, nigger?" He leaned down closer to his ear, his words chopping rasps of sound. "You hear me?"

The Nightman, his eyes filled with fear, painfully nodded his head. "And I don't want to see you pushing that goddamn shit no more, you hear me?" Again the head moved in acknowledgment, the cheek scraping against the cold cement. The detective, satisfied, pulled him roughly to his feet. He weaved and started to go down again, but caught himself. The Negro detective in the car had watched the grotesque charade through the rear-view mirror and now backed up the car to them. Sullivan took the money out of the wallet, grabbed the wind-blown coat and jammed the billfold back into The Nightman's pocket. He pushed the crumpled bills through the car window to his partner. "Here, Owen, my contribution toward your retirement." Sullivan sensed the unasked question. "Don't worry, Owen," he said. "I got more than my share tonight; I got me a talking pigeon that's going to let me win a few prizes in the foreseeable future. . . ."

The same fists, the same spot. The future was here, thought The Nightman as his eyes, lidded and heavy, moved past the closed door of the poolroom toilet and settled on the iron bars covering the back window. "You

94

tryin' to get me killed, man? You two come walkin' in here and start pumpin' me in front of people." He shook his head and looked directly at Sullivan at last. "You want word should get around I'm whorin' for the law, man? If that gets around you wouldn't have to frame me, I'm out of business like maybe permanently. If you wanted to talk to me I woulda met you on the q.t. like in the past, you know what I mean?"

"You lyin' bastard," Sullivan said, still hefting the cue ball in his hand. "If you had any idea what I wanted and had time to think about it, I wouldn't have found you for a month."

"Well, could you blame me? A little man like me should get off the street when the big boys start to play and this is the biggest I ever heard of. I hear they got almost half a million and left more bodies around than a battlefield." His dignity seemed restored by what he felt was inside knowledge, and he picked up the cue stick and thoughtfully began to chalk it. "I also hear Doc's got his boys out in force; they lookin' all over Harlem. He's actin' like he knows something your boys don't; like it's a local deal."

"Hey, punk, tell us something new." Bill Pope's strident tone cut through The Nightman's thin display of self-assurance.

He looked past the detectives to make sure they were alone. He could see the owner's grizzled head through the front windows, see him stop a couple of players about to come in, motion toward what was taking place; the players took a furtive glance then quickly walked on. "Well, maybe what I got ain't new," The Nightman said quietly. "Like it didn't happen tonight and it could be just— what ya call it?—yeah, just a coincidence, but if it's true it sure could be worth a lot of blackmail loot to some- body who wanted to push it. But it's not my stick 'cause a man could become dead out of it. Like I say, maybe it ain't worth nothin' but you're welcome to it." He looked at Frank Sullivan. "About two, two and a half weeks ago, I'm coming' out of the Calypso Room. I turn the corner and I see big Jim Harris comin' my way. I say 'Hi, Jim,' but, man, this cat looks the other way and just passes by like I'm a total stranger. I never real friendly with him,

95

but it still figure kinda flaky, you know what I mean. Like we know each other enough to say hello. I know he was busted and did a little time recently so I figure he be happy to say hello to me."

"Maybe he's seen some of your hags." Pope's face remained impassive, but the caustic humor could be seen in his eyes.

An indignant look spread across The Nightman's thin face. "I'm just a little guy tryin' to make his bread and I don't like handlin' any bad-lookin' bitches either, man, but sometimes they're the best bangs of all. . . ."

"What's the Harris history?" Sullivan's tone snapped The Nightman back from his digression.

"Oh, he's a small-time cat, just one of the army, that's why you don't know about him. He was workin' for Doc around the same time I was. You know the way Johnson uses his guys, a little strong-armin' or collectin', or even usin' them to protect the transfer, and in that way he can always use a guy anywhere he wants him. But this Harris he don't work for him too long before he get busted on some kind of charge."

The detective felt his interest quicken but he sounded matter-of-fact as he asked, "What makes you so sure this Harris could be one of the guys in on this hit?"

"Hey, I'm not sure of nothin'. I just thought it funny the way he act that time I meet him and then I forgot about it until tonight." The knowing wisp of a Harlem hip smile touched the corners of his mouth. "Yeah, tonight with all the talk and excitement and everybody wishing they were in on it, but they don't know nothin' of how really good that job was. When I heard about it, I'm thinkin' it took Superman to walk in and kill all them guys, includin' them downtown grays, and take all that money, and then top it off by killin' some cops." He shook his head in respect and awe. "Yeah, a great big coal-black Superman. And then it starts to fall in place, real slow at first, like ones and twos, 'cause to make somethin' like this go was knowin' Doc's setup. And this Harris he gotta know it. And then, man, you gotta have the desire and be plenty sharp. You need all that plus bein' a no-carin' mother fucker, and this cat's got the rep of a tiger."

The Nightman's Harlem knowledge had the sound of truth. It was a lead that had to be followed.

"Okay, so where do we find this Jim Harris?" Sullivan kept his voice indifferent.

"I sure enough don't know." The Nightman shrugged phlegmatically, but he wasn't fooled. He knew Sullivan was more than interested. Score one for me, he thought. "Don't even know if it was him," he continued lazily, "but if I was you two I'd sure enough look for him."

"You're a big help," Sullivan snarled, trying to mask his appreciation of what The Nightman had already given them.

"Oh, I may be yet," The Nightman answered a little too quickly. "He used to be kinda sweet on a B girl over at the 7–11 Club. Her name is Ivy something or other, I forget now." He shifted his eyes to the table and gently rolled a ball toward a corner pocket. "The reason I know about this chick is I tried to get her for my stable. She kind of a fine-lookin' bitch and she would've fit in real good. One night he told me to lay off and I did without any questionin', if you know what I mean?" He looked up. "Hey, you two act like I'm puttin' you on."

An impatient car horn sounded through the open door and echoed back across the empty felt tables. A couple of flies had found the light above the table and buzzed in and out of its brightness. The Nightman's face was polished in sweat, the perspiration under his arms began to darken his light suit. He tried to read the faces of the two detectives, but their expressions told him nothing. There was a gnawing doubt that maybe he had lost Sullivan, that he had told him too much and should have left some gaps in the story to make it more believable. He held up his right hand, his left holding the cue stick, in what he hoped was a reassuring gesture that would soften the detective's disbelief. "Man, what I tell ya is the gospel, nothin' held back."

Sullivan had used The Nightman only twice before, both times successfully. Good things come in three, he thought, incongruously associating it with the Holy Trinity. Sullivan's lips barely moved. "Nightman, you never had an honest day in your life." His tone epitomized that of the professional cop.

"I'm levelin', man. Why you wanna fight the truth?" The Nightman's voice was a pitch too high.

The detective turned to his partner. "You think he's telling the truth, Bill?"

Pope caught the inflected mockery. The few months that he had worked with Sullivan had taught him how to judge the moments for subtle play. "Well, we're sure going to find out if he is."

"Yeah, we are that," Sullivan answered, his face still sustaining the impression of dissatisfaction, "and if this punk is giving us the wrong lead, he better start running right now."

Chapter 10

Up past the pyramiding bottles in the center of the circular bar through a haze of smoke, revolving light and loud talk. Women on cushioned stools, their gleaming heads moving with the tempo, and men in tropical suits, standing beside them, reaching for laughs with movements of exaggerated humor. Quick bartenders and hustling waiters, diluted booze and crowded tables. Over it all rotating disks slowly splashed prismatic blues and reds and yellows across black faces.

The drummer rolled a crescendo of introduction, forcing heads to turn up to the small stage above the bar. The piano player leaned into the mike.

"And now, ladies and gentlemen, the Club 7–11 proudly presents Miss Bobbi Watkins."

The room went dark, then a bright spot flared through the smoke, and lights came up from beneath the plexiglass stage, and she came on. The long white gown, cut low at the breasts, clung and pulled across the full body as she mounted the steps to the throbbing, driving beat of "Night Train." Her magnetic sway pulled the dusky room to mesmerized silence as her arms lifted seductively from her body. Her green-shadowed eyes almost closed and the slender, graceful fingers curved over the breast down the salaciously rolling stomach, moved across the round, supple hips and somehow opened the clip that released the shimmering gown down her body in tantalizing, erotic waves. Male faces hung transfixed above their drinks, each isolated in a common thought, as their eyes roamed greedily down the voluptuous body to the gown at her feet. She worked her bunned hair loose and it fell down her back. The full, pointed breasts, their nipples covered by the stickers the law demanded, bounced to the rhythmic drive of the hips. Her head went back, mouth parting to show white teeth, white as snow against the brush of a wet pink tongue that caressed her lips. The musicians played on obliviously; the drummer bending over his drums belted the mounting beat into a sexual frenzy that drove the chocolate-skinned body sensually higher. And no one moved. Waiters hung back against the walls, bartenders didn't serve and the women in the room were as motionless and quiet as the men. Her buttocks tightened, then went slack and tightened again, her belly rising and falling and quickening still further. The spotlight gave way to the rotating disks, but this time the spinning gels revolved to the pulsing tempo of her movements. And her body was sheeted in a kaleidoscope of blues and reds and yellows. Beads of sweat popped out across her body, gathered between her heavy breasts, rolled down across the belly catching the navel, then down once again and into the moist G-string between her legs. She ground to a scorch of climax, stopped suddenly, her arms and legs tautening in a culminating stretch of imagined copulation, and she held the G-string in her hand. The lights switched off, cutting the room to blackness. There was a moment of silence, then through the darkness the spontaneous applause reached stimulatingly for her. The lights flashed on again; she was gone. She had disappeared into the stifling cubicle of a dressing room beneath the bar.

The talk and laughter picked up as before and a couple got up to leave. Waiters who had held back during the act now floated between tables, pushing the watered-down and overpriced drinks.

"Hey, Frank, how ya doin', man?" said the mustached manager, standing just inside the glass doors. Here comes trouble, he thought, forcing a smile across his dark face as he watched Frank Sullivan push into the club. "Long time no see," he added, and hoped the smile looked convincing.

Bill Pope came up beside his partner and they both squinted in the haze, letting their eyes become accustomed to the dimness and smoke.

"How's it going, Eddie?" Sullivan asked, not looking at the tuxedo-draped manager, for he was too busy, out of pure habit, trying to make out the faces along the bar and tables.

"What you boys checkin' on, business or pleasure?"

"What do you think?" Sullivan said tonelessly, and added to the discomfort behind Eddie Whitfield's smile. A few heads had turned from their drinks to peer through the bad lights at the men by the door.

"Well, I think I'm going ta have an empty place if you two keep standing here counting the house." The manager slapped him a little too affably on the back. "Come on, let me buy you two a drink."

"This is a business call, Eddie."

There was a noticeable hesitation, the smile disappeared, and the manager's eyes went to Pope and back to Sullivan. The reflected light over the entrance glared much brighter in Eddie's mind, spotlighting him and the law for all to see. "So my business is pleasure. Come on, I'll have one with you," and he started toward the tables.

"You got a girl name of Ivy working in here?" Sullivan's question turned Eddie around, his eyes showing concern.

"Maybe," he said guardedly. "Why, what'd she do?"

"You can relax, Eddie, this is no collar. We just want to talk to her." But worry was still visible on the manager's face. "Just talk, you understand," Sullivan said, trying to reassure him that there would be no arrest scene, no duplication of the violence he had once visited upon one of Eddie's felonious patrons who wouldn't come quietly: Sullivan had promptly put bullets into the man's leg and hip.

100

"Yeah, yeah, I understand, Frank," Eddie said slowly, "but she ain't here. She works here, all right, and her last name is Roberts, but she's not here yet. She's due in a little while, so why don't you two take that drink. When she comes in I send her over, okay?"

They nodded agreement but Eddie Whitfield didn't move. "Frank, you do me a favor, okay? Talk to her like quietly. I got a good house goin' tonight and if you start flashin' your badge . . . You too, huh?" He took a quick look to include Pope so that it wouldn't seem like such a direct plea to the white detective. "A gun would scare the hell outa half o' the crowd and I wouldn't see them around for a while. You know what I mean, man? You know the trade I get."

Sullivan looked at him and smiled. "Sure, Eddie, nice and quiet."

The manager turned and was leading them past the bar to one of the rear tables in the darkest corner of the club. "This is good, Eddie," Sullivan said, stopping at the bar. "I don't want to take your four-dollar cover charge away from a table, and besides, we can see your customers better from here."

Space opened to them as patrons pushed subtly against each other like people in church pews making room for latecomers. But it was not the attitude of share a space, for some knew who he was and the rest could smell cop. They shied away from the white odor of force, though to most of the people at that end of the circular bar, Bill Pope didn't count, maybe because he was a black man and didn't have the look of law. Tall, studious, dressed in conservative clothes, he might have been a social worker or maybe a reporter covering the ghetto scene for one of the white papers. But the bartender remembered Sullivan only too well, and without asking what they wanted went for the uncut stuff and set a fresh bottle of J&B before them. A heavy-set man in a sharkskin suit, laughing loudly as he admired the crossed legs of a tawny bar girl looked up and the laughter caught and died in his throat as he recognized the white detective staring at him. He finished his drink and quietly walked away from the bar. More heads turned toward

101

the detectives and their space at the bar expanded; they were fast becoming isolated.

"You know, Frank"—there was a waggish grin on Pope's face—"if we were really conscientious cops we'd bust everybody in here who looks suspicious."

The joke was based in reality, for though the 7–11 Club was overpriced enough to appeal to some of the newly arrived Negro middle class, its patrons were mainly a crowd of well-heeled dope dealers and numbers men, bookies and guys who'd broken through and had some illicit bag going for themselves, as well as the would-bes and hangers-on who still hoped to make it illegitimately.

"If we did," Sullivan answered, "we'd be leaving Eddie here all by himself."

"Hey." Eddie smiled, not too assuredly. "You cats pull something like that and them white boys who put up the money and own me and this club would have a new front goin' for them tomorrow. And besides, you wouldn't do it. They're holding my mother for collateral. You close me and she never gonna get free from cleanin' their houses."

The three of them laughed, but Pope felt self-conscious. His easy response to such jokes seemed to be fragmenting principles built on the foundation of an eleven-year-old boy slowly awakening to find he lived in a white world . . . Bill Pope, nurtured by Northern apartheid and bias, and driven by anger and the hardships his family endured to ensure that the first male in their family tree was able to jump down clutching a college diploma. Now he sipped his drink, half listening to Sullivan and Eddie Whitefield talk, half hearing the music and laughter in the background and remembering that it was before the cause and black militants and civil rights marchers, before the sit-ins and riots and death in the streets. When he lived in a far younger world, where they had gathered surreptitiously in threes and fours away from their white so-called fellow students. He could still see one particular black, standing like a bantam rooster, his hand strangling a beer can, as he held forth as their leader in his high-pitched vitriolic voice. "I'll tell you, Billy, I'll tell you. The ones I respect are the Northern crackers that can't stand our black asses. I really do, Billy, and I'm gonna tell you why. Because there's at least no bullshit in how they feel. They've drawn the line and try their best we don't cross it. Oh, yeah, I can live with that because I don't have to see them every day to know the score, because I know they're always tryin' to pitch shutouts."

He remembered the way his friend used to rise up on his toes, his brown eyes glowing in righteous indignation. "Now I'm gonna tell ya who bugs me more than the crackers. And, man, once you get to know them, baby, you really know them. You know they're on the other side of a two-headed coin. It's them so-called liberal bastards that I can't stomach. They pick up our slang and act like white niggers. It's a kick for them, man, when they can say to their white middle-class elders, hoping for shock, 'Why, some of my best friends are Negroes.' These freckled Irish cats come on and tell ya about their history in this country and how tough it was for their ancestors to make it. Or the Italian about his grandfather with the pick and shovel. And the bagel babies always comin' around hung up on guilt and cock and the only good thing about them, they like to fuck. But, Billy, they all turn, because when they start to climb that white-world ladder and move to the suburbs, their liberalism turns off like the hose on their front lawns. And who have we got left, huh? Well, I'll tell ya: it's the kooks, the wild-eyed whites, schizos and paranoiacs, the sickies lookin for a cause, any cause. Now it's liberalism and we're their baby. In the thirties and forties, they were the Marxists talkin' about spreading Mother Russia's legs around the world; now it's sing along with the black man. Who needs them, man, and who needs the politician who promises anything for a vote? What the Negro needs is some sleek black cat who could organize like a Walter Reuther or a George Meany and put us more than twenty million people together into a massive economic and political voting block. Then, baby, oh, then you would see things change."

Well, the black power advocates who had come along just as his school buddy, Bobby Davis, had hoped knocked the majority of white liberals right out of the civil rights movement. And Bill Pope wondered if that was real wise. So far Davis himself, the man who was going to lead

103

them out of the black wilderness, had failed them. He had taken a federal job for security and got strung out on his own guilt, living in neither a black nor a white world but on a precipice of gray that borrowed from both. And Billy Pope had copped out, too. His ambitions and drives were too strong for him to end up walking a beat as a civil servant. He had majored in humanities and had young idealistic hopes wrapped in the mist of an uncertain future. In a wildly changing world he knew he wasn't going to move mountains, for he had no fanatic's drum beating inside him. But he felt he could contribute by working in a black environment among his own people, who needed their own to surmount its walls of ignorance and poverty, to fight for better education and housing jobs, to put its men back as the heads of families and to pull its women out of whitey's dirty kitchens.

But somehow Billy had lost his way and had found himself sitting with five hundred other men taking the police examination. For kicks, he told himself; I'm curious how I will make out, but he had studied the manual diligently before taking the test and had scored well. And had then looked for a rationalization. A man can maybe do more for his own being a— Who am I bullshitting? Full salary in three years, time and a half for overtime, use the education to advance and out in twenty on half pay. Security—what do they say?—cradle to grave. But, baby, a voice would echo out of his past, there's no real security for a black man because you can't lose the color of your skin. Then equality, goddammit, that's what I'm looking for, my own personal equality, the same kind of security the white man seeks in civil service. I just want what's due me, that's all.

But he had not found it. In its place he had discovered something in the job, something he had not realized had existed in him until his promotion from uniform and disarming a holdup man on a crowded street in Bedford Stuyvesant, and his subsequent assignment to Harlem. He found an expanding ego; now he walked among his own but with a heady authority, feeling the gun on his hip and the badge of entrance in his pocket, and experiencing the ambivalent respect and fear this black community had to offer. The equality he had been searching for had paradoxically transformed itself into the guise of superiority. He was sickeningly aware of this self-importance, having seen and hated it in other Negro cops. He wanted to excoriate it, to find where it began and burn it out, this malignant tumor of arrogance. . . .

The trio was taking a break and in the room conversation levels dropped without music to compete against. The manager of the 7–11 Club tilted the bottle of Scotch for a second time, filling the shot glass above the false white circle. He leaned toward Sullivan and started a bawdy joke, openly playing for a laugh to soothe the silence of this unpredictable white man.

Pope listened to the joke, trying to gauge the reaction on Sullivan's face to see how far his partner had come back from his personal loss. Sullivan's eyes in the flickering light were patches of faded blue in an overcast, melancholy sky. Only his mouth reacted, twisting in a brief smile, not in response to the dirty punch-line but to let Eddie the manager relax. Pope guessed that Frank had not come very far from his sorrow, and he wondered if it was possible ever to recover completely from such a tragedy, such deep remorse. But he knew his partner had control now; at least the wild sickness of his grief had been dissipated. Bill Pope was pleased about that. A few months ago he wouldn't have cared if Frank Sullivan lived or died. At that time Pope had cataloged him in his mental file under "racist," just as he separated and docketed blacks according to his own categories. He knew the fallacy of such an index, that there was more to people than surface judgments could yield, but he also knew that external images and performances reflected basic truths. Yet this elusive white man, by some action, a casual remark or a psychological slip, would break out of the tidy stereotype, would have to be tested against truth, to be placed somewhere else in the Negro detective's vault of people. At times he was sure he had closed the lid on him, for wasn't he the classic cop too quick with his hands, always ready to beat the black man for information? Then there was the arrogance of the man, cutting a wide swath of reputation through Harlem that would have done justice to a Southern deputy patrolling the black shanties of a cracker town. Now I got you, Sulli-

van, you fucking fascist, you Northern honkie cracker.
. . . But Pope's indictments would be jarred at the sight
of a tough black youth sticking his hand out, shaking
Frank Sullivan's hand, telling the white detective that the
job he had set up for him was working out fine, just fine.
Pope would case the kid's smile for a put-on and would
find only warmth, for the chance he'd been given when
he had no more hope.

Sullivan had known how Pope felt about him and he
purposely kept the barrier up, sustaining it with a deliberate aloofness that strained their relationship to just
barely above a working association. And Pope waited for
the precinct commander to tell him he had been transferred back to uniform, back to a beat in the black sec-
tion of Brooklyn. He knew the standard words that were
going to be used against him: "surly," "uncooperative,"
"psychological block." But the ax never fell. Only the
gulf between them was widened still further by the Negro
cops in the precinct, bad-mouthing among themselves
about their fellow white cops unnecessarily throwing their
authority around and singling out Sullivan as a prime
example. "You watch yourself," he was told by a young
Negro detective who had been assigned to the precinct
shortly before he was. "That man you're teamed with, he
looks for trouble like he don't care. He steps on a lot
of toes and I hear he's been bounced out of this precinct
once already. So you watch yourself with him, you hear?"

But what had finally brought their sour partnership to
an ugly head was Sullivan's seeking out a particular
pusher, a two-time loser who bragged around that he
wouldn't be busted a third time without some cop dying
for the effort. The two detectives were on a side street
just off Lenox Avenue when Sullivan spotted him dealing
his bags defiantly out in the open. The pusher ran into a
tenement when he saw them and was almost out a rear
door when Sullivan cornered him. The frightened Negro's
hand went to his pocket and the detective hit him before
the gun could be pulled. He fell back against the door and
Sullivan's hands tightened around his neck in blind, uncontrollable fury. "He's out, he's out! What's the matter
with you?" Pope cried. "Let him fall!" He had to pry the
fingers away from the unconscious man's throat. Then

Sullivan looked for the gun that would rationalize the rage, but he found none. The pusher had only been going for a cover of money, to try a payoff in his panic.

They had finished their tour together in silence. As they came down the precinct steps Sullivan watched his Negro partner walk abruptly, disgustedly away. "Hey," he called after him, "how about a drink?" Incredulously Pope turned and stared. "I want to talk," the white man added, his face offering an open token of friendship that made Bill Pope curious. Their drink turned into a five-hour marathon of talk and whiskey, in the beginning mostly Sullivan's, as if his dammed-up emotions were suddenly released in a flood of words. Pope could never again file this man away under "racist," "prejudice," "hate." He told him, as best he could, of the angers that consumed him and drove him to flare out, at times blindly, against the excesses that were an affront to his basically puritanical nature, of impulsive acts that he recalled later in shame, then tried unsuccessfully to bury. Of his stevedore father who drank and the discontent and gloom of his mother, which helped put her in an early grave. A high school diploma and military service at eighteen and an anonymous civilian at twenty. Jobs for a few years that went nowhere, then the cops, and finally it all seemed to smooth out. He had a happy marriage and a family to look forward to, though it took three miscarriages and eight years before their first was born. It was too hard a pregnancy. The doctor told him there should be no more or she might die.

It had been an extraordinary monologue, this self-revelation in the booth of a Spanish Harlem bar, Sullivan exposing his trepidations and small victories and the uncertainties that were common to all men. Above all there was the pride, the uncontrollable consuming pride, which he used, at times brutally, to prove he was a man trying his best. It had gained him recognition—first grade detective. But he knew he would go no higher. Though still in his thirties, he was an anachronism; the department of the future would shy away from men like him because he barely accepted the changes that had already begun. He talked of throwing in the retirement papers when he did the twenty and getting out, to where he didn't know. Pope wondered if this violent man could ever retire. He realized Sullivan was an unconscious seeker of trouble and excitement, and would be out of step in a world of middle-class calm. He was a boat rocker, born a hundred years too late, a marshal in a frontier town who should have been locking up drunken cowboys or shooting red men instead of punching contemporary black ones. The ideological chasm rooted in the color of their skin and their backgrounds dictated their approach to life and the job. But the honesty that barriers, and Pope's partnership with Frank Sullivan took on new dimensions thereafter.

Their tours in the seamy jungle of whores and pimps, pushers and wasted junkies, petty assaults and hysterical murders passed quickly and solidified them into a team. Slowly Bill Pope began to see the job through his partner's eyes as somewhat of a dedication. He wouldn't tell anyone that for fear of their laughing in his face, but he was taught more about police work in that brief span of time than an entire course at the Academy could have taught him.

And then Sullivan's tragedy. Pope went to Queens, to Schaeffer's Funeral Parlor. He said a prayer over the two caskets lying pathetically side by side. Frank stood lost in the corner of the crowd of mourners, unable to talk or even look up, just barely erect when the priest came in to chant the rosary for the deceased. He took just enough time off to bury his dead, and came quickly back to work, hoping to dull the cutting edge of his grief by routine, to still the accusing voice that tore at him inside. But his anguish and guilt were too consuming and fought for release. Exploding in a rash of violence, he checked off what he felt were the bad niggers and went after them a self-styled avenger who ran roughshod over everyone. Complaints came across the captain's desk and the gun started to come out with a frequency that alarmed Pope for his own safety and Frank's. The climax erupted in the ugly needless shooting at the 7–11 Club. The stink would have dumped the average cop into a suspension, or maybe out of a job. But Captain Paul Matthews understood and shielded him, quashing the grumbles with the higher-ups and easing him into a protective thirty-day sick leave. "Lose it in a bottle, take a walk in the woods, or hit your head against a wall, but don't come back with it, Frank. I won't be able to save you again. . . ."

As Eddie the manager talked, Frank's affable nods and conversation lacked that terrifying tension. Yes, he had control now, Pope thought. His partner was all right, he was going to make it back from his sorrow. The manager, too, realized it was a different Sullivan who had last visited his place, and he dropped the guarded small talk.

"This wantin' to talk to one o' my girls, it have anything to do with what happened earlier tonight? You know, about the killin's and Doc Johnson gettin' robbed?" The detectives looked at each other, then at him. He knew he had said the wrong thing. His hands went out in physical apology. "Hey, man, I'm not pryin', it's just that it's on everybody's lips about some cat scorin' big against Papa Bear."

The buzz of conversation around the bar and tables, punctuated by laughter, blended with the rhythm and blues flowing from the multicolored jukebox, which covered the entertainment break. The manager's eyes circled around the room, then rested on the full shot glass before him. He lowered his voice. "Some o' Doc's men were in to check the house; they gave it a pretty good lookover. They said Doc's layin' out money for information, he's tryin' to buy some leads." He felt uncomfortable under their silent stares and decided it was wise to drop the subject. He lifted his glass. "Well, anyway, here's luck to ya."

"What else do you know, Eddie?" Sullivan's tone stopped the Negro's hand halfway to his mouth.

"Not a thing," he said, and shook his head. "But I wouldn't've laid big odds nobody coulda ran up a score like that." The glass continued upward and he drank.

"I guess that was why it worked," Pope said, taking Eddie off the hook. "They didn't think anyone would ever try."

"Man." The manager looked at Pope. He felt he could express himself better to a fellow black. "The guys that pulled it have to have balls made of cast iron. You know what I mean. Like that money had to be covered like Fort Knox. You got to give them credit." For a moment his admiration made him forget who he was talking to. "Well, yeah, you know it's too bad them cats cut down the cops. If they coulda made it without hurtin' anybody . . . like who were they takin' the money from but a guy who can afford to lose it?" They were both staring at him coldly and he vainly tried to dig himself out of the hole. "The guys upstairs, they shouldn't've been killed, either. It's only money and no life's worth that, right?" Eddie stumbled, trying to smooth it over. His head twisted to the door. "Hey, fresh money." His tone brightened as he motioned toward the entrance at a party of four just coming in.

The two men at the door, draped in up-to-the-moment fashion, looked like shiny copper pennies. Sullivan recognized them as numbers runners putting on a front. Their bewigged sleek women were duplicates of the other girls in the room. "You're goin' to have to excuse me, boys; business is exceptionally good tonight." He didn't bother to finish his drink. "When that gal comes in I'll send her over." He turned, happy to leave.

"Remind me, Bill, will you?" Sullivan asked seriously, but his eyes were soft with amusement. "Next time I'm drunk take me in here because I'd like to shoot this place up just for pleasure and I'd start off by puttin' a bullet up our friend Eddie's ass."

Pope's mouth curled into a grin and he shook his head slowly. "The hell I will. The next time you go drinking and want some action you're going to do the scene yourself, because my old, gray-haired Southern mother told me to stay away from drinking white men with guns."

Sullivan snorted an easy laugh. "Well, then, at least help me drink some of Eddie's private stock." He tilted the bottle of J&B and filled their shot glasses.

Above them the musicians came back on the bandstand, the slowly turning colored disks reflecting off the dark glasses. The piano player hunched across the keys, leaned into the mike and purred Ellington's "Sophisticated Lady" with a pleasant huskiness. Sullivan looked at his watch, then glanced at the entrance. "If this bitch don't show in another fifteen minutes, I think we're going out to look for her."

"You think The Nightman was putting us straight, or just making up a convenient story?" Pope asked.

"I don't know." Frank shrugged. "But it's the only story we got so far, so we might as well stay with it."

Pope's fingers worked a cigarette loose from the pack he had thrown on the bar. "Well, one thing: we're a damn sight better off sitting here drinking free booze than running around pulling in punks and going through the question bit with them back at the station house."

"That's for sure," Sullivan said. "The atmosphere's a lot better here than back in that squad room." His head motioned to the music. "But I wish that drummer would play a touch softer."

The match illuminated Pope's high-cheekboned face. He exhaled and the smoke rolled up through the revolving spots covering the bandstand. "I guess we should be thankful for knowing blacks pulled this off." The music blared over Pope's voice, making Sullivan incline his head toward him. "If whites ever made the hit, the department could have ended with an unsolvable on their hands."

"What makes you think it still couldn't end up that way?"

"No." Pope shook his head. "Black men with the kind of money they're holding eventually have to stand out like sore thumbs. Oh, they can be swallowed up for a while; any good-size city like Washington or Philadelphia or even Newark with their big Negro populations can help lose them just by sheer numbers. But they can't stay submerged too long."

Sullivan thought Pope's judgment was sound, for in most instances blacks wouldn't have the patience to sit back for any great length of time, and would tend to spend the money a lot more quickly than whites but he felt his partner might be underestimating the perpetrators. "You could be right, Bill," he said thoughtfully, "but give the devil his due. I think they're too sharp to blow this in an insane getaway against a thirteen-state alarm. Even a short run to Newark or Jersey City doesn't figure, because what you said about losing themselves in a crowded ghetto is the key and Harlem is made to order for them. Half a million people crowded into six square

111

miles—this has to be their best bet, at least for a while." He wanted to add, So go ahead and find them, but it would have been a lame joke on him as well as Pope and every man on the job. Instead he continued to dissect his young partner's theories. "And about them bringing suspicion to themselves with a quick itch to spend, I think we can forget it because I agree with Matthews: they didn't plan on killing any cops and that has to make them a lot more cautious in how they behave from here on in."

The fact of Sullivan's experience made Bill Pope reconsider. "Sort of like lost in an anonymity of blackness," he said, then thought of the analogy, Like niggers in a coal pile, but he didn't say it. "Maybe this thing will start to crack from within," Pope added. "They took a lot of money; what was the rough estimation, four hundred thousand? How long do you think they can hold that kind of fortune without something giving?"

"I think that's hoping for a lot," Sullivan replied. "They're not about to fight among themselves. The way they went after the money indicates they were willing to sacrifice themselves for it. And we've got to presume these hard-nosed bastards didn't stop thinking now that they've succeeded, and each day they hole up makes the odds a little bit better for them." He seemed to sigh. "So we better enjoy Whitfield's liquor while we can, because unfortunately I think this is going to take a lot of leg work and maybe an equal amount of luck to crack."

"That kind of talk makes The Nightman's story hold up. It sounds like you bought it."

Sullivan shrugged. They became silent, watching the bartender refill their glasses.

Under the noise and music, a short, thick-set muscular man had shuffled up and now stood almost on top of them. He pushed his hand into Sullivan's back. "Hey, man," he said in a grating voice. The small eyes scowled out from under scarred, fissured brows with the dullness of two unpolished stones.

"Hello, Clubby," Sullivan said amicably. "Where have you been keeping yourself?"

"Who dis guy?" the squat man asked belligerently, his finger pointing suspiciously at Bill Pope.

"This is my new partner," the detective answered soberly. "Say, I haven't seen you around in months, Clubby. How've you been doing?"

The man pushed his face in close; the chipped teeth in front were turning bad. "Is he a good guy, Frank, this new partner of yours? Can we talk in front o' him?"

"Sure, sure we can." Sullivan glanced at Pope but there was no wink; his face stayed serious. "You can say anything you want."

The broken face relaxed. "You wanna paper, Frank?" He whipped out a night edition of the *Daily News* from the bulky bundle he carried under his arm.

"No, thanks, Clubby."

"Yeah." He spread his legs and shifted his hip into the papers. "Yeah, they don't spend no mother-fuckin' money on wages down there, baby. I dropped a few of their lousy dishes and dat swank hotel he don't fire me because he remembers who I was, but I end up polishin' all them goddamn sheeny shoes. I shine every fuckin' shoe in that goddamn hotel for one lousy year, man, until I say, No more, no more. Go home, Clubby, I tell myself, to where you belong." He paused, tongue running over his lumpy lips. "You sure you don' wanna paper?" and he pushed one at him. "Here, here, man. I give you a freebie."

"No, Clubby, I don't—"

"When you goin' ta lock my manager up, huh? Last time I see you you say you're goin' downtown and lock him up."

"He hasn't handled you for a long time."

"I know, man, I know." His free hand moved a couple of times in front of his face. The eyes rolled back in his head as if he was trying to clear his thoughts. "That white rapin' bastard. I told ya—didn't I tell ya?—about how he done give me plenty wrong counts when that long green was rollin' in. He still got my money. He get rich on my dough. You the law, you lock him up."

"I got a couple of days off next week. You want me to lock him up next week, Clubby?"

"Yeah, next week, man." His head bounced affirmatively. "You know where he hang out, man. Downtown. West Forty-ninth Street, with the rest of the fight crowd."

113

Then he stopped, his eyes blinking in the cavernous sockets made hollow by built-up scar tissue. "But maybe he ain't around there no more. They say there ain't no more real fighters, no more action. You know they tear Stillman's Gym down and there's no more Garden down there. No more Stillman's; like everything's dead, you know what I mean, man?" He stood there broodingly for a couple of long seconds, his eyes going to the floor. Then his head popped up. "But he have a business, yeah, somewhere down there, I think, he have a business. Well, it don't matter, you just hold him for me, Frank. I'm goin' ta get that money that's due me." He pressed his head in close. "You sure you don't want a paper?"

Sullivan's eyes went to the money on the bar and he remembered he was drinking for nothing. His hand dipped into his pocket and came up with a couple of singles; he stuffed them into the ex-fighter's sweat-stained shirt pocket.

"Hey, man, I make out okay. I don't need no handout."

"Who said you did? It's just a loan."

"Well, okay then, okay. Just a loan." He seemed about to say something more, but he lowered his head, turned and started to shuffle away. Then he stopped and looked back. "You get me in the morning', you hear? We'll go downtown together and grab—" Someone called for a paper.

The detectives watched him move down the length of the bar, instinctively slouching forward in the hunched-over style of his past. Somebody recognized him and patted his back as he passed and the smattering of applause for the trio suddenly became explosive greetings from tiered thousands. A match flaring in the shadows of the tables was the hundreds of continually lighting cigarettes fireflying a darkened stadium. He stood down at the other end of the room, a subdued light above his head making him barely visible through the crowd, and the light seemed to intensify into many lights that beat down on his jet sleekness while his manager and seconds hovered about him and people screamed his name. And he stood down at the other end of the bar selling his eight-cent paper for ten cents. "Ten years ago," Frank Sullivan said reflectively, "he was beautiful."

It was the tight green dress that Bill Pope saw first. She was on the thin side, but the flashy dress swelled and curved in the proper places. She had turned her head, listening intently to Eddie, then, following his quick motion, picked Sullivan out through the dim lights. The manager walked away from her and she stood uncertainly for a moment. "We don't have to wait any longer," said Pope. "Here she comes now, Frank."

Sullivan turned and watched her approach. There was an outward appearance of calm, but as she came closer he could see concern in the brown eyes. Her nose was maybe a little too wide for the slender face, but her jawline had a delicate firmness that accentuated the full, almost sensuous lips. The straightened hair wasn't too long and was pulled back from her face. In the shifting lights of the room, with her sleek hair and her tawny complexion, she looked Oriental.

"I hear you boys want to talk to me," she said to Sullivan. Her voice was unruffled.

"If your name is Ivy Roberts," Frank said quietly, "we want to talk to you."

A forced smile touched her lips. "That's what they call me."

A few people had turned from their conversations along the bar and were staring curiously at the three of them. Sullivan reached out and pulled an empty stool between Pope and himself and motioned for the girl to sit down. She seemed thankful for the partial obscurity, which made her feel less conspicuous.

The detectives watched her open her bag and dig down for cigarettes. Neither man offered her a light; they watched her fumble for matches and light up. She looked at them, all traces of a smile gone. "You'll have to excuse me; it isn't every night I jeopardize my job by talkin' to cops. I think I'm goin' to have to do a lot of explainin' to Eddie when you boys leave. He don't like the help being questioned, especially in front of the customers. Bad for business, you know." She tried to break the constricting mood by an effort at levity. "He thinks he's running the Copacabana." It didn't work. They stayed coolly expressionless and she looked at the white detective. She hadn't been there the night he had

115

walked into the club and put a couple of bullets into a man and pegged shots about the room, but she knew all about him. Rumors floated about that the shooting was tied to some kind of payoff, and he had coldly tried to kill the man before he could talk and expose him.

"If you're clean, baby, in whatever he's gonna question you about," Eddie had said to her, "you get that bastard out o' here fast; I don't want him around here. But if he's got you for somethin', you go quiet, and don't try askin' for no help from somebody at this bar. You understand what I'm sayin?"

She studied the inflexible face; his guarded eyes offered no key to his feelings. Dropping her gaze, she took a long drag on the cigarette. "Okay, what can I do for you, mister?"

"We want to talk to you about your boyfriend, Jim Harris." The detective emphasized "boyfriend."

Her brow furrowed into a question and she looked up. "My boyfriend? Mister, you got the wrong girl."

"I'll ask you again, only this time we want a straight answer." Sullivan didn't raise his voice.

"Now wait a minute, fellas, please." Her hands inched above the bar, palms held out loosely in a stop signal. "Let's slow it down, huh? You're goin' a little too fast for me because, if I remember correctly, that boy is doin' time and if he broke out of jail he sure enough didn't come running to little ol' Ivy to hide him, I can guarantee you that."

Sullivan and Pope looked at each other. "How do you know he was serving time?" Bill Pope said it as if it were a casual question, but it came at Ivy like a loaded hose.

She looked at him really for the first time and was surprised to see how young he was.

"Mister, you don't work in a place like this without knowin' what's goin' on. Every racket man, big and small, makes the scene here one time or another and they talk shop. Like who's strung out and which is the latest cat to be busted. You know, things like that. And that's how I hear about Jim Harris."

From their inquisitive stares she knew they were far from satisfied with her answer. She would have liked to

116

leave it like that, for it touched a period in her life she felt was no one's business but her own, but they were The Men, and she knew she had better answer their questioning silence.

She took another long drag on the cigarette as though gathering her thoughts. The exhaled smoke rose slowly above her head. "Look, I won't deny Jim Harris took me out a few times. Any one of the girls around here will tell you that. But that was about a year and a half ago, then we stopped seein' each other. It was no fight or anything like that; he just stopped comin' around the club and that was the end of it. Just passin' time; a few laughs, you know, nothin' serious. It was a little while after that I hear he got messed up with the law and got sent away." She tilted her head toward Pope and shrugged. "And that was the end of Jimmy Harris as far as my life was concerned, until you two mentioned his name now. It was like a long time ago."

"We hear he's back on the street and was seen about a month ago, and this was told to us by the same person who said you were his girl." Pope spoke slowly, watching her eyes for a response, but there was only a firmness that helped attest to her denial.

"Well, I can't help what you hear, but if somebody says they seen him with me in the last month or so or any time since we stopped datin', they're puttin' you on. Why they mention my name with his now I sure enough don't know. But it's playin' a lousy trick on me, I can tell you that."

Pope looked at Sullivan. Pope felt she was telling the truth but he avoided saying anything, lest he might have misread something in her words or mannerisms that Frank's greater experience could detect and now would use against her. Ivy Roberts became awkwardly aware of the white detective's steady gaze. She wanted to turn to him, stare him down, shout her fear and embarrassment and frustration out for everyone to hear: You got nothin' on me, cop; leave me alone, just leave me be! But she could combat it only by riveting her gaze on the trio softly carrying the beat of the music through the room.

"You're sticking with that story, honey?" Sullivan's flat voice forced her to turn around.

"If you take me in," she drawled slowly, measuring her words, "I can only repeat to you what I already told you: he was just a guy I dated a few times and then it was over. And I have nothin' to add to it because what I said is the truth and I think you two know it."

The music and talk and sound of laughter ceased, shut out of her mind by Sullivan's intense skepticism. "Are you goin' to take me in?" she asked in a voice that might have been a child's.

He shook his head. "No, no, I'm not," he said, and turned and motioned to the bartender with his thumb and forefinger, indicating that a shot glass be put in front of the girl.

She didn't show the relief she felt. She had never been locked up before but she knew girls who had been and the booking, fingerprinting and legal arraignment seemed a humiliating and revolting thing to go through. She waited until the bartender moved away from them, then had to say something to break the silence. "What's Harris done?" she asked, and caught the look that passed between the detectives. "Hey, if I'm out of bounds just forget I asked. It's just that I got to be curious, seein' that I'm bein' questioned about him. And besides, I just don't feel like makin' up no story for Eddie, 'cause I'm gonna get that question myself after you guys leave and I'm goin' to have to give him some kind of a straight answer."

"Maybe nothing," Pope said, "or maybe he was in on a robbery tonight that involved a lot of money and a number of people being killed. This guy Harris could be clean, but until we find out, he's a suspect."

Her hand picked up the drink. Some of it spilled over the top and ran down her fingers. "There, you see." Her lips went into a quick smile. "That's gotta prove you boys shook me up. Well, I sure earned this." She nodded and drank it down.

"What kind of guy is this Harris?" Sullivan asked casually as he poured out another drink for her.

"Oh, the usual type that comes in here. Flashy dresser, swinger with more loot than the average uptown cat."

118

She paused, her head imperceptibly going to the crowd of well-dressed blacks spaced around the bar. A couple of stools away, a diamond pinky ring caught the spray of changing light, gleaming while it rode up with the other fingers wrapped around a tall glass of gin and tonic. "But I wanna tell you," she said coldly, "they buy you a drink and even though they know you're shillin' for the house they think they own you. After a couple o' drinks they're grabbin' your thigh and tellin' ya what great big successful men they are. And the ones that ain't sure they goin' ta have the money to keep a room over their head by the end of the week, they start talkin' about the day they goin' ta break through and they're gonna remember me when they get on top." She snorted, a jaded sarcastic laugh.

Sullivan contemplated his drink to cover the surprise of her unexpected frankness. It was a putdown he rarely heard, as if she forgot for the moment they were the law and that she spoke in front of a white man. But he was cognizant of her anger and embarrassment and the degradation of being questioned, of what she felt to be an indictment of the hustle she worked, and she seemed to be reaching for a public assertion of self-respect that under normal conditions she would have kept to herself.

"What about Harris?" Bill Pope asked. "Was he like that, too, a would-be big man who thought he knew all the answers?"

"No," she said softly, her fingers making abstract designs in the spilled liquor. "No, he seemed a little different; I guess that was one of the reasons I went out with him. Oh, he talked about doin' big-time things, you know, like everybody else. But it was kind of a cool approach, like he really was goin' to make it, maybe in the straight world." She looked at Pope and shrugged. "Oh, I knew he was somewhere in the rackets. It seems like half the guys uptown got something illegal goin' for themselves, and I guess if they didn't they wouldn't eat. You accept it. It's a way of life. I guess you know what I mean." The changing light coming off the bandstand caught her eyes, reflecting her somber tone. "Yeah, maybe that's the real reason I dated him; maybe I believed he could do what he said and I could ride out with him into a world he talked about. But nothin's lastin' with me. When we stopped datin' it was him that ended it, not me. His plans sure didn't include me, so the hell with him."

Frank Sullivan listened quietly. Given the nature of his calling, people generally went to the other extreme. But now he felt that he had caught her in one of the rare moments of self-revelation that people permit themselves. Like a stranger sitting beside you on a bus, unexpectedly telling you intimate details of his life and his problems, talking to you as if you were a cherished old friend, then, a few stops farther along, getting off and disappearing into a crowd, never to be seen again. In this loquacious mood she warranted one more question. "Do you think this Harris is smart enough to plan a big robbery and have the guts to pull it off?" he asked.

She turned to him. "Oh, he's sharp enough to do a lot of things, but if you're askin' if he's capable of killin' somebody to get what he wanted"—she stopped as though running the question around in her mind—"I don't know, I really don't know. That's a kind of loaded question I just ain't able to answer. I'm not runnin' away from an answer, mister; it's just that I wasn't around him that much to make a guess on somethin' as deep as that."

The drummer rolled a sudden beat of attention, the rotating gels gave way to a white spot coming out of a darkened corner, and the piano player leaned into the mike. "Ladies and gentlemen, the Club 7–11 proudly presents, direct from her successful Baltimore engagement . . ."

Ivy's voice could barely be heard above the amplified introduction and the detectives bent their heads down to her. "Maybe I can help you boys out," she said. "He has a sister who plays piano for the church of Preacher Gregory. It's the Tabernacle of Moses over on Lenox." She stopped, her soft brown eyes apologetic. "I know it ain't much, but it's all I can offer." She took the shot glass from the bar, dipping it toward them in a brief toast—"I wish you boys rich"—then continued it on up to her lips.

Chapter 11

"Rufus," the high-pitched voice yelled, the squat body leaning over the bar. "Hey, you, Rufus. Goddammit, man, hear me." Sweat rolled down the black face. "What's that mother, he deaf or somethin'?" he asked the four people crowded around him. He called again, and this time his voice carried and caught the bartender's attention. "Hey, man, come on." His hand waved above the empty glasses. "Hit us again, will ya?" Henry Jackson turned back to his party. His protruding eyes were glazed by liquor, while his head moved to the recorded beat of the jukebox as it banged out along the length of the whiskey-smelling room. Here the men pressed against the bar shunned Edwardian jackets and Italian silks in favor of the open-neck sports shirt of the laborer. The women, some standing, some sitting on the worn wooden stools, wore the bargain-basement specials of Madame K's on the Square; their hair was unstraightened, not because of a defiant pride in their Afro heritage, but mainly because of the scarcity of money. The music bounced off a wall that needed a paint job, off the back of the bar, vibrating and weaving between the rows of glasses and the bottled lineup of Schenley and Carstairs and Dixie Belle gin. The voice on the record was singing an up tune; it was their song and they knew it. The night was trying to forget the long hard day. Here there was no need to force the laughter; it came easy and natural and the talk was honest. In this bar they were among their own.

"You sure a goer tonight, Henry," the big-busted brown girl said. She sat on a bar stool, her legs crossed, the miniskirt showing generous thighs. "Where you get all this walkin'-around money?" Her mouth parted in a derisive grin and she glanced at the other girl sitting on a stool beside her and at the two men standing with Henry, letting them all enjoy her open tease. "You hit a number today, baby, or you jump some rich ol' gray or somethin'?"

"Maybe he usin' bad dice in a good crap game," the tall, dark girl on the other stool said, and they all smiled.

Henry had his back to the bar and was enjoying the jesting attention. He bent forward, his hand grabbing the waist of the abundant brown girl who led the ribbing. "Laurelene, honey"—he pushed his face close to hers—"you better be nice to me, because Henry's through bein' a pauper. From now on things are goin' to be silk an' satin, baby, you hear? From now on all you people"—his head went in the direction of the two men—"are goin' ta see a new man." The bartender put down a fresh round of drinks, reached for the money one of the other men had laid on the bar. Henry spun around. "Hey, Rufus, don't you touch George's money; it's no good here. This here is my round." His arms swept out importantly, pushing a couple of bills from his own change before him on the bar, and he capped his generosity by adding a tip. "Keep the change, man." Rufus the bartender took the money and stood there smiling. He seemed about to say something, then shook his head amusedly and walked away to ring it up in the register.

"If this is the new man you gonna be, Henry," Laurelene said, her eyes wide with exaggerated awe, "you sure gonna find a lotta new friends quick. You're gonna end up the black pied piper of Harlem and all them drinkin' people are gonna point you out and say, 'There he go, Henry the new man.' "

She softened her scoff with a smile and reached out to snuggle around Jackson's neck, while the others laughed. Henry had laid himself open to their ridicule. They had been drinking together for the last hour. As one quick drink led to another, Jackson's restrained jubilation in his new-found wealth had slowly seeped out in boastfulness about a happy future, guarded at first, then expanding in defense against Laurelene's good-natured needling.

The tall, yellow-skinned man standing next to her smiled. He had been masking his annoyance at Jackson's expansiveness; since he was drinking on him he would let the phony mouthings pass. But as the rounds continued to flow, Henry started to grab for the big-titted girl and it churned the man's irritations still more. Now he decided to puncture Jackson's bullshit balloon, cut him down to size.

"Now, Laurie, baby, you go easy on Henry," he said, the smile never leaving his face. "His old woman she gonna be hard enough on him. She gonna be real mad when she finds out he's throwin' more money across the bar than he more than likely gave her in the last month. So I think we better let him finish his drink and go on home, 'cause I don't wanna be no part of breakin' up no marriage."

Jackson looked up at him, his eyes narrowing in anger. He didn't mind Laurelene's ribbing; in fact he found the backhanded attention she gave him flattering. But he had just enough drink in him to resent the man's chafing sarcasm. He rode up on his toes to gain some height. "Well, I'll tell you, man, I don't have to push no goddamn clothes rack through that downtown Jew garment district for my bread like some cats I know. And I ain't boot-lickin' some white man for shit money either. I make mine by usin' my brains."

The other man in their party shook his head and gently touched Jackson's back in a soothing gesture. "Now why you want to go and get mad for, Henry. Cass don't mean nothin', he just havin' some fun. We all just havin' some fun and nothin' serious meant. We're all friends here just tryin' to enjoy ourselves."

Henry held his belligerent stance, his boozy eyes glaring at Cass. "Well, I don't like bein' made no fool of, man. Them days is gone, too, along with a lotta other shit in my life, 'cause I don't have ta take it no more." He turned and looked disdainfully at the four of them bunched in tight around him. "And I don't give no good goddamn, you believe me or not, because action speaks louder than words. You'll see. You all see soon enough what I'm talkin' about." He reached out against their silence for his glass and gulped it with righteous indignation.

The song on the jukebox ended. Talk and light humor ran the length of the bar, but the four people crowded

123

around Henry were momentarily silenced by his words, their thoughts so similar that they might have been reading one another's minds. They all knew Henry to be a quick squanderer of paychecks from a long list of menial jobs that he now scornfully denounced. They had heard his empty optimistic talk of a fanciful dream world of plenty many times before, but never before had it had quite such boisterous conviction. It was against the familiar tedium of his tall tales that they had aligned their whimsical putdown, but this time, unlike most kidding, it drew no line in its roughness and slopped over the boundaries of mockery into raw meanness.

Laurelene's eyes fell on the remnants of Henry's twenty lying on the bar. She was having too good a time to let go this easily and she moved to keep the party going. "Hey, Henry." The skirt slid further up the brown legs, holding for a long second at her crotch, then slowly she got off the stool. "What say you and me pick out some songs and add some life to this dead-ass party?" She laughed and her arms went around his neck.

Jackson had been pacified by what he considered their respectful silence. He smiled back at her, then scooped some change off the bar and stuffed it into her hands. "Yeah, baby, you load that money-grabbin' music box while I become the middle-man with the men's room in the back."

"Now, Henry"—her face became serious—"don't you go and fall in because I can't save ya, I don't know how to swim."

Jackson swept his arms about the girl and they bent to fresh laughter. Then he eased out of the tight circle. "Hey, if you get that lazy-movin' Rufus' eye, order another round and I'll be right back. And if I'm not, then you know I blew my bladder on the way."

Joe Logart also stepped away from the bar. He had been standing only a few feet from the quartet, nursing a drink in apprehensive silence as he listened to Jackson's building braggadocio.

It was empty in the darkened rear, by the toilets, and he waited in a booth. As Henry strutted past him Logart grabbed his arm and stood up, blocking the narrow

124

passageway. "Henry' let's get the hell out of here, huh, it's too—"

Jackson pulled his arm away with a quick flash of anger. Joe Logart might have been a stranger. "Hey, man, don't you touch me. I don't like bein' pushed, you hear?"

The sudden bluster stunned Logart. He stared at Jackson, studying the protruding drink-blurred eyes. He wasn't surprised that Henry had momentarily forgotten about him, for after he had been introduced at the bar he drifted to the fringe of the party, staying just close enough to hear the talk, mindful of the unpredictable personality of the drinking Jackson.

"I'm not pushing you, Henry," Logart said soothingly. "I just want us to get out of here. You know what I mean, man, like we shouldn't be here this long. Come on, let's go. If you wanna drink more, I'll buy a bottle and we'll drink up in my hotel room, okay?"

Jackson, mollified, shook his head sadly at what he felt was unnecessary concern. "What you frettin' about, Joe? Everybody know me here. I'm among friends. The trouble with you is you don't know how to relax. Come on, man, join the party and let's have some laughs." He leaned closer and lowered his voice, as if to impart a secret. "Look, Joe, we could push them two cats out. I know them two guys and they're nothin'. It'll be easy to grab their cunt for ourselves. That Laurelene chick, man, she'll blow your mind. But you got to join the fun and spend a few bucks first. You know, you got to impress them and then we'll have these bitches made real quick."

"I'll have my laughs, man, but not here." Edginess crept into Logart's tone. "No, you finish your drink, Henry, kiss these people off and let's get movin'."

Jackson could sense the anger behind Logart's surface calm. In the short time they had been thrown together he had taken a strong liking to this quiet man. Even though they would be parting after taking their shares, in all probability never to see each other again, he didn't want to end their friendship on a sour note over something he considered merely foolish overcautiousness. His hand went up to Logart's shoulder. "Joey, you the biggest worrier I ever did see. We all got away nice and easy and

125

that gotta be the toughest part of the whole bit. You listen to me now when I tell you you gotta stop seein' the gloomy side. Jim Harris, maybe he got somethin' to worry about 'cause he got a record. But we, we should be celebratin'." He closed his eyes for a moment, his head swaying as if to some rhythm only he could hear. "Man, man," he drawled with a grin of delight, his thoughts vicariously reliving the earlier excitement, "we showed them all tonight. Didn't we, Joey? You and me and Jimbo." The smile widened and he could barely control the laughter. "And, Joey, you know what the best thing is, the best thing of all: The cops ain't goin' ta tie me into it. They don't have a sheet on me, man. I never been locked up in my life so I don't even have to worry about the fuzz. I won't even be pulled in for questionin'." His laughter bubbled up and he began to rock gently to its gratifying pleasure.

Logart wanted to shake him, to rattle the crazy optimism from his liquor-addled brain, to pull him back down from the rose-colored fog that seemed to be carrying him further out of reach. Disgust smeared across Logart's scarred face, his mouth twisted ironically. "Henry, I'm from outa town and I'm clean with the law, too. But I'm still worried about them." The heavy beat of recorded music began to pulse up from near the entrance to the bar. "But I'm not half as afraid of them as I am about Doc Johnson if half the stories I heard about him are true. And knowin' all the cats he got workin' for him up there, he got to be a bigger danger to us than the law. So why buck the odds, man? In a couple o' days we'll be outa here, so let's lay low like Jimbo says."

Henry Jackson straightened up to his full height, his eyes fixed on Logart, the laughter replaced by quicksilver anger. "They can come lookin' for me, every last goddamn one of them," he snorted in contempt, his hand patting the gun stuck into his waistband beneath the jacket. "I'm packin' this here piece and if any of them boys of Johnson's comes a-callin', I'll shoot their mother-fuckin' eyes out. You hear me, man? None of them bastards scare me. None of them."

Then they both were quiet, watching a burly man in work clothes squeeze past them to the gray door that hid the privy from the patrons. Insistent beats and talk and laughter filled the gin mill with a gaiety that was jarring to Joe Logart's mounting nervousness. Drink had transformed the docile Jackson into a schizo ready to fight the whole damn world. "Henry, you gotta listen to me, and listen to me good. Do you wanna jeopardize everythin' we knocked our brains out for?" Logart appealed to him in a firm, even tone. "It's not only yourself to think about, it's me and Jimbo and all the sweat and strain we all went through to score. And even now that we crossed the finish line big winners, the race still ain't over with, 'cause there's too many guys that want to put a claim against us and they still got the power to make us losers, Henry." He softened his voice. "All them good things we talk about, man, they all up front waitin' to be enjoyed. Good days ahead with enough money to buy all the women and laughs you want. You know what I mean, man? But tonight ain't one of them. So don't you blow this thing, baby, not now."

Jackson listened and he remembered Logart's eyes having almost the same look when they gazed hauntingly above the money in Jim Harris's apartment an hour or two before. "I don't agree with your thinkin', Joe," he answered slowly, "but like you say, I gotta consider you and Jim. If for no other reason, man, than that big bastard's still holdin' on to my share. Okay." He nodded in agreement. "Okay, you can relax, man. I'll have that final drink with my friends and I'll go with ya." He buttoned the top of the jacket, then brushed his hand back over his hair. "Besides, I got too many things to straighten out than to be wastin' my time around this here dump. But you do me one favor right now, okay? You stop worryin'. Everythin's all right, Joe, you know. And that's the way it's goin' to stay."

They left the toilet and went out, to be met by Laurelene, who had hipped her way from the crowd up front. "Hi, honey," she said, sliding in between them, her arms going about Henry, her wide mouth parting in a smile. "I was beginnin' to think maybe you really drowned. We got a drink waitin' for you. What's takin' you so long?" She purposely kept her back to Logart; from their silence she sensed an argument. "What's the

127

matter with your friend here, Henry? He antisocial or somethin', or maybe he afraid of women?"

"No, baby." Jackson winked at Logart. "He not afraid of women, he just a worrier."

She tilted her head, her round face exaggerating the question. "He a what?"

"A worrier. You know, like the atom bomb that ain't ever goin' to drop."

Her eyes narrowed suspiciously as she looked for the joke. She glanced quietly at the unsmiling Logart and then at Jackson, and grew annoyed because she couldn't see the humor. "Now don't you try and get deep and mysterious with me, Henry. That ain't your style. If your friend is a drag, let him stay by himself, but you got a drink on the bar that's paid for and that music fillin' this here joint you paid for, too. So let's go up front and enjoy it." She took him by the hand. "Come on now, no more serious talk. That the surest way to break up a good time."

Jackson, delighted by her exaggerated attentiveness, winked again at Logart as his hand slipped around her waist and nestled up under her tit. Near the jukebox a couple had picked up the infectious sounds and begun an improvised dance. A few people turned from their drinks and grinningly encouraged them.

"I can do better than that black bitch," Laurelene said back at the bar, prodded by the liquor.

"You sure can, baby," Jackson answered absently, still caught up in what Logart had told him. He laid his finished drink on the bar with finality, straightened up and looked toward Logart to let him know they were leaving.

"Well, then, let's both show them, eh, Henry? Let's show them what we both can do." She grabbed his hand and began to pull him to where the other couple danced.

"No, baby, I gotta cut out, I got things—"

"Come on now, Henry. I need a partner."

"Here." He motioned to the man beside him. "Here's Cass; he dance with you."

"I don't wanna dance with Cass, I wanna dance with you," and she dragged playfully at him.

"Hey, you, mama!" Her voice threw its husky sarcastic challenge over to the other girl and twisted heads along the length of the crowded bar. "You move your black hide out of the way because I'm goin' ta show you how it's really done." She turned to Jackson. "You ready, honey?"

A silly, uncomfortable grin went across his heavy lips. "Well, baby, I . . ." The whole place seemed to be staring at him in anticipation.

"Are you gonna dance with me, Henry, or are you chicken, or maybe you startin' to turn queer or somethin'?" A few people started to laugh.

"Okay, Laurie," Henry said, accepting the dare. "If you wanna dance, I'm with you."

She stepped into the thumping music, her hips snaking into erotic rhythms that brought hot smiles to the line of watchers. Liquor had stripped her inhibitions, letting impulse drive her body to the sensual solo of a wailing trumpet. Henry's ponderous dancing, as he tried to follow her, brought sweat out on his brow and it rolled down his face. The flashing neon in the window of the bar vibrated from the cadence of clapping hands as the aroused audience goaded them on. She moved in a small circle, perspiration running down each side of her body from the sweating patches of hair beneath her uplifted arms. Grinding lustfully, she thrust her body at Henry, pressing almost against but never touching him, and throbbed the closing beats in a climactic ending, and they fell laughing into each other's arms, enjoying the appreciative applause.

"Come on, baby, give us a second helpin' o' that."

"Sock it to us, baby."

"Yeah, an encore, mama, give us some more!" Laurelene, her dress hugging her sweating body and her bosom heaving, raised her hand for silence. "Boys, if I give you two treatments o' that, you stalkers wouldn't let me outa here alive."

The bar roared with laughter and Henry Jackson felt inches taller as he swaggered back with her arm in arm to their own waiting party.

"Hey, Rufus," Jackson called impatiently, "set up a round of drinks here."

"Take it easy dancin', man," Cass said, ridicule in his

129

voice, for he was still smoldering from their earlier exchange. "What the big rush for, boy? We still got some." He raised his almost filled glass.

Henry did a slow theatrical turn and stared pompously at the other man. "Man, I didn't ask you to buy, did I? And when I do that'll be the day." He cocked his head toward the bartender, who stood, arms folded, amusement on his face, enjoying Henry's stagy manner. "Rufus, you back up a round for them because this is my last one; I'm cuttin' out."

"Hey, where you goin', honey?" Laurelene protested. "It's plenty early yet, the night's too young to end it now."

"I got some important things to do, baby. I got a lotta things to square away."

Rufus hadn't responded. He held an old tab of Jackson's that he had written off to experience and now he didn't feel like starting a repeat performance. Congeniality disappeared from his face as his eyes dropped down to Jackson's money on the bar. There was only change left.

"What you tryin' to tell me, man?" Henry grew visibly angry at the insinuation that he was a deadbeat. It was degrading, especially in front of Laurelene. "You sayin' like I can't cover it, is that what you tryin' to tell these people?" He dug into his pockets and came up with a roll of bills flashing in his hand. He peeled off three twenties and threw them angrily on the bar. "And when you finish gettin' our drinks you just keep on servin', bartender, 'cause I'm goin' ta do somethin' you never do in this dump. I'm buyin' the house a drink. And if any of these people jump from beer to the hard stuff, you still serve them," Jackson added nastily, going for the overkill with a flourish. " 'Cause most of these people that keep you in business are my friends. And friendship is somethin' you know nothin' about." He slowly creased the money in his hand, studiedly, conspicuously placing it back in his pocket. "Now you hurry up, you hear me, bartender?"

"I'm hurryin', Henry." Rufus gave a grin to the others as he turned to fill the orders. "I'm hurryin'."

Laurelene raised her brow exaggeratedly at the girl beside her and motioned admiringly at Henry. "There's

130

nothin' tight about him; when he got it, he swing." She looked around her. "There's no tomorrow with Henry, that's what I always say about him. He goes for the moment. He know how to live, 'cause he know how to spend. And that's a real indication what a man is, is what he do with money." The conviction in her voice dug deeper into Cass's irritation.

Jackson lit a cigarette and blew the smoke importantly toward the ceiling, awash in the enjoyment of what he felt was a big-time display of style.

"This is just openers, Laurie," Henry said, catching a corner of his own reflection distorted in the mirror by the stacked whiskey bottles. He liked what he saw and stopped a second to admire it. "Yeah, honey, this is just the beginnin'. But I'm goin' to be concernin' myself about the tomorrows comin' up because I'm going to be operatin' my own business pretty soon."

Cass didn't like Henry with money, particularly when he had none himself. The ten that he had put on the bar when they came in was safely folded away back in his pocket, keeping company with a lonely single. He was losing out, and he wanted to salvage his prestige along with the bed he was hoping to share with Laurelene. "What kind of business you think you goin' into, Henry?" he said, baiting the trap with a smile.

"A business like this," Jackson answered, his hand going in a grand sweep about him, "only a bigger and nicer place than this that's kinda well-established with a good spendin' crowd of steadies. You know, somethin' a man can be proud of ownin'."

Rufus happily hustled the drinks along the span of the bar, motioning to Henry as the benefactor of it all. A few drinkers, after they received his gift round, raised their glasses in his direction. Henry acknowledged them like a bored philanthropist. He picked up his own drink, tilted back his head, glassy eyes rolling to the gray tin ceiling, and swallowed his whiskey neat. He laid the shot glass down with a finality that seemed to signify an exit.

"That's nice," Cass said, "because it take a smart man to own a gin mill like that. But you ain't it, because a business like that gonna cost more than you ever gonna see in your whole life." He shook his head sadly. "I sure like to know what you're smokin' there, Henry, that can fill your mouth with so much bullshit."

The ridicule jabbed into Jackson's alcohol-swollen ego and he glared furiously at Cass. His jaws snapped open a couple of times and then hung there, exposing a mouthful of bad teeth. But, somehow, he checked the rush of anger, the corner of his mouth twisted up, and he closed one eye in a drunken blink that he thought conveyed his mysterious, important message. "Man, I got it," he snarled. "I got all the money I need right now to buy anything I want and that includes buyin' and sellin' the likes of you."

Joe Logart had moved up from his half-concealed place at the bar when he had seen Jackson finish his drink. He stood now just behind a lean dark girl and her boyfriend and flinched at Henry's boast. He signaled with his head to the door but Jackson was too preoccupied with his punctured dignity to see the motion.

"Now, Cass, you stop ridin' Henry," Laurelene said. She didn't believe him either, but she had jumped to Jackson's side and was trying to ingratiate herself, eager for some of the money on the bar and what was still in Henry's pocket. "Honey, when you get this place you talkin' about"—she smiled—"you gonna let us drink for nothin'?"

"Yeah, baby, I'll let you drink all you want and won't charge you a dime, but you're goin' ta need carfare to travel for it. I'm buying that bar in Chicago."

Logart took a conspicuous step back, his anxious gaze seeking Jackson's. They caught and Joe's raised hand beckoned to the street, but Henry, drunkenly determined to leave big, pulled his eyes away and reached for a fresh drink that somebody had sent to him in reciprocation.

"Now wait a minute, baby," Cass said to Laurelene, the booze starting to slur his words. "I'm not ridin' him." A caustic smirk crossed his face. "Maybe ol' Henry here did catch ahold a somethin' big. Maybe one of them rich relatives of his drop dead down in Alabama and left him a talkin' mule and a golden plow and he gonna exchange it for a big fortune."

132

The other couple laughed and even Laurelene smiled, as Jackson swallowed the drink in fuming silence.

"Henry." Joe Logart's imperative voice turned the four of them around and they stared in surprise at the strained, intent face. They had forgotten about him. "You comin' with me, man?" His tone was almost a plea. "Let's go, huh? You have your drink, let's get out of here."

"Man, you stop buggin' me," Jackson snapped, his temper now blinding him to the undercurrent in Logart's words. "I'm goin' when I feel like goin' and that ain't now. If you wanna leave, go ahead, go ahead. You don't need me to protect ya."

Cass could see he had him at last and he began to turn the stiletto of his mockery deep into Henry's exposed ego as revenge for playing it big in front of the girls, for his flashing the roll of bills and buying the house. And for that last eleven dollars in his own pocket. "All I'm sayin', Laurie, is who's this boy tryin' to put on?" He spoke to the girl but kept his scowling gaze on Jackson. "Because we all know this tomcat's nothin' but a gang of shit. If his old lady didn't get the welfare checks the first and fifteenth of every month they'd all be sleepin' in the street."

Jackson's temples throbbed, his eyes narrowed against the smoke rising from the cigarette hanging in the corner of his mouth, as he thrust his face up to Cass. "I'm going to tell you somethin', boy, and I don't give a good goddamn if you believe me or not." The intensity in his voice made some people turn and stare at him. "You couldn't count how much money I got comin' to me. I hit the mother-fuckin' jackpot tonight for more sudden gold than you ever gonna see in your stinkin' life. So big, I won't ever have to bother with a boot-lickin' nigger like you no more."

Joe Logart turned, trying to get away from the high-pitched drawling voice, but it pursued him along the bar, came over the heads of the people, followed him through the door and chased him down the street.

Chapter 12

"The man is sapped with the booze, like his brains are comin' out of his mouth. I tried to talk to him, honest to God, man, I tried to tell him. But he just don't wanna listen. He too wrapped up in actin' big man and tryin' to make some funky bitch of a whore." Logart stood in the middle of the rotting oilcloth floor, his words tumbling out under the jaundiced light twisted into the kitchen ceiling. The tattered shade was still pulled down, dishes cluttered the sink as before, and the empty glasses sat before the half-filled bottle, but the money was now piled back into the duffel bag. "Jimbo, you should've seen him getting drunker by the minute, struttin' and dancin' and big-mouthin' it, and I couldn't believe it when he brought out the whole roll of money you gave him and bought the bar a round of drinks, then standin' there acceptin' the thank yous."

Jim Harris's body felt unhinged. The fingers of his hands started to twitch. He stuffed them into his pockets so they wouldn't be noticed, and lowered his eyes so Logart wouldn't see what was taking place inside him. "About the job." His voice was hoarse, almost indistinct. "Did he say anything about the job?"

"He's drunk, but not that drunk," Logart answered quickly. "But if he gonna stay there, I wouldn't bet against it. He liable to say anything that come into his head."

Harris eased his breath out and put his hands flat on the table. He lowered his head and closed his eyes and wished he could close off the sound of Joe Logart's fright just as easily. It was all falling apart about him: the cops, the unexpected cops appearing out of nowhere in the hall, who had made him throw away a timetable of escape that had taken months of thoughtful planning, that was supposed to leave a route open that he could travel. And now a drunken Henry Jackson, who had stayed so beautifully sober up to then and who was so essential to the scheme, was forcing him to make another unanticipated change. It was too soon, too soon. Doubt gnawed away in the back of his mind, devouring his confidence, leaving anxiety and anger.

"I'm sorry, Jim, I just couldn't help it," Logart said regretfully. "He got away from me, I couldn't get him back. It's not that I didn't try. I did every—"

Harris whirled around in a rage. "What the fuck you tell me you couldn't help it?" The cords of his neck bunched and throbbed. "I ask you to watch him, to make sure he don't give us any kind of unnecessary trouble, and you come runnin' back here to me like some kid cryin' he was too much to keep an eye on." He turned back to the table, grabbed the duffel bag of money, and held it up in front of Logart's face. "This is my whole life, my whole future, and it's yours, too. I planned this mother fucker for over a year, I put it together like a clock that ain't goin' ta ring any alarms without me knowin' about it, and the whole fuckin' thing worked, you hear, it worked. And now you tell me that lousy lush is blowin' it on me." He turned and flung the canvas bag back toward the table; it hit the wall and fell to the floor, scattering some bills. "I asked you to watch him for just another lousy thirty-six hours more, another day and a half, that's all I need. And now I got a new worry that's bigger than the cops and Johnson put together."

A shock of sickness cut across Logart's stomach. "Take it easy, will ya, Jimbo? I'll tell ya what happened and then you tell me if I did wrong, okay?" Logart's words tumbled out in a rush of justification. "It was one of them happenin's that just built outa nothin'. We were walkin' over to his pad, and we get to his neighborhood, and as we pass this bar a cab pulls up and two guys get out with a couple o' chicks. One of the bitches gives him a big hello and asks how come they haven't seen him around lately. Well, he starts to strut—you know how he is, man, like the way he was actin' up here before—and then he tells them he was busy workin' on somethin' big." Harris grimaced. "The way you look is just the way I felt, Jimbo, 'cause I'm standin' there not knowin' what to do. Then they invite him in for a drink and he

135

shakes them off but they start kiddin' around with him, you know, like they're goin' ta carry him into the place no matter what. That's when I stepped in. I tell them we gotta go someplace and don't have the time. And all the time I'm talkin' he's eyein' up this big, fine-lookin' bitch. He musta had just enough juice sloshin' inside him that he couldn't resist their invite. He turns to me and says, 'Let's have one drink,' but he wasn't askin', 'cause in he goes without waitin' for an answer, leavin' me standin' in the street."

"You shouldn't've let him go in there. You shoulda laid the little bastard out and thrown him in a cab and carried him back up here."

"How the hell could I, man?" Logart's shoulders shrugged like a sigh and his hands went out for understanding. "I don't know this cat that long for me to know how he was goin' ta act inside, and besides, it woulda looked crazy if I did, with the street so crowded, people hangin' around outside. I didn't want a big commotion goin' on. When he walked in there I think he have one, maybe two drinks and we'd be on our way, nice and quiet like. So don't blame me for losin' him; I don't deserve it 'cause I never seen that cat drunk before. I didn't know how he gonna behave. If I had any idea how he was goin' to act, he wouldn't've got mixed up with no people in any bar."

Joe Logart's face was a combination of resentment and concern. There was nothing he could add and now he stared unblinkingly back at Harris. Between the walls loose plaster fell, nudged by the scurry of a rat. A woman's laugh sounded across the courtyard and Harris's face, rigid in accusation a moment before, softened in thought.

Harris sighed. "Yeah, you're so right, Joe, you ain't to blame. It's my fault, not yours. I shouldn't of gave him money. But I couldn't very well give money to you without givin' some to him because he woulda got suspicious. I—I thought it would be safe, it would look natural and be a good cover. The trouble is I figured him too fine; he's comin' on too soon."

"What you mean?" Logart asked, perplexed, watching Harris bend down to the overturned bag and pick up the scattered money. He put it absently back into the duffel bag, and replaced it on the table. Then he slumped tiredly into a chair.

"He's our patsy, Joe," he said softly.

"Huh? Patsy? What the hell you talkin' about, man?"

Harris looked up pensively at him. "How long do you think it's goin' to take Doc Johnson to put this thing together and figure out it was me that engineered this hit tonight?"

Logart was confused by Harris's apparent lack of concern as he asked the frightening, foolish question. "Well, I'll tell ya," he groped, "I'll tell ya how long—like maybe never. And if he do put a fix on you, it'll still be enough time for us to be long gone from here that it don't really matter."

"Maybe," Harris said, then shook his head, "but I don't think so. Doc Johnson's a sharp man. He might even have me pegged right now."

It was said too casually; it was like a throwaway surely not to be taken seriously, and Logart searched for a sign of humor on the somber face. But all he could see was distress. Fresh beads of sweat ran down his body and his mind filled with the memory of the weeks of work that lay behind the money in its bloated bag on the table before them. The time it took to case the transfers, acquire the uniforms and the guns, and all the talk and planning that meant a perfect job. But most of all the fight all that time to control the nerve that gave him the impetus to push up the stairs, and permitted him to go through with something so big that the very thought of it had kept him awake with visions of failure. And now this cold bastard of a man was telling him their accomplishment was to be short-lived, clearly knowing that to be caught would mean finish in its truest sense. After the hard reality of the drunken Henry Jackson, the strange detached unconcern of Jim Harris was more than he could take. Joe Logart's tongue darted across his dry lips a couple of times before he was able to speak.

"If you knew all this from the very beginnin' and you still went through with it knowin' we're not goin' ta get a chance to run, that's gotta make you the lowest crawlin'

137

bastard that ever lived." His pointing finger punctuated the awful bitterness. "Because you conned me, man, you conned me, and Henry, too, into somethin' that was too fuckin' big for me and him to get hooked up in. From the very beginnin' it was way over our heads. Why you done it I don't know. The only thing that's clear to me now is you dealt me a mother-fuckin' bad hand."

"No, I didn't, Joe," said Harris. "This was all figured in, man, everything was real thought out, even right down to this here conversation." His face was expressionless, but his voice was understanding. "I didn't leave you out on no tree to be shot down by Doc Johnson. I give you the same kind of consideration I give myself and I ain't about to commit suicide." There seemed to be a greater tone of confidence now and it seemed to check Logart's fluster. "Joe, did you ever wonder why I picked a cat like Henry for somethin' this big?"

"Yeah, yeah, maybe a little, but I was wrapped up enough just to think about if we could pull it off and what was goin' to happen after. He didn't have very much to do, all he had to do was drive that car, so I didn't think too much about him."

"Well, I did. For a straight twenty thousand I coulda picked a hundred different guys to wheel for us, and they woulda been fallin' over each other for the chance. But I had to know my man real good. How he gonna behave, because I needed a drunk with a braggin' mouth, but a special kind of boozer, one that could stay off the juice for weeks. Then when he goes off the wagon he falls so loud everybody's goin' to notice him."

"Well, man, you sure got one," Joe Logart said.

"Your fears cloggin' your ears, Joe. You still ain't hearin' me. Don't you see what I set up, don't you see, man? He's this lamb we're goin' to leave sittin' for Johnson to slaughter."

"Lamb for slaughter," Logart repeated to himself, "lamb for—" Then the full meaning of what he was being told suddenly hit him with an excitement that sent him pacing around the room. Not taking his eyes off Harris, he walked to the table and sat down opposite him. He wanted it confirmed, he wanted to yell, "Tell me, tell me it all, let me hear it!" but instead he held onto a facsimile of cool and tried to provoke Harris into an explanation by shaking his self-assurance.

"You're forgettin' one important thing, Jimbo: to set up Henry, he's got to stick around Harlem and he don't intend no such thing. I heard him tonight, man, he's headin' for Chicago. He all wrapped up in buyin' him a bar."

Harris laughed scornfully. "I know that clown, known him for fifteen years, and I can tell ya exactly what he's goin' to do and one of the things ain't gettin' outa town. He knows nothin' but Harlem and at his age he's not about to change. I'll tell ya what's goin' ta happen to him, Joe. Once he gets his cut, he's goin' to go crazy, he's goin' to throw money around like it's goin' outa style and people are goin' to start to wonder about him. Then they're goin' to talk, because Henry Jackson never had more than two nickels to rub together in his life and all of a sudden he's actin' like a rich man and when he drinkin' he got a mouth on him, man, which you found out tonight. He can't help himself. And the cats he's hangin' out with are gonna put it together and it's all just a matter of time till Johnson grabs him."

"Till Johnson grabs him," Logart repeated aloud. No longer able to look directly at Harris, he lowered his head, dismissing any remaining doubt he had about Harris' coldly brutal abilities. He screwed him, oh, man, did he screw him, he thought, and again he smelled the sickening gunpowder, saw the bodies spinning and smashing against the windows, thrashing on the floor, again heard their cries and Harris hunched above the butchery, his face, when he turned to him, like nothing he had ever seen before. A fresh rush of suspicion swamped Logart. Watch out, watch out, he cautioned himself.

"What's the matter, Joe?" Harris asked softly. "You worried about him?" He knew by the silence he had jolted Logart, but he didn't realize how much he had shocked him until Logart raised his head once more and he saw the apprehension in the trouble-scarred face.

"How come you didn't tell me none of this until now?" he asked accusingly.

"For the best of reasons, man." Harris ignored the insinuation. " 'Cause I needed a guy that wasn't known around Harlem. It was like a lifetime ago when we did the army bit together but I remembered a lot of things about ya. I remembered what you was made of. How you'd gamble on something big like this and that you'd hang tough against real bad odds."

"You're right about one thing," Logart said sadly. "It was sure a lifetime ago, 'cause the guy you remembered is as scared as hell right now."

"If you weren't, Joe, I'd sure be worried about your sanity. Only some kind of a fool would sit here and not be scared. I didn't want no local brave boy, and most of all some cat that knew Henry. It seems like everybody knows everybody else up here and I didn't need no friends workin' for me." Harris's hand went around the cap of the whiskey bottle and absently began to turn it "You see, I trust you, man, but you got a fault I had to watch out for. You too quick in givin' a guy a break. For the last few weeks you and Henry been thrown together pretty close and I didn't know how friendly you would get with him and all I needed was for you to hint what I had set up and give that drunk a chance to get away. Yeah, I'm usin' him, man. I'm goin' to waste him to give us an edge—if I can't leave some kind of a barrier behind us I don't think I would never got into this thing." He leaned forward, his large hands extending and spreading, almost touching Logart. "Now you see, Joe, it wasn't us goin' up there to make the hit; I felt right along we grab them by surprise we can do it. The key to this thing was pushing that lush into the spot I got marked out for him so it give us a good runnin' start."

Logart looked at the bag of money, and he reached out and touched it, fondling it as a man would stroke a woman. He peered at Harris. "Jimbo, you coulda been relaxin' all this time, because when you called me in Detroit and told me what you were puttin' together and asked if I wanted in, you were givin' me my only chance that I'd rise above the shit, and now there's a hundred grand o' my money here and for that kinda scratch I wouldn't tell Jesus Christ they was goin' to crucify him." He shook his head as though he had begun to appreciate fully what Harris had done, but he couldn't shake away the doubt in his eyes. "Now I see the whole thing, Jimbo,

I gotta hand it to ya even more. From the start, right down to Henry you put it together, like nothin' I ever see or hear about before. But I think you're forgettin' one thing. If they grab him like you say, he goin' ta tell him who we are sure as we're sittin' here talkin'."

"So what?" Harris snapped. "We won't be around. Look, man, they're goin' to bust their hump tryin' to find us, they're gonna be lookin' all over, and when they come across Henry he's goin' to be a real find 'cause he's goin' to end up a bigger man dead than he ever were alive. Johnson's gotta waste him big. Ol' Doc, he gonna get the only thing he'll be able to make a show of."

"Because they grab Henry, that's goin' ta stop them?" Logart asked. "Man, we hit the mob and that ain't no local black operation. Them dagos are everywhere. They're still goin' to come on after us."

"Sure, sure they will, but not half as fuckin' hard," Harris said, raising his voice against Logart's carping anxieties. Then he choked back his irritation. "Man, you're askin' for guarantees. Well, I can't give 'em to ya, never could. Because you don't go up against these people and grab their money without trouble. But we gave them a local problem and that's what they got to think about. It's here right in Harlem that they gotta look good, and that means Johnson's gotta look good, because he's their representative, and believe me, after he gets ahold of Henry and saves some face for his white bosses, it's just got to cool them off enough to where they're gonna sit back a little and wait. Johnson's their man. He got one and he's gonna get the rest, 'cause it only natural they're goin' to think the money's still in Harlem. And, baby, that's the edge I'm lookin' for, 'cause they got to be like most whites, they're gonna sell us short as dumb niggers. Time, man; that drunk he buys us time."

The tone and knowledge of Jim Harris's logic should have been comforting to Logart, but he was still worried beyond the sacrifice of Henry, the retribution from Doc Johnson and Italian mobsters. It tore Harris's blueprint, months of planning didn't mean much now, for unexpectedly it had all changed and he had to say it. He took a deep breath. "Now I know the whole thing it makes good sense, Jimbo. Honest to God, man, I don't think many guys coulda thought it out this way. It took a rare cat to do it and in its own way it's kind of a beautiful thing. It's just"—he lowered his eyes—"just that it's a shame it had to kick bad at almost the last second, 'cause things would be a lot easier now if the law didn't have got in our way goin' down them stairs." He could as easily have said "got in your way," but he was glad it came out as it did.

The chair creaked under Jim Harris's weight, and his face reflected some of Logart's stress. "Yeah, yeah, I know," he said, his voice a mumble, as he tried to keep his own gnawing worry from engulfing him. "I didn't want that, Joe, I sure never meant them to be in on this. If it'd worked the way it was meant to they wouldn't hardly have taken no notice. I mean my play shoulda been only against Johnson and the Syndicate and they was goin' to be rough enough to lose without the law houndin' after our asses. But you're so right, they're in it now, they goin' to tell us how and when we spend it because they goin' to have this case still open, hangin' over our heads for the rest of our lives." His voice grew grave and bitter. "And it don't matter where you light to 'cause you ain't goin' to buy anything big with cash without that white man noddin' and smilin' and figurin' out the bill, without thinkin' where this black man got his money, while somebody is in the back maybe callin' the fuzz. You goin' to have to bury it, man, use only just enough to live, but bury the rest until what we pulled off is just some kind of a faded memory. And all that time you gotta be thinking' about the day you dig it up, that there be no more workin' for short money, no more bullshit hearing somebody tellin' you to get at the end of some goddamn gray line, no more nothin'. And when that day comes, you celebrate, you drink one to yourself and you think of me because we done something that you just got to feel proud about. You and me we beat the system, man, but until that day we gotta cool it behind a workin', square front. It's like we both got to have patience and play it real smart and we got this thing made."

Joe Logart, as he listened, watched the sweat trickle down Harris's almost flat nose. He watched the hand rub the sweat off and drag across the wide-boned face. He could smell the stink of garbage, paper-bagged, at the door and the silence of tenement, sullenly holding back its constant minute noises as if it were monitoring this hard moment of angry confidence that came at him across the table like a bracing wind.

Logart knew everything would be all right. It *was* all going to work.

"I guess I'm too keyed up, Jimbo. I"—the corners of his mouth pulled his scarred face into a sheepish grin—"I sometimes get like this when things get too tight. Like I said before, man, this was too big for me. I tried to kid myself, but now I know. I was afraid you might notice and get some other cat in my place." His shoulders moved apologetically. "I guess I'm still sort of up tight; guess that's why I kinda got flaked out listenin' to Henry. Most likely ain't nobody goin' ta pay that loudmouth no heed. They're just gonna go on thinkin' he's just so much drunken bullshit and that'll be that. I wouldn't be surprised tomorrow mornin' he knockin' on my door apologizin' and tellin' me to keep quiet to you about his drinkin'." He waited for an answers, a confirmation, but Harris kept a brooding silence, as if there was no more to say. Joe Logart wanted to linger, to talk, to dig more of this self-assurance, but now, reluctantly, he stood up. "I guess I'll head me over to the hotel; I sure as hell can use some sleep. It's been some day. Way I feel, I think I'm goin' to sleep right through tomorrow." He stood awkwardly at the table waiting for Jim Harris to rise, to slide the bolt from the barred door and let him out into the darkened hall.

"Jackson has fucked us into the ground, Joe," said Harris softly. "He's cut down our runnin' time to where you ain't gonna do any sleepin' tomorrow."

Logart squinted questioningly as though he had not caught the full meaning of the words.

"Yeah, he sure pushed up our timetable," Harris went on. "I didn't think he'd jump the gun on me, not on a lousy few hundred. But I shoulda known, man; I had his track record; I shoulda known that."

The restrained almost indifference in Harris confused Logart completely. "But, Jimbo, they're not takin' him serious, they're like laughin' at him. You know, it's like

I told ya, maybe I blowed it outa proportion, like I saw things that ain't happenin', you know what I mean?"

"I'm not about to rely on a drunken Henry Jackson to keep his braggin' mouth shut," Harris answered in the same dry, toneless voice. "Oh, you could be right, man, but I ain't waitin' around too long to see if you're wrong." Logart's mouth opened like a fish, but Harris signaled him to listen. "I know Doc Johnson. Money's everything to him and he knows what it can buy. It's only natural he goin' to put a price on our heads and with that old mother fucker Henry runnin' off at the mouth ain't anyone not our enemy. Johnson would lay a good price on any cat that could rat out the kinds of information that's goin' to help him grab ahold of any one of us."

Logart's face twisted. "Then what the hell are we waitin' for, huh?" he cried. "What're we here sittin' talkin' all this shit for when all this shit is goin' on in your mind? For Christ's sake let's get outa here. Let's get the fuck on the road, man, and put some distance—"

"Huh, man, where you goin' to run to right now, to-night?" Harris asked evenly as he stood up. "The police, they just got to have every exit out of Manhattan covered; you couldn't buy a subway ride now without a cop lookin' ya over, wantin' to know who you are. And all the time we were carryin' a big bag of money." He turned away from Logart and took a couple of steps and stood facing the door for a moment before he spoke. "Joe, I want to get out, too, I'd like to run right now, man, tonight." He turned back to him slowly. "But when you move you going to need you a crowd to get lost in and that means tomorrow mornin' when the streets is busy with people headin' for work. It'll be a lot easier to lose yourself durin' the rush hour, man. No cop's apt to be noticin' a workin' black man in no crowded train. The odds is still with us, baby, and we just got to gamble a little bit more. I doubt they could of marked him this quick. There's a hundred Henrys drinkin' in dozens of bars up here every night." He raised his arm and seemed to block out the rest of the room as he pointed toward the entrance. "But if they did, man, ain't nobody gonna come through that door alive."

144

There was no braggadocio in his voice. Joe Logart knew he meant just what he said. This impoverished flat, facing reeking alleys and set in the center of a sordid ghetto, was guarded by a man willing to die for the bag of bulging money lying on the table before him.

"What I'm tellin' you is what I'm goin' to do. But you can take your share right now," Harris said, "or you can stay here till mornin', take it then and cut out when I do. Don't matter to me; any way you want to do it is okay with me now, man."

Logart shook his head. "We both need some sleep, Jimbo. If I stay here I'm goin' ta talk your head off and in the mornin' I ain't likely to be concerned about payin' no hotel bill. No, I'm goin' over to the hotel and try to get me a couple of hours sleep and check out nice and proper. No sense in raisin' anybody's interest in me by jumpin' the tab. You said that, remember?" and he had to force it, but he smiled. "Man, you must want me to be robbed by some no-good-doin' cats up here, because I'd be a walkin' target with money bulgin' outa my pockets." The strained smile disappeared. "No, I gotta get me my clothes and an old valise layin' in back of the closet and pack my share in."

"Okay, Joe," Harris said. His hand came up and touched Logart's arm. "I'll see you back here in the mornin', but you make it no later than eight o'clock, you hear?" The large hand tightened, turning and moving Logart in step with him to the door. Harris was physically spent and wanted him to leave, he had no more strength to give to this docile man groping for assurance against the army of his fears. And he wondered where the courage he had remembered so vividly as a part of Joe Logart had gone. "Just a few more hours"—he heard his thoughts ticking off the time—"until tomorrow," and he slid back the bolts, one above, one below the knob.

Logart stood behind him watching the muscles contract against the T-shirt covering his broad back. They bunched and rippled at the neck as Harris inched the door open and peered out. For an instant there were bodies again twisting and spinning, disbelief freezing the faces in terror, and then slamming against windows and wall.

Jim Harris turned and looked at him. "You okay?"

Logart nodded. "Yeah, I'm okay."

"Now don't you forget, Joe," Harris whispered, "that's eight o'clock, man. Anything later and I ain't goin' to be here." He sensed a question and forestalled it. "No more talk, I can't take no more of your talk," he said, and opened the door wide enough for Logart. The light from the kitchen illuminated the darkened hall.

"Don't worry, Jimbo, I'll be here a lot earlier than eight o'clock," Logart whispered as he passed Harris. Behind him he could hear the bolts click like muffled .22s and the lock tumble. I got a question, Jimbo. He could feel his mind formulating it. Tonight, up in that room, when you had those guys covered, I thought that white man had the gun, he had control of the gun, Jim, and he wasn't about to turn it on us. He was lettin' us take the money and, man, man, all of a sudden they were dead. Were they meant to die, Jimbo, was that in your plan, too? Were they meant to be dead?

Harris could hear the footsteps recede on the other side of the door. He closed his eyes, leaned back against it for a moment and took a deep breath, filling his lungs with the stench of desolation. He opened his mouth as if to scream, then closed it very slowly, and the silence and loneliness moved down upon him.

Chapter 13

His coat was open and his sweat-stained shirt was bunched over the belt. The cigarette smoldered between his fingers as he worked his thick pink tongue across his lips, picking up a loose piece of tobacco and spitting it free. He staggered, reached out and grabbed the bar for support, then dug his hand clumsily into his pocket and pulled out some money. Extracting a crumpled twenty, he threw it on the bar. The crowd had thinned out by now, and back near the booths where he was standing there was room around him and the girl. The jukebox was still playing and people laughed, but Henry Jackson was too

146

drunk to know their laughter was forced and the talk strained. He had not seen the car stop outside, nor the three white men come in and talk to the colored stranger who had been sitting near the door nursing a drink. He had not seen the Negro nod subtly in his direction and then step out to the street, to say something to another equally well-dressed black. Then the two of them diligently, silently covered the entrance.

At first the customers thought that the whites were The Men, that it was some kind of stakeout and they were going to collar somebody in the place. They had that kind of fatalistic cop calm about them and maybe a pusher was being busted. Then, as the patrons sneaked further glances and sized them up, they sensed that this wasn't the law, they were just grays, and probably the Negro they had talked to was setting up an evening of pleasure. Black women or pot or—it didn't matter what; most of the people lined along the bar had to face Mr. Charlie during the working day and they didn't want to look at no goddamn white face at night, not on their home ground, not in a gin mill on a side street in Harlem. Times had changed. What were they? Stupid? Don't they read the papers? No grays allowed. Finish your drink, whiteys, and get out. We in no mood to hear your liberal slop and smell your stink because we going to let you know you not wanted. But as the customers took a further scowling look their contempt dissolved and they become thoughtfully quiet, staring down uneasily at their drinks as they grew aware of the morbid attraction Henry Jackson had for the newcomers. The whites stood near the entrance holding glasses that they didn't bother to drink from.

Laurelene's loud laugh faded boozily as she turned toward the door, sensing the chill at the other end of the room. One by one the people fell silent. Even Henry, in his drunken haze could feel the atmosphere change and he bobbed his head fuzzily, seeking the cause through the smoke and flashing neon light. The song ended and the jukebox colors dimmed, making the silence complete. A room that had been gay minutes before was now deadly still and the patrons waited. They weren't sure what they were waiting for but they all sensed that the lethal answer lay with the three swarthy white men near the door.

"Hey, nigger." The flat, brutal tone carried to Jackson at the back of the narrow room but it seemed to be calling them all as well, for heads twisted and turned toward Difalco, the eyes suddenly blazing a silent answer of hate.

Henry Jackson's bulbous eyes peered at them and tried to keep them in focus. As he squinted along the bar he made out the sallow faces beneath the hats. The cops. He muttered, half to himself, "Yeah, yeah, they're The Men. The fuckin' fuzz. I'm clean, nobody seen me. They don't have nothin' on me. I don't have no record and who the hell do they think they callin' nigger. . . . If you talkin' to me," he snarled at them, "the name's Mr. Jackson."

"Yeah, shine, we're talkin' to you."

The barkeep Rufus moved to the club he kept among the rags beneath the bar; his hand went around the handle, and he sucked in his breath and waited.

"You going to buy us a drink, nigger." Difalco's voice cut into everyone along the bar. "I hear you been buyin' everybody else a drink. And then I want to hear you talk again about all the sudden money you made in a big score tonight. Is that right, nigger, is that what you been sayin'?"

Jackson's fogged, sodden mind wobbled. If they goin' to take me in for questionin'—the thought formed slowly, they shouldn't treat me like this. Like a man I gonna be treated. They got to give me respect.

A confused Laurelene swayed on the wooden stool to get a better look at this white man who had turned a barroom of partying blacks into a funereal stillness. She shivered as his gaze swept across her.

"If you think you got something on me, man, you go ahead and pull me in." Jackson raised his hands in mockery. "Come on, cop, come on. Put the cuffs on me, but you leave out that 'nigger' shit talk. I don't take that, you hear me?"

"Oh, I'm goin' to do better than pull you in, shine," Difalco said solemnly. "I'm going to lay you out in a pine box." And he stepped away from where he was standing and walked slowly toward Jackson, followed by the two hulking whites. As they moved past the sullen customers, now hunched silently over their drinks, a few lifted their heads, letting their puzzled eyes, some seething, others awed, follow them, knowing not only that Henry Jackson was being humiliated unmercifully, but that all were being abrasively put down. But nobody moved. This kind of attention meant something far more ominous than white men taunting a Negro. That wasn't done up here. Not in Harlem. But every last one of them heeded the credo of the street. Whatever it is don't get involved; let it be.

Laurelene had not taken her eyes off Difalco and now as he approached she slid off the stool and edged back toward the empty booths. Then suddenly her hands went to her face and she screamed a warning. "They not the police, Henry! They not the law!" Her shrill cry reminded him that Jim Harris had given him a gun. "If they catch up to ya, use the gun." People pushed away from him and Henry Jackson stood alone, filled with the blind false courage of drink. He lurched, almost staggered away from the bar and took up their challenge. His hand groped inside his waistband, reaching for the gun. But it was too late. Difalco's fist caught him across the side of his face, slamming him back against the bar, and the gun fell to the floor. He stood braced against the counter, his mouth agape, the eyes clouded in a whiskey stupor. Frantically he looked down for his weapon, but it was too far away; he could never reach it. Then, suddenly, Henry realized the hopelessness of his fight; he panicked and started to run. But another punch snapped his head back across the bar and Difalco stepped away to give his two button men room to work. One hit him, then the other. Jackson went down sprawling on his face. They pulled him up. His lips were cut and blood ran from his nose. His eyes were turned up and he moaned as the bull-necked torpedo held him propped against the bar while his partner pumped his right hand into Henry's stomach, doubling him into a dry retch. He was struck again, and then again. The sickening silence of the room was broken only by the thud of the blows and the grunts of an unconscious man.

Some of the customers had started to edge for the door when Jackson pulled the gun, but one of the outside Negroes watching the street had come back in and he held them inside the entrance by his appearance alone, because somebody had recognized him and whispered he worked for Doc Johnson. The word spread like a combustible fire. They all stood while punches pounded and tore Henry Jackson's flesh.

Only Laurelene, pressed up against a booth in the rear of the bar, could not take it and she vented her horror at the sight. "You lousy white mother fuckers!" she screamed, but still nobody moved to help him. As the echo of her shrill voice died against the silence of the room, Difalco snarled, "Okay, that's enough," and they stopped their hatchet job, letting the blood-smeared Jackson slump to the floor like a crushed balloon.

A large man in a maroon sports shirt stood not quite lost in the tight-lipped crowd, for he was half a head taller than the others. His eyes had smoldered in rage as he watched the white professionals work over the drunk. He was going to let it pass, let them walk out, because it was obviously meant only as a brutal lesson. A man can recover from a beating. But when they lifted Jackson, lugging and pulling him like a slab of gored meat, and followed the sadistically smiling Difalco, he could not overcome the throbing pulse of anger. He stepped out in front of them, his fists clenched like locks of black stone, and his face showed the loathing that Laurelene had cried out to the muzzled room moments before. The unconscious Jackson was eased to the floor and the hoods moved up behind Difalco. But a gun was already in his hand. He raised it slowly, pressed it almost between the eyes of the Negro and cocked the trigger.

"If you want your black head blown off, shine, you just make a move to stop us."

The muscles in the Negro's arms twitched and he stood for what seemed an eternity facing the ugly barrel in the terrible hush of the room. Then he gave way; he stepped back slowly and Difalco's gun followed him, pushing him up against the wall. One of the hoods grabbed Jackson's collar, and dragged him face down to the door,

where the other picked up his feet and they carried him
out. The breathing of the people in the room halted and
slowly Nick Difalco lowered the gun from the terrified
black man, turned and walked from the bar.

Chapter 14

> "I wanna walk up.
> I wanna walk up.
> Oh, Jesus, Jesus, hear my plea.
> I wanna walk up them salvation stairs."

The black cloth rolled to the movements of the shuffling
body and the inky face was thrown back toward the
paint-chipped ceiling. "Jesus, Jesus." His voice strained
in its reach, the sweat rolling down his face, catching on
his jowls, then dropping to the floor of the shabby stage.
He finished the solo against a continual clapping rhythm
produced by robed sisters. A girl, a virginal white cassock
covering her skinny frame, stepped forth and belted into
the sublime reaches of the spiritual. She bent and rose
and threw her arms above her head, and her fervor
moved the sparse, ragged congregation, sitting in rows of
straight-backed chairs in front of her, into bellows of redemption. The singers behind her caught the spirit of
the rollers up front and as if one pushed the other, they
merged into cries of rejoicing that lifted them above the
poverty and strife, the dole and depression, to an elation
that they were sure brought them to the very threshold
of Christ. On and up and still higher they moved and
the badly tuned piano banged along in accompaniment.

The clerical smile was frozen beneath the flaring
nostrils and the mustache as he came at them like a
practicing undertaker. His hands were clasped and he
wore the traditional black smock of pious dignity.

"Good evenin', gentlemen. My name is Curtis; I'm the
church deacon. Can I help you, please?"

Bill Pope's hand went into his pocket and he flashed

the badge strictly for formality, for he knew the deacon had him and his white partner made as The Men.

"You got a Miss Harris here?" Pope asked, while Frank Sullivan looked at Deacon Curtis and thought he had seen him before. It must have been in some old ID file, he decided. Well, each to his own bag. He smiled to himself.

The cleric's eyes widened theatrically and he looked astonished. "You mean Miss Lucy Harris, who play piano for our tabernacle choir?"

Neither man answered him.

"That's a good-doin' woman. She never get in no trouble."

They remained silent.

"You'll find her a very religious person."

They stared at him.

"I'll go get her."

The storefront church was on Lenox Avenue, four floors of sordid walkups above it. Its window, flaked with grime, bore a crude painting of Christ lofting an avenging sword while at his feet lay a severed serpent's head. Over the entrance hung a sign: "GOD LOVES YOU. HE WHO ENTERS WILL BE CLEANSED." The detectives stood just inside the door. The main hall, running to the back yard, was partitioned off from the entrance by blinds that masked the sight, but not the sounds, of redemption. To their right was a white-walled makeshift parlor, empty except for a desk, a couple of chairs and a settee.

The deacon led her formally by the arm. She was a stout woman in a white robe and her eyes were enlarged by the lenses of her glasses. Fortyish and prim, and her round face was indignant.

"This way, gentlemen, if you please," the deacon whispered. "I think y'all be more comfortable in our sitting room"—he took a look back toward the singing congregation—"and more private. People sometimes get nosy about these things, you know."

The detectives followed them into the room. The deacon, still guiding the woman, led her to a chair, then walked back and shut the parlor door. It filtered out most of the sound. "That choir, when they catch the true spirit like they got tonight, they kinda move our membership to enthusiastic response," he said, and came back to the center of the room. His lips smiled down benevolently at Lucy Harris. Then he turned toward the men. "This here is our semimonthly special nighttime service. It is quite popular with our congregation. Why, we have people who moved out of the community to Brooklyn and the Bronx who still come for this upliftin' service."

"Are you the preacher?" Sullivan asked tonelessly.

"Oh, my, no, no." His eyes rolled in denial, as if embarrassed by the thought. "No, I'm jest his assistant. The pastor, Gregory, he gonna speak after the singin'." His hands were clasped together, lost in the folds of his robe, and he leaned forward earnestly, as though imparting a great truth. "I only hope you gentlemen got the time and will stay and hear him. He truly one of the most elegant speakers you could ever want to hear. Tonight he goin' to be specially good 'cause he goin' to speak on 'God, You and the Devil.' "

Both detectives stood looking at him, Sullivan not sure whether they were being put on. Bill Pope, having heard this kind of talk before, turned to the woman. "Miss Harris," he said, and the deacon turned his head as though not to miss a word and gazed serenely at the detective, waiting for him to continue.

Frank Sullivan pointed his thumb toward the door. "Okay, assistant, if we need you we'll call you."

The deacon stared into the suddenly congealing blue eyes and the ecumenical look drained from his face. "Of course," he mumbled, "of course," and walked out of the room.

A flick of humor flashed in Bill Pope's eyes as he glanced at Sullivan. "Miss Harris, my name is Pope. This is Detective Sullivan." He motioned toward Frank, who had moved away from the questioning and now leaned against the edge of the desk, lighting a cigarette. "I'm sorry we have to intrude on you this way," he said courteously, "but it's necessary that we ask you a few questions about your brother, James Harris."

She tilted up her fleshy face, her eyes glaring through the glasses, hard and ungiving and coldly assessing his authority. "Never"—she shook her head—"no, I never goin' to live this down. What the congregation goin' to

153

think when Deacon Curtis tell them their music player bein' questioned by the law like some common thief? Can you answer me that? Can you tell me what I'm goin' to say to all them hard-workin' decent-livin' people inside?" And she sat there with all the moral strength of a crusading evangelist directed against this onslaught of the heathens.

The detectives knew about the Lucy Harrises; Sullivan from observant distance, and his Negro partner from up close. Every family seemed to have its religious enthusiast who would venerate the virtues of a lean, white, dead-bodied Christ while he or she moved through the live swamp of stink in a black ghetto. Most of them were strangely anesthetized to the roar of the corner bar, the big H popping in punctured and withered arms, the hooker working her trade in the back of a hall, and the drunks they had to pick their way through on Sunday mornings, still lying in the vomit of Saturday nights. To hell with the sinners, they seemed to cry from their high protective walls of self-righteousness that isolated them from the grinding impoverishment. They were blind to it all and without compassion, for they lived only for the serenity of that beautifully nebulous day when they would rise gloriously from it to meet their maker.

Bill Pope tried again. "If this was a normal police situation, Miss Harris, where we had the time to speak to you at your home, we would have done so. We don't like to embarrass you like this, but it's very important that we locate your brother, so if you will answer a few questions I will try and make this as quick and painless as possible."

"Why?" she snapped. "What you want to speak to my brother James for?"

Pope was relieved that at last there was an opening and even though she led the way he was glad to follow momentarily. "Well, it's quite possible he committed a very serious crime."

"What you mean when you say serious?"

"Seven men were killed tonight during a robbery. Your brother is suspected of being one of the men who pulled it off."

She sat in her sulking silence, the enlarged eyes behind

154

the glasses unblinking, the black face unmoved by the terrible accusation. Pope could almost feel a barrier slam down between them but he continued. "And he's going to stay suspected until someone can check on his whereabouts earlier this evening. That's what we're attempting to do right now. And the quickest way to do that is to speak to him. So if you can tell us where he's staying at the present we could—"

"I don't know where he livin'."

Pope, exasperated, half expected Frank Sullivan's voice to come angrily over his shoulder at her. He knew why Frank was holding back his aggressiveness but wondered how long he could keep it up.

"It's not necessary that you know his address," Pope said, adding more authority to his tone, "if you know where he might hang out or the names of some of his friends. What I'm asking for is simply some information that could lead us to your brother."

Beads of sweat were on her forehead but the crumpled handkerchief in her hand stayed on her lap and her face did not change. The choir and the shouts of religious frenzy coming through the walls were muffled and melancholy.

Pope's initial look at her had convinced him that the woman was incapable of duplicity, that she was too deeply religious to cover for her brother once she heard the charge. Now he wondered whether he had taken too much for granted and was treating her too gently, whether behind her piety was evasiveness. "If your brother is our man and you're holding back information," he told her, "you could be placing other people's lives in jeopardy, because I don't think any of the men involved in this would hesitate to kill again to avoid being captured. And I don't think you're the type of person who would want that on your conscience, relative or not." He waited for an answer but she gave no acknowledgment she had heard him.

"Bill," Sullivan called, and Pope held back a second before he turned, not sure of what kind of look he would receive. But there was not a trace of criticism in his partner's eyes. The ruddy face was subdued. "I'd better get with a phone," Sullivan said easily. "I'll let the precinct know what we have so far and see what's up."

He turned from Pope and opened the door and a heavy bass voice inundated the parlor with syrupy words of thanks to the singers for their wonderful hymn to Jesus. The door closed but the voice was not to be denied: it seeped through stubbornly.

Bill Pope relaxed his lean frame and lit a cigarette, letting the irritation subside as he pulled slowly on the butt before he spoke. "I can understand how you must feel about the police, under the circumstances of being questioned right here in the church, and to be questioned about someone close to you in connection with such a bad crime. I know it can be a very tryin' experience, but you gotta understand, Miss Harris, I'm just one o' the hired help tryin' to do a difficult job in the best way I know how. All I'm doin' here is checkin' out leads. Your brother happens to be one of them. He just a suspect and not a strong one at that. So if you can see your way in helpin' us to eliminate him off our list it would be well appreciated."

Pope watched the emotionless face for a reaction. But it did not change. He might have been some despised door-to-door white peddler trying to collect payment on an overdue bill. In the silence, the preacher could now be heard bellowing a parable to the assemblage behind the thin walls. Bill Pope decided he was wasting his time with Miss Lucy Harris. Frustrated, he turned toward the door to seek out Sullivan and the street.

"Mr. Detective," she said roughly; he turned around to her. "You don't know how I feel about nothin'. You don't even know me but I'm gonna tell ya somethin' before you leave." Her voice was touched by a bitter honesty that held him riveted. "I'm a religious person who give my time free to the church because I believe we all bein' judged every day of our lives, how we behave, by a Super Bein' that's above us all. And sometime people say, 'Because you devout and all the time runnin' to church and prayin', you stupid.'" She pushed her heavy body forward in the chair. "But if you think I'm goin' to tell ya somethin' because that white man done walked out of the room, you the one that's stupid"—she

156

snorted her contempt—" 'cause you can save that 'all us colored folk' routine for where it might do more good. You don't need to use that darky stuff with me because I got news for you, baby: if I knew James' whereabout I wouldn't need no promptin', I'd tell ya." The crumpled handkerchief she had worried with her fingers at last rose and dabbed at the dark, intense face.

Surprised by the sudden burst of denunciation, especially of her brother, the detective kept silent and watched her eyes.

"I stopped talkin' to James a long time ago, even before he done went out and spread his wings on big-shot ideas. I wash my hands of him. I'm the oldest in my family and when my mother die I help bring up my brothers and sisters. And I do all right 'cause they all turn out good, hard-workin' folks." Her voice thickened. "All except that James. Even then, even when that boy were a child, he always gettin' messed up in all kinds o' trouble. I told him he goin' to end up bad. He gonna end up a bum. I told him, and you know how I knew?" Her tone moved higher, the evangelist showing more clearly in her eyes. " 'Cause as a little boy he never opened his heart to God, he have no room for religious understandin'. He was always runnin' around the streets with a lotta other little bums and stealin' just about everything he can get his hands on. How could he grow up right leadin' that kind of life? A person that denies his soul to God is goin' to end up in hell and that sure enough where my brother James Harris is goin' to go."

". . . and now Deacon Brown will move out amongst you good, God-fearin' people and anything you can give will kindly . . ." The door had opened. Sullivan came in. The muffled oratory of a moment before now boomed through the parlor as Preacher Gregory moved among his congregation to get the collection.

Frank Sullivan received Pope's negative glance. He looked down at the woman, whose body was perched forward, her fingers kneading the wet crumpled handkerchief. A lousy waste of time, the black bitch, he said to himself, and looked up at his Negro partner. "If you're finished with Miss Harris, Bill," he said affably, "there's something I want to see over on Park Avenue." He turned and started toward the door, while Pope held still, looking at the woman, who had stiffened into a statue in the presence of the white man.

"If you do hear from him, Miss Harris," he said, "you can contact us at the local precinct." She answered him with a cold silence that turned him toward the waiting Sullivan.

"Mr. Detective." They were both at the door by then, and stopped and looked back at her. "If you come across my brother James will you do something for me?"

"Sure," Pope answered her.

"You tell him for me, 'Satan damn it, God save it.'"

Fire and brimstone leaped past them through the open door as the voice of the preacher came at them in imploring cries of "Repent, repent," and sorrow rose from the pews in answer: "Amen, amen." And the fat lady, her black face shining with sweat, stared with the eyes of a true believer.

Chapter 15

The siren was nudged on Lenox Avenue. It goaded an opening in the traffic and they turned left past Mount Morris Park with its sparse trees, their twisted branches reaching out as if trying to flee the frightening nightmare behind the rusted fence. They rolled past Madison Avenue, down a garbage-littered side street, past rows of dismal brownstones and tenements.

The tunnel began in the midtown labyrinth of Grand Central Terminal, running beneath the manicured shrubbery of Park Avenue and three miles north the tracks came out at the other end of Park Avenue. Out of the pit the commuter trains climbed the track over the iron and concrete girders, and the passengers, absorbed in their evening papers, or their drinks in the club cars, did not bother to look out the windows. What was there to see but the same ugly buildings with their grime-pitted windows pressed in along the tracks, the garbage, long overdue for pickup, piled overflowingly along the curbs, the abandoned cars and back yards and lots filled with debris. Then the trains started their long screech for the local 125th Street stop, showering sparks down on the closed secondhand stores and open bars beneath the elevated tracks.

Pope maneuvered the car around an iron girder and under the el. The light from the overhead street lamps that ran parallel to the tracks was lost in the grayness under the viaduct. A red-and-amber light revolved in the distance. The radio car, its doors open, stood empty, facing a dark blank wall that formed one end of the station. Pope eased to a stop behind it and doused the headlights. The whirling splashes of light atop the patrol car picked up two uniformed cops, whose cigarettes were hastily dropped and stomped out. Both men stiffened as Sullivan walked out of the slush of shadow past the patrol car.

"Oh, it's you, Frank." The larger one relaxed and his voice seemed sorry he had dropped his smoke.

"You got a DOA here?" Sullivan asked leaving out the salutations, his eyes going to the ground in front of the patrol car, searching the shadows for the inevitable blanket-covered body.

"Take it easy, Frank," the other cop greeted the detective. "This jig ain't going anyplace."

Bill Pope had emerged slowly, from the other side of the car. The cop had uttered the flippancy without remembering that the white detective was teamed with a black. He realized he had spoken too quickly as Sullivan's eyes moved past him to Bill Pope coming around the front of the patrol car. The cop turned and looked into Pope's stare. In the silence the patrolman's embarrassment turned into defensive anger. Fuck him, one could almost hear him think. His sallow face tightened as if daring Pope to do something about it. Pope accepted the challenge and took a step forward.

"What have you got, Molloy?" Frank said to the other white cop, his voice a quick pitch of warning to Pope to forget it.

"We got a lulu, Frank." Molloy had picked up Sullivan's cue and moved between his uniformed partner and

Pope. "It's really wild." He turned to his partner. "Show him, Pete."

For a moment the young white cop held his ground, then slowly, unwillingly he took his angry eyes off the Negro detective. But Bill Pope didn't move and the cop had to walk around him, making sure he didn't brush against Pope on his way to the driver's side of the patrol car. Then he leaned in and turned on the headlights.

The body was crucified, pressed against the wall. The head was pulled back, held in position by a rope looped tightly around the throat, then tied to one of the numerous spikes that protruded from the wall. It looked as if the body had been garroted, then strung up, but the grotesqueness did not stop there. It was suspended three feet from the ground and supported by a file-sharpened steel spike that ran through the back of the body, sticking out gruesomely above the stomach.

Murmurs rose around them and Sullivan turned quickly away as the headlights clarified the grisly form before them. He squinted out from under the el. He had not noticed the onlookers before. They had been standing in silence along both curbs of the street. Now, under the impact of the macabre sight, a ripple of noise grew stronger.

"Turn it off," Sullivan said sharply. The patrol-car lights went off but the flurry of voices could still be heard along the curb.

"They're not pushin' in close to this, Frank," Molloy said. "It's kinda weird. They stand there like they want to see, but they don't come under the tracks. Oh, a few kids came running over, but most of the older people stand around like they were at a funeral. I can't figure it."

"Gimme your flashlight, Jack," Sullivan said, and took it out of the cop's hand.

He didn't switch it on. His eyes were becoming accustomed to the darkness and the flashes of light rotating atop the patrol car outlined the brutalized form. He turned over an empty garbage can, pulled it next to the body and climbed on top.

"Check his pants; I'll get the coat," he said to Pope, who had moved up alongside.

When he turned the flashlight on he saw a horror movie in closeup. The arms were spread in unnatural slackness from the sides of the body and supported by some of the spikes that ran, like many ladders, to the top of the el structure. Sullivan pushed the flashlight in close, but kept the beam away from the bulging, unbelieving eyes. The lips were parted across the gaping mouth in a terrifying silent screech and adhesive strips still clung to the frayed mustache where they had been applied to muffle the screams. Blood from the cuts on face and scalp had started to cake in brown streaks across the ink-black face.

"Hey, you can't touch the body," the voice of the younger cop barked nastily behind them. "What are you two brains tryin' to pull? We're not lettin' nobody touch him until—"

"Shut your mouth," Sullivan snarled as his hand went inside the dead man's jacket and pulled out a wallet. He was about to jump down, then twisted back to the body. He held the flashlight straight down. In the dim light his hand moved to the crushed face and his fingers closed the eyes.

Sullivan held the flashlight while Pope went through the wallet, flipping the cards. He now held one card closer to the light. "Here it is, Frank," he said. "Henry Lamont Jackson, 561 West 146th Street." He looked up. "That's over past Amsterdam Avenue."

Sullivan waited for him to jot down the name and address, then switched off the light. Their faces were blurred in the murky grayness that filtered in under the el. The two uniformed cops stood watching curiously but they couldn't see the excitement beneath Bill Pope's apparent calm. The uniformed cop could have no idea that Henry Lamont Jackson in death had given a clue so solid Pope felt he could stand on it. Nor could the two cops peering at them see the respect he felt for Sullivan's gutter perceptions during a telephone conversation while Pope struggled in the storefront church against the blank black wall of a woman's hate and fanaticism.

"What's happening, Connolly?" Sullivan had asked the desk sergeant when he phoned the precinct, and

161

was filled in on the normal routine of a summer night in Harlem. A DOA, death suspicious—a ludicrous legal understatement until a medical examiner stamped it violent. A liquor store broken into on Saint Nicholas Avenue. A knifing outside the Convent of the Sacred Heart; the sisters called, alerted by the screams. And in their prayers they would remember the scream and pray for the dead as well as the living. A husband-and-wife scuffle in the Green Towers Apartments, that high-rise middle-income development with a façade of snobbery in the turbulent surrounding sea of want. Yeah, she used a broken bottle and slashed up his face. And Connolly had droned on in a bored monotone reciting his tally sheet of violence.

"You think there's a connection?" Pope queried, acting out a charade in front of the inquisitive patrolmen. It was obvious that they would check out the address, but it was Frank's play, his intuition. Pope fed him the line, knowing what the answer would be before he even spoke, letting his senior partner dictate the move that had already begun, letting his six months uptown as a third grade detective be subordinate to the hard white man's first grade status and five years in the ghetto; letting him lead the chase.

"I don't know, it could be." Sullivan shrugged, also underplaying, conscious of their audience. "What do you say we check it out for the hell of it, anyway?"

He looked back to the harpooned remains stuck brutally against the wall. A memory gnawing in the back of his mind suddenly crystallized and now he knew what it had reminded him of—an army checkpoint long ago on a rural road in an almost forgotten country. The bamboo house behind the guard point, where friends and relations had gathered—cheerful slanted eyes, white lace shirts and frilly dresses and no shoes. It was some kind of holiday, or maybe it was a wedding; he wasn't sure. But he remembered the men tying a pig to a tree and taking festive swigs from a bottle while they waited for the hog to calm itself. He had turned away after the first badly aimed sledgehammer blow had failed to knock the animal out. The front legs went out from under it, the head split open, the blood running down the pink skin and over the beady terrified eyes, and Sullivan

162

had turned away, revolted. He waited for the second blow, hearing the piercing squeals of pain, then the hammer fell again, bringing a sickening, almost human screech. And they had to strike a third time. Finally silence, and despite himself he looked. A pole, sharpened at one end, was held at the backside of the hog and then driven into its rear, suddenly reviving the animal into terrible shrillings of agony, and then it seemed to die again. Each sledgehammer blow riding the spit further into its innards would bring it to agonizing life, to scream again, and he had had enough, enough. The .45 came out of his holster, he slammed the slug into the chamber and walked into the middle of their holiday, stunning them into silence. They backed off, not sure of what he intended to do. The gun went to the head of the pig and they all began to speak excitedly. "No, Joe, no." He looked up into the face of an old man, the yellow skin so tight it looked as if it were ready to tear open. "No good, Joe." The old man shook his head frantically. "No good, no good." The gasp at his feet brought his eyes back down. What life remained expired in a terminal snort, the head flickering in a final quiver. Blood ran down its flesh, across the eyes, down the sides of the snout into the petrified open mouth.

Patrolman Molloy's voice brought him back to the present. "What's the big deal, Sully? Hey, Sully," Molloy said, his broad red face pushing in close.

Frank Sullivan turned away from the outlined body. "Were you two the first on the scene?" he asked.

"Yeah. A guy flags us down on the Avenue. He's kinda wild-eyed when he tells us there's somebody strung up under the tracks. We think right away we got a nice quiet suicide, maybe with a little more imagination than the average leaper. There's not many that take the out in the street. That takes a little showmanship. But after we see the body"—his head motioned to the wall—"I wasn't about to pull him off the hook. We got to wait around for the medical examiner. I'll let him take it down." Molloy paused and winked at Sullivan. "You know, he might have to make a report that the deceased didn't put himself up on that wall."

Sullivan ignored Molloy's sardonic gibe, but he knew

163

what he meant: he didn't want to get caught in a coroner's inquiry, court appearances and all the legal red tape a murder like this could entail.

"Any of the brass been here?" Sullivan asked casually, trying to hide his interest.

"Why should there be? DOAs don't bring out the gold badges." Far off a dim rumble was heard. "You know what we get up here, Frank, better than I do. Maybe five or six stiffs a week are part of the job." Molloy smiled. "It takes a big deal to pull them gold badges off their asses. They don't come to Siberia for something like this." The din in the distance grew louder. "In fact, I'm even surprised to see you two here." Molloy, hands on his hips, now had to raise his voice to be heard against the swelling crash of sound. "It takes something big for them to make an appearance like"—his eyes narrowed shrewdly in the wide florid face—"like"—and he had to shout the words to be heard above the thunderous roar—"like that shooting earlier tonight." Above their heads bedlam, then the screech of iron wheels locking against the rails and sliding like chalk against a hundred blackboards. Lights in the train window reflected off the vibrating third-floor windows of the tenements. The New Haven train made its 125th Street stop.

Frank Sullivan had no more questions to ask. He turned and walked past the patrol car to their own unmarked sedan. But Pope stood and looked at the young cop Molloy had called Pete. "Here," Pope said, holding the wallet out to him, "put it back." The cop glared at him, as if debating whether to take it, then hesitatingly his hand came up. "He won't hurt you." Pope's tone was sheeted in sarcasm. "He's just a dead black man," and he slapped the wallet into Pete's hand.

Frank was already behind the wheel and waited for his partner to get in before he turned the motor on. Molloy had followed him. He bent his broad frame and looked into the car as thought he wanted to pursue the idea sparked in him by the detectives' brisk search of the body and Sullivan's much too casual queries.

"You know, I helped scrape a lot of stiffs off the sidewalks up here," Molloy said, looking at both of them but talking to Sullivan. "I did the death watch on some real

164

weirdos, a couple maybe even crazier than this." His brow wrinkled in speculation and he shrugged. "I don't know, like there's something awful offbeat here. You know what I mean?"

The veteran cop caught Sullivan's interest. His hand moved away from the ignition. "Was there anybody acting suspiciously around the body when you pulled in, Jack?"

"No, not suspicious." He shook his head. "But that's it. That's the trouble, Sully. It's the way the crowd was actin' when we came in under the tracks. Somebody had a flashlight on the stiff and maybe there's fifty, sixty guys all talkin' real low to each other. Generally, when something like this happens, it's tough moving the crowd. Like they all want to stay in close and watch the whole procedure. But they all went back nice and easy without any coaxing." He jerked his head toward the cluster of watchers huddled along the curbs, now in subdued conversation. "It's like word is being passed around not to get too nosy. The crowd's gotten a little bigger but nobody's getting curious enough to come across the street. It's like something's telling them to stay away from this."

The detectives sat and watched Molloy's broad freckled face struggle to articulate what had started out to be routine. His was purely an objective view, that of a cop assigned to stand the death watch over another violent dispatch in Harlem. Just another one of the more than two hundred and fifty murders recorded in the uptown police ledger each year, murders that rarely made a line in the New York papers. Frank Sullivan was becoming impatient to leave, for he felt Molloy had no more to tell him. Then the cop said something that made him look at Pope to see if he had picked it up.

"The guy who flagged us down said the call came to a nearby gin mill." He pointed to a bar located at the corner. "The caller told them to take a look at what was under the tracks. I never heard of anybody wanting a body found before, did you?"

Bill Pope caught his partner's look, a signal exchanged. Then Sullivan turned the key in the ignition and peered up at Molloy. It was likely that much of his excessive interest was an excuse to break up a disagreeable duty.

He'd forget most of this with time. Maybe over a beer he might tell someone else, but there-after it would fade and be just another memory. The detective made a mental note that when this was over, he and Pope owed the big cop a drink to tell him how sharp his perception had been and what he had contributed. But he played it cool now. "I think you must have seen too many of them movie spy thrillers, Jack. You're letting your imagination run away with you." Molloy straightened up from the car and gazed down at the detectives.

"Yeah, yeah, maybe you're right," he said dryly.

And the look in his eyes made Frank Sullivan think that Molloy's story might just make it across the sergeant's desk at the end of this tour.

"Hey," the driver called out of a car that had pulled up on Bill Pope's side. The street lamp washed the car in light and the lettering on the door read. "THE DAILY NEWS—NEW YORK'S PICTURE NEWSPAPER." "What's with the crowd?" He leaned out of the window. "You guys got anything we can use?"

Blacks kill blacks, fuck it. Blacks kill cops, sells newspapers, Pope thought.

Sullivan deliberately turned on the low beams and backed the sedan slowly from behind the patrol car. In the grizzled darkness the revealing light turreted on top of the police car streaked past the wall.

"Huh?" They heard a surprised sound from the reporter. He then twisted the small spotlight that was on the side of his car and threw its beam against the wall.

It picked up an arm. He worked the handle and the jarring brightness pinned Henry Lamont Jackson in its terrible glare. The whistle came low, like the sound little boys make between their teeth. "Holy Christ," he said. "Hey," he yelled to Pope, sliding past, "hey, what's the bit? What's the story on this?"

Bill Pope raised his arm out of the window and pointed to the young white cop he had handed the wallet to. "Why don't you ask him? He's got a lot of mouth."

Chapter 16

The flashlight beam picked its way across the broken mailboxes. Some of the small doors were jimmied, others were torn away. The name was blurred across the smudged adhesive: 5B—always the top floor. The vestibule door of the tenement was open and they walked into the blackness. The flashlight in Sullivan's hand cut a slow bounding circle of white up the wooden steps, which creaked beneath their weight. They leaned cautiously into the wall in a slow ascent, neither man trusting the bannister, for more than one cop had taken a vicious header when rotted wood gave way in their hands. The smells of chitterlings and pork and urine filled the hall and the usual cans of garbage on the landings stood in an overflow of chicken bones and roaches. The cry of a baby was heard and the voice of a drunk called a woman a whore and she answered him, "You nigger mother fucker." Television and radio noises mixed with the sound of running water from a broken flush. Sullivan was familiar with the fetid smells and snarling frustration that filtered dejectedly through the impersonal walls of all the tenements he had walked through in his time, dense, mean, raw. Without hope or a chance for dignity.

The crippling, melancholy surroundings made his breath come like a sigh in the darkness, as he followed Pope up the stairs.

On the fifth-floor landing his foot stumbled against a garbage can. Casually he played the light on it. A rat rose up suddenly, its fat gray body, which had been wallowing in the filth, now tensed and reared back in a squealing snarl. The small, blood-red eyes in the pointed fur face recoiled in the light, the mouth flashed yellowed fangs. Sullivan's flesh crawled as he steadied for its spring. The rat wheeled and jumped, landing on his leg, clung for a frightening instant, then slipped down and across his shoes. He could hear it scurry along the hall and down the steps.

"Frank, here it is. Five B." Pope's words came from the other side of the hall.

Sullivan eased his breath out slowly and then turned, flashing the full beam on him. Pope was fixed in its round glow like an actor in a theatrical spotlight. There was no answer to his knock. He tried again, this time louder, more demandingly, so that there would be no mistake about its gruff authority. He looked at Frank and was about to rap again when light showed through a crevice at the bottom of the door. Feet shuffled across the floor inside. "Who is it?" a tired voice asked. "The police," came the reply. There was a pause. Finally they heard the familiar scrape of a police lock sliding from its notch in the floor. The lock on the door tumbled and the door cracked open. Concerned eyes squinted around its edge in a dark sleep-leadened face. Sullivan lowered the flashlight to the floor. She was silhouetted by the light behind her, hands high, ready to slam the door back into its locks.

"Mrs. Jackson?" Pope asked.

She stared at them for long seconds as though she hadn't heard him, and he had to ask her again, his tone taking on an official tone. "Are you Mrs. Henry Jackson?"

"Yes, I'm Mrs. Jackson," she answered slowly.

Pope was about to show the badge, then realized it wasn't necessary. "We'd like to speak to you."

"There's no trouble up here." Weariness was in the voice, but the dark eyes became circumspect as she peered past Pope at the white detective. "I didn't call no police."

"It's about your husband," Pope said.

Her hand moved around to the edge of the door and clung there for support. In the dim light her eyes seemed to blur as she stared at them, not sure what to say or do.

"We'd like to talk to you inside," Pope said.

Her face hung there for a moment more, then she opened the door, closed it behind them and led them down the short hall of a railroad flat and into the kitchen,

168

the soft slap of her slippers filling the hall. They had no warrant so there could be no search, but Sullivan instinctively looked about for anything abnormal. He flashed the light into the darkened room beyond. There were four children. The oldest turned restlessly on a cot; the other three, their slack bodies beaded in perspiration, slept on a bed pushed against a window, where a fan on the sill flipped the curtain and moved the summer heat around the humid room.

A shabby robe hung loosely about Mrs. Johnson's skinny frame, and her feet shuffled across a piece of torn linoleum as if trying to cover her impoverishment. Paint was peeling from the walls and a frayed cord hung from the chipped globe on the ceiling. But the curtains were clean and the kitchen had the heavy antiseptic smell of too much detergent.

She slumped down at the table. The thin somber face looked up at them, searching their silence. Then, as if she found the answer, her wan voice rose out of a pit of premonition. "Something has happened to him, hasn't it?"

Bill Pope could answer only by nodding his head.

For an instant her body seemed to sag, but her face gave no indication of emotion as she continued to look up at them.

"He's dead, isn't he?"

Pope nodded again. "Yes," he said, and stopped, waiting for an outcry of sorrow. But none came as she lowered her head to the faded tablecloth, on which stood a small vase of artificial flowers. She leaned down against her skinny arms, as if the weight of her thoughts were unendurable. Pope glanced at his partner, but Sullivan was peering stoically down at the bowed head.

Encouraged by her restraint, Pope went on. "This is a bad time to ask you questions, but your husband didn't die under natural causes. The circumstances of his death . . ." He stopped, disliking the sound of his own voice. "I'm sorry, but it's necessary we ask a few questions."

No grieving, no sad sobs, just the dreadful silence. And to Pope, the death of Henry Jackson had suddenly become the detestable job of telling a woman she was a widow.

"Are you all right, Mrs. Jackson?" he asked. There was no answer and he paused, taking a breath like someone about to plunge into cold water, wishing that it was over and done with. "What we'd like to know is if your husband had any dealings with a man called James Harris. It is believed that Harris had recently been released from prison and he could have been in contact with your husband."

Slowly she raised her head, the dark pinched in desolation, and tears ran down her cheeks. "How did he die?" she asked. The grieving query reverberated off the washed-down walls and echoed corrosively in the poverty-smelling rooms. And the detectives knew they had blindly run into a depth of sorrow from which there was nothing to do but retreat, retreat, retreat. But leave her with a shred of kindness.

"He was hit by a car, a hit-and-run," Frank Sullivan said.

Her hand brushed away a tear as she strove for control in front of these strangers. "He weren't living home with us," she murmured, and lowered her eyes, embarrassed by what she was about to say. "I haven't seen him in over a month. I don't know where he was stayin'. I hear talk he took a furnished room someplace, but I don't know where. I don't know." She shrugged hopelessly and looked up at Sullivan. "But if you find out his address I'd like to know. I'd be grateful so I can go over there and get what little belongings he had."

She had gotten to Sullivan long before her words did. Her sorrow had reached gropingly toward him like a supplicating hand. Maybe she had seen commiseration in the blue eyes, maybe to another sufferer he wore his own loss like a black armband of grief.

"He were always talkin' about doin' things. He wanted to be somebody," she said quietly. "I guess he felt the children and me held him down. Me, I don't know. Maybe he were right. He'd go on about that sometimes when he had too much to drink, tellin' how he coulda done this and that if he didn't have to care about us. But I loved him and so did the kids. And when he left us this time I know he come back to us like he always do. But I didn't think it would be like this." A spasm shook

170

her and she sobbed, her mouth tight over her mournful memories.

Sullivan's intuition still told him he was right. He felt they now had the first jagged piece of the sordid puzzle, but without names to follow up and add substance to a hunch, it had no immediate use. And now it was dying against this blank wall of a widow's lament. His tongue was dry. He had to lick his lips to speak.

"You'll be able to claim his body at the city morgue," he said, and watched her lower her eyes, her fingers tracing an aimless design on the worn tablecloth. "The coroner's office will most likely want you to identify him. They'll get in touch with you." He knew the words were calloused and cold, but there was nothing else he could think of that could comfort this tragic figure. He had had enough, and turned to the door, away from the heavy smell of cleanser fighting its losing battle against the roaches now beginning to crawl out from under the sink and the stink coming through the open windows from the filth and rubble that rose from the decaying yards.

"I—I mean we"—her voice followed down the hall after him, touching him like a cripple's crutch, making him look back at the weary face straining for words difficult to express—"we never do get married legal-like; we always had an understandin' about that, like it wasn't goin' to make me love him any more than I do." She halted, struggling with her embarrassment, her dark eyes searching his. "Will there be any fuss when I go downtown? You know, like they goin' to ask for some kind of proof Henry and me were married?"

"No, it'll be all right," Frank answered. "They won't question you."

"Mama, Mama!" The cry in the darkened adjoining room came frightened from the edge of a dream. "Mama, you out there?" A frantic, sleepy voice cried for reassurance.

"You go to sleep, Mama's here." Soothingly she answered the call for protection. Then her thin arms went about her stomach, trying to hold herself together for a moment longer, and her head lowered to the table.

They shut the door gently and stood outside in the darkness hearing the halting cry; then quietly, as if embarrassed that they were listening, they started down the steps.

Chapter 17

A warring party of young hoods, black dew rags tied about their straightened hair like arrogant shields of self-esteem, walked the hot night looking for sport, but the sentinel's hand came up quickly in warning and they became ominously silent. They had spotted an enemy. Lowering their heads, they walked past, trying to hold on to their swaggering cool. But it was sham. They turned thankfully at the corner and disappeared. The laughter and talk of the people sitting on stoops, drinking beer out of cans against the late summer heat, had subdued into a hush of Harlem hip. Two lovers moved apprehensively out of the shadows of a building, the boy looking nervously over his shoulder; and he banged into a strung-out junkie, almost knocking him against the nondescript sedan with the big antenna. When the junkie looked up, his habit was down on him, and alarm spread across the cocoa-skinned face as he blinked at the men who stared at him through the front window of the car. He stood still, unable to move, his fingers scratching the wide, ever-itchy nostrils, then he turned awkwardly and stumbled away.

The detectives were still wrapped in sullenness, remembering the grieving woman and a lead that had led nowhere. A police dispatcher's scratchy voice could be heard from the dashboard radio. But they didn't notice it, their ears attuned only to their squeal number; the rest meant nothing.

Bill Pope took a long pull on a cigarette and out of the corner of his eye looked at his partner. Sullivan's reddish face was shadowed by his hat brim, but the street lamp threw enough light into the car to illuminate the

172

irritated tic at the edge of the jawline and the brooding, deep-set eyes. Pope knew why the street gang cooled it when they passed, why the boy with the girl was so concerned and what made the addict get so frightened. Sullivan had the kind of face the Negroes viewed with trepidation. They had seen it before over Southern badges marked "Deputy" or "Sheriff" or "Chief," or over Northern numbers in silver pinned on blue shirts and coats. Pope flipped the butt into the street, annoyed with himself for letting his thoughts take off in such a flight. This was no up-North Mr. Charlie; this was a man whom he'd seen only a few minutes ago touched by kindness. After all, wasn't he The Man, too? Harlem was looking at him as much as they were looking at Sullivan and maybe with more hate. For *he* stared back at them from a black skin.

People passed in singles and couples, their eyes glancing furtively toward the car, sharp to the law sitting ominously quiet on scabrous side streets. "Watch your step, man, watch out. They're on a stakeout. They're bustin' everybody who looks suspicious tonight. Or maybe—yeah, yeah, that could be it—they just waitin' for a pay-off. You know what I mean, man. Like business as usual. Like they're bagmen for the precinct. It no matter though; you still watch out."

Sullivan had watched the lanky youth pressing his body against the girl, moving under the shadow of a stoop in a cadence oblivious to the surroundings. Then the boy, somehow sensing they were being watched, looked up and dragged the surprised girl by the hand away from threatening eyes. Through the windshield, the addict with his gaping mouth and bulging eyes appeared to him like something flushed from beneath the rocks, floundering, death creasing the brown face, then as quickly being washed from view by a wave of panic.

The bells of Our Lady of Lourdes, a couple of blocks away, rang through discordant streets, and its dirgelike tolling sounded so strangely similar to the retreat bells of the abbey that the miserable street on which they were parked seemed to disappear. Frank Sullivan could visualize the gentle countryside, and a monastery almost isolated from the world. . . . He had tried to drown the

173

voices with whiskey, but out of the hollows of empty bottles he heard their laughter, their faces vibrant with life, and then the frightened aftermath: a stalled truck, a car skidding and slamming metal into metal, and then deadly silence. The scene would come at him drunk or sober, repeating its dreadful sequence over and over. At last it drove him to his knees in a retreat among the cloistered. He knelt with other troubled outsiders, hunching forward with clasped hands across wooden pews and praying to a nailed Christ stretched and bleeding above the altar. He listened to the monks talk of afflicted life and the salvaging hereafter. He sought their counsel and submerged himself in meditation, prayer and tranquillity. Then slowly, slowly, the remorse began to drain away, the frequency of seeing their faces, of hearing their voices and tasting the salt of his grief gave way to a melancholy he could endure and the knowledge that a lifetime on his knees could never completely erase the guilt and that time and activity were the best cure of all. But his working world was called Harlem. He had approached his return to active duty with misgivings, his controlled emotions in doubt. It was too easy in this repellent boxed-in ghetto to flail out, to indict others and cover it with neurotic rationalization. Control, control. Play it by ear.

Now he could feel the bad taste in his mouth from too many cigarettes and the dryness that too much whiskey had put there. His mind ran back up the cancerous steps, past the locked door and into the room where the woman sat with bowed head. It all seemed a waste: the retreat, the prayers, the acceptance of his grief. It was as if he had deceived himself with elaborate lies. If a black woman who meant nothing to him was capable of ripping away that easily the careful veneer he had built around himself, he knew it was going to take a long and painful time before he could really come back.

He could feel the paradoxical anger as he watched the people passing along the sidewalk, some like primed peacocks but most with the head-down shuffle of struggles long given up. He thought of their exploiters, the dope dealers making addicts, numbers runners and strong-arm guys who worked their bags on human frailty. And Doc

Johnson, the biggest black bastard of them all, sitting high on top of the heap of Harlem punks thinking he couldn't be reached because of connections and money. Johnson . . . He rolled the name around in his mind. Johnson. Johns— His churn of frustration was suddenly arrested by an exciting idea, a haphazard whim. It was balls and crazy and was just the thing that might be expected of him. But under the circumstances, yeah, it could work. He could feel a fever sweep through him as if his body accepted the risk before his mind did. Yeah, just the right amount of pressure properly applied could do it. But it has to be done right now, now, now.

He was about to turn to Pope to voice his speculations when cold reason washed over him. Bill Pope might not want to take such a gamble, for to lose could be hazardous to his ambition, maybe even end his career in the Department before it ever really began. He knew his partner liked the plain clothes of a third grade rank and the times were right for the Bill Popes. The Negro with a college education could look past promotion to first grade detective, past even the gold and silver bars to the rarefied air of an inspector's world. He knew Pope had the brain and ambition that could capitalize on the new interest New York's liberal politicians had in such men as he. Now more than ever they needed to showcase ebony talent to the city's million blacks.

Sullivan was aware of the talk that was whispered behind his back, of his reputation for seeking out trouble. But he also was known for making the big arrest, the kind that could mean immediate recognition, the kind that made third grade plain-clothesmen into first grade detectives overnight. Now he intended to work this on his partner. He was going to use him, he had to, for to go it alone would be to court the danger of political reprisal. What he needed was a strong witness to what he intended to do, and if it turned bad, someone with enough guts to back up his play.

A kid not more than seven, wearing torn sneakers and shorts, halted in his mad dash of night play. Holding his cap pistol straight down from his body, he looked into the squad car. He stood there, brows knitting, as if debating whether to shoot the bad guys. Then he turned and ran off into a garbage-littered lot near the end of the block.

Frank stuck a cigarette in his mouth, his hand going around the match. He took a long drag before he looked at Pope. "Of all the guys in the precinct working on this case, I would say we have the hottest lead so far. But I don't think we have a chance of catching up to whoever done it." His voice gave no indication of what he was driving at. He looked away. "Oh, we might see them but I think we'd have to take a ride down to Bellevue's morgue to get a real close look. Because if they're found, they're strictly going to be DOAs."

Bill Pope sat quietly, weighing Frank's pessimism. "I don't know," he answered finally. "We worked the leads to where we're inclined to believe this Jackson's part of it. Maybe somebody else in the squad is working from a fresh angle and could be breathing down Harris's neck right now. That is if it's him. Look, somebody could get lucky. Maybe it could even be us. Who knows?"

Frank blew out a stream of smoke indifferently. It hung for a moment about their heads, then worked its way out of the car windows. "I think we're going to have to make our own luck if we want to turn up any action on this. We got to start throwin' our weight around, and I don't mean against some punk stoolie."

Pope was bothered. He knew obscurity was not Sullivan's style and he respected him for it. "If you have something, Frank, let's hear it." He stuck a needle in his tone and watched it pull the white face around.

"I got a hunch," Frank said, and the pretense of casualness fell away. "I realize that better than ninety percent of hunches are horseshit, but I know who I can book this one with. How do you feel about playing long shots?"

"You should know me by now, Frank. I don't go by form."

"You may very well this time, because we'd be running against an odds-on chasing. Johnson can buy a hundred informers for every one a guy in the squad can scare up. He's got a working capital that has bought a lot of people, even some we work with." Sullivan did not sound bitter; this was stated as fact. But what he didn't say was implied: that black responded to black, and in particular that a success symbol as outstanding as Doc Johnson was far more formidable to the people of Harlem than the police, white or black.

Pope had been witness to a few of Frank Sullivan's hunches' working out in the past. But his gnawing doubt persisted. This was far too big to be followed up on only a whim. Too many important people in the Department were watching, and Frank had given him no substance; for they had no actual clues to connect with Doc Johnson.

Pope spoke quietly. "Frank, I heard a lot of things about that man and one of them is that he's no fool. I've got to presume you know what you're doing, because if we start to suggest that he committed a retaliatory murder we wouldn't have a legal leg to stand on if he hollers for a lawyer."

Sullivan ground out the cigarette in the dashboard tray. Pope's caution bothered him. But he was determined to give it another try, for by now he felt it was too good an idea to let die from cautious talk. "Bill, I'm going to try something that was never pulled on him before. I guess you could call it reverse extortion—and maybe I won't be able to back up everything I'm going to tell him. But I can tell you this: I'm about the last person he wants to see walk in on him, because he can't afford a boatrocker who's trying to throw him to the sharks. Not tonight he can't. I'm telling you, Bill, the more I think about this the better I smell a deal. And if it works it could be one of the best collars we could ever hope to make. It's the type of thing that pulls publicity. A bright guy like you, just starting out, he sure could use it as a steppingstone."

Pope had always guarded against revealing any personal goals, for it was too easy for a man to be tagged by his failures; the precinct and the Department were loaded with those who had. Until now he'd thought this white man knew nothing of his aspirations. But here was Sullivan openly, bluntly working on his ambitions, digging into what Pope had thought were hopes buried deep in the privacy of his own mind. He had underestimated his partner; had he been overestimating himself? He was annoyed.

The street had become oddly quiet. A few stoops down, the beer drinkers had drifted off to a more congenial atmosphere, away from a couple of intent detectives staring moodily out of a squad car.

"Before you say anything, Bill," Sullivan said, as if measuring the words, "I want you to know I detest the black son of a bitch. But I'm not using it as an excuse to pay off an old debt. Because there could be a loser's side to this gamble, far beyond just no deal. I already got some scars from his string pulling, so I'll be straight with you. If this thing turns bad and if he wants to, he could hurt us. And you, being new, can be hurt a hell of a lot more than me. There are a couple of gold shields down in Centre Street that I think I can hide behind until Johnson stops throwing his political bombs around. But you could end up a casualty."

Pope realized his courage was being tested by this blunt, single-minded man, over an idea that at very best was a long shot. It sounded as if he was being given a choice, but there was no choice. He resented being forced into an awkward position, with no out, for no matter how he answered there would be a transformation in their relationship. In fact, Sullivan's impatient probing had already changed it.

Pope was silent too long and Sullivan felt let down. He tried to keep the disappointment out of his voice. "It's too wild. Yeah." His hand went around the steering wheel as if he was about to start the car. "Yeah, it could be too big a gamble. Like I said, the most sensible thing to do is forget it."

"You're full of surprises, Frank," Bill Pope said evenly. "I could sit here and give you a half dozen more reasons why we shouldn't take Johnson on. But I don't think you'd want to hear any of them. I thought I had you figured out at last, but you keep on slipping out of the mold. I guess I could give myself a couple of easy clichés why you want to buck the odds, but I don't think they'd cover you on this." He paused and seemed to sigh. "Okay, Frank," he said quietly, "you want it this way, we'll see Johnson. I'll back up your play."

If he had known of the hate that simmered in his partner, of the retaliation that Sullivan had been sub-

178

consciously preparing for and was still trying to conceal from himself by lying now about the merits of longshots and gambling, Bill would have held his silence, would have let him drive off in the opposite direction from Doc Johnson, and would have let this white think whatever thoughts he wanted to about his black partner.

Chapter 18

In the blackness the shrill laughter echoed down and his head twisted frantically in the darkness for an escape. He covered his ears, but the hideous squeals went on, reverberating and tearing at his senses. Suddenly a grisly light materialized out of the darkness. The laughter ceased. He could see a dingy figure stumble toward him from far back. The rough black face, brutal and violent in its drunkenness, lurched to a stop. It was then that he recognized the craggy head. But the eyes were different, strange and sad, as though they didn't belong to this man in a rage, raising his arm in fury. "No," he whimpered, "no, Pop. It's me, Jamesy. It's me, it's me." And he reached up, tenderly grasping for the elusive distress in the broken face that at last he understood. But as suddenly as it appeared, the screen darkened and he twisted and turned in the blackness. "Where are you, Pop? Where are you?" But all he could hear were the muffled cries of children. Pitiable, tear-stained cries. The sounds were behind him now and he whirled around and saw them weeping in the front row of wooden chairs. They sat mourning the frail body encased in a casket that was no more than a wooden box. A single bouquet of flowers was at its feet and the preacher mumbled the eulogy to a handful of blacks. An older sister held the youngster in her lap and a distressed little boy at the end looked familiar. He walked past them and stared down into the box, down at the cheap dress covering the haggard remains, the face powdered like a clown's. Compulsively he bent down, his lips seeking the dead. Then a hollow knock and as he looked up he was in a kitchen with children crowded about a table. The knock again and the oldest sister rose nervously, her finger motioning across her mouth for silence and remembered behavior before she would open the door. And the white man with his black leather book walked around the winter-cold rooms taking his inventory, asking his questions and making his check marks. He scowled at the demolished drunk lying in a stupor. The oldest child's eyes stared shamefully at the floor while the children she had cautioned peered wide-eyed from the other room. Their shame and impoverishment was being exposed by the man from Welfare. Incensed, he shouted, "Get out. Get out." And he rushed at the man, but nobody heard him, nobody knew he was there. The crash of laughter returned, tumbling him back into his pit of darkness. But he could still hear knocking, pausing, then coming on again. He opened his eyes, still caught on a periphery of dreams, his body beaded in sweat, his mouth dry.

Then he heard it again, this time not so blatant, its restraint sending shivers of apprehension up from his bowels. He rolled silently off the bed, stood in the darkness, the pounding of his heart filling his ears. His hand groped back to the bed and found the gun. His finger flicked off the safety. The click, in his mind far too loud, rebounded off the walls. In his stocking feet he crossed the floor into the kitchen, but the break of worn wood betrayed his movement, freezing him. He held his breath. The gun, clammy and slippery in his hands, rose and pointed at the door; his finger tightened about the trigger.

"Jim," he heard the imploring voice through the door. "Jim, open up. It's me, Ivy."

His body went slack and he stood tasting the bile of his fear. Then he took a deep breath and unbolted the door. She held back in the darkened hall as if afraid to step into the room, afraid to confront him. The faint light sneaking in through the window behind him glimmered on the hard, metallic submachine gun in his hand.

"Oh, my God, Jim!" Her voice was a throb that pulled her into the room, her arms extending toward him. But he brushed past her, shut and rebolted the door.

She stood there, afraid to speak, intently watching him

turn on a low-wattage lamp that hung on the wall above the table, which made his shadow loom against the opposite wall. Pushing the safety back on the gun, he placed it on the table next to the bag of money. She stared for long seconds at the bulky duffel, but for her it did not have the reality of the gun; the bag was too full, too fat to contain anything of value. And if it weren't for the greenish bills showing through, it could have been a bag of dirty laundry.

"The police were over to the club to see me," she whispered, and saw the muscles tighten through his sweat-stained T-shirt. "It's okay, honey. It's all right. Nobody knows I'm here. They were two plainclothesmen. I don't know how they connected us, but it didn't seem they had much to go on, and I—" She stopped, her voice breaking into a sob. She remained silent until she had control of herself. "I'm sure I threw them off. I don't think they'll come back to question me, at least not for a while anyway. And then it won't matter." He turned and looked at her impassively. "When the detectives told me what had happened, I wanted to run. I wanted to run up here and prove them wrong because I never thought you'd go through with it." She shook her head as though searching for the words that would clarify her disbelief. "I—I never knew how serious you really were. I thought all this thinkin' and plannin' was just wild talk, somethin' you would let go after you seen how crazy it all was. I never took it like it was. . . ."

He moved away from her, walked to the window. His hand pulled back the edge of the shade as he leaned against the frame and stared out to the tenements on the next street.

"We didn't need it, Jim. We coulda made out okay." In the humid heat, the discord in the courtyards filtered up. "You said you were through with it all, the rackets, the hustle. You told me that, and now this terrible thing." The cadence of late tenement flowed across to him from the other buildings. "Why, Jim? Why did you go through with it when you knew it was insane?"

He turned away from the depressing sights and sounds and smells. "Insane," he said, examining the word for honesty. "Yeah, maybe you're right. Maybe I am a

181

crazy man grabbin' for somethin' that wouldn't cross a normal cat's mind, somethin' so far up in the sky that for the last few weeks I could barely sleep or eat for thinkin' about it. Thinkin' that I lose my cool, make one little slip, I'm gonna be a dead man. But I still went for it 'cause I could taste it. I gambled it all—you, me, the future—on one big chance, and now you talk like I lost. I won, Ivy"—his hand motioned to the money—"and so did you, baby. It's all gonna turn around for us now. You'll see. Everything's gonna be fine."

"How good can it be when I see you like you were a few minutes ago," she said, "standin' there with that gun in your hand and your insides all flarin' up and it all showin' in your face? You talk about a future, but the cops they seem to think you done it, and the people you took the money off of, they ain't just goin' to forget it. Do we build a normal existence on that kinda worry? You tell me, Jim: how far we goin' to run on top of dead men?"

"What the hell you want, Ivy?" he asked embitteredly, his voice rising. "You sound like you want me to give up. Is that what you want? That I should turn myself in?"

"I just want you to save yourself, honey." Her tone grew mollifying. "This thing is—it's too big for me. I don't know what to think or even say to you." Her voice trailed off. She averted her eyes and sat down despondently at the table, rummaging through her plastic handbag. He watched her nervous hands struggle to light a cigarette.

"Ivy." She looked up at him. "You sound like ninety-nine percent of all the blacks I ever knew when they come on something big. It's the same cry: Man, man, I can't make it." His mouth twisted with disgust. "They been niggers so goddamn long they think black. I just did it all, made the kind of grand slam score any thief in the world would be proud of, and you come runnin' scared in here tellin' me I don't have much of a chance to make it all the way. I don't need you to tell me that and I don't need no sermon on what'll happen to me if I'm caught." Perspiration clung to her upper lip as she took a long drag. "I expected more, a lot more than that from you, Ivy. I always think you a step and a half ahead

182

of the pack and now you come on like some black bitch cow, too shocked to dig what's goin' on. Well, baby, you knew what I was up to right along. 'Cause I didn't fill you in minute by minute don't make you clean, so don't you get holy on me now."

The abrasive sounds of tenement seemed to suspend into unusual quietness as if everything ceased, waiting for her answer to this angry man standing before her.

"Yes," she whispered to him, "yes, I'm real shocked." There were tears in her eyes. "Not because you stole, that don't bother me. I been seein' people steal my whole damn life. The only difference between you and them is that you did it big. Maybe I should give you credit the way you went out and took it. But that's just the thing that scares me. I'd've bet my life that the Jim Harris I knew wasn't no guy to kill the way I hear you did. I guess I just don't really know what make you go inside. I thought I did, but now you plain frighten me. The change it's been too quick and I just don't understand it."

Her disconsolate indictment of his violence melted his anger. He wanted to go to her, to put his arms tenderly about the slim body so she wouldn't slip further away from him, to continue to soothe her with lies about how nothing had changed. "I didn't want to hurt no one, Ivy. You gotta believe that." He had to make her understand, see it through his eyes, feel it as he remembered. "I planned it, I thought, where I could get at them with surprise. Be in and out of there without firin' a shot. You know what I mean, quick-like, and no cops in it. That the last thing I wanted. Like I told you before, I didn't lose my nerve? Well, I did. I know that now, yeah, because I should been able to handle it better up there. But that room was too hot. I felt like I was chokin'. I . . ." He seemed to leave her, his eyes moving above her head, seeing it all happen once again. He continued to talk, but so soft that she had to lean toward him. "It was the money, Ivy. It was my pot of gold layin' out in fives and tens and twenties, all just piled there just waitin' for me. More than one year plannin' and the minute I walk in that room sure God I knew it was mine and they have to kill me for it. I was thinkin' about this thing so long, figurin' every angle, everything except what happened.

And when it come at me I couldn't handle it because I was lookin' at all that money, only this time it was for real. And then somebody decided to stop me." His eyes closed against the playback that was so vivid in his mind. He swayed there before her, hearing again the sounds of the dying and seeing again the blurred, startled faces in the blue uniforms just before they fell.

"If only I believed you when you told me," she whispered. "I don't know how, but I'd have stopped you from goin' through with it. I would've showed you we didn't need a lot of money for us to make a life together." Her tawny face was sad for the dreams of her tomorrows. "Even if you stayed workin' for Doc Johnson with the worry of you bein' picked up by the law and doin' more time, I could've lived with that because it still would be better than what we got us."

"Ivy, when I got busted and done that year I laid awake nights doin' a lot of thinkin'. You know what I mean: like I thought about you and me and where we headin'; for the first time in my life I seen myself and it was no good because what I seen was nothin' but small-time nigger muscle and I knew I wouldn't be anything more than a scuffler when I get out, no matter how I hustled. Doc Johnson could pick my type off of any corner any night. I was holdin' on to the real low rung of a ladder, and now with a rap against me I wasn't even sure of stayin' there. I was the kind of cat the cops pick up and work over." His voice was so sharply bitter that it was as if he were cutting himself open for her to see the flaws inside. "When you come over to visit me that time and like I told you I was through with it, that there wouldn't be no more, I meant it, every word. But I wasn't quittin' to be no porter, cleanin' up after some goddamn white man; not this boy."

Slowly he took a step toward her. "I hear somebody say once, 'Anything you ain't never had you never miss.' Ivy, that is one damn lie. I wanted a lotta things I never had and I was goin' for them in one big grab. It was either that or die tryin'. And I did it, baby, I did it. I made it work. And now I'm quittin', but on my own terms."

The sounds of tenement now started to pick at their

184

privacy: the muffled, wanting cry of a baby, and some-where across the yards canned laughter from a TV set.

"Yeah, you're one smart man, Jim, but I don't have to tell you that. You proved it tonight, and a few other things." She shook her head sadly, slowly. "No, you got a lot more to offer than bein' a porter. If you put your mind to it you could've done so many things: you'd've latched on to the right job. It was all just a matter of time. Sooner or la—"

"Like what, huh?" His voice was a harsh grating sound that barreled frustratingly up from deep within his chest. "Doin' what? Like workin' in a car wash, or maybe de-liverin' coffee for a downtown restaurant to one of them big office buildings?" He raised his arms as he took a step further into the light. "Look at me, Ivy. Just look at me. A thirty-four-year-old nigger with no schoolin', no trade, and an ex-convict. Who the hell would want me for anythin' but swingin' a pick? Get out of your white-woman dream world, baby. It's about time you grew up, because your life was never goin' ta change by me goin' straight. It would be one shit job after another and you'd still be workin' in that club, still bein' propositioned every night and, baby, when we get up tight with money, and that would be like from the start, I'm gonna tell you to bed down with some of them cats because I'm goin' to have you out whorin'.'"

He turned from her and began to pace the shadowed kitchen. "Or maybe I'd start dealin' drugs on some street corner. Yeah, it would be either that or me back with a gun lookin' for a small quick buck 'cause I'd be tryin' to hold on to some kinda manhood." He moved about almost silently in his stocking feet like an irritated caged animal. "And where we goin' ta live? Tell me that, huh?" His hand swept about the room. "In some stinkin' trap like this? Take a real deep breath sometimes, baby, 'cause I don't think you ever have. And come winter you goin' ta be pushin' rags around the windows and under the door to keep from freezin'. Yeah, I done a lot o' thinkin' when they bust me for that year. I turned it over, tried to see it from your side, rememberin' all the crap you used to tell me. But no matter how hard I looked, I couldn't see us goin' no higher than the gutter." He moved into

185

the light. "In six months we'd be at each other's throats, in a year we'd be through. And that was just about the last thing I wanted to happen." His hand reached out tenderly to her face and his fingers moved gently across the slender hollows and down along the delicate firmness of the jaw.

The weeks and days and hours of anxious preparation and then the unstrung climactic strike that left him with memories he could not erase now were too heavy a burden to carry alone. The armor he had encased himself into melted from the heat of tears burning in his eyes. Suddenly all the strain, all the terrible guilt caved him to his knees. "Ivy, Ivy honey, I'm scared." He could taste his tears and his hands grasped her waist.

She sat there staring down at his head burrowed into her lap, not quite believing the transformation, for there had never been anything in the past to indicate that this tough-minded man would ever expose his frailties or break down. All her thoughts about what had happened and her fear of the immediate dangers that stalked them disappeared. Maternally her arms went about him, pressing him closer to her. At that moment there were no bad dreams; no sitting alone at the table facing the door with a gun in his lap, his insides jaggedly turning at every sound, his eyes, heavy with fatigue, watching the roaches move across the table as rats scurried in the sink, gnawing at the crusts of food on the unwashed dishes. Exhaustion filled him, his head dipping toward sleep and fitful dreams.

Tears ran down her face and her arms stayed protectively about him. In the doleful light they clung to each other. She lived in three rooms in a middle-class building just off Riverside Drive. It had a doorman and an air of respectability and it was worth the high rent that she could barely meet each month. She'd been late that day and she had dressed hurriedly and come straight to the club and her job: flashing her legs at black rubes who would pony up a dollar and a quarter a shot for watered-down whiskey; tight dresses and suggestive talk; then fighting off the squares who thought she was available.

"The men want to speak to you, baby," the manager

had said. "You got a little evil bag goin' on the side, honey?" He smiled, but she could see his annoyance at having the law sitting out front. She was sure as she approached, watching the young Negro detective look her over, that it had happened. It was not a premonition or some kind of psychic knowledge. Hadn't she heard the story often enough? All the twisted talk: Jim had picked the two that were going to help him and he was setting up one to take the fall. Jimmy Harris's Sky Pie Plan. It was just something to build himself up with, and that was all right, because it would pass, because nobody would . . . She felt her legs go weak as the white detective turned to look at her. He stared and she felt certain he was in no hurry to go anyplace, but was there just to tell her her Jim was dead. How she made it to the stool she didn't know. Hiding behind the slow act of lighting a cigarette, afraid her fear would show, then elated: "He's alive, he's alive," the words almost bursting out in thankfulness. She had to go to him. Maybe he's hurt. Maybe he's . . . But not now. Cool it. Wait. Wait.

And she bogused a smile, listening to the big dude customer at the bar until her nerve ends were jagged from being chipped away by the movements of the clock. Finally the anxiety was too much and she left. Eddie the manager disgruntled by her sudden sickness. Walking against the traffic, afraid of being followed, she watched the street for the fuzz while her thoughts raced ahead to her Jimbo, knowing her hopes had been kicked in the stomach. Hopes put together from his words through wire mesh in the Rikers Island prison. "No more, baby. From now on things are goin' to be different. We're goin' to make it. You'll see." She banked his optimism, putting it toward expectations of a new life, in which their two legitimate salaries would combine to pull them out of the swill and satisfy her passion for respectability, move them into the middle-income life of the newly emerging Negro. But his release had buried her dreams under an avalanche of plot. He told of his plans and she waited patiently for him to awaken to reality, never really believing he would dare go through with it.

At the corner she had cased the street, trying to assess the parked cars hugging the curb for the one or two that

187

might be on a stakeout. "Hey, mama, you lookin' for a good time?" a big teen-ager had said, laughing, and he gestured with the forefinger of his right hand, which brought dirty laughter from other boys standing with him outside a candy store. To Ivy the street was nothing. Radios blared from passing cars, but the music was like a dirge without beat. The people moved lethargically in the summer heat, oblivious and lost in thought. Cautiously she walked a block past the tenement, stopped for another look around, and then came back. As she had climbed upstairs, her tears turned the steps into muddled pools, and she knocked. . . .

He jerked in her arms and cocked his head warningly toward the door, letting go of her waist and standing up. His body tensed forebodingly as he listened to the sounds of footsteps climbing closer. Then a door closed on the floor below. Commonplace sounds had turned into threats. Sounds he had never even noticed now battered at his nerves, shouting their nonexistent dangers.

He was only an arm's length away, but he appeared distant and distorted. Ivy knew his moment of dependence had passed. He was again the vigilant, frightened man she had seen earlier in the darkened room ready to use the ugly gun.

"It's okay, honey. It's all right," she whispered, knowing the reassuring words were falsehoods she didn't believe herself. "I guess maybe I helped shape what happened tonight. With all my real fancy talk about a bright new future, you went out and did somethin' about it. I guess I was cheerin' you on all the time, Jimmy, and didn't know it until now. And now that it's here, I—"

"Well, you still hold on to that big hope of yours, Ivy," he said gently. "I think we goin' to need some of it, 'cause things have been happenin' that make some of my figurin' dead. Logart's been here and tells me Henry's hittin' the sauce. He's startin' to shoot his mouth off."

"Ain't that what you wanted him to do?" Her brow furrowed. "You said you wanted him to cover you with a lot of drinkin' and talk. Didn't you tell me that, didn't you?"

"Yeah, I did. But he's bustin' up the scheme. I had him thought out right but he's comin' on too soon. I can't take the chance now of sittin' it out here like I wanted. That's why I'm dividin' tomorrow. I'm givin' Logart his cut in the mornin' and then you and me are goin' to run for it, but quick, baby."

He saw it in her face, a moment of indecisiveness in which her eyes searched his curiously. "What's the matter, Ivy?"

"What would've happened if I didn't come up here tonight? There would be no way of me knowin' you changed your plans. It would've been a bad time for me, Jim, because I would've had you dead someplace. Weren't there no thoughts of how I would feel not knowin' what happened to you or where you were?"

He shook his head slowly, admonishingly, at her, then showed the edge of a smile. "Don't you fret, girl, I was goin' to knock on your door in the mornin' with a bag over my shoulder like some big black Santa Claus and you would've been dressed and out of there in about three minutes and movin' with me." She started to speak but he motioned her to listen. "No, baby, it ain't that tight yet. A lot of things are still like I told you. That big suitcase I stashed at your place, you just bring it here tomorrow mornin' at eight-thirty. And no packin', Ivy. We leave with the clothes on our backs. What we need we can buy, 'cause I want plenty of room for—"

"Jimmy," she said softly, "I want you to go without me."

Her voice came up, striking and stunning him. His eyes clouded and he stood there like a defenseless fighter, his arms slack at his sides, beads of sweat on his bewildered face. "What—what you tellin' me, baby, huh? This was part of the plan. You forgettin' that? I'm just speedin' it up, that's all. Nothin's changed that much, Ivy."

"Jimmy, I meant it when I said you couldn't lose me." Emotion thickened her voice and her hand grasped his. "But I'm not like you. You know what I mean. I can't control my fright. Right now I feel I'm comin' apart. If it really come to where we was bein' pressed in, I wouldn't be no help to you, and that's the truth. I'd just be scared baggage slowin' you down to a walk. When things stop movin' so fast, when you don't have to run from every suspicious footstep 'cause it might mean somebody comin' at us, I . . . What—what I'm tryin' to say is just give me time, Jimmy, to take this in my mind. I'll come to you, no matter where you are. But when I do I wanna help not hurt you."

His face was still and they looked at each other and his hand eased out of hers. "It's not goin' to work that way, baby," he said tonelessly. "You're askin' for somethin' that ain't goin' to happen. That money is goin' to make me a runnin' man the rest of my life. No matter where I go, Ivy, I got to be listenin' for footsteps behind me. Oh, it'll ease and I'll get me some breathin' room, but it's never goin' to be the kind of safe you talkin' about." She sat forward in the chair, her hands clenched on her lap. Her gaudy clothes looked incongruous next to the innocence and fear on her face. "Now, Ivy, I need you now. Don't come to me when things have eased. You know how I feel about you. Everything I done was for both of us right from the start. But, baby, I beg you only once to understand what I done and I ain't goin' to beg you again. It's either you pull out of here tomorrow with me or you turn around and walk back down them stairs and we end it right now."

"Oh, Jimmy, it's not what you thinkin'; I wouldn't know how to walk out on you." She rose from the chair as if physical contact was necessary to prove her words. "I just thought you could get a good jump in the beginnin' without me, that's all I'm sayin'." She took a step and closed the distance between them. "You my whole life. I'd do anythin' to see that you're not hurt." She stood in front of him, wanting to touch him, to reach up and put her arms around him. "Oh, Jimmy, honey, I love you so much. Oh, God, if you only knew how much."

Slowly Jim Harris's hand lifted and touched her face, his thumb tenderly brushing away a tear. He lowered his head and kissed her. Their arms went about each other and they melted together in a compulsive urge for refuge.

"Ivy, Ivy. Without you, what the hell does it all mean?" His urgent mouth pressed against the dampness of her neck. The dingy light distorted their erotically swaying shadows against the floor and walls as his hands unfastened the dress, pulling it down off her shoulders; it hung about her hips for an instant and then fell at her feet. His lips went across the full breasts, pausing on the swelling nipples, making her body pulse. His mouth tasted the brininess of her sweat as it moved across the swell of her stomach. She spread her legs and her fingers pressed his head urgently against her straining body. He pulled her down to the floor beside him. She grasped his throbbing hardness and inserted it and they rose inflamed sheltered in passion, which suspended fear and desolation. It engulfed and cradled them, up, soaring, being carried to the top of a searing sensation of climax. Then down, down, the quick fall, the ebbing wave breaking and plunging them back into the jarring sounds and stenches of tenement, then down even further into a personal abyss of despair and dread.

Chapter 19

"We want to see Doc Johnson." Frank Sullivan's voice carried the impersonal hardness that announced them as cops, but the tone seemed wasted on the towering black standing before them, his wide frame blocking the door. His small eyes, sentinel slits, darted to Bill Pope, then back to the white detective. Sullivan's demand seemed to roll loosely around in the big shaven head as though the appearance of fuzz was more than he could comprehend. The three of them stood pinned under the greenish light that hung above the garage doors. At the corners the lights of street lamps barely outlined the lofts looming heavily up into the darkness. Behind them, across the cobbled avenue, decaying piers thrust fingers of blackness out into the polluted river. There were no cars or people in the streets.

"You heard what I said. We want to talk to Johnson." Sullivan's tone grew more abrasive, but the big beefy Negro held his silence. Frank had recognized the gargoyle-faced giant who answered his knock, recognized the cauliflower ears and battered features of the hulking ex-fighter turned chauffeur and personal bodyguard to Johnson. The dull-witted nigger bastard, he thought; he must know I'm from precinct.

"You can't be as stupid as you look, boy," the detective snarled, digging the degrading Southern putdown into him. "I'm going to ask you just once more, you hear me, Sam?" He watched the Negro's mouth tighten in angry response, then the man answered begrudgingly.

"He ain't here. Nobody here, man." The words came up basso from the broad chest.

Some of the light spilled inside and reflected off a couple of limousines parked in the garage. Beyond that was darkness, except for a thin thread of light under a closed door at the rear of the building.

"Okay, Sam," Frank said sarcastically, "we'll just wait for him inside." He took a step toward the door.

The guard stiffened and seemed to grow a couple of inches taller. "Doc say he don't want nobody comin' in here that ain't supposed to."

Sullivan stopped. He could feel the familiar flash of heat spread out across his body. Now it didn't matter if Johnson was there or not, for his authority was being checked. Even more, it was as if this thick-set black had challenged his masculinity. "Get out of the way," he snarled, and his hand shoved into the guard's chest, forcing him back a step.

"You ain't comin' in here, man," the black said in a low tone, his face screwed into a scowl of hate as he shoved the detective's arm away from his body and reclaimed the entrance.

"Doorman, we're the police and we're comin' in." Sullivan spat out the words, fighting back the fury now storming in his eyes.

"I know who you are, man, and I don't give a motherfuckin' sh—"

Sullivan threw the punch, a rising right that had the snap of his body behind it. It landed with a dull, sickening thud of bone against bone across the guard's mouth, and drove him back into the garage. But the detective knew he had missed the one-punch argument. The guard shook his massive head, his shattered lips splattering blood down his shirt, and bellowing in rage blocked Sullivan's follow-up punch and threw his own, with all the skill of a pro, into the white man's stomach. The detective shuddered, doubled over and gasped in pain, his hat toppling from his head. The big guard shuffled professionally into position for a finish, but Sullivan suddenly shot his head up and caught him under the chin, slamming him back against the side of a car. The guard's hand went to his throat. He was gagging and coughing and spitting blood as the detective hit into the body again with a left hook, then a right. Bill Pope stood sentinel as if on the perimeter of a pit, a billy in his hands. Goaded by punishment, the Negro pushed away from the car and threw a vicious downward blow that banged across Sullivan's face, dropping him to his knees and into a stupor of pain and the smells of oil slicks and gasoline. The black twisted around to Pope but he found no spectator. The short club was already coming down. It crashed across the guard's face, spinning him, staggering, back toward the darkness. Down again, the billy finding its mark this time, down across the head, forcing a gasp from the torn lips of the guard, and he toppled, face forward, and lay like a dead man.

"Frank, Frank, are you all right?" Pope bent down to his partner.

"Yeah, yeah, I'm all right," Sullivan mumbled, and got to his feet slowly.

Pope watched him for a moment longer to make sure, then squinted in the dimness, searching for his partner's hat. Behind him the big black form twitched to life; his fingers clawed in the oil-soaked ground and his arms tensed and began to push up from the floor. He was almost to his knees when Frank Sullivan saw him. The detective took a couple of steps, gained momentum, and kicked him in the back of the head. He fell forward, his face smashing into the cement floor.

The darkness suddenly flared with a brightness that momentarily blinded Sullivan.

"Well, if it isn't Harlem's flashiest cop." The caustic voice snarled mockingly and turned him around to the back of the garage. Doc Johnson stood, like a sovereign, outside the door. Spread out from him were two of his men, one holding a .38, the other a Beretta. On the word "cop" they lowered their guns but didn't put them away.

"You better have a warrant on you, Sullivan, or you're goin' to be in trouble in another direction."

"No warrant," Sullivan answered coldly, "If this was official I would have already bagged them two ugly-lookin' bastards standin' beside you on a weapons charge."

The .38 went inside a coat; the one with the Beretta continued to hold it.

"All I want, Johnson, is talk. Just talk."

Doc Johnson's face soured. "What would I have to talk to somebody like you about?"

"You might be surprised."

"Life's full of them," Johnson retorted automatically, but the shrewd eyes studied the wrinkled suit and the bruised face. No, he told himself, he's not on the make. Not this white son of a bitch, not tonight. He was about to tell him to get the hell out when he remembered the young Negro detective's contemplative stare, and the image of Nick Difalco crossed his mind. Tonight everything was off center, already moving out of his confident grasp. It had to be something really big to make this gray come on the way he did. It was all too strong. "Yeah," Doc Johnson said grimly, "life's full of surprises. You wanna talk, huh?" He shrugged. "Sure, why not? Who knows, you might even have something to say—but I doubt it." He turned and opened the office door. The Beretta was pocketed now and his two blacks started to follow him inside.

"Alone," Frank said sharply, his tone turning Johnson around. "We talk alone, without the two punks, or we don't talk at all."

Doc debated the request for an instant, resenting the dictate. But a private talk with cops always meant one thing: a deal. He nodded toward the busted-up chauffeur, whose head lay in a spreading pool of blood. "You two," he ordered his stoic gunmen, "clean him up and wait out here."

Inside, Johnson leaned his heavy body back against the closed door, watching the detective take in the air-conditioned room, the pine-paneled walls, the wide desk, the dark leather chairs. It was Pope who lingered over Johnson's portrait hanging over the bar.

"Okay, cop, you wanted privacy, so go ahead. Talk.

Make your pitch, but it better be good, 'cause I'm not in the mood for the likes of you to take up my time."

In the car Sullivan had decided to play it by ear, not sure of how Johnson was going to act once they were alone with him. But their entrance, which had gound one of his men to floor, dictated the only approach Johnson could take—blunt and direct—and Sullivan accepted it readily.

"For openers, let's start talking about two dead cops that got gunned down by thc guys who knocked you over tonight," Sullivan said flatly.

Johnson was startled. He had expected something else, but his face remained blank. "A couple of cops got killed, you say?" He made a clucking sound with his mouth. "Ain't that too bad. So what do you want me to do? Throw somethin' into the pot for the widows? Yeah, you look like the type that would start a collection like that." He snorted. "Just so long as I can have a receipt for it for my tax man, you know. I wanna be straight with the government."

Sullivan could feel his anger at Johnson swell with the galling sarcasm. But he controlled his temper and tried to continue as if Johnson had never spoken. "Okay, then, let's talk about a mutilated corpse I seen about an hour ago strung out against a wall under the el of the New Haven tracks."

"Man, I don't think I'm hearin' right. I heard you blew your mind and were out on sick leave. Well, you're still sick to think you could walk in here and ask me a question like that." He began to shake his head disapprovingly. "If this is what you fought your way in here to talk about; then all I can say is, Massa Charlie, youse is in da wrong place. Us poor colored folk, we know nothin' 'bout nothin'." And he smiled, a full-toothed smile of contempt.

"Don't you pull that jig jazz on me," Sullivan snarled, momentarily forgetting the deal he had come for. The hell with it, let it go, it wasn't worth it now. "You know goddamn well what I'm driving at, and if you don't then I've been overestimating you, because you got nothing but a piece of black coal for a brain and you deserve everything I'm going to throw at your tar man."

195

Doc Johnson moved away from the door, his stout body somehow stiffening into a hardness that lent credence to his reputation. "You watch your mother-fuckin' mouth, white man." The growl peeled away the polish. "You may be somethin' to the small-time thieves you work over in some back alley, but you ain't gonna get away with that shit on me. The only reason you in this room is 'cause I let you, so you better know your place and remember who you're talking to, somebody that can put your ass in a sling like I done to you once before."

Frank Sullivan could almost taste the animosity, like bile in his throat that he had to spit out. "I'm not on your grease stick, Johnson, so I don't have to listen to you tell me what a big shot you are because I know you're nothin' but a shine that got lucky." Sullivan was too aroused to care about the color of his partner's skin. "Things have changed for you, fat man. Tonight when you lost that payroll and the Syndicate lost two of its collectors, the secure little wall that you built up between you and people like me started to crack. Don't press your luck by threatening me. I made this unofficial, but you push and I'll collar you and the hell with the consequences, because I don't give a good fuck who your protection is."

"Don't press my luck!" Johnson echoed sarcastically, and his face showed disgust, as though Sullivan were something loathsome. He walked and sat down behind the desk, apparently in full command of the situation. But the detective had got through, had shaken him with his reference to the Syndicate. Johnson wondered just how much the cop knew, and he saw again the images of Nick Difalco, but this time as if it were stitched across the flushed face of the detective before him.

"Your partner here," Johnson drawled deeply, turning his back to the white detective and swiveling his heavy frame in the chair toward Pope. "You know what he is?" His hand pointed, the diamond on the small finger sparkling in Frank's direction. "He's a racist. You know that?"

Pope, who had stood by watching what seemed a personal conflict, was about to deny the accusation, to defend his white partner. But he didn't say anything.

"Or he hates me," Johnson continued gruffly. "I haven't

figured which. I got a feelin' it's a little of both. I'm gonna tell you something about him, sonny." Doc's tone carried the authority of an arrived, legendary black talking to a young, ambitious one. Pope remained silent, almost mesmerized by the incredible display of Johnson's emotions. "When this gray first made the scene up here he makes a couple of quick flashy arrests on two of my top guys. You understand how I pay good money to keep my key boys operatin' loose without having to worry about being picked up on shit charges. You know what I mean, sonny? So I get my downtown sheeny shyster and he talks both cases out of court. But does that bother him?" A derisive smile moved the corners of Johnson's broad lips while he tried to gauge the effect his words were having on Pope. "No, not him. He still goes on trying to make a white world work in a black ghetto. But now he starts to make the arrests a little more shrewd, a little more annoying, and he's usin' his hands a lot on my guys and along the way he makes first grade detective. And pretty soon I got all my numbers guys and runners and like all my people tellin' me how the son of a bitch was buggin' them. Maybe I'm a little slow, I tell myself. Maybe this great arm of the law was sendin' me a massage. So I decide to put him on the take and at a price above the going rate. And you know what he did, sonny? He beat up on my man and put him into the prison ward at the Harlem Hospital." Pope was amazed that Johnson was speaking so candidly, though he assumed it now must be open knowledge to the older men in the precinct. But still . . . He sneaked a glance at Frank Sullivan, who stood silent, almost passive, except for vitriolic eyes riveted on Johnson. "So I set him up. I rigged something where he punches around an innocent plant. Now I get him on a police brutality rap. Then I made the phone call. He was moved out and busted to second grade and buried in Queens. That gray he must have a rabbi, because, like a bad penny, he bounces back about a year later, first grade and all, and not one bit smarter, because he must think I can't get him now."

He turned in the chair, and looked at Sullivan, like a fighter sensing the finish of a not too dangerous opponent. Annoying, yes. But now he was going to finish him, put him away for good. Johnson knew Pope would un-wittingly tell of this confrontation; it would be too big to contain. He was betting on it that his remarks would taint Sullivan as a fraud and give Pope something to gnaw on.

"Yeah, I think he's a cat who never grew up to the facts of life. While everybody else is grabbin' and tryin' to line their pockets with a little gold, he's still playin' cops and robbers. Up until tonight I figured him nothin' but one of them—whatta ya call it?—moralists, trying to whitewash the world with some of that phony gray phi-losophy and his fists. But now"—he stared malevolently and his tone grew meaner—"now I think it's more than that. When I heard he blew his cool and shot up a joint I knew why. Because he wasn't big enough to take his losses like a man. He always needed a head shrinker, but he may be too far gone for that because"—and Johnson's finger pointed at Sullivan, emphasizing the final accusa-tion—"you're nothin', Sullivan, but a sick white bastard. Now take sonny here with you and get the fuck out of here and consider yourself lucky I'm lettin' you leave under your own power."

The rage inside Frank Sullivan blazed up uncontrol-lably. He took a couple of quick steps and closed the distance between himself and Johnson. His hands went flat on the desk and he hovered ominously above the black man.

"You know what I feel like doing to you?" he snarled savagely. "I feel like knocking your goddamn head through a wall."

Johnson stiffened, his hand reaching out to a drawer. He slid the drawer back far enough so he could grab the handle of the exposed Colt if he needed it. "Don't try it, Sullivan"—his tone was as hard and metallic as the gun, only inches from his hand—"or they will be scrapin' up another dead cop."

"You go for that gun and I'll put a bullet in your rotten nigger head." Sullivan's voice was a guttural, chal-lenging tone that slammed and vibrated and caromed off the walls and about the room. And in the appalling silence, the echo of his words resounded again and again in Doc Johnson's mind.

"And I'll kill the first guy who comes through the door." Johnson heard Pope back up the challenge, but he couldn't take his eyes off Sullivan. He could see the veins in the neck bulge out against the collar, the jawline pulsate in erratic tics and, in the air-cooled room, a trickle of sweat roll down the side of his face. But it was the eyes, mainly the eyes: red-rimmed and narrow and psychotic. And the mouth was parted, showing the teeth. It was the face of a deranged animal on the verge of a leap.

Then sounds, momentarily suspended, filled the silence: the hum of the air-conditioner, the metronome ticks of a clock, a breath being sucked in abnormally Doc Johnson was shocked to realize it was his own mouth that made the gasping sound.

"You really tryin' to force my hand. You want me to go for the gun," Johnson said in a tone of disbelief. "You'd kill me if I gave you half a chance." He could feel the rancid taste of how close he had come to being shot if his hand had moved a couple of inches closer to the revolver. He slowly, cautiously, closed the drawer, leaving the gun in the desk. "Well, cop, I'm not giving you that chance." And he leaned back in his chair, not taking his eyes off the detective, seeking deeper reasons on the frenzied face, something he could accept, for the challenge that had just been hurled at him had been too vivid, too chilling to dismiss with the simple word "sick." "Everybody's lookin' for somethin' in this world," Johnson said quietly. "Some guys want money, some power, and others just want a good woman. But you, you want to die. Well, you keep it up, keep doin' what you been doin', and somebody is goin' to make that death wish of yours happen."

Johnson, backing off that way, took the edge from Sullivan's anger. But in the second of silence before he could answer, Pope tried to salvage his partner's long shot.

"Jim Harris," Pope said, and watched for a reaction as Doc Johnson turned an expressionless face at him. "We want Jim Harris," Bill Pope repeated, and this time Johnson didn't disappoint him. He nodded his head affirmatively.

"Already a make, huh?" and his tone carried a modicum of respect.

Johnson again surprised Pope with easy acknowledgment of Harris's name. The young detective could feel the stimulation as the long shot broke late but well from the gate. "No, not yet," Pope answered evenly. "He's just a name going through a teletype. Tomorrow he'll be everybody's collar. Right now he's our and we want him."

"In a blue or red ribbon?" Doc mocked his eagerness. But there were no signs of humor in the heavy-jowled face.

"Any kind; it doesn't matter," Pope said, "just as long as it's a live package."

"Not this one, sonny, 'cause you're stickin' your nose where it don't belong," Johnson retorted, and the thought of Nick Difalco out on the street made him pause. The idea of his guys guiding a white hunting party through his black domain rankled and toughened his voice. "When he's found, he's going to be cold turkey."

"Call off your hounds, Johnson," Sullivan broke in, feeling a responsibility to shield Pope against political retribution that Johnson might throw at them later. "The Department wants him more than you do. You already hamstrung one message tonight. You got what you wanted; now you leave Harris to us."

Doc Johnson didn't answer, didn't even look at Sullivan. He sat there almost indifferently, unwrapping a cigar, biting the end and sticking it unlit between the loose lips. Another time, he thought to himself, I'd throw him at you. You're right, I don't need to impress uptown with what I can do; they all know. Yeah, another time . . . And he could taste the submission.

"Because if you don't"—the white man's voice came through Doc's brooding speculation—"you're going to get more pressure than you'll know how to handle. The two cops getting killed on a robbery of money you milk out of uptown is going to make a lot of other cops in Harlem feel you're open season."

Johnson removed the cigar from his mouth. Twice, he thought, twice in one night. Threats from opposite worlds, but were they that far apart? He could see very little difference in their strong-arm pressuring methods. Though with the Syndicate he had to sit still and listen and do their bidding until . . . But he had to be sure of such a grand design before he would go up against them. He'd continue to play the puppet for the downtown string pullers—but for this punk cop? Never.

Johnson came forward in the chair, contempt in his face. "If you think I'm goin' to be shaken up because a couple of dumb cops didn't know enough to walk the other way and ended up bein' killed," he snorted, "you got to be a joke. You must see yourself as some kind of a noble avenger tryin' to wow the crowd with a grandstand play. Well, you ain't wowin' nobody, because your stink is just as bad as the fuzz I got to pay off every week. The only reason this operation stays in business is because the law lets it. They're my partners. If somebody tries to deal drugs on a corner that don't belong to them, or tries to compete with my numbers bank or bookmaking or you name it, my partners they bust 'em. They grab a headline for themselves and keep the competition out. And I pay big for that kind of service. I shove money under their nose, from the cop on the beat right on up to downtown Centre Street. And they're grabbin' like the thieves they are. And everybody in Harlem knows they're bought. But I can understand them grabbin' for some of that green. Yeah, I can take them because they're honest about their stealin', it's part of the business. But there is always somebody out of step, and that's you. And I don't have to take you now or any other time. If you weren't so sick you'd be a laugh." He stood up behind the desk, his tailored bulk dominating the room, and his scowl turned into a snarl. "Okay, cop, I'm through talkin'. Your audience with me is over with. Now you get the hell out of here."

Frank Sullivan didn't move. There was still tenseness in the body and his coat was open and the gun could be seen in the snubnose holster, but the fury that had almost made him grab for it was gone now, replaced by the knowledge that he had won in his showdown with Johnson. For the brooding pauses and half-concealed disquiet on the Harlem ganglord's face made Sullivan feel that at last Doc Johnson was vulnerable to the kind of squeeze Sullivan could apply.

"You're nothing, Johnson"—the detective's voice was expressionless—"you're nothing but colored help. And that white Syndicate you work for don't like being robbed. From now on they're going to be watching you real close, and I'm going to give them something to look at." He turned to Pope. "He sounds like he got the whole precinct on the take, doesn't he? Well, he's full of shit. He didn't mention the guys he couldn't buy, white and black, who are just waiting to tear him down."

He looked back at Johnson. "You don't know it yet, but your days of being a big man in Harlem are numbered. Oh, it won't happen tomorrow or next week or next month, but it's coming, because each day a little piece of you is going to be chipped away until nobody will bother to stick their greasy necks out to protect you, because you won't be worth the effort. You're going to be a liability." The chilling calm of his voice carried more of a threat than if he had thundered. "Every time one of your men is on the street he'll be picked up. If he's carrying a weapon you lose him. We'll hit your numbers men, the collectors, the pushers, the whorehouses, your whole rotten bag. Yeah, you'll get your sharp lawyers and you'll get most of them out. You'll move around the drops in the operation and you'll stay in business. But you're going to sweat to do it. And the money will start falling off each week and you won't be able to explain it to your white bosses because they're going to know you're the chief cause of their trouble. And you know what they're going to do then?" the detective's voice rasped. "They're going to look around for a new boy. And he's going to be picked right out of your ranks and then you're going to get something for all your years of valuable service. They're going to put a bullet in your head, fat man. You're dead now, only you don't know it."

Frank Sullivan smiled. It started slowly, the lips pulled back across the teeth and the corners of the mouth stretching taut, while the eyes continued their burning, vindictive stare. His face was like wax and the cadaverous smile was not meant for sound or laughter. And then it was gone, but it had told everything.

Doc Johnson had listened unmoving. It wouldn't work, he thought to himself, I'm covered too good; he couldn't

202

get away with it. But as the words piled one on top of the other, he realized that it could happen. Maybe not exactly that way, but close enough, close enough. This lousy white bastard was crazy enough to push it and he'd need only a handful to get it going, and then maybe it would snowball, and Doc Johnson remembered all the toes he had stomped on, and would it be JJ or Swinger or somebody else just biding their time, eyeing his chair, ready to jump into it once the word came across from Jersey that he would have to be killed. . . .

And now he realized that the night's chain of events, in which he had unwittingly been caught up, the robbery and Difalco and now Sullivan, had combined to force him into a decision he had been putting off for a long time. The odds against it didn't look so big now, as it all suddenly fell into place. He could see it working; the auspicious time had come. He needed the field clean. The stakes were too big for him to be sniped at by a fanatic. Sullivan was now a calculated risk Doc Johnson could not afford.

"Sullivan." There was something in the tone of his voice that stopped the detective at the door. It made him look back at the imposing figure standing in the ornate room. "Everybody's got their price. I know I can lay out enough money to put you in my hip pocket until the day you retire. I can own you. But I don't think you're worth convertin' so I'm gonna do the second thing. If you try to fight me it won't be a phone call, and no transfer to Queens this time; I'm gonna have you killed. I'm going to cut you down as sure as Christ made sour apples." He paused, his face almost doleful and his voice even softer. "And, Frank, I'm not kidding."

Chapter 20

"Three hundred and fifty years usin' the black to build the most powerful country in the history of the world. Three hundred and fifty years of holdin' us down, of rapin' our women, exploitin' our children, and tryin' to rob your eyes, brother, so we blind to everythin' but shantytowns and slum ghettos, tellin' us to come out when he want somebody to clean up his garbage, then you get back in that hell, but that was yesterday, brother, today, today things are happenin' and tomorrow goin' ta bring the change, we on the rise against the white devils, we on the rise in a black movement that goin' ta rock the very foundation of this here country, that goin' ta shake the structure of the whole white world." The desperate thin face was pinched with fury and the black bony arm rose like a sword and swayed above the heads of the upturned, many-hued Negro faces. "He first get his warnin' in Harlem, and he got it in Watts. He ignore Boston and Chicago and a hundred other places. He didn't listen in Newark or Detroit. And a presidential committee come out and tell him he livin' in a racist society and he just better change, change. And in the nation a great voice was tellin' us black men to cool it, cool it, we goin' to make it in a passive nonviolent way. And now Martin is dead and his dream is dead along with him, murdered by a white world that ain't goin' ta give us nothin' but the heel of their shoe. Well, they got a sample of the answer while the King laid dead. And that ambush in Cleveland was just the start, because the biggest explosion of all is yet to happen." His arm stopped waving and he pointed at a white uniformed cop who stood to the side of the small gathering stifling a yawn. But the cop's eyes were fully aware of some of the faces that turned toward him in hate while the speaker's voice became a chant. "There'll be no more beggin' for decent housin', no more bad schools or closed white unions, no more racist cops or white bosses shoutin' you out, or families being smashed because of no money. And no more listenin' to them Northern big liberal politicians tryin' to kiss your ass and tellin' ya to take it slow while they take your vote."

A jagged streak of lightning cut across the heavy sky. Its answering growl of thunder was hollow and distant in the heat. In front of him the people stirred and the youths lounging at the soft-drink store across the street seemed to come to life as they looked up at the murky clouds, then started to walk away down 125th Street.

"Because, brothers, a mighty black fist will be formed

by an angry army of over twenty million black people. We gonna rise together and demand the white devils give us our rightful share in a society that growin' rich and fat while we stand around outside lean and poor. And if we don't get what we want, that black fist goin' ta cripple this country. We can start it on its downfall. We can bring it to its knees." His listeners began to stray off in ones and twos, leaving him with a remnant who stood and waited, their silence asking for more. He peered down at a cocoa-faced youth. "Do you believe me, soul brother?"

"Yes, I believe."

"You better, brother. You better go and get a gun and be ready to kill them white devils, take ten of them for every one dead black, because that's the way it's goin' ta be wrote when they write the final chapter of this here mother-rapin' country." He stepped down, tucked the necessary handkerchief-size American flag into his pocket, folded his ladder, picked it up and walked off.

The white cop yawned again, looked at his watch and headed toward the call box. The traffic had thinned along Seventh Avenue. Raucous bars still held their quota of night people, but the congestion on the streets had given way to isolated stragglers. A couple of hookers shook their breasts defiantly as they passed. But he didn't notice, for he was looking over the three white men who were approaching him. Whites who moved with swaggering authority through Harlem after dark were always suspect. As they came closer he dismissed his suspicions. Fight manager, he thought, with a couple of his tigers. Uptown for a drink at Sugar Ray's. But if he had turned around he would have seen that they walked past Robinson's through the thinning crowd and disappeared around the corner, turning in under the marquee of the Lorelei Hotel.

The knock came nervously, apologetic for its intrusion. There was no answer, then the knock again, loud enough this time to stir a drowsy voice inside.

"Who's there?"

"It's me—Arthur, the bellhop."

"Who?" the sleep-heavy voice called through the door.

"The bellhop, man."

"What do you want?"

"I got a message for you. The man say it important."

There was a wait, then the door opened partially and Joe Logart, with just shorts on, looked out sleepily, his mind working with the sluggishness of one who wakes too soon.

"Yeah, what is it?"

The tall, skinny-framed bellhop looked from side to side as if about to impart a secret. He opened his mouth, his enlarged Adam's apple bobbed a couple of times, but he didn't say a word.

Logart, irritated, opened the door a little farther and leaned toward him. "Man, what the hell do you want? . . . Why, you stoolin' black mother f——." They jumped from the sides of the walls, misshapen and big, their white faces blurring. He tried to slam the door, feeling fright scream across his body. They pushed against the door and he knew he couldn't keep them out. He released the door suddenly, throwing the two men staggering into the room. Frantically he whirled and grabbed for the gun lying on top of the night table, the gun that would hold them off, give him a chance to escape. He started around with it when he felt a blow of pain in his arm and stunning numbness smash against the side of his jaw. The floor came spinning up in a rush of gray carpeting and slammed into his face. He rolled over, still conscious, somehow still holding the gun, and a new shock wave of pain tore through the arm. His fingers uncoiled slowly from the weapon and it lay useless in the palm of his hand. It was taken away and his eyes started up the ponderous foot that pinned his wrist to the floor. Up the spiraling leg and soaring mountain of body to a head that seemed to brush the ceiling. Beside him was the other man, just as towering. And they stood poised, ready to tumble down on top of him if he dared move.

He lay there waiting for them to bend down and snap the cuffs about his wrist. Resignation stilled the fear now that he had been caught. He twisted his head to where the bellboy stared at him in open-eyed wonder. Nick Difalco, who had leisurely followed his muscle into the room, now took out his wallet with the casualness of one paying a gratuity for an expected service. He ripped

206

the hundred-dollar bill in half and held it in front of the bellboy's face.

Joe Logart closed his eyes against the terrifying realization and a new, much colder fright swept across his sweating body. His legs began to shake.

"Man, I didn't see a thing," the bellboy said nervously, greedily pocketing his half of the bill, and he turned quickly back to the elevator. Nick Difalco shut and locked the door.

The night lamp had been knocked over on the table, casting Difalco's elongated shadow up against the wall as he stood motionless, his eyes taking in the sparsely furnished room. The suitcase near the door was closed and ready for travel. He opened it and emptied the contents on the floor. Looking in the closet, he found a jacket and pulled a wallet from it. Silently he read an identification card, indexed the money with his thumb, then returned the empty wallet to the pocket. He was in no hurry as he peeled the mattress off the bed, then let it slide back in place. He stepped over Logart to the dresser and checked the drawers. He stopped, looked around, but there was nothing else to search. Then he stared down at the reddish-black face. The twisted scar on Logart's face made him look as if he were smiling back.

"Pick him up," Difalco said. They pulled him to his feet and he stood there rubbing his wrist, trying not to show his fear. Difalco motioned to the bed. "Sit down. I want to talk to you." The voice was hard but it carried no urgency and sounded almost like a request. Fright showed in Logart's eyes as he sat hunched on the edge of the bed watching Difalco pull a chair up close to him, turn it around and straddle it, his hands hanging loosely over the backrest.

"I had a talk with one of your playmates a little while ago. A boozy jig by the name of Jackson." The searing almond eyes watched him, but Logart sat there as if he hadn't heard. "It took us a little time to make him talk. We sort of had to take the story out of him piece by piece, you know what I mean." He nodded knowingly as if to dismiss any doubts about his ability to get a man to talk. "He told us about you and the other shine. We got his name but didn't catch his address. It seems your pal Jackson died suddenly of a stroke." Difalco's tight, swarthy face showed its disgust for a moment, as he glanced up at the thick-set man standing beside him, then it turned slowly back to Logart with a suggestion of a smile. "But it don't matter now, because you're going to tell me his address and you know why: because I'll let you walk away clean from this. I'm going to trade your life for the money and the guy that rigged up the hit. So you be a real good nigger and do as I say, and if I get what I want I'll let you live."

Joe Logart had not taken his eyes from Difalco's. His only response was the sound of his breathing, which mixed with the faint noises that drifted through the old hotel—an elevator door closing, a toilet being flushed in the room above.

"All I have to do is give you the address?" Logart was surprised at the strength of his own voice. Only moments before he had been almost too scared to think.

"No," Difalco answered in a self-assured tone. "It's not that easy, pal. You're going to open the door. You take us to where this guy's holing up, and like the bellhop you get him to the door, then we take over."

"Then I just walk away, is that it?"

"Yeah, that's it, pal, you just walk away."

"You must think I'm really stupid," Logart said quietly. "I wouldn't get more than two steps and you'd cut me down, and you know I know it."

"What the hell, you want it in writing?" Difalco's voice turned ugly. "I'm offering you the best deal you ever had, your life for his. That's simple enough to understand, ain't it?" His tone smoothed out again. "There's only one way you can save your ass and that's do as I say. I don't want you, I know how it was put together. Jackson was nothing and you weren't much more on this. I want the guy that thought up this caper. He's the one I want to bleed, so it makes no sense you going down with him. Right?"

Logart tried to calculate his chances to get past them to the hall and down to the lobby. Then he stared forlornly at the worn carpeting and let go the futile thought of escape. His only hope was that the bellhop would have a change of mind. But he remembered the eyes as the bell-

208

boy fingered the torn bill and knew that was a possibility beyond real hope. Henry Jackson was dead and Joe Logart knew these men were going to kill him, too. They had to; there was no other way. They couldn't afford to leave any witness who could go against them if something went wrong. And now to crawl to this white man— for what? So he could live another twenty minutes, the time it would take him to lead them to Jim Harris's door —and the money? The money. All his future hopes and plans had hinged on how he was going to spend it. And even if there were some kind of miraculous escape, there would be no dreams left without the money. The best he could hope for now was his life, and a dragging on of a wasteful, hateful existence. His chance for something big was now gone, over and done with before it had ever started. It all seemed so futile. Henry was dead and this man was demanding Harris's address so they could go up there and kill him, too, along with all their efforts and hopes. Somehow it didn't seem right. Even the way it was happening now. If he had to die, let a black man do it.

Then, very slowly, he realized something was wrong. This white face pushing in close to his should have been Johnson's or one of his guys', and for the first time he appreciated what Harris and he and even Henry had done. The excitement they had spread, not only in Harlem, but also in that mythical Mafia world that he hardly believed existed. Yet here they were, smelling of Caucasian sweat and garlic. He knew that nothing like this had ever happened before in Harlem. The story would be told over and over, and eventually they would hear about it in other cities wherever black men gathered, telling of how they carried out the robbery and of the dead and dying they left behind. But was the ending going to be that they all wound up dead and, worst of all, all the money was returned?

A macabre pride filled him and he looked up. A lifelong hatred of his terrible existence, of countless humiliations, now became his strength. It combined with his accepted faith, and firmed and bolstered his courage, lifting it beyond anything he had ever experienced.

"So come on, come on, you dumb shine bastard, what's your answer?" Nick Difalco snarled impatiently.

"Fuck you, white man," he said softly. The acrid words were bony and black and carried Logart's hate of the white world.

Difalco hit him. Logart had turned his head, but the punch stretched him groggily across the top of the bed.

"What the hell are you waiting for? Go ahead," Difalco barked at his underlings, and kicked the chair he had been sitting on into the corner.

The bigger of the two, Morello, pulled Logart off the bed, propped him up from the rear, pinning his arms in a bear hug for the bull-shouldered Parini, who, as emotionless as a fighter pounding a bag, pumped a right into the body that tore a gasp out of the victim. Repeatedly he hit into his stomach until Logart's cries filled the room. Difalco's hand went to the radio on the dresser and turned it on, the volume up to cover the sound. ". . . and Dixie Girl pomade will guarantee to take the wrinkle out of that unruly hair. Yeah, baby, if you want that great big cat of yours to touch a handful of soft, glowin' hair, you go out and buy a jar. And hey, you guys, too. If you want to keep the pompadour soft and silky, don't forget Dixie Girl pomade. It's guaranteed or money back." The slurring Negro voice played down its education, wrapping itself in colloquial phrasing and booming out of the speaker. "And now Number eight and movin' up fast, Little Leonard and the Dream Drops . . ."

"Okay, take it easy," Difalco snapped. "I lost the other one too soon; I don't want to lose him."

They released Logart and he crumbled to the floor and lay on his back, his eyes squeezed tight with pain, his open, taut mouth struggling for breath in a room suddenly devoid of air.

The tip of Difalco's polished shoe nudged his ribs. "If you want it to stop, nigger, all you have to do is lead me to Harris." Joe Logart's arms clasped across the scorching pain that was his stomach. He tried to speak, but could only gulp out low, indistinct sounds that forced Difalco to lean down to him to make sure he would hear against the crash of music. "What do you say, pal?" he said. "We got a deal, right?" Logart shook his head from side

210

to side. "Dumb," muttered Difalco, "dumb, that's what they are," and he kicked Logart in the ribs. Morello and Parini hit him as he lay there, taking turns with a cruel proficiency that had nothing to do with sadism. They were indifferent professionals. Logart meant nothing to them, merely that he was meant to bleed. They worked the groin, the stomach, closed the eyes and shattered the nose, impervious to the yells of pain.

"Hey, hey, in there, cut out that noise, you hear?" A muffled voice from the next room shouted irritably through the wall. The two hoods, leaning above Logart, stopped and quickly looked to Difalco.

"Put him on the bed," they were told, and they threw the bleeding Negro on top of it like a discarded rag doll.

Difalco took a pitcher of water off the dresser and emptied it into the brutalized face. Some of it slopped past the torn lips and ran down his throat. And in limbo, somewhere between coma and awareness, Joe Logart tumbled back through the years, back to a wiry-bodied adolescent being held beneath the water's surface by the strong hands of the big Italian kid. Again he could feel the panic. The three of them had hitched a ride behind the trolley and ridden it all the way out to the beach on that hot summer day long ago. Their black skin had stood out in the pallid sea of white flesh. "Hey, niggers, this here's a white man's beach." And they were surrounded at the edge of the surf. His companions had wisely retreated back through the sand, but he was slow in complying. "A wise guy, huh? Okay, nigger, we're going to teach you a lesson you don't forget." They grabbed him and carried him farther out into the water. He kicked and squirmed and fought them off, but the Italian kid was too big, too strong to shake loose, and he plunged his head below the water. He twisted and tried to wrench free, but the powerful hands held firm. Terrified that he was really drowning, he bit at the shimmering finger beneath the surface, clamping and grinding until the pressure on his head was released. And he bounced, gasping for air, above the shallow water. But he still didn't let go of the finger. The white kid threw frantic punches at his

211

face while the rest of them stood back. And he remembered the yell: "Please! Please!"

"What're you holding out for, pal? Come on, smarten up." The voice came through the subconscious and pulled him back. Logart's eye turned down out of the top of his head. The skeletal face above him, which stared down with savage persistence and flaring nostrils, moved in a slow, nauseating circle. A film of sweat covered it, making it appear plastic, unreal. It was an aberration, a bodiless, demonic horror hovering above him, and he cried out in his terror in a piercing screech. Nick Difalco's hands covered his mouth, muzzling it into silence, as he waited for Logart to return to him completely. The swollen eyes began to clear and Difalco took his hands away and leaned down close to him.

"You're taking a beating for nothing. You know that, don't you? Because I'm going to end up with what I want. You proved you can take a pounding, but any dumbhead can do that. So do like I say. Play it smart. When you take me to him you're out of it, you understand?"

Logart's face was numb, pain crowded his body, blood ran into his mouth from his torn lips, and he tried to swallow it away so he could speak. But even behind the cut and puffing slits his eyes burned up at Difalco with a fury that made him alter his demand. He wanted it over and done with, and expediency edged into his voice.

"Look, I'll make it easy for you. You just tell me where he's located. That's all. You don't even have to come with us. You stop holding out and tell me the address right now and I'll give you back that five hundred and throw in another thousand. I'm going to let you out of this with fifteen hundred in your kick, and you don't even have to leave the room. You stay right here. How do you like that, huh?"

Logart raised his head. The muscles in his throat tightened but only a mumble emerged. He pressed his lips together and anxiously Difalco pushed closer to be certain to hear him. Joe Logart spit. The saliva and blood and mucus splattered across and hung in globs on Nick Difalco's face.

"You black bastard, you!" Enraged, he straightened up, fumbling for a handkerchief.

212

Morello and Parini moved in mechanically on the prone Logart, but there was a difference in their movements now. The professionalism and the lack of emotion remained and their blows were as painful as before, but somehow their effect was dulled by the enigmatic pride Joe Logart had wrapped himself in, and sloppily they let him slip into unconsciousness far too quickly.

It was like a second drum, flat and out of beat. They didn't hear it at first, for it got lost in the music. It came on again, its pounding audible this time above the din, and accompanied by the voice shouting from the next room.

"Hey, hey, you in there, if you ain't goin' to cut out that racket I'm goin' ta have the manager call the police. You hear me?"

Morello and Parini became suspended, their fists drawn back, their punches halted, and they stood for a long moment like deranged statues.

Parini's fighter's face peered anxiously at Difalco. "We're takin' too much of a chance, Nick," he said hoarsely. "We stay here much longer, we're goin' to get ourselves jammed up, but good."

Tony Morello wrinkled his forehead as though he faced a complex problem beyond his reason, and he shook his head. "He ain't goin' to talk, Nick. We're just wastin' our time." His tone was more surprise than statement of fact.

Logart lay like a dead man, his eyes swollen and closed, blood flowing from his shattered nose and lips down the sides of his face and onto the water-soaked bed.

Difalco walked to the window and looked down onto the darkened roofs of the closed stores. Lights and neon signs still flashed up from the bars and theaters. The noises from the still busy avenue could hardly be heard for Difalco stood twelve floors up in the slight breeze blowing in across the river from Jersey. A flash of light blazed above the Palisades cliffs as he pushed the window up all the way. He turned around. "Dump the bastard," he said flatly.

They dragged the limp form by the arms. As they passed Difalco he kicked Logart in the side in what seemed a senseless display of frustration. But it was a

213

businesslike blow, a check to see if the unconsciousness was faked, for diligence was one of the enforcer's fortes. The legs were pushed slowly through the window; he was going out feet first. Then the unexpected happened. Joe Logart regained consciousness. Minutes before he had resigned himself to death, but now, irrational and frenzied, he was vitalized by the will to live. He grabbed for the sill and hung with the impossible strength of the insane. He shrieked the profanities of the condemned as they worked frantically to pry his fingers from the wood. Difalco reached for the open window and yelled, "Watch out." They pulled their hands back and he slammed it down with crushing force. The fingers disappeared beneath it, but the closed window could not shut out the screams of Joe Logart as he hurtled down to the pavement of 125th Street.

Chapter 21

She stood motionless under the shower trying not to think, but the needle spray massaging her skin could not wash away her despair, and at last she turned off the water. Lightning flashed against the frosted-glass window, startling her. She caught her reflection in the mirror and it looked like someone else's face. A chill rippled against her nakedness and she had to turn away from the sight of this distressing stranger who seemed to be pathetically begging for her help. She put on a robe and stepped out of the bathroom.

She put a spoonful of instant coffee into the water still bubbling in the cup, stirred it and then she sipped it, flavorless and synthetic as the retreat she had tried to make out of the small apartment. At times it had worked as a sanctuary, giving her a sense of attainment and some glimpses of a better life. Now, though, the windows might as well have been barred and the light-blue walls painted the gray of a cell. She was locked in. She waited through the hours, ticking off the time until she would run into

214

a future utterly alien to her nature simply because he wanted her with him. Yet that was enough. If he had gone off without her she knew now she would have followed him. She stood up and walked tiredly into the bedroom. Her body ached for want of sleep, but her mind, filling alternately with hope and despair, would not let her slip into momentary escape. The world was big, she told herself; there were a hundred places they could settle in where they could still put a life together. Everything was going to be all right. But as she stared up at the dark ceiling she could see the other side to this reassurance. There could be no end to their flight, for there would be no way ever to hide from something as personal as fear.

Jim Harris thought he heard a sound, and stiffened in the chair. His hand went worriedly across the table and touched the gun. He switched off the safety. Its click frightened a rat rummaging in the bag of garbage next to the door; it scurried across the floor and into the wall. Harris snapped the safety back on, pushed the gun away from him, disgusted at himself. After Ivy had left he had tried going back to sleep, but the remembrance of her warmth and his anxiety about the drunken Henry and the beautiful money exposed there on the kitchen table made his senses acute, his body too keyed up. Now he sat in the darkened kitchen, a bottle of beer in front of him, turned warm because he forgot to drink it, too preoccupied with the isolated sounds that were magnified by the silence of the now sleeping building.

The sudden splash of light and roll of thunder made him wish for a rain that would last well into the day, heavy and unrelenting, and would wash the cops out of the streets. A deluging rain, his ally, which would give him a slight edge of extra cover among the people going to their jobs amid the normal activity of the daytime streets.

And again his thoughts turned to Ivy. How fair was it of him to ask her to share the terrible insecurity and physical threats that lay ahead of them? He knew the right thing would be to go now, to be gone when she arrived in the morning, and the hell with Joe's share. Hadn't Logart thought that might happen? It was a natural assumption for him to make after what he had been told about the setup for Henry. And that, too, ran through Harris's mind as he sat morosely in the dark.

"Yes, I heard about it on a news broadcast earlier this evening," the resonant voice said, and even in a casual telephone conversation it carried a touch of stentorian opulence. "Well, with that kind of money at stake I guess one must accept the hazards that go along with it, eh, Doc? But its adverse publicity, I believe, is going to give our community another black eye. It's too bad." Johnson envisioned the face at the other end of the line wearing a sarcastic smile. "Tonight? Well, I don't know about tonight, Doc." The voice parried, trying to pin Johnson into a verbal corner. "Tomorrow? No, no, I'll be going back down in the morning and I'll be tied up with work for the next couple of weeks. Could it hold till then?"

The man sensed the irritation in Johnson, and not wanting to lose him, he amended, "Say, I'll tell you what. Why don't you come on up? No, no, it's nothing that won't prevent us from having a chat. It's just a few friends over for a social get-together. We'll have time to talk, I assure you. . . . Fine, fine. Then I'll expect you."

Doc Johnson slowly replaced the phone under the small bar. It was a private number that he rarely used. He knew it wasn't tapped because one of the people he spread money on would have told him. After what happened tonight it could be bugged, he thought, but what's the difference? In a few weeks it's going to be no secret who I'm aligned with.

He made himself a tall drink. Leaning his heavy bulk across the bar, he felt the exhilaration that at last it was beginning. He had thought maybe he was getting too old to buck the house and that had frightened him. His eyes ran up the knotty-pine wall to his portrait. The man staring down at him wasn't as heavy and his hair wasn't as gray and Doc Johnson wondered if he was the same person who had ten years before posed for a local artist. The painting had been done as a gag, but as time went on the picture took on dimensions to Doc far beyond the Negro artist's talents and intentions. For the last year or so he had been tempted to take it down and hide it

216

because it was too much of a reminder to him of what he used to be. But now he held the glass up to it and toasted himself, accepted the spectacular robbery pulled off by long-shot bettors, accepted the arrogant Nick Difalco sent to humiliate him, and even accepted the fanatic Frank Sullivan. And Doc Johnson, who hadn't been inside a church since he was a child but had retained his belief in the Almighty moving in unexplained ways, knew the time had come to set the grand design in motion.

Frank Sullivan sat eating in a booth by himself. There were a few people on stools along the counter, and the diner was filled with the smell of greasy cooking, which was somewhat alleviated by the large rumbling fan blowing toward the open door. The Greek owner, who sometimes sat with him, telling of the troubles a white man had owning a business in Harlem—and who sometimes picked up the tab, which was rarely over two dollars—now busied himself behind the counter. He had seen something in the detective's face that had made him shy away from him.

Sullivan could hardly eat the breaded veal cutlet and steamed vegetables, for his interview with Doc Johnson had left him with a bitter taste. He criticized himself for not being smart enough to ignore a black widow in a tenement and for not being able to control the inexplicable rage that, at times, blinded him to reality. He had shrugged off Johnson's threat, though he knew that for his assassination to be even remotely considered, something a lot more important to Johnson than having some of his boys busted had to lie behind it. He had dismissed the menace as so much bullshit shoveled up by a man trying to convince himself that the bottom of his world wasn't shaking, that he could still threaten and live up to his threats. But Sullivan wondered if he could actually muster a force to harass Johnson; it seemed much more difficult in retrospect. How many guys would go along with him? Damn few, maybe none. And what if he was able to dump Johnson, get him washed down into a one-way sewer? Someone else would rise out of that filth and it would be as if nothing had changed. . . . A vivid vein of light split the night sky and its echoing thunder pulled his eyes to the window and the street, where his partner sat in the prowl car.

Pope's ears barely registered the toneless voice cracking in the static of the radio, dispatching the interminable number of police cars to an endless number of addresses. They had driven away from Johnson's place each keeping his own counsel. Anything they said would have been anticlimactic after such a confrontation. But Pope wondered if he should have given more support, been more vocal in his denunciation of Johnson. But wasn't it Frank's show? Didn't he set the scene, relegating Pope to a bit player. Oh, he knew it was probably to protect him from retaliation by Johnson, and that part had seemed to work, for he had walked away without a finger being pointed at him. But if Frank went through with it and it came to a showdown, Johnson would win. Johnson would stop and wait and let the situation dictate his next move, knowing Sullivan would continue to charge bluntly, unheedingly, ignoring the obvious pitfalls of going up against somebody you just couldn't beat. Pope slumped deeper into the seat. Their leads were exhausted. There was nowhere to go now but back to the station so they had stopped to eat.

Then the voice on the squawk box mentioned the Lorelei Hotel.

The streets were in motion, filling the windshield of the car. Tenements slid back around the side windows, wrapped themselves smotheringly around them while the impending storm announced itself in flashes of light and rumbled growls that thinned out the corner gatherings and moved people a little quicker along the avenues.

He looked at Morello and Parini, sitting like statues in the front seat. He knew they would whisper of their night ride through Harlem, tell of how they had worked with the enforcer, for he had caught the stealthy looks they gave him and each other. And that was all right. Yeah, wasn't he Nick Difalco, the professional robot who never questioned an order? He wanted to call the old man, to wake him out of the sick sleep of the dying, to tell him he didn't have the guy that rigged the hit or the money, but fuck it, he had had enough and he was coming back downtown. But he knew he never would make such a call because he remembered nodding his head affirmatively at what he was told to do. In the beginning he had silently disagreed with Giaccano, and as the night wore on it had become even clearer he had been right. This was not the way to do it, this symbolic message of dead men used as a warning. Those it was intended for were so far removed from Doc Johnson's fat world that the warning was practically meaningless. He saw it now as a compromise. The old man had backed off from what he should have done: told Johnson he was on trial, or killed him one way or the other. But the businessman in Giaccano had taken charge, had dictated the instructions, because Doc Johnson was a good administrator, made a lot of money for the organization, and the old man was out of touch; he knew of no one he could replace him with. Instead he had heaped humiliation on him, nothing more, actually, than a slap on the wrist and business as usual. So let Morello and Parini talk, let them shout through The Family, let them build up Nick Difalco. He didn't want what he was doing to be forgotten with a pat on the back or a few Italian adjectives laid on him privately by a dying old man.

Chapter 22

"Yeah, he called about half an hour ago and asked specifically for you." Frank Sullivan could barely hear the desk sergeant's familiar monotone and he had to close the phone booth door to shut out the noise that surrounded him. "No, he didn't say what it was about, just that he'd meet you over at the Apollo for the last show. He said he'd be in the back of the theater."

Sullivan looked at his watch, thanked him and slid the door back. Bill Pope stood in one of the clusters of police in front of the manager's desk. The lobby wasn't big and they overflowed into the street. The precinct detectives, with badges pinned on their civilian jackets, had taken over. One of them, his hat pushed back, took notes as he leaned on the check-in desk. The night manager, a meticulously dressed Negro wearing heavy-rimmed glasses, listened attentively, along with the detective, to a bellhop.

"There was something about them, man, when I take them up in the elevator, like they ready for anything. I figure them the law, like they real quiet, real mean. You know, man." For an instant he forgot he was talking to the law. The enlarged Adam's apple began to bob above the starched uniform collar. "I think they goin' ta bust him and I'm goin' ta see them pull this cat through the lobby with cuffs on him. But when they come down they alone and not the same guys I took upstairs. There was something nasty about them now, like, man, their eyes, like they could scare ya to death just by lookin' at ya. You know what I mean! And then I see spots of blood on the two younger cats. I hadda look fast, man, like they actin' like they want to get away from somethin' real bad. It was then I think they bookmakers and that guy upstairs he renege on a lot of high bets he made downtown and they come around to rough him up to make sure he get up the money. But the way they move out of here, I say to myself maybe that boy upstairs really hurt and he need some help."

But the bellhop didn't tell how he waited outside the elevator, nervously fingering the torn hundred-dollar bill in his pocket and refusing calls from the desk, afraid that he would miss that man and the other half of the bill. This he didn't tell, for the C note was united now and lay silently in his wallet.

"It was at that particular point that Arthur told me his suspicions, that we should check 1202," the night manager cut in. The bellhop looked disappointed that he couldn't continue. "I had received a complaining call from the adjoining room about the excessive noise. There was no follow-up call, so I presumed the disturbance had stopped and I dismissed the matter." He nodded toward the bellboy, light catching the lenses of his glasses. "I was quite busy and didn't see the three men leave until Arthur alerted me. I hadn't realized what was taking place, but once upstairs it only took a moment to evaluate that the poor misfortunate in 1202 had met his death at the hands of those men. The room was in terrible disarray. We looked down into the street, but all we could see was a small group of people surrounding a horrible-looking—"

"Yeah, that right," the bellboy broke in. "That cat he musta hit and bounce six feet in the air fallin' from so far up."

The storm was about to break when Pope and Sullivan stepped from the Lorelei. It had brought a coolness that felt good after three days of abnormal late-summer heat. They were going to walk the one long block to the Apollo, but decided against it as the first few drops of rain started to fall.

Sullivan swung the car in a U-turn and made a fast grab for the wipers as the rain pelted the streets clear of pedestrians. A number of people who had ducked under the marquee eyed them silently as they pulled up in front of the theater. The detectives walked between the people past the closed box office and into the long narrow lobby. They heard the orchestra theme signifying the last show and, stepping into the interior of the theater, stood for a moment letting their eyes adapt to the darkness. The music ended and the master of ceremonies came through the curtain; the silk suit sparkled in the spotlight as he did a little two-step and flashed a good-looking brown face into a glittering smile. Pope and Sullivan started to walk to the back of the house, looking for their man.

"Welcome, ladies and gentlemen. The Apollo Theater once again proudly presents Amateur Night in Harlem. From this stage a lot of people have been launched into the stratosphere of stars. People like Sarah Vaughan, Sammy Davis and Pearl Bailey, to mention just a few. And maybe tonight we got somebody who is going to start the hard climb up. But that's not for me to decide. It's you, the audience, who will indicate by your applause who will be the winner and take that first step up the ladder of show business. And now, before the contestants run out of the stage door with fright, I think we better get on with the show. Vivian, will you please bring on the first contestant?"

And bring him on she did. She came from the wings, but the eyes of the audience staring up out of a sea of black faces were not on the square-looking Negro she had in tow. The tight dress amply outlined her sensual body, its low-cut front leaving little to the imagination. She placed the contestant in front of the microphone, handed the MC the introduction card, tossed her straightened long hair seductively toward the audience and continued offstage. The master of ceremonies followed her off with his eyes, then turned his head, then his body, until he stood looking into the wings. He twisted his head back at the audience and deadpanned, "Oh, yeah." He shook his head affirmatively. "Oh, yeah." The crowd loved it. He turned again, looked at the contestant and jumped back startled.

"How the hell did you get out here?"

The amateur stood in the glare of the spot, his brown shoes mismatched to the blue, ill-fitting suit. He rolled his eyes nervously toward the balcony.

"That girl she done brought me out."

The audience roared and the MC joined in, bending over with practiced laughter. He straightened up, raised his hand, hushed the crowd and looked studiously at the card.

"Well, let's see who you are. Ladies and gentlemen, our first amateur tonight is George Davis." He looked at the contestant. "Where are you from, George?"

"Montgomery, Alabama."

The master of ceremonies quickly grabbed and shook his hand. "Welcome to America, George."

Their man was sitting hunched down in the last row; there were empty seats on both sides of him. And when Pope leaned over the divider and tapped him on the shoulder, The Nightman flinched. Turning and recognizing them, he smiled his relief. He slid out of the seat, came up the aisle and stepped between the detectives. The three of them, their arms on the divider, casually faced the stage.

"You wanted to see us?" Sullivan's voice barely carried, for the band started the refrain of a standard and George began to sing an octave high and a beat off.

"Yeah, I sure do."

222

"The way you jumped, you must have expected some-body else," Pope said, taking a side glance at him. "Why the edge?"

"Hey, man, I didn't know if the message would get through to you in time and I wasn't sure who would be comin' at me in the dark," The Nightman answered, continuing to look at the stage. "The way you two shook me down in the poolroom, you never know. Word could get around I'm stoolin'; I could end up with a shiv in me."

"You told us that before." Sullivan's voice had turned nasty. "What have you got?"

George from Montgomery was taking the quick hook, Apollo style. The judge who decided the fate of the contestants sat high in a side box just off the stage, in full view of the audience. He had on the black robes of a jurist and the white wig of an English court. He had stood up, after the struggling amateur had tried a couple of mangled high notes. Looking at the audience, he had shaken his head sadly, then with a sigh reluctantly raised to his lips a battered trumpet that blared the command for a sticklike elongated man to come charging down the aisle dressed in the shrunken uniform of a Keystone Kop. The stick man swan-dived over the footlights and slid on his stomach along the stage. The band had hit a wild, discordant beat, as the clown constable got up and did an improvised dance while firing blank cartridges at the terrified contestant. George from Montgomery, wild-eyed and confused, held on with both hands to the microphone until his fingers were pried loose by the Keystone Kop and the master of ceremonies. They picked him up bodily and lugged him off into the wings.

There was no way to be heard over the roaring laugh-ter so the three of them watched the action on stage, know-ing George from Montgomery was a plant.

The Nightman, hunched over and almost lost be-tween the detectives, felt conspicuous even in the back of the darkened theater. But to continue his hustle on the streets and in the back alleys of Harlem, it was neces-sary for him to pay his premiums on a freedom insurance policy Sullivan held over him. He was never sure when this white would let the policy lapse. After tonight he would be Pope's pigeon, too, and under his breath he called them both mother fuckers. But he had no illusions. He was a working informer and it had its compensations. If he was busted by another cop, Sullivan would get him out of it and keep him in circulation, because that's the way it worked. He had hustled for the detective knowing that the two dead policeman had made it a big one and Sullivan would have to remember. Both cops would have to owe him a large favor now, for in the jungle of The Nightman's world, where the unexpected was a normal way of life, it was a future edge on anything short of killing a man. Because what he had come up with he felt was good, very good.

A girl singer with a passable voice had been introduced, and the crowd sat respectfully silent, listening to her.

"You know, when you guys left me I got curious and started to check around." The Nightman spoke softly, forcing the detectives to lean toward him. "I figured I better get closer to something as big as this. It could have its advantages, you know." He stole a look at Frank Sullivan, then quickly looked back at the stage. "So I remember a chick by the name of Gloria that used to work the Seven–Eleven Club. She leave there a while back. She doin' her thing at another club now. But she used to be a good girl friend of this Ivy. Well, Gloria she like owe me a favor, so I decided to take it out in talk. She don't wanna tell me nothin' at first because she still tight with Ivy. But I remind her of that favor and told her I want to be paid now. And, man, she fill me in real good about her. She say Ivy's been over to see Jim Harris a lot of times when he was in jail and that Ivy and him are still more than friendly since he's been released. They got to be, man, because they married."

Chapter 23

The apartment house went up into the darkened rain clouds, wet and majestic in its niche among the other

224

scrupulously cared-for buildings high in a block in Sugar Hill. It looked down to the hushed, tree-lined street, down past the hill to the ball fields and playgrounds, to the West Side Drive and to the river and beyond, where isolated lights glowed through the rain high on the cliffs of Jersey. But behind the building were rows of tenements like veins across a boozer's face. And if you took a deep breath, really deep, you could smell the stench of death.

The Negro doorman moved instinctively to the shimmering black limousine before it rolled to a stop. His smile became surprised as he opened the door and saw Doc Johnson emerge.

"Good evenin', sir," the doorman said. His old face grinned like that of an adolescent seeing a fabled hero.

He trotted ahead, pushing open the door to the cavernous lobby, which was furnished elegantly with large pieces of modern furniture. Ordinarily the doorman would have asked, "Who are you visiting?" and would have used the lobby switchboard to call the apartment above to see if the visitor should be admitted. But now he was already pressing for the self-service elevator.

"Summer sure hangin' on, sir; it's a hot night, but I guess this rain it'll cool it off some."

Doc Johnson turned away from admiring his own image in the full-length mirror on the opposite wall and nodded.

As Johnson disappeared behind the elevator doors, the old man watched the floor indicator, but there was no need; he knew where it would stop.

The top floor was divided into two separate penthouse apartments. To the left was the quiet, dignified residence of a Negro jurist of the appellate court. Johnson turned to the right, where a door was open, letting out laughter and the sound of piano music, Ellington's "Sophisticated Lady." A large geranium plant, in the arid white foyer, was partially obscured by a tuxedoed white man pressing a stylish mulatto girl against the wall in what seemed to be mutual seduction. He walked past them and stood looking down into a sunken living room filled with mixed couples. Their animated chatter and laughter, a touch too loud and forced, was apparently helped along

225

by a tray of drinks being served by a white-jacketed Negro. The guests came from backgrounds of prominence and influence. There was a Wall Street broker with ties to the federal government; a Negro administrator of local housing and urban renewal; a state senator and his pallid wife, laughing too soon, jumping the punch line of a joke told by a colored balladeer who had become famous for his black Southern folk songs. Off to the side of the room was the appellate judge who lived at the other side of the building, his aging intelligent face working as he talked with a nodding white man. And circulating among the other guests, their breasts and their smiles bared just enough to add an aura of sexual parody, were a number of beautiful Negro women, elaborately dressed, while heard over it all was the piano player's almost white music.

Some heads had turned, the whites following the glances of their colored companions at the fashionably dressed large middle-aged Negro who had just come in. Most of the blacks in the room knew who he was and a couple of whites did, too, but there was no wave of acknowledgment, no one asked him to join them in a drink.

"Don't spit, you'll down them all." Johnson's thoughts were put in words. He turned and stared into narrow, mocking eyes. The nose, broad above the full mustache, seemed compensation for an almost bald head. But the ruffled shirt, laced with silk, fronting the evening suit was exactly right for the strong dark face.

"Hello, Doc." The lips spread across capped teeth and the face now looked almost Oriental. "Glad you could make the party." The suave Negro shook his hand as the piano player hit some wrong keys. "How about a drink and I'll introduce you to my guests." The smile became broader. "It's been a dull evening so far. Maybe them meeting you will give the party a touch of life. I know it'll give them something to talk about on the way home."

Johnson knew it was the character of the man to flaunt someone like himself to a roomful of influential New Yorkers. His host would enjoy moving Doc, an infamous black tom, among the pompous fat cats with whom he and Johnson had never appeared together socially before.

Theirs, until recently, had been just a casual acquaintance built on mutual respect. For the only thing they seemed to have in common was the blackness of their skins; this sleek, urbane man moved in a rarefied world far removed from the likes of Doc Johnson.

Five years ago the black magazine *Sable* had hailed him as their man of the year. A man who put in twelve working hours a day and seemed to swing as many at night. A realtor and landowner, they said, an industrialist cut from the same pattern as the Hugheses and Gettys. And they seemed rightfully proud to make the comparison to white men, for to Walker Lewis it had all seemed to come easy, as he had that unique talent for making money that few men in the world possess.

A business administration degree from New York University, a war on, three years in the service and out as a second lieutenant. At twenty-five an opportunist looking around impatiently for a beginning stake. His father, a postman, had scrimped to buy the brownstone they lived in. The rents covered the mortgage and a profit was seen. He talked the old man into taking a second mortgage. "I'll pay you back double, Pop." And he took the money, put down payments on a couple of tenements, renegotiated loans and bought a couple more. It was too easy to be spotted as a slum lord, so he hid behind a corporation. Bust a block in Queens, pay a hundred percent above the price for a house, put in a black family with a mess of kids, then wait and buy out the whites, who sell at a loss. Then do it again, this time in the Bronx and then somewhere else, because blacks were willing to pay the exorbitant prices for houses, spread-out over thirty years, to escape the hated ghetto slum lords.

There was talk the third avenue el was going down. The whole rotten Irish area was going to be torn down. And new apartment buildings would replace their tenements and the East Side was going to be the new gold coast. Walker Lewis bought that information from a functionary in the city administration long before it became a fact, and bought up tenements and waited for the money combines to come around and offer ten times his buying price. "Amateurs," he said, "the bastards are amateurs." And he went into the construction business when he saw how it worked. Out of the rubble of tenements he built sparkling new high-rise apartment houses and called them Manhattan Towers and Manhattan View, and there seemed no limit to what he could charge for rents.

And once he was sitting on money, other money was attracted to him, smelling at his rear end like dogs ready to mate. Land in Arizona and California, motels, a company bought here, stock manipulations there, and three marriages. The country was booming and Walker Lewis rode its crest into New York and Washington's most plush clubs. For he was an oddity, a black multimillionaire who summered on the Riviera, had an apartment in Paris and a penthouse, in a building he owned, high above Sugar Hill.

But Doc Johnson knew him as something else, a greedy man reaching out abnormally, far beyond the need for money. In Harlem society their worlds rarely crossed. But they saluted each other with cursory words, each respecting the other as an authentic success. But all that had changed the night Walker Lewis invited him up to the apartment. "There's something I want to talk about, Doc." At first Johnson thought he was being sparred with, as Lewis told about his political awareness early in his financial rise. Of how he had looked around for a candidate to back, realizing the apathetic Democrats from downtown could be beaten, for they took Harlem residents for granted as sheeplike voters. He told of how he had found his man, a young lawyer destined for nothing higher than claims court, fighting for a piece of insurance money. Lewis ran him for Congress as an Independent Liberal. He spread his money around, brought in professionals to run the campaign, and his man won in a tight race. Once in office he became a caustic voice that people identified with. In the quickly passing years his reelections became easier and his seniority piled up and he became a head of an influential committee and Walker Lewis owned him, lock, stock and vote.

So what? Doc thought. So he owns a congressman. But Lewis continued to talk and Johnson could feel a beginning fervor at the enormity of what was being proposed, the stimulating talk grabbing and filling his mind with excitement. Thoughts he himself had wishfully entertained for a number of years, and he told Lewis about them and in the end he played it all down with "I'll think about it," trying to cover it over with indifference. But Johnson had lain awake that night tossing the immense partnership offer over and over, and in the end he had put it aside as something just possibly too big even for their combined efforts to take on. He hated himself for backing away.

"Come on," Walker Lewis said, "I think I'll introduce you to the judge first."

Johnson could hear the laughter in the voice as the hand on his back began to maneuver him past the white wrought-iron fence that fronted the living room. His body stiffened, the look in his eyes announced impatience. "Not tonight, Walker," he said softly. "Maybe some other time you'll give me a chance to converse with some of them sleek white and black cat friends of yours. Tonight I just wanted to talk to you and you know what about."

The smile came off Lewis's face, his hand slid away and then the brown narrow eyes seemed to take on a fresh glow of anticipation. Slowly the smile returned. "You should learn patience, Doc. I waited a long time for you to accept my offer. Now you won't let me savor it. You should let me sniff and inhale it like good wine for a few minutes, because taken too quickly it might be too intoxicating."

Johnson's broad face hardened. He didn't like Lewis's glib word games that passed for sophisticated wit. Save it for Negro judges and white bankers. Use it to impress the heads of management and labor, but not me, he thought.

Walker Lewis read the flash of fleeting doubt crossing Johnson's mind and he turned him around to the door that led to the study. "You're right, Doc, it's about time we talked, and besides, you're not missing much by refusing that introduction to my guests; they'd bore you to death."

Lewis was a short man, but sitting behind the desk he appeared taller. "I was a little surprised to receive your call tonight, Doc"—the desk lamp spilled off the scattered papers and open attaché case as he rummaged through a drawer for a light—"because I had my doubts we could ever get together and that would have been disappointing." He lit a thin cigarillo, then snapped his lighter shut and gazed inquisitively through the smoke curling up from his lips. "Tell me, Doc, what was it that made you make up your mind?"

"Let's just say my mind was made up for me by a combination of things," Johnson answered evenly.

"You don't mind a curious but natural question. Tonight, when you were taken, did you set that up yourself?"

Doc's mouth gave the impression of a smile. "Why should I do that, Walker? With you backing me I can go for it all, the whole operation. I'd be foolish to jeopardize something like that, wouldn't I now?"

Johnson sat a little away from the desk. The fleshy face was obscure but his eyes, despite the smile, stood out like an omnivorous black bear's in a dimly lit cave. There could have been mockery in the answer; Walker Lewis wasn't sure. But he did know that an alliance with this man would be bound in tenuous threads and he wondered if time and their mutual commitments could ever change it. He shrugged. Who says I have to like him? I only have to make money with him, he thought, and flicked ashes into the tray.

"I don't really care what happened up to now, Doc. All I'm interested in is that we have a firm understanding of the parts each of us will have to contribute to our enterprise. There can be no referring back to a contract, or even a meeting to iron out any future difficulties." The eyes in the good-looking dark brown face suddenly hardened. And his voice left the culture; it moved down to the tough nitty-gritty of Harlem talk. "So if there's any bitch, man, you let it come now, you understand? This deal's too big to have you walk out of here dissatisfied. I don't want to hear you wailin' after we start dividin' the marbles. Now's the time, baby. So if you got something to say, let's hear it."

Doc's eyes went past Walker Lewis through the opened sliding door that led to a patio. The rain could be heard falling rhythmically on the outdoor glass table. "I think you're askin' for too much, Walker," he said dryly, and looked back at him. "What you're doing is important, but not fifty percent important. This thing is going to be

230

won or lost out in the streets, not in a penhouse apartment or from some office in Washington. There's over a couple of hundred people working up here, from runners to managers, and I'm going to have to be movin' among them to make sure they don't decide to go in business for themselves while the war is on. What I'm saying is, I got to keep a smooth-runnin' organization while I fight a battle and I wanna tell you that dago is goin' to lay a price on my head that's goin' to be large enough to interest a lot o' niggers and maybe some of the law up here. Yeah, Walker, I'm the one that's going to be in the middle runnin' it all and that's got to make me more than just an equal partner in the business."

There was a long abrasive silence while Walker Lewis watched the smoke rise and twist erratically up from the smoldering tip of his miniature cigar. At last he lowered his eyes and they locked with Johnson's.

"You make out a good case for yourself, Doc. A very good case," he said, measuring the words like the calculating businessman he was. "When I approached you"—he motioned toward Johnson and himself—"about us going into a partnership in taking over what should rightfully be a black man's business, you were very enthusiastic about the idea. You told me that this was in the back of your mind for a long time. Well, I want to remind you, Doc, that without me it still would be in the back of your mind, because if you think this thing is going to succeed by your bravado of replying something out of a nineteen-thirty-eight gangster movie, you're in for a bad surprise. Oh, you might do pretty good in the beginning. You kill a few, they kill a few. But in the end you're not going to beat them. Their money can buy a lot of black men. They'll chop you up and every one of your guys, and I think you know it. No, this great battle you anticipate is going to be fought by intimidation and backed by the power of politics. It's true, we're going to need a very strong show of force. And when you have aligned behind you people you can trust, and are prepared to physically tell our Mafioso friends that there will be no more money coming out of Harlem for their coffers, I will then make a phone call to my prestigious committeeman in Washington. Whom I have fully briefed on what is going to transpire. Then he's going to quietly get in touch with Giaccano and tell him exactly what I told him to tell him. That he is backing our stand and if they insist on fighting us, he will prepare to go against them politically."

The thin cigar moved to Lewis's mouth, the exhaled smoke went across the desk, hung for a second in a cloud below the lamp, then was ripped apart by a breeze moving in through the open patio door. "What we're taking on, Doc, as you well know, is a national underground organization with a take that is possibly even beyond my imagination. They got such a lock on this country with their control of all the illegal operations—and it's being barmitzvahed into straight businesses—that if you told the average taxpayer he wouldn't believe it. But—and here's the guts of our fight—their one big fear is publicity. The sectional heads of the families, like Giaccano, and their chief lieutenants know that too much of it would destroy their power, because the organization is bigger than the individual, and they'd be willing to take a loss to preserve their anonymity."

He leaned across the desk and the eyes seemed much younger in the middle-aged face. "In that phone call, Doc, I'm going to have my man tell Giaccano that he will pull some political strings and help create a congressional committee on crime of which he will become chairman, and he will move the committee into Foley Square with television sessions. Then they will subpoena Giaccano and everyone high up in his Family in an investigation of not only New York, but the whole East Coast right down to Miami. They'll dig in Las Vegas, the West Coast, touch every base. It's going to be a three-ring circus that will make the old McCullen Investigating Committee and the other investigations look like they were on the take. And they won't let it die because out of it will come legislation; the public will *finally* become aware of how much organized crime is costing each and every citizen in this country and they're going to clamor for prevention and he's going to make sure they get it. The Syndicate's a bunch of bright people, Doc; they know an investigation of this size has to cost them millions of dollars and the inevitable rolling of heads."

Lewis's voice lowered into a conspiratorial tone, deep and resonant, and came at Johnson like a cadent banging drum. "And then he's going to tell Giaccano that the only way it can be stopped," he paused for emphasis, "is for them to get the hell out of Harlem; that it's a black man's domain and black men are going to run it." He nodded toward Johnson. "And that's you and I. No, Doc, it's not going to be your guns in the street that's going to chase them out of uptown; it's going to be me, Walker Lewis, controlling a congressional committee through my puppet in Washington, and you can consider yourself lucky I'm letting you be associated with me in this great venture."

An awkward quietness, broken by the erratic rhythm of falling rain out on the terrace. Walker Lewis leaned back, the cigar going to his mouth, and he waited for a response. But Johnson's impassive ash-dark face gave no indication of what he was thinking.

"I believe now we have a clear understanding of our relative merits"—Lewis's voice became more temperate —"but I don't undersell you, Doc. If this is any consolation, you're the only man I would ever go into this with. You have the rare combination of intestinal fortitude and brains and a willingness to gamble for high stakes, and that's the ingredients that are necessary to take on something as vast as this. But like I said before, if you're not happy with arrangements, if you think you're being given the short end of the stick, then let's forget the whole thing right now."

Slowly Johnson nodded his head. "Okay, you've got a deal, Walker. We'll get along."

Lewis's face broke into a broad smile. The teeth below the brush mustache were like a dental ad, laugh lines crinkled at the eyes and the nostrils flared beautifully. "I'm sure we will, Doc," he said, "I'm sure we will." Somehow the face didn't convey a feeling of humor to Johnson.

She came through the door and she stood looking at them for a moment before Walker Lewis saw her.

"Oh, Loretta, I want to introduce you to Mr. Johnson."

She walked toward the desk. She was about thirty-five, and was wearing a shoulderless pink evening gown

233

that complimented her figure. Her fair complexion went with her shoulder-length blond hair. And Johnson remembered the wedding; the *Amsterdam News* had made quite a social event of it.

"Doc, I would like to introduce you to my wife."

Johnson came out of the chair and smiled an acknowledgment. Loretta Lewis gave a terse nod of her head, added Johnson up, then dismissed him by turning to her husband, who had remained sitting.

"Some of your guests are starting to leave."

Walker Lewis smiled at her. If anything the smile was more synthetic than the one he had given Johnson. "I'm in conference, dear. When I'm finished I'll be out."

"There are some important people out there, Walker." There was petulance in her tone. "Don't you think you should say good night? You *are* their host, you know."

"I think you can do a far better good night than I can, my dear, so will you please convey to them my apologies for not seeing them to the door and my wishes for their safe journey home."

She stood in the half light coming from the desk lamp and stared chillingly at Lewis. Then she looked at Johnson, who had remained standing, and bent her head slightly. "Good night, Mr. Johnson." She turned and went out to the departing guests.

Walker Lewis contemplated the closed door. "Women," he said tonelessly. "If a messiah's hand could miraculously sew up the lips of their vaginas, they'd be through." He looked at Johnson. "Using a golden thread, of course."

Doc smiled. "I guess I should be going, too, Walker. There's nothing more we can add to what's already been said. I got a lotta work ahead of me. It'll be two, maybe three weeks before I'm ready to roll."

"Take your time," Lewis answered, coming around the desk. "Just make sure of the men around you and when you're ready you let me know. In the meantime, I'll see that there's some early noise in the papers about an impending crime investigation." His hand came out, Johnson took it and they shook firmly, their eyes holding as silently they wished each other luck.

Doc was at the door when he looked back. "Oh, by the way, Walker, I'm going to have to kill a cop. I'll frame
234

it so it'll look like an addict killed him, but it's gonna cause a stink. But a necessary one. I want this detective out of the way before we start."

There was a silence while Lewis's eyes swept across him. Rain had spotted Johnson's shoes and put some creases in his suit, but the garish diamond on the hand holding the doorknob glimmered dimly back across the room.

"All right," Walker Lewis answered slowly. "If you think it's a necessity I'm sure it will be handled in your impeccable good taste."

Chapter 24

"You lied to us once tonight, bitch. Just don't you try it again. Because I got you halfway into a prison cell now. You lie and I'll help close the door on you for the next ten years of your life, even if I have to frame you to the wall."

Ivy sat bunched over on the edge of the sofa, too frightened to look up. She was barefooted and her robe was pulled tightly around her slim body. She had lain in bed trying to fight her way into evasive sleep, trying to close her mind to frightful reality. Then, as the thankful blanket of sleep had begun to cover her anxieties, she heard the knock and bolted upright in bed. For a few bewildering seconds she didn't know where she was or the time or why she was being awakened. The demanding knock came again and suddenly she knew it was her Jim at the door, that he was there to take her away, their plans abandoned, and that's the way it would be from now on. . . .

"We know you've seen him." Sullivan's voice hammered at her relentlessly. "When we went back to the club to take you in for questioning the manager said you went home sick. And that was shortly after we had talked to you. But you didn't go straight home. The doorman in the apartment here said you only arrived back in the building about an hour ago."

"I was walkin', like I told you," she murmured. "I just felt like walkin' and gettin' some air."

They had put it together. They knew who she was but they could only threaten and guess the rest. Hold them off, she told herself. Hold them off, just a few more hours, that's all he's going to need, and maybe this was the best thing she could give him: a chance to run without carrying the extra burden of her fear. Ivy had always hated her cowardice. Now she was determined to fight the fear, choke back the timidity, hold off the verbal assaults with stillness, denials and open antagonism.

"I want to tell you something," the detective said irritably. "You don't know it but you're doing him more harm than good. Because I don't give him no more than forty-eight hours to live unless you play it smart and give him up."

She raised her head slowly and stared blankly at Sullivan. "Give him up." She repeated the words to herself. How do you do that, white man? she thought. She studied the rough-hewn face and wondered if somebody as hard as this had ever been in love—where everything else was secondary, and that included your willingness to say the hell with your own safety.

"You know he can't get away. Only a fool would think that," Bill Pope said. He had hung back and now stepped up next to Sullivan. "By tomorrow afternoon his picture will be on every precinct bulletin board in the city."

"If you really want to help him, this is your chance. Because, believe me, if there was ever a man marked to die, he's it. He's killed two cops and nobody is going to forget it when they take him. You cooperate with us right now and maybe we'll still be able to get him without firing a shot."

He wasn't conning her and Ivy knew it. She lowered her head and closed her eyes and wanted to put her hands to her ears. And shut out those words about him dying. Oh, Jimmy. She almost said his name.

Lightning filled the windows and snarling thunder rolled across the storming night sky.

236

"You won't have it easy if we take you in like this," Pope continued quietly. "You'll be considered an accessory for holding back information that's helping him escape. You could really end up doing a long time in prison and that's not an idle threat. That's a fact that—"

She looked up quickly, suddenly finding strength in unexpected anger. "I don't care what you do to me, you hear me?" she shouted. "Why you two keep comin' at me? I'm—" there was a catch in the voice and her hand brushed at the corner of her eye—"I'm not goin' to tell you where he is 'cause I don't know. You understand that? And even if I did I wouldn't tell you, 'cause I'd try to help him by giving him all the life I can. And if that's just another week, another day or even just another breath, he can have it. But it will be as the free man he always wanted to be. And I don't care how long you question me, I'm going' to say the same thing—I don't know where he is—over and over. So take me in, go on, do it now, and let's get it done with."

Bill Pope looked exasperatedly at Frank. Probably any further talk would be a waste of their time. But her stubbornness seemed out of character to the older, more experienced Sullivan. The style didn't match the woman he had remembered from earlier in the night. And Sullivan had noticed other things: the orderly apartment furnished in inexpensive good taste, where nothing was pushed into a corner or against a wall just to fill a room; the crucifix tacked to the wall just inside the door, and the faded silver-framed picture of a brown child holding the hand of a dark man, both wearing their best in front of a church on some Sunday long ago. He suspected that locking her up would mean little to her and even less to them. Booking her on suspicion would remove them that much more from Harris. He knew he had already played one of his hunches and Doc Johnson had exploded it in his face. But now he felt they were so close, a few minutes more wouldn't matter.

"You have a choice," he said, his voice softening, looking down at her as one would gaze at a disobedient child. "You can stay with the idea that he can get away and we'll take you in. You won't make the bail because it's going to be too high. And you're going to sit inside a cell

237

dreading to hear that your husband was shot dead trying to escape an all-states alarm. Or you can tell us where he's hiding out, where something can be set up that will give us a chance to take him alive, without anyone else being senselessly killed."

She thought she could see sympathy in his eyes, but if it was sympathy she didn't want it. Not from him, not from him, not from these two. "Oh, sure I can help him. That is, like if I knew where he was at you would want me to turn him in, that it? Like help set him up to die in the electric chair?" She smiled bitterly. "Mister, I know the chances for him to get away are maybe like a hundred to one and hardly nobody wins at them odds, but as long as he's free he's still got that one chance."

He shook his head. "I don't think you have a very clear picture of what's happening. Your husband was in on this with at least two accomplices that we know of. Well, we're reasonably certain who they are. In fact, we've seen Jackson and Logart tonight."

Her eyes had moved away from his but now the casual mention of those names pulled them back to him and despite the previous denials her face unwittingly showed concern.

"I think you'd have a rough time recognizing them now, because they both were killed brutally. One ended up with a spike driven through his body, nailed to a wall like a warning to someone. The other one was thrown out of a window twelve floors up. He must have been half dead before he hit the street from the beating they gave him. They were both obviously meant to suffer before they were killed, and they did." He watched her closely.

Jackson and Logart. She felt sick. They *can't* be dead. She searched his expressionless face to see if he was lying and could see nothing. He's trying to trick me, that's what he's doing. But how did he know their names? She could fight off the rough questions and the threats of what was going to happen to her, could even fend off their changing tactics of sympathy and soft words, but her mind couldn't blank out the picture of Jim Harris lying dead between the other two. She tried to erase the picture but she couldn't. There would be no way to expel it. Her mind was preconditioned to accept the worst.

"And they weren't blacks that killed them. They were white men. White professional killers"—and Sullivan emphasized "white" by holding the word a touch longer than he had to, letting it fall against her like the rain outside pounding down onto the street. "It was more than the money they're trying to recover. It was even more than the straight murder of retaliation, because they could've killed them a lot easier with a quick bullet in the back of the head. But they purposely made them bleed and suffer first and left them in the cruelest way they could think of. And by now they know Harris was the one that put it all together and they're sure as hell not going to stop until they get him. It may not be tonight or tomorrow or the day after that, but you can be certain they're going to get him and when they do they're going to do a special job on him, too."

Pope stood back and watched Frank Sullivan's cold professionalism beat her down. He watched her bowed head, pulled protectively into the hunched shoulders, and the clenched hands, pressed together as though in prayer. And he pitied her involvement in something that seemed beyond her needs or conception.

"They're going to torment him by tearing him up a little at a time," Sullivan went on in a dry, matter-of-fact tone that was somehow making it sound even more shocking than it was. "He's going to beg them to kill him and he's going to get his wish, but only after they've had their fun. And when you get him back you're going to have to keep the casket closed because nobody will have the stomach to look at what's left."

She got up from the couch, pulling the dressing gown even tighter about her shoulders and moving like a sleepwalker caught in a dreadful dream that she was incapable of waking from; went over to the half-open window, where she stood staring down into the rain-drenched street.

"You say if you turn him over to us he's going to get the chair. Well, if any man should, he deserves it. Only law is a complex thing. There have been a lot of very strange court verdicts and decisions in the last couple of years. If there was no proven premeditation, if they can prove he hadn't planned to take the patrolmen's lives, then maybe he can beat the chair and get life in prison.

But that is only the slimmest of hopes, because in all likelihood his sentence will be death. But it won't be tonight in some rainy gutter. By the time he goes through all the legal work of a trial, the appealing and the final setting of the date, it could add months to his life." She stood stiffly, her back to him, and there was no way to read her thoughts. "Now it may not sound like much, but it could be time he could use to make his peace with God and to die like a man with some dignity."

The curtains caught the breeze of the storm and whipped up about her. A shaft of light covered the window, then there was a burst of thunder and then a ponderous silence broken only by the torrents of rain.

He spoke again, slowly. "It's your decision, Ivy; you hold the answer. You can give him maybe a year more of life or certain death in the street like some half-crazed dog."

Sullivan looked at Pope and they both held their breath and stared anxiously at her, waiting in the suspending hush for her response.

It was low, then piercing, and it tore the silence like the sounds of a wounded doe, mournfully crying through the long frightening night to be let free from the cage of words that lay the dreadful future smotheringly out before her. She lowered her head, her arms going about her stomach, and her body began to rock with sobs.

"Where is he, Ivy? Where is he located?"

Chapter 25

"Six forty-seven Lenox Avenue. Yeah, yeah, I got it," Nick Difalco said too casually. But he repeated the address appreciatively to himself. "Nah, we won't need any of your guys. "What's that? No, I won't be goin' back to your place. When I finish up here I'm going' to sleep for a week. But you can do me a favor: don't lose any more money, huh?" He was about to hang up but an afterthought made him hold on to the phone for a few more seconds. "And oh, yeah, Doc, thanks for the help. I'll let the old man know. He'll most likely give you a call after I fill him in."

He slipped the receiver back into its cradle and stepped out of the phone booth, squinting against the slanted rays of the hot morning sun. The rain that had ended a couple of hours before had not brought the expected relief to the sweltering streets. Difalco could feel the wilted shirt cling to his body as he walked among men in work clothes, young girls in fresh sleeveless dresses, and older, more plainly dressed women. They were all moving unsmilingly with the unhurried steps people use on their way to work. Most of them were being swallowed up by the cavernous entrance of the Interborough Rapid Transit subway. The few that looked at him didn't notice the tiredness in the eyes beneath the brim of his hat or the stubble of beard on the swarthy olive face. It was more of an abstraction that caught their quick glances, for they sensed the white antagonism that was passing them during the morning rush hour.

He moved unhurriedly through the crowds and eased into the back seat of the waiting car, and they twisted around to him.

"It looks like we're going to put a finish to this. I just got the address where the bum's holed up."

There was relief in Morello's and Parini's faces. Moving through the thin cover of darkness in Harlem was one thing. The night people who swung in its bars and assembled on its corners were a different breed than the somber workers who passed them now. (The first one had been easy and exciting, taking him out of the bar under the threat of leaving behind a couple of dead nigger boozers. They worked him over at the end of a deserted pier, but he died too quickly from punishment and maybe fright and it was then that they found out why they were being paid big bonuses. They listened, nodding and asking no questions as Nick Difalco explained that the body, rolled in a blanket in the trunk of the car, would have to be shown in such a way that there would be no mistaking the message. But the Lorelei had been something else. Hard work had turned the excitement off. The bastard wouldn't talk, the noise was too loud and the

241

pounding threats coming through the wall too close. It was there that they both found out why Difalco's reputation as an executioner was talked about through the New York Families. The long Harlem night had turned into discouraging day. The street seemed too crowded now with black humanity and the white faces in the blue uniforms with guns strapped to their hips stood out too vividly against the choking gray filth. And Difalco was at last ready to turn back for downtown after he made a final call.

"Remember that reward money Johnson mouthed about? Well, it paid off," Difalco said, unnecessarily cupping his hands around a match; it never wavered in the breezeless heat as he lit a cigarette. "I'll tell ya one thing: you got to hand it to that black son of a bitch. He got Harlem knocked up." He leaned back—he was in no rush now—and shook his head in wonder. "It's like they're waitin' in line to do him a favor—for a price, that is. It seems like one of his boot-lickin' jigs lives in the same building this Harris has holed himself up in and was kind of suspicious of him the way he kept to himself and stayed in the apartment a lot. Well, last night he spots the bum with another guy comin' up the stairs. They're carryin' what looks like a pile of clothes in a laundry bag. But it's dark in these dumps and he wasn't sure what he had seen, but he remembered the guy following Harris up the stairs mumble something about cops and Harris telling him to shut up. Then they slammed and bolted the door. It wasn't till this morning that he heard about the reward money Johnson was offering around and he called Doc on the chance there may be some kind of a connection." He paused. "Nice and simple, huh? All the time people are lookin' for hard answers, but in the end it's always simple, because there's always some punk ready to spill his guts for a price. We get him at six forty-seven Lenox Avenue, top floor rear."

Morello, eager to get it over with, turned the key in the ignition and started to pull the car away from the curb.

"Hey, where you goin'?" Difalco didn't raise his voice but his spare, bony face showed the dissatisfaction. "Did I tell you to move?"

"No, but I thought . . ." The driver didn't turn around, he looked in the rear-view mirror, and when his eyes caught Difalco's face he stopped talking.

"You're goin' to ride over there and knock on the door, huh?" Difalco snorted disdainfully. "It's a good way to get your head blown off. This one is maybe not going to be as easy as the first two. This shine is more than likely sittin' on top of the money with a cannon in his hand and maybe a headful of H, ready to blast anything that moves. I think we're goin' to have to take this bum straight because the main thing here is to make sure we can get at him and still give ourselves enough room to maneuver if things get tight. So we're gonna' look the joint over real good before we do anything."

The bullish-looking Parini, his hat pulled down over the rough face, walked authoritatively down the steps of the stoop. It was filled with gossiping women, who turned off their talk, watching him as he passed a couple of baby carriages. They noticed his rumple, sweat-stained clothes, made a couple of wry remarks, then forgot him. On the sidewalk his shoulders synchronized with his aggressive steps along a half block active with school kids, old men, city noises and more women.

Difalco watched him come around the car, open the front door and sit down next to Morello. He took off his hat and wiped his brow, then turned slowly to Difalco. His narrow eyes were alive in the pug face.

"It looks all right, Nick. We can come across the roofs to his building," he said quietly, but his voice wavered and tipped off what was happening inside him. "There's a fire escape that leads down the back right into the apartment."

"Have any trouble?" Difalco asked.

"Nah. I told the old jig super I was a building inspector checking the roofs and fire escapes and he knocked himself out showing me the place." He took a quick look at Morello. The driver's eyes were boring into him as though asking for more assurance. "It's okay. It's deserted up there." He turned back to Difalco. "We can get this guy without anybody knowin' what's goin' on. And it's a break for us. I could see the window open; he's not goin'

243

to be expecting anybody to be coming through it. I think we can even hit him from the fire escape before we go into the room."

Difalco sat silently, turning over the enthusiastic suggestions. It seemed the quickest and best way to do the job. But though it sounded logical, he didn't like the concealed flutter in Parini's voice or Morello's overconcerned expression.

"Well, do we go, Nick?" Parini asked.

"Okay," Difalco said coldly. "You both hit him. Nothing fancy; just a straight blowout. And don't bother goin' back over the roofs again. Go down the steps and out the front entrance. If the bum runs on you, follow him out the door, but"—his hand came up, his finger pointing truculently at their faces—"don't forget to grab the money. If he takes to the street there's only one way he's likely to go and that's to me. I'll be waiting in front of the building and get him comin' down the steps. And don't be far behind him. I'll be movin' this heap right after I make the hit. You both understand?"

They both nodded that they did, but each weighed the rigid orders. Morello lowered his dark curly head, not wanting Difalco to sense the gnawing question that ran through his mind. What if we run into trouble up there and it takes more time than expected? How long would he wait for them?

Parini averted his eyes from Nick's and stared past him out the rear window of the car. "It should be okay, okay," he said reassuringly to himself.

Maybe it was the pale-blue dress against the amber skin or the shapely thinness that moved inside the dress. Whatever it was, she stood out from the squalid street and drab tenements. He watched her take uneasy steps like some frightened tropical bird alarmed by the jungle of noise and people. As she crossed the avenue the brakes of a car screeched against a changing light, made her raise the suitcase in an impulse of protection. But she had lifted it too easily for one so lean, and as she came toward him the suitcase did not extend her arm fully, as a full valise that size should have. It was off its normal plane of carry, riveted there without a sway above the hot pavement. He could make out the features now and was surprised by the good looks of her angular face. But the hair, pushed back, seemed to pull the full mouth too tight and her eyes jumped in quick, birdlike fashion, taking in the whole street in flicks of hesitation as if seeking something.

She was almost parallel to the car when Parini motioned his head toward her. "Hey, Nick, get a load of this."

Difalco looked over his shoulder. As she started to pass them she turned her head and glanced nervously into the car, hesitated for a noticeable second, then picked up the pace of her walk and continued on.

"That broad's scared of somethin'," Parini said, his eyes following her as though mesmerized by the nervous prance that moved her away from them.

"That's just another high yella bitch," Difalco snapped irritably, annoyed that Parini was so easily distracted.

"No, no, Nick, it ain't that. It's the big suitcase and the way she's checkin' the street." His answer had the excitement of discovery in it.

"What about the suitcase?" Interest crept into Difalco's voice and he leaned forward as she glanced back apprehensively at the car and almost stumbled.

"Ever know anybody, Nick, who carried an empty suitcase through the streets like it was gold? It's something wrong here. She's scared to death. You see the way she looked at us when she passed?"

Difalco nudged the wheel man's shoulder. "Follow her."

"We'll stay off the street so he won't suspect," the white detective had said. "You've got to walk him around the corner. That's where the stakeout will be. There'll be a lot of plainclothesmen around. They'll move in and grab him before he knows what's happening. There won't be a shot fired. He won't be hurt. It'll be easy, easy, easy." But why did they have cops sitting almost in front of the place? The cops had said they'd be off the block. Jimmy's going to spot them, he's going to fight. The empty suitcase seemed incredibly heavy. She felt like switching it to her other hand but held on to it even more tightly as she glanced into the car. Why are they looking at me? They're not supposed to recognize me. "I promise you we will do everything we can to avoid firing a shot. But, Ivy, you've got to follow everything we tell you. You've got to make sure to walk him around the corner. That's where . . ." Oh, Jimmy, why should they change their plans? It doesn't make sense, unless—unless they don't want to take you alive and they're setting you up to force you to use a gun and try to run for it. She could feel their eyes digging into her and she had to look back, she had to see them once again. Then the shocking awareness exploded in her mind with all its frightening meaning. She swayed for an instant, almost falling into darkness, feeling the sudden sickness knifing across her stomach. Her impulse was to run, to warn her Jimmy. No, take it easy, easy. They don't know who I am. They don't know who I am. They don't know. They . . .

She heard the car start. She looked over her shoulder again to be sure and felt a new wave of fear. The car was inching doggedly behind her. They don't know who I am but they're following me. I'll pass the house. I'll keep going. They'll think I'm somebody else. What did that white detective say? They would have something special for Jim. They know he'd planned it, they'll make him suf . . . But if I pass the house they'll go up after him. . . . Oh, my God. Jimmy, Jimmy, you've got nobody to warn you. I've got to help. I've got to tell you. A sob tore from her lips. She dropped the suitcase and began to run.

Difalco had the door open before the car stopped. He snapped at Morello to stay behind the wheel. Parini was right behind him as they rushed into the tenement, whose front door Ivy had just flung open.

Through her tears the gray interior blurred and whirled and hurtled past the climbing panic that made her gaping mouth choke for air. On the landing above them she could hear the pounding steps reaching terrifyingly for her. And she shouted his name in a dread-stricken voice that filled the foul building with awareness of the horror coming up after her.

She was only half a flight ahead of them as she reached his floor. "Jim, Jim. They're here!" Her shrill cry tore at the door along with her fist. "They're goin' ta kill you. They're goin' ta kill you." Petrified, she whirled around. Difalco and Parini, breathing heavily, hesitated. She moved back away from them, sliding along the wall, not taking her eyes from theirs, and suddenly she began to scream. It was high-pitched and eerie and it filled the hall of the tenement. And for an instant it held the two men frozen. Difalco took a step toward her, curled his fist and punched at her face, but the sweating Parini's gun was far quicker, the bullet blowing the screech from her lips into echoes bounding down through the building. The bullet had struck her chest, pinning her against the wall, then slowly she slid to the floor, her eyes holding them with a look of disbelief, her mouth still parted, still moving in a silent screech, though somehow they still heard a scream, which now rode up the stairs at them stridently from the street. It took them a moment to understand the sound.

"Nick, do you hear that? It's the cops. Goddammit, the cops." Parini's pug face compressed, his marble eyes jumped wildly in his head. He took another look at the girl, then glanced back to Difalco. He started to say something, it came out mumbled as, lost in his fright, he whirled and ran down the stairs.

Nick Difalco looked at the door, which was still locked, and the girl, slumped against the wall apparently dead. He could hear his underling retreat and he cursed him and cursed the closed door and cursed Harris in the room behind it. Then he turned and ran down the stairs.

The wail of sirens ascended, pitch upon pitch, higher and higher, coming from all directions into a growling crescendo.

Tony Morello had already started the car to pull away and save himself when he saw Parini come dashing crazily out of the front door with a gun in his hand. Morello hit the brakes and threw the back door open to him as the first patrol car came into the block from the wrong direction and skidded to a halt, emptying out two cops with drawn guns. Their shouts to stop were lost in sirens and more grinding of brakes as two more prowl cars bounced to skidding stops.

Nick Difalco emerged from the entrance and took in

247

the odds, seeing Parini, oblivious to a second warning, reach for the car door as the police guns opened up, puncturing the street with a dozen clattering explosions that spun Parini around and staggered him off into a different direction. Then he stumbled to his knees and his face slammed into the pavement. He was dead and the front windows of the car were shattered. Morello his throat and one of his eyes shot away.
throat and one of his eyes shot away.

Nick Difalco's hands reached up toward the oppressive heat pouring down out of the bleaching sky. Guns extended stiffly before blue uniform shirts and beneath visored hats were strained, expectant faces, their alarmed eyes all looking the same as they came slowly up the stoop for him. And he knew, even as they twisted the handcuffs about his wrists and pulled him down the stairs, that an old man in a palatial house high on the cliffs of New Jersey would take the lock off the treasury and buy him the best legal brains in the country.

He had eased her head into his lap, gently brushing the hair back from the perspiring face. "Baby, you're goin' to be all right, you hear. You're goin' to make it," he said, trying to hold back his grief as his eyes went to the blood drenching the front of her dress. The snarling cracks of gunfire came muffled up through the hall as her almost closed eyes stared cloudingly up at him. "Everything's goin' ta be okay, honey. Everything—" His voice broke. "Just—just you hold on, Ivy. They'll get you to a hospital."

Her parched lips, caked with saliva, murmured feebly and he had to put his head close to hers. "Promise me you'll give up now," she said in a hoarse whisper. "You can't win, it's too late for you, Jim." Her hands suddenly clawed the air, her face twisting with the scourging pain. Her body stiffened against the new charge of suffering. He kissed her tears, his arms going gently about her, trying to hold her back from the deeper torment she was plunging into. He heard the door slam far below them and the distant hurry of feet on the stairs.

"Oh, Jimmy, I love you," she murmured.

"And I love you, too, baby," he answered, and began

248

to sob, tears rolling down his face he he tenderly placed her in a sitting position against the wall and slowly stood up.

Her lidded, glazing eyes reached pleadingly up to him. She tried to get up but she began to cough and pressed her bunched hands against her chest, fighting the pain.

The surging steps were louder now, heavily echoing up for him. He wanted to speak, to tell her so many things, but there was no time, no time. And in spite of his terrible guilt at seeing her lying there spilling out her life onto the filth of a squalid floor, he had to appeal to her for a final understanding of what it was all about.

"Baby . . . baby, I can't . . . I . . . You don't understand. I can't let go now. I come too far. I gotta play it out because that's the way it gotta be. Forgive me, honey, please forgive me."

They could hear the door slam above them. Bill Pope was in the lead and took the last flight of steps two at a time. They reached the landing out of breath and looked down at Ivy, her eyes begging, pleading for clemency for Jim. Bill Pope turned to the door.

"Wait, wait!" Sullivan's voice snapped a hushed warning and he pushed his partner back against the wall; then, flattening himself out against the opposite side of the door, he reached out his hand and slowly turned the knob. It opened a few inches, then stopped. Harris had had time only to put a chain in place. "We go in together," Frank whispered. "Go right to the floor." He motioned with his hands as if he held a machine gun, showing how he felt it would rise. Pope nodded tensely and braced his body for the signal. They hit into the door together, snapping the chain from the frame, smashing the door against the wall, but as they staggered in neither man had to hit the floor. The room was empty. They went through the bedroom, the closet.

"The roof. He's gone on the roof," Pope yelled from the kitchen window.

Jim Harris was already stepping from the fire escape over the ledge to the top of the building when Frank Sullivan followed Pope out the window.

"There he is, Frank," his partner yelled, pointing to the running figure two roofs away. Harris's left arm was

249

wrapped around the duffel bag of money, his right hand held the machine gun and he moved like a big black bear, low and hunched. A couple of kids who'd been on the roof had scattered in fear from his approaching frightening desperation. Pope's warning shot cut into the cloudless sky. Harris crouched down still farther, running wildly, like an animal trained to move faster at the cracks of a gun. Sullivan knew Harris's goal had to be the last house on the block, the farthest the roofs would take him from the crush of cops in front of the building he had just left. Once down those stairs, he could bury the gun in the duffel, then try to lose himself in the crowd that the shooting had attracted.

The white shirt ahead of them bobbed between television antennas, worn chimneys, pigeon coops and rooftop sheds, then suddenly his cover disappeared. He was in an open area between ledges and he straightened up for more speed. Sullivan stopped, steadied the gun and squeezed off a shot. He watched Harris stumble forward, the bullet kicking him to his knees. He turned to see where Pope was and when he looked ahead again he was astonished to see Harris rise unsteadily, still grasping the duffel bag, twist and fire a burst wildly from the gun, then continue on.

The blotched red back simmering in the heat of the tarred roofs bounced distortedly in front of Bill Pope. Harris, laboring onward in a crouch, knew he couldn't outdistance them now to the end building. He veered to the back to the roof he was on, seeking another fire escape down which he would go to get into an apartment, then to the stairs and the street. Pope stopped, aimed carefully and fired. The bullet turned Harris around, his mouth tore open and his shout of anguish and frustration and failure vibrated across the roofs. He dropped the submachine gun and squinted at the advancing silhouettes coming at him in an agonizingly slow, cautious tilt. The sky and roof behind them began to rotate, whirling into a blur that altered their civilian clothes into bulky blue uniforms. He could again feel the chilling cold of another roof twenty years before, could feel the fright of a skinny adolescent trying to contain the fear of being caught for some misdeed committed in the jungled streets

250

below. Even the tears felt the same running down his face, burning into the black skin. He staggered back toward the end of the roof, still clinging to the sack of money. And suddenly his mind cleared and he saw it all, saw at last the fallacy of his scheme, which had been based on guts, the only thing he ever really possessed, and which was now pushing him into the final escape of certain death. But he didn't care. The hell with it all. It didn't matter now. Not a fucking thing mattered, and he reached for the .38 that was tucked into his belt. The bullets caught him across the chest and stomach, spinning him and driving him back. He hovered for a second, his thick muscular frame mutilated and bleeding, and then he tumbled over the end of the building. The fire escape a floor below caught his body. In the darkness that started to shroud him he realized that the duffel bag had fallen with him and that the .38 was still clutched in his hand. With one terminal effort he raised the gun. He wanted nothing to be left, determined that it should end now. He could barely make out the blackened shadows against the blinding sky and fired up randomly. The sounds of the returning shots cracked and echoed across the roofs, the bullets puncturing, ripping, tearing into his flesh. Jim Harris's life was blasted from his body, his head, grotesquely twisted to the side, faced into the massive courtyard. The eyes, wide in their final stare, had brought through the surging blackness his last conscious thought: The money he had gambled his life for was falling away from him, for the duffel bag had torn open.

They were lined two abreast, one behind the other—fifteen-hundred of them, all teen-agers, all black. The local high school was starting its school day. When the shots had vibrated down from the roofs they had grown quiet, each listening, looking up, wondering what was going on. Then the climax emerged above them. They were awed at seeing Harris's form teeter at the edge, topple and fall while guns flashed. But as the first few bills came gently down, there was a slight stirring as they awakened to what was lazily tumbling and turning and being carried toward them. At first there was only an isolated shout as the money thickened, then a rumble coiled across the yard, building into a bellow of excitement

251

that exploded in the throats of hundreds of young blacks. They broke from the lines, pushing, clawing, straining up to grab for the slothful treasure that flowed steadily down upon them. A rush from the rear knocked down those in front and they pulled the money out of each other's hands, punching and kicking and turning the canyonlike schoolyard into a rapacious pit of greed.

Pope, leaning over the edge, could hear the heavy steps coming across the roof from all directions. The steps stopped and the men gathered about him, but still he couldn't take his eyes from the violent students reaching up for the remaining rain of money.

"Goddamn, Frank. Did you ever?" Pope said, finally looking up. "Did you ever see anything like—"

He stared into drawn faces, blacks and whites in blue uniforms and in civilian clothes, with shields hung on their lapels. Then he caught sight of Sullivan. He recognized the suit, now smeared and dirty, lying at their feet. He took a slow step toward him and could feel the sickening apprehension start in the pit of his stomach. The others gave way and now he could see his face. Frank Sullivan lay on his back, his eyes open, but he lay as if in sleep. The puckered mark of the single bullet seemed only a mild incision. A trickle of blood seeped from his mouth and Pope had the impulse to wipe it clean. And as he bent to him, he saw that the back of Frank Sullivan's head was blown away.

The sun beat down upon them, throwing shadows of the men across the body. Pope tried to hold back the wrenching sob that seared his chest and throat, and he could feel the scalding run of tears blurring his sight. His fingers spread as though in absolution and his hand benignly moved to Sullivan's face, and gently, oh so gently, the dark hand closed the eyes of his white partner.

☐ **HOT SUMMER KILLING** by Judson Philips

". . . the struggle for racial justice often gives a sense of driving urgency to a suspense novel. Such is the case with this book." —**The New York Times** (63-379, 60¢)

☐ **MAGGOT** by Robert Flanagan

A ruthlessly honest novel of Marine Corps basic training, where the recruit is not a man but a **maggot.** (66-741, $1.25)

☐ **THE ONLY WAR WE'VE GOT** by Derek Maitland

"Savagely funny is the obvious way to describe this elaborate put-down of the whole Vietnam mess."—**Publishers' Weekly**

(65-638, 95¢)

☐ **STRANGERS AND COMRADES** by Alfred Slote

A compelling novel of America in the full fury of war on the home front and battlefield: (65-148, 95¢)

EXCITING BOOKS FROM THE WORLD OF SPORTS!